poison ivy
THORNS

# poison ivy
# THORNS

written by
## KODY KEPLINGER

illustrated by
## SARA KIPIN

colors by
## JEREMY LAWSON

letters by
## STEVE WANDS

Sara Miller *Editor*
Diego Lopez *Associate Editor*
Steve Cook *Design Director – Books*
Amie Brockway-Metcalf *Publication Design*

Marie Javins *Editor-in-Chief, DC Comics*

Daniel Cherry III *Senior VP – General Manager*
Jim Lee *Publisher & Chief Creative Officer*
Joen Choe *VP – Global Brand & Creative Services*
Don Falletti *VP – Manufacturing Operations & Workflow Management*
Lawrence Ganem *VP – Talent Services*
Alison Gill *Senior VP – Manufacturing & Operations*
Nick J. Napolitano *VP – Manufacturing Administration & Design*
Nancy Spears *VP – Revenue*

POISON IVY: THORNS

CONTENT NOTES: The following story includes depictions of sexual harassment and parental abuse. To anyone impacted by these issues, you are not alone. We encourage you to use our list of resources at the end of the book for support.



DC Comics, 2900 West Alameda Ave., Burbank, CA 91505
Printed by LSC Communications, Crawfordsville, IN, USA. 4/23/21.
First Printing.
ISBN: 978-1-4012-9842-5

Library of Congress Cataloging-in-Publication Data

Names: Keplinger, Kody, writer. | Kipin, Sara, illustrator. | Lawson, Jeremy (Cartoonist), colourist. | Wands, Steve, letterer.
Title: Poison Ivy : thorns / written by Kody Keplinger ; illustrated by Sara Kipin ; colors by Jeremy Lawson ; letters by Steve Wands.
Description: Burbank, CA : DC Comics, [2021] | Audience: Ages 13-17 | Audience: Grades 10-12 | Summary: Even though Pamela Isley spends most of her time caring for a few small plants and does not trust other people, when cute goth girl Alice Oh comes into her life she starts to open up, but the dark secrets from home could destroy the one person who ever cared about Pamela, or as her mom called her, Ivy.
Identifiers: LCCN 2021001514 | ISBN 9781401298425 (trade paperback)
Subjects: LCSH: Graphic novels. | CYAC: Graphic novels. | Family secrets–Fiction. | Self-realization–Fiction. | Love–Fiction.
Classification: LCC PZ7.7.K455 Po 2021 | DDC 741.5/973–dc23
LC record available at https://lccn.loc.gov/2021001514

PEFC Certified
This product is from sustainably managed forests and controlled sources
PEFC
PEFC/29-31-337
www.pefc.org

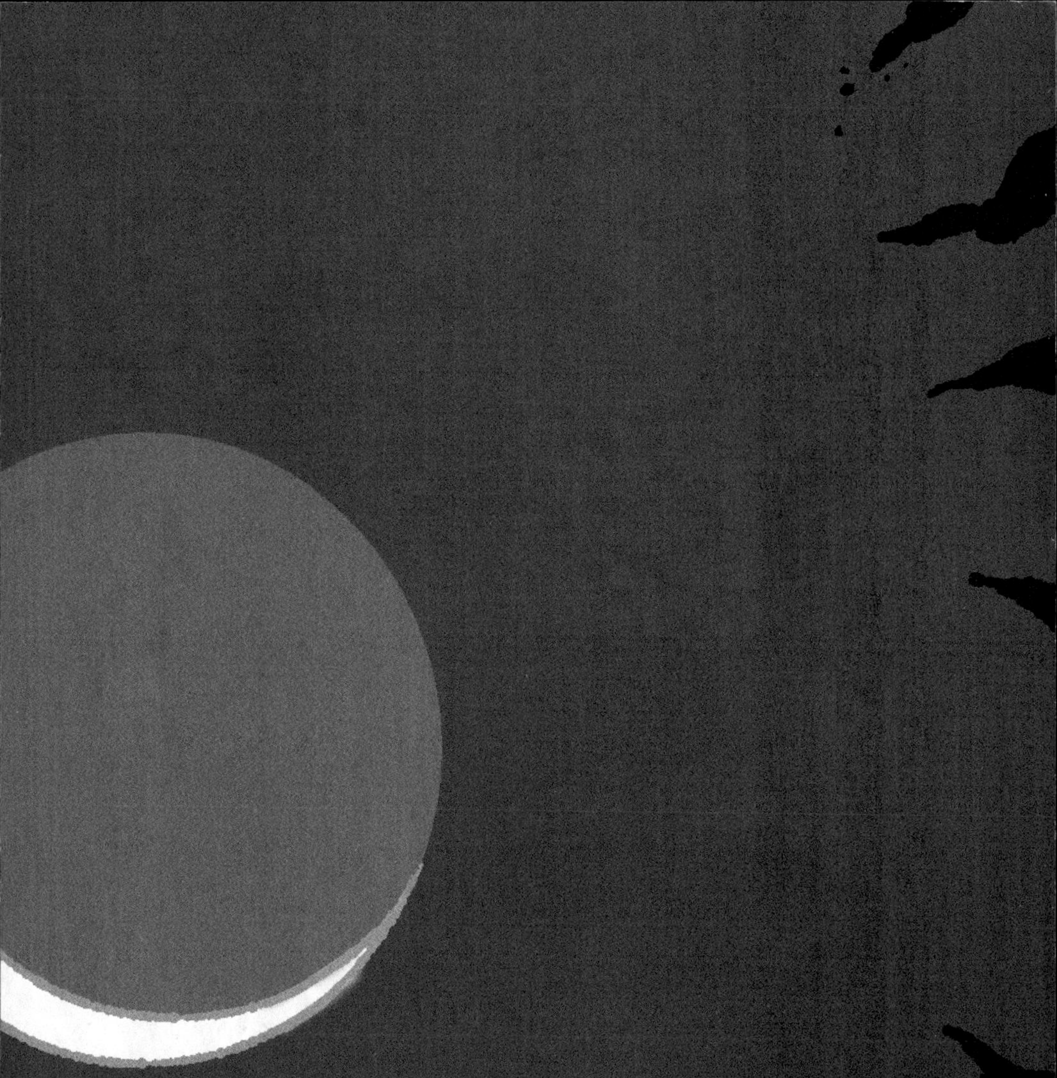

For Wendy, who is
always an inspiration.

—Kody

For my family and friends
who've supported me over the years.

—Sara

# TABLE of CONTENTS

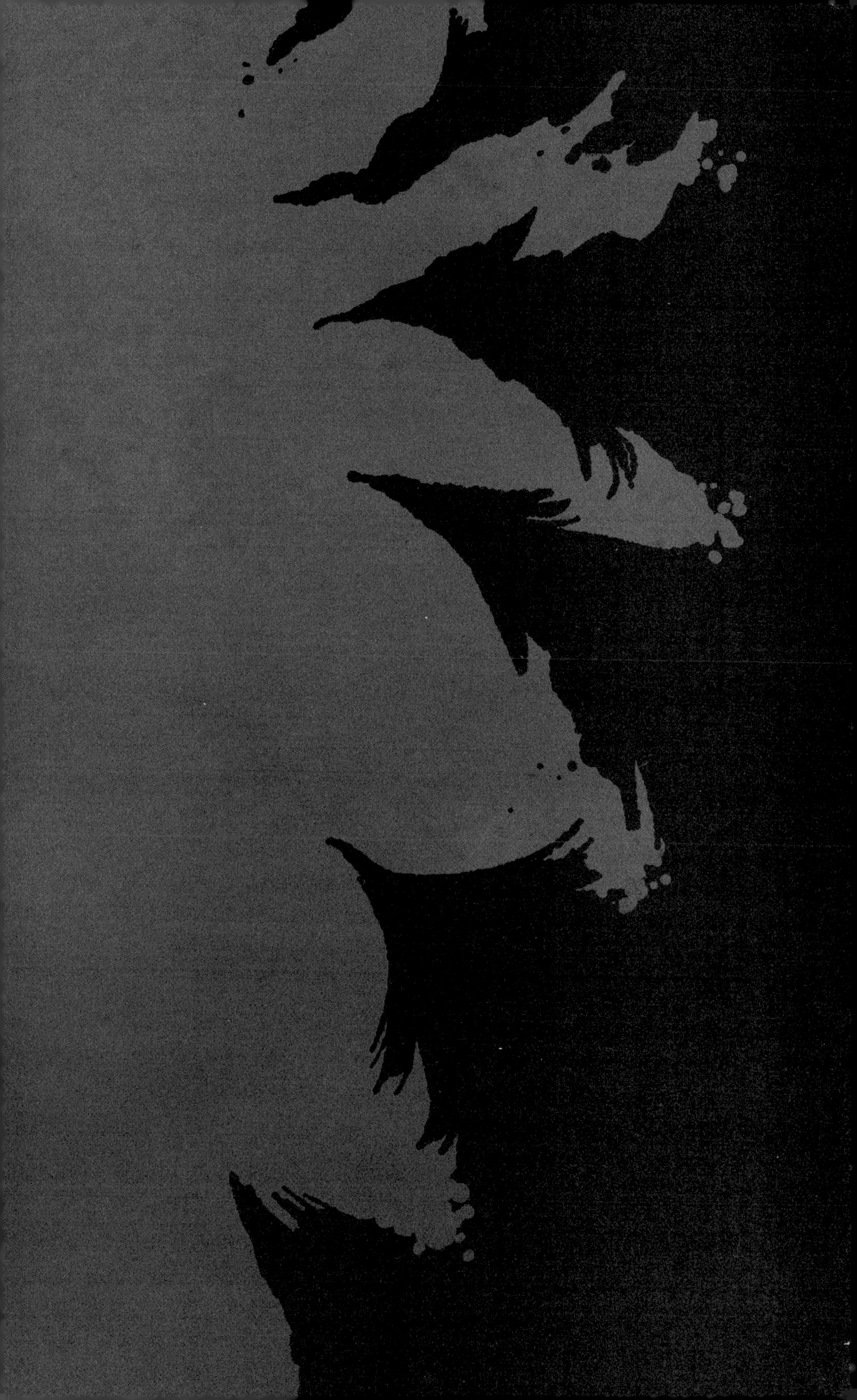

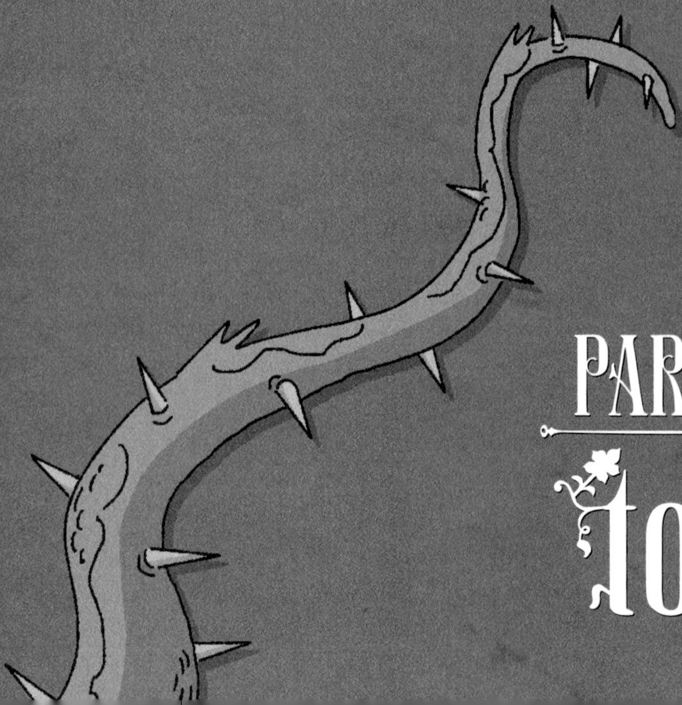

# PART ONE

# toxic

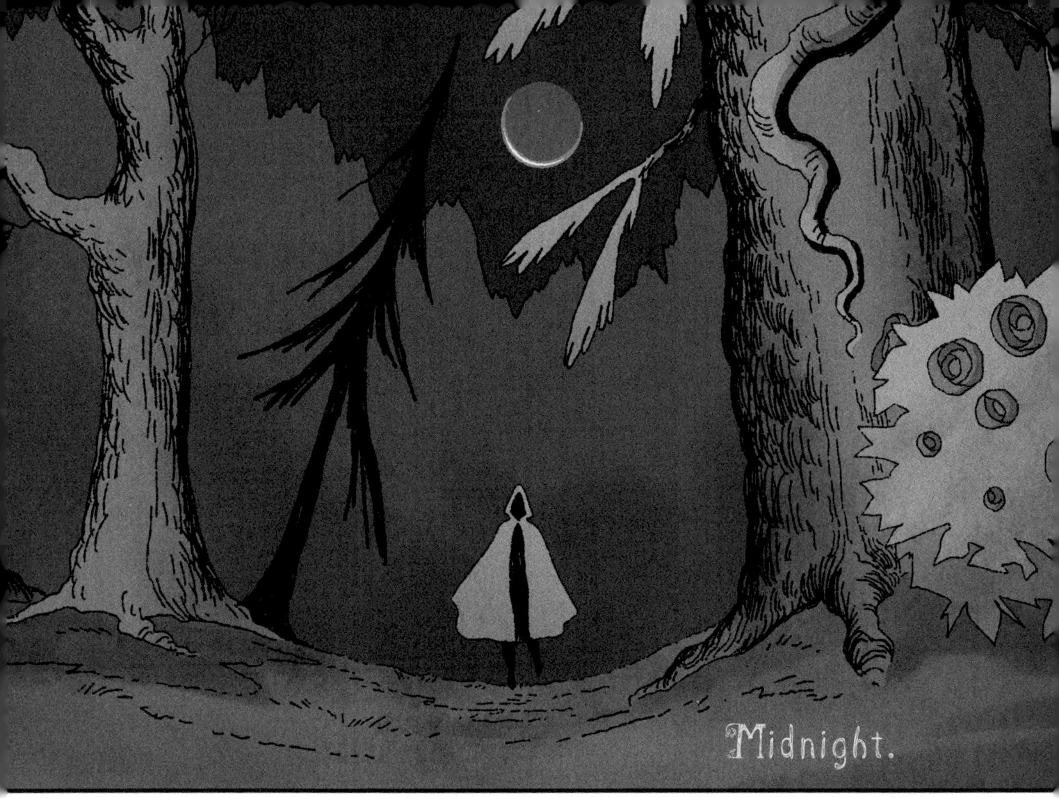
Midnight.

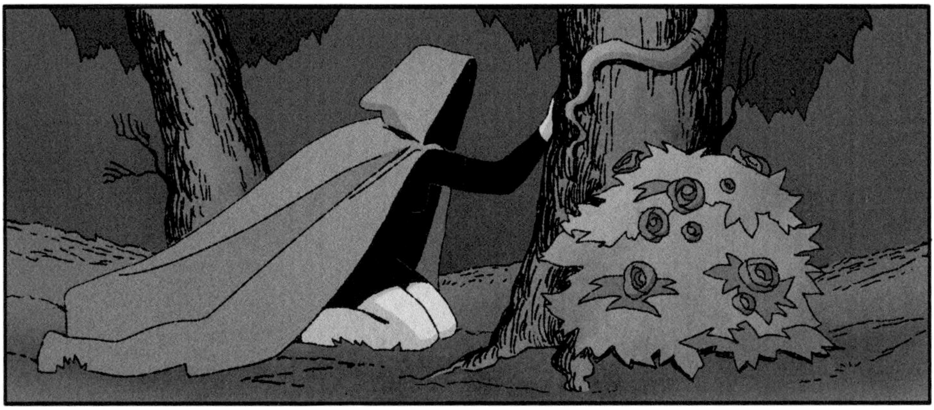

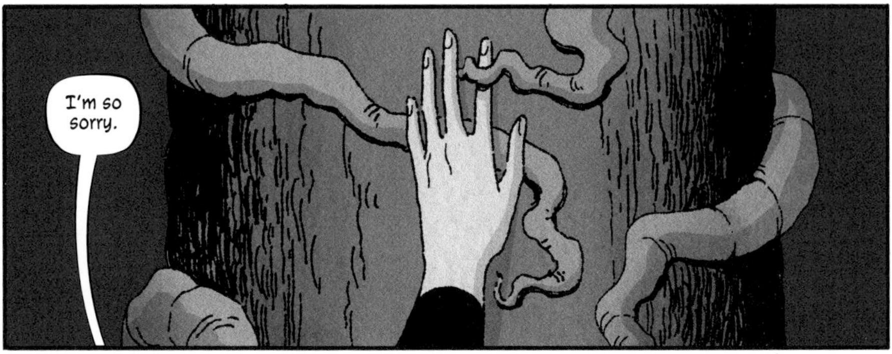
I'm so sorry.

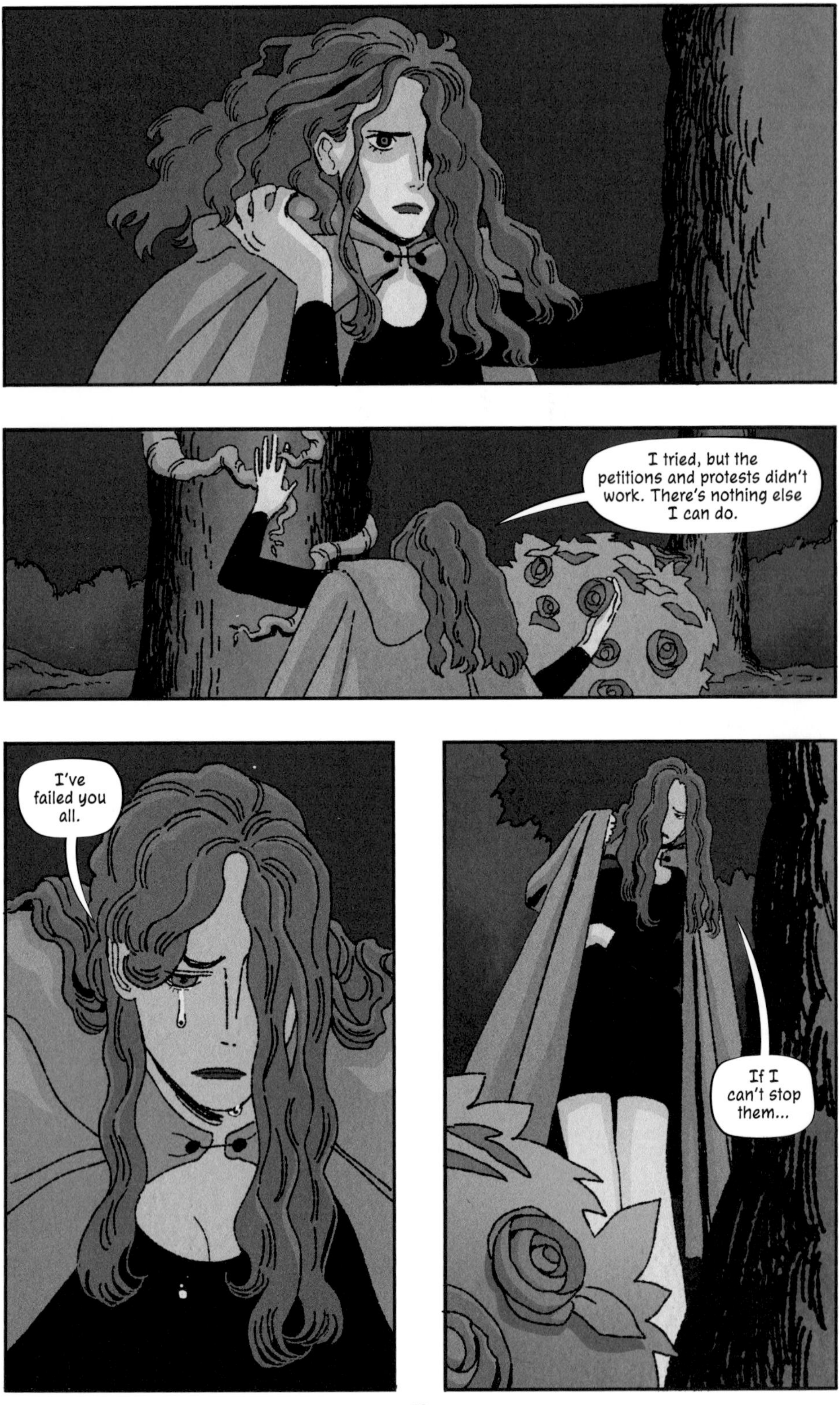
I tried, but the petitions and protests didn't work. There's nothing else I can do.
I've failed you all.
If I can't stop them...

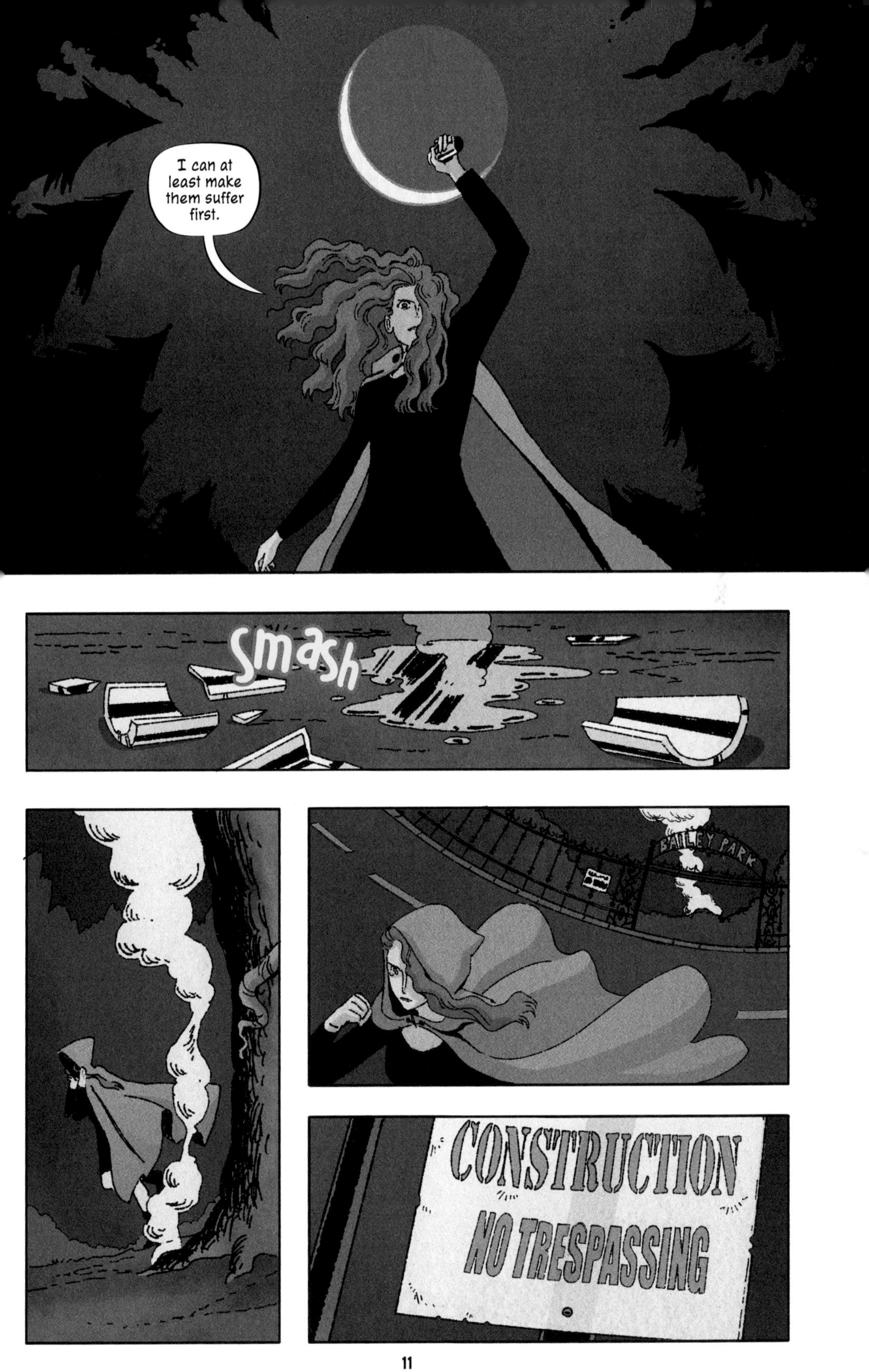
I can at least make them suffer first.
Smash
BAILEY PARK
CONSTRUCTION
NO TRESPASSING

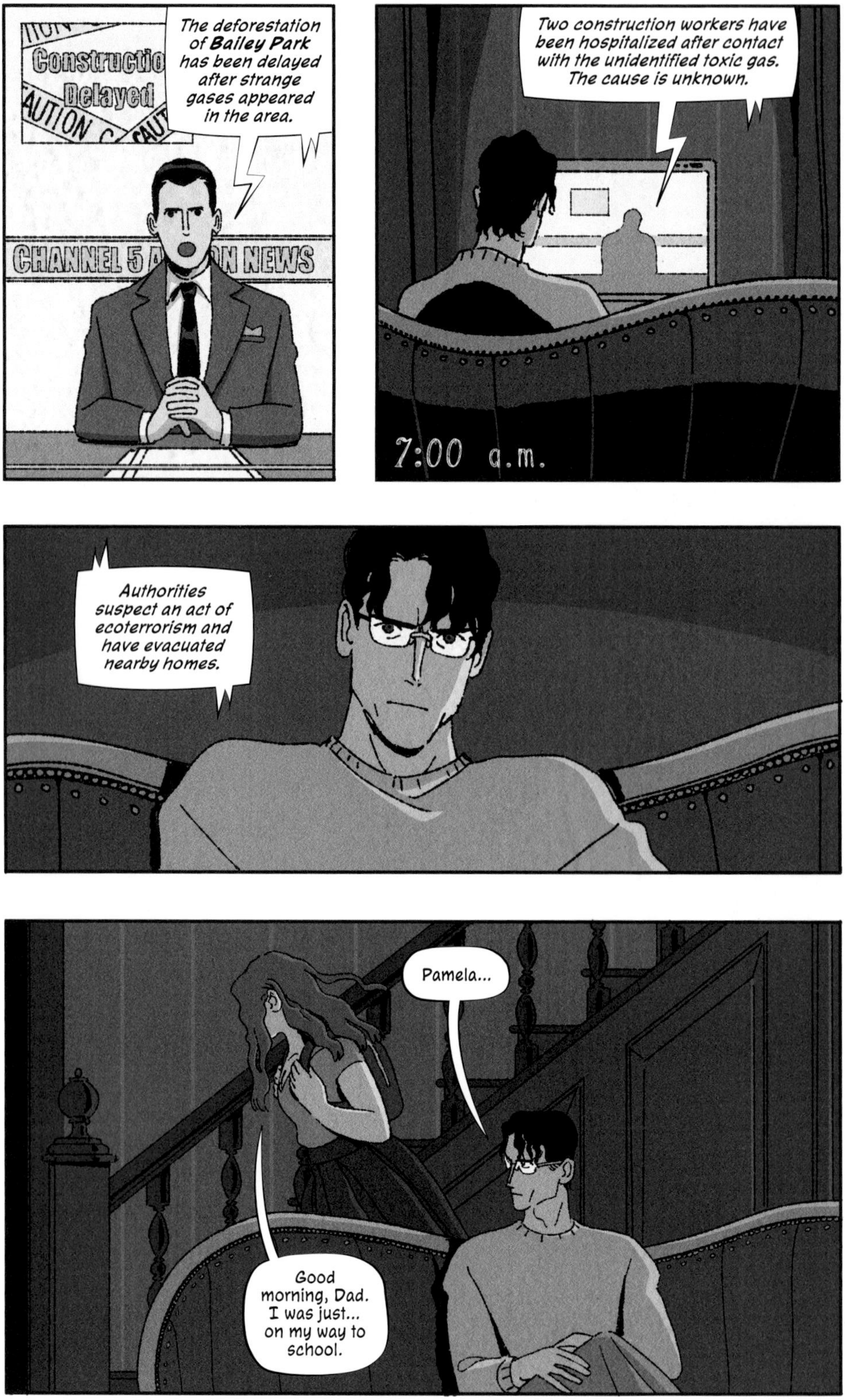
Delayed
CHANNEL 5
NEWS
The deforestation of **Bailey Park** has been delayed after strange gases appeared in the area.
Two construction workers have been hospitalized after contact with the unidentified toxic gas. The cause is unknown.
7:00 a.m.
Authorities suspect an act of ecoterrorism and have evacuated nearby homes.
Pamela...
Good morning, Dad. I was just... on my way to school.

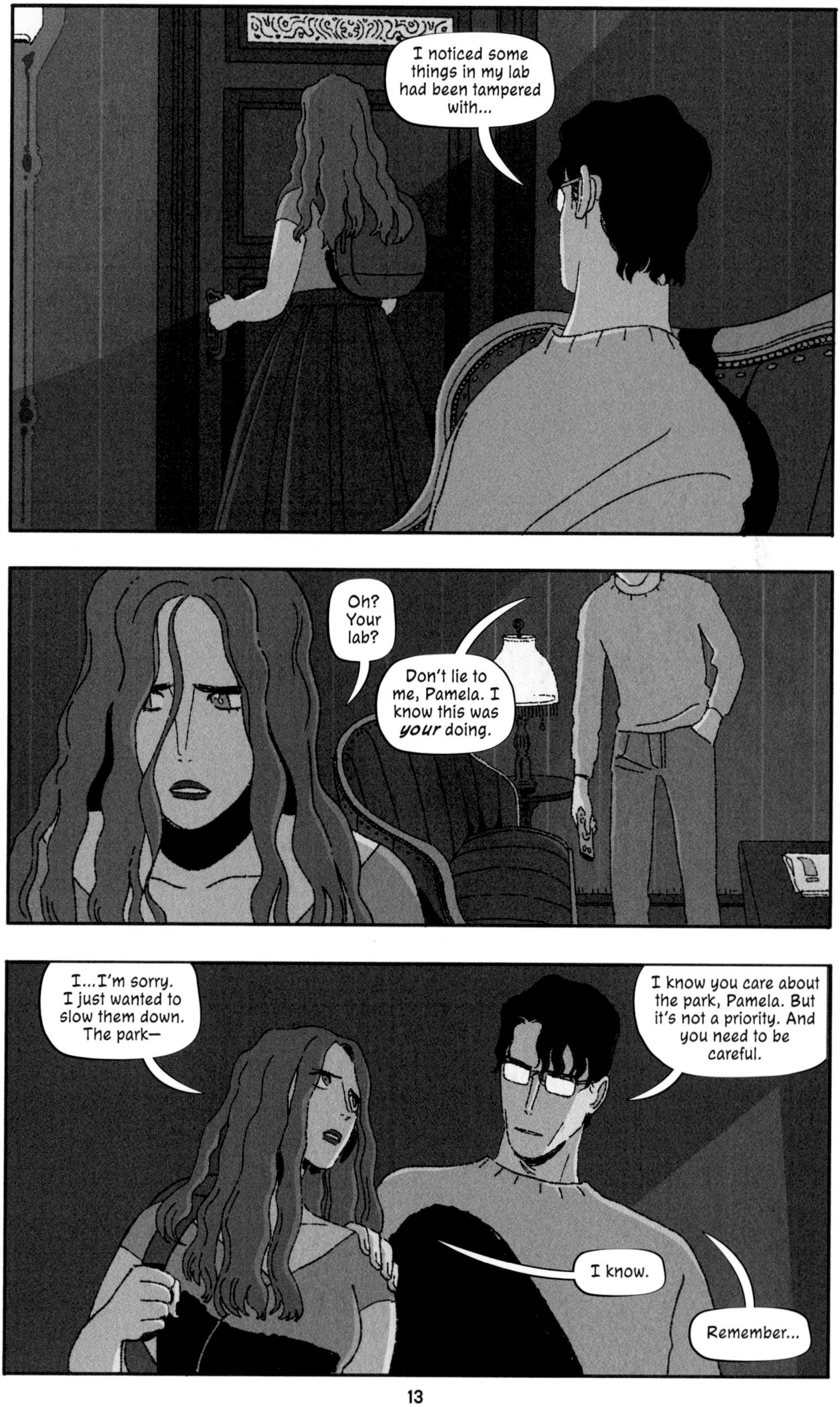

I noticed some things in my lab had been tampered with...
Oh? Your lab?
Don't lie to me, Pamela. I know this was *your* doing.
I...I'm sorry. I just wanted to slow them down. The park—
I know you care about the park, Pamela. But it's not a priority. And you need to be careful.
I know.
Remember...

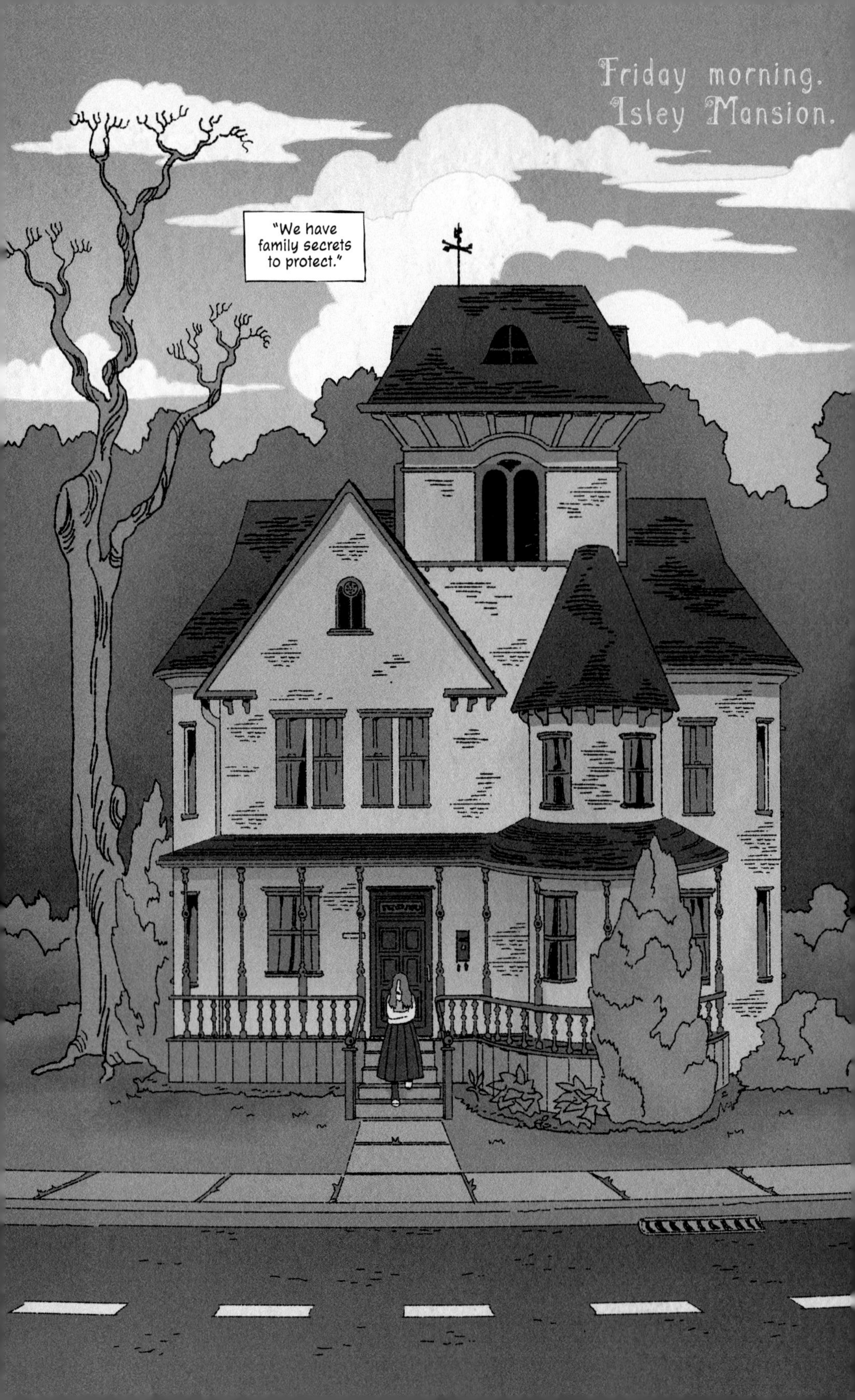
Friday morning.
Isley Mansion.
"We have family secrets to protect."

7:20 a.m.

Huxley High School.

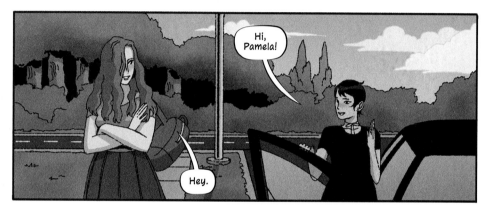

Hi, Pamela!

Hey.

Did you have fun at homecoming, Brett?

The real fun was after, if you know what I mean.

Hey, wasn't that your homecoming date?

Huh. She must be in a hurry to get somewhere.

God, she's hot. But kinda weird, y'know?

15

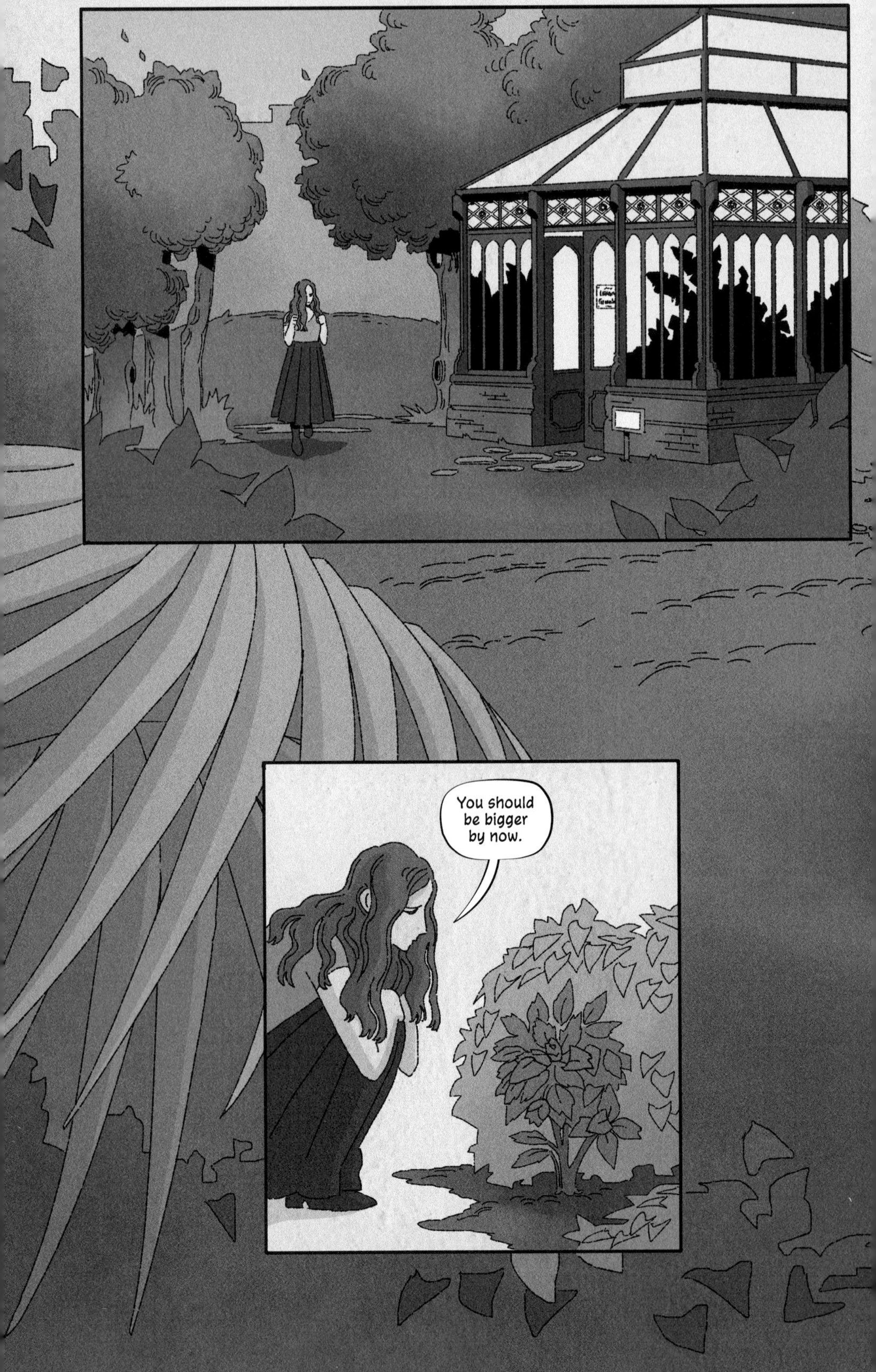
You should be bigger by now.

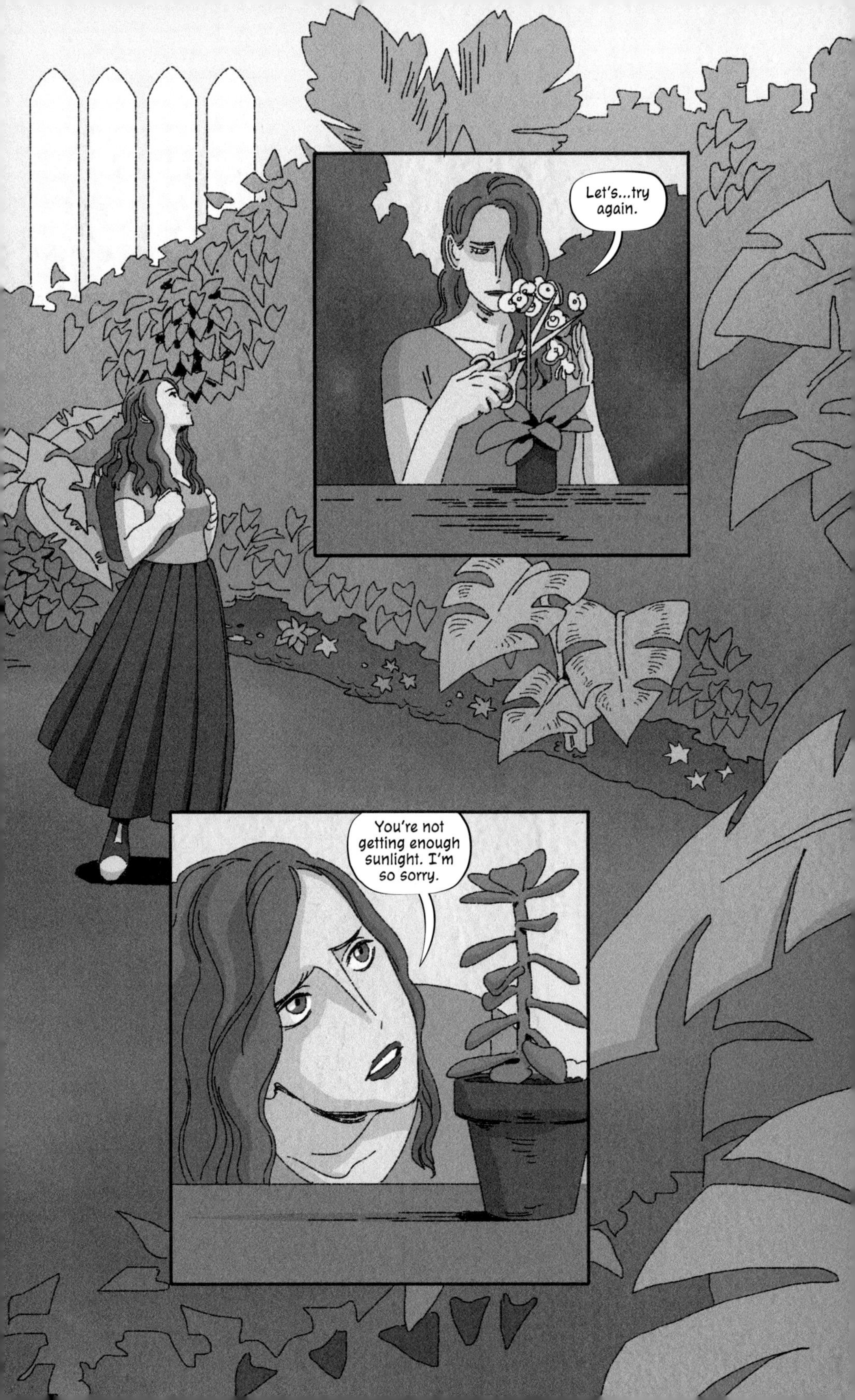

Let's...try again.
You're not getting enough sunlight. I'm so sorry.

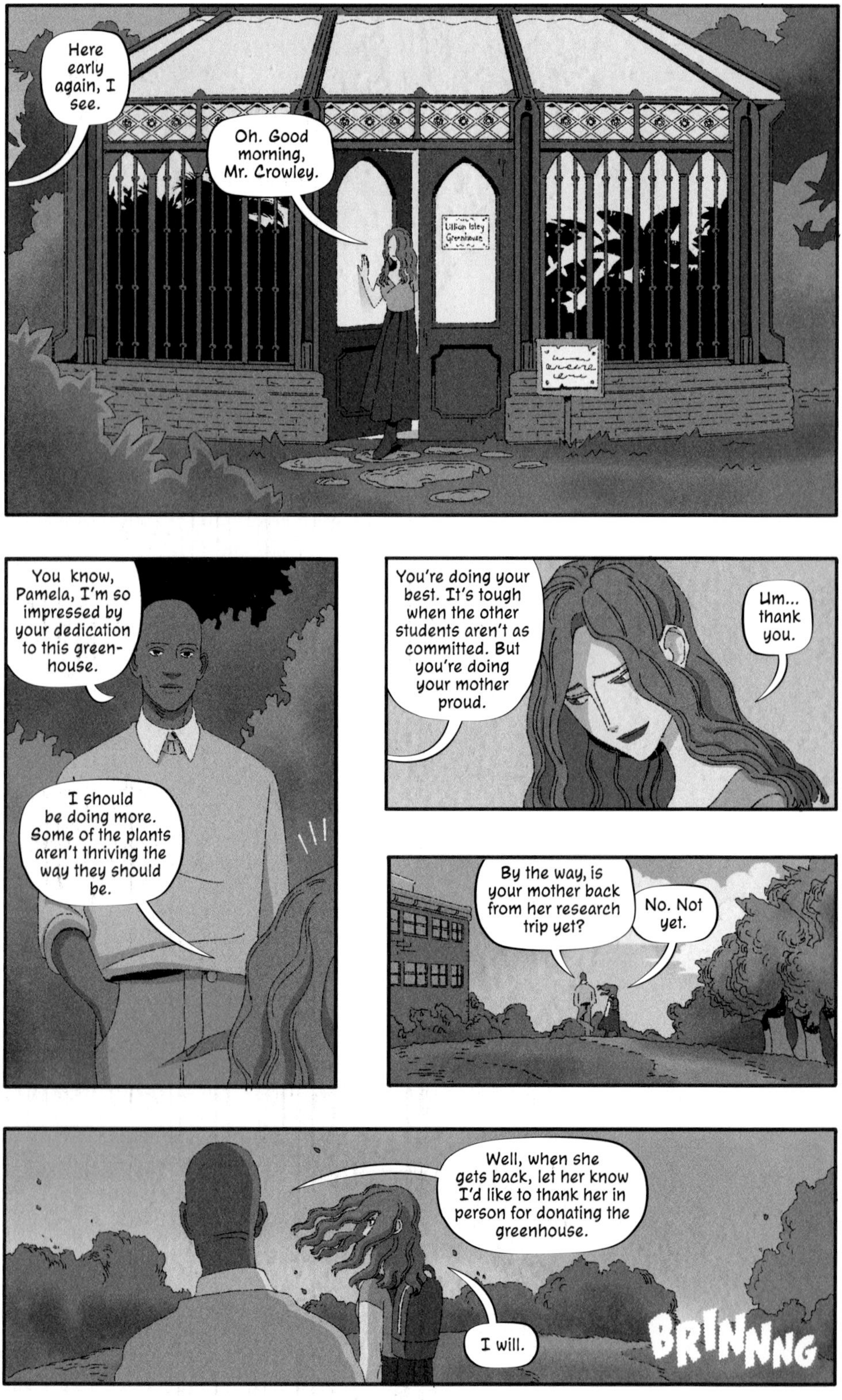
Here early again, I see.
Oh. Good morning, Mr. Crowley.
Lillian Isley Greenhouse
You know, Pamela, I'm so impressed by your dedication to this greenhouse.
I should be doing more. Some of the plants aren't thriving the way they should be.
You're doing your best. It's tough when the other students aren't as committed. But you're doing your mother proud.
Um... thank you.
By the way, is your mother back from her research trip yet?
No. Not yet.
Well, when she gets back, let her know I'd like to thank her in person for donating the greenhouse.
I will.
BRINNNG

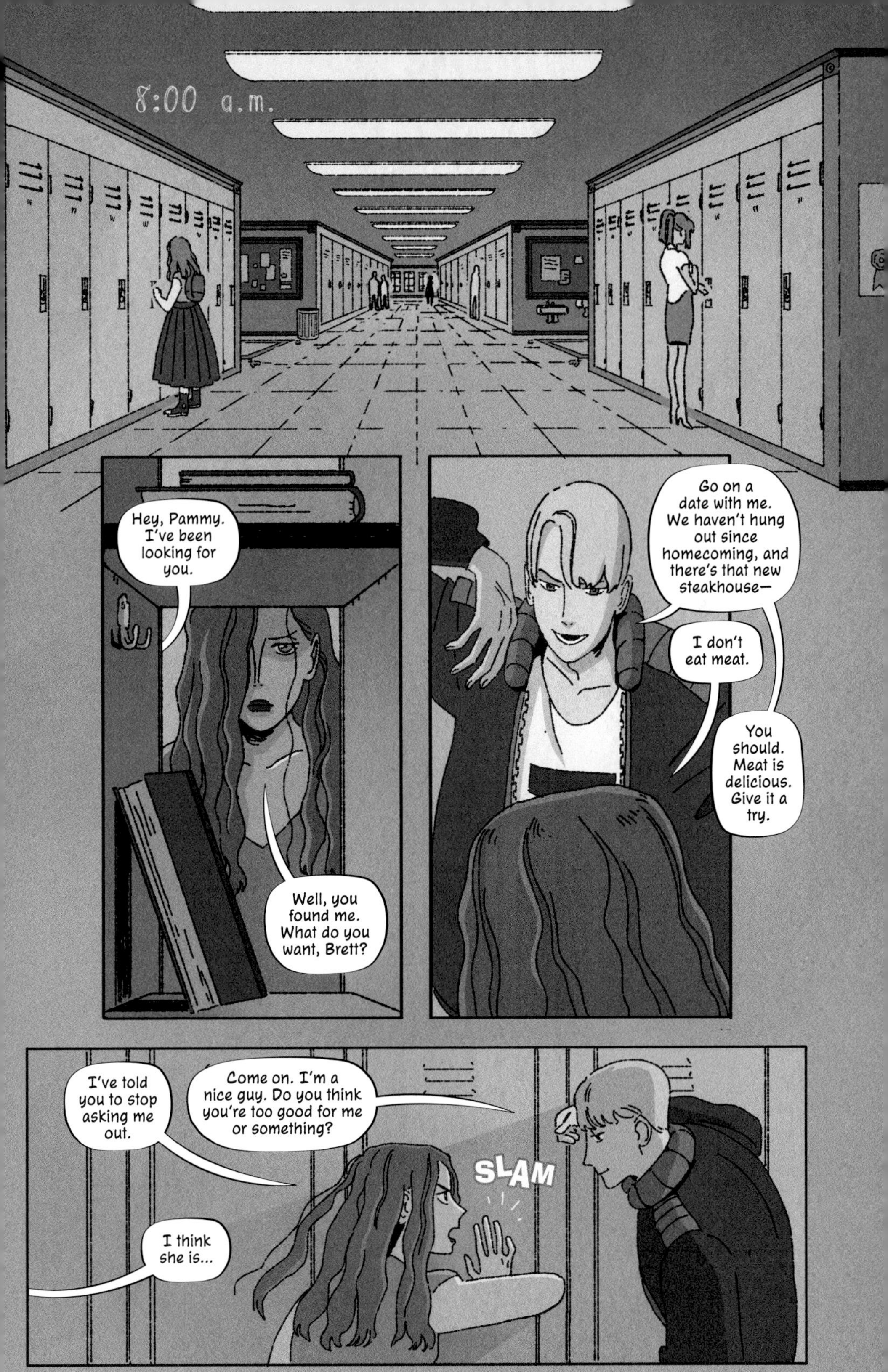
8:00 a.m.
Hey, Pammy. I've been looking for you.
Well, you found me. What do you want, Brett?
Go on a date with me. We haven't hung out since homecoming, and there's that new steakhouse—
I don't eat meat.
You should. Meat is delicious. Give it a try.
I've told you to stop asking me out.
Come on. I'm a nice guy. Do you think you're too good for me or something?
SLAM
I think she is...

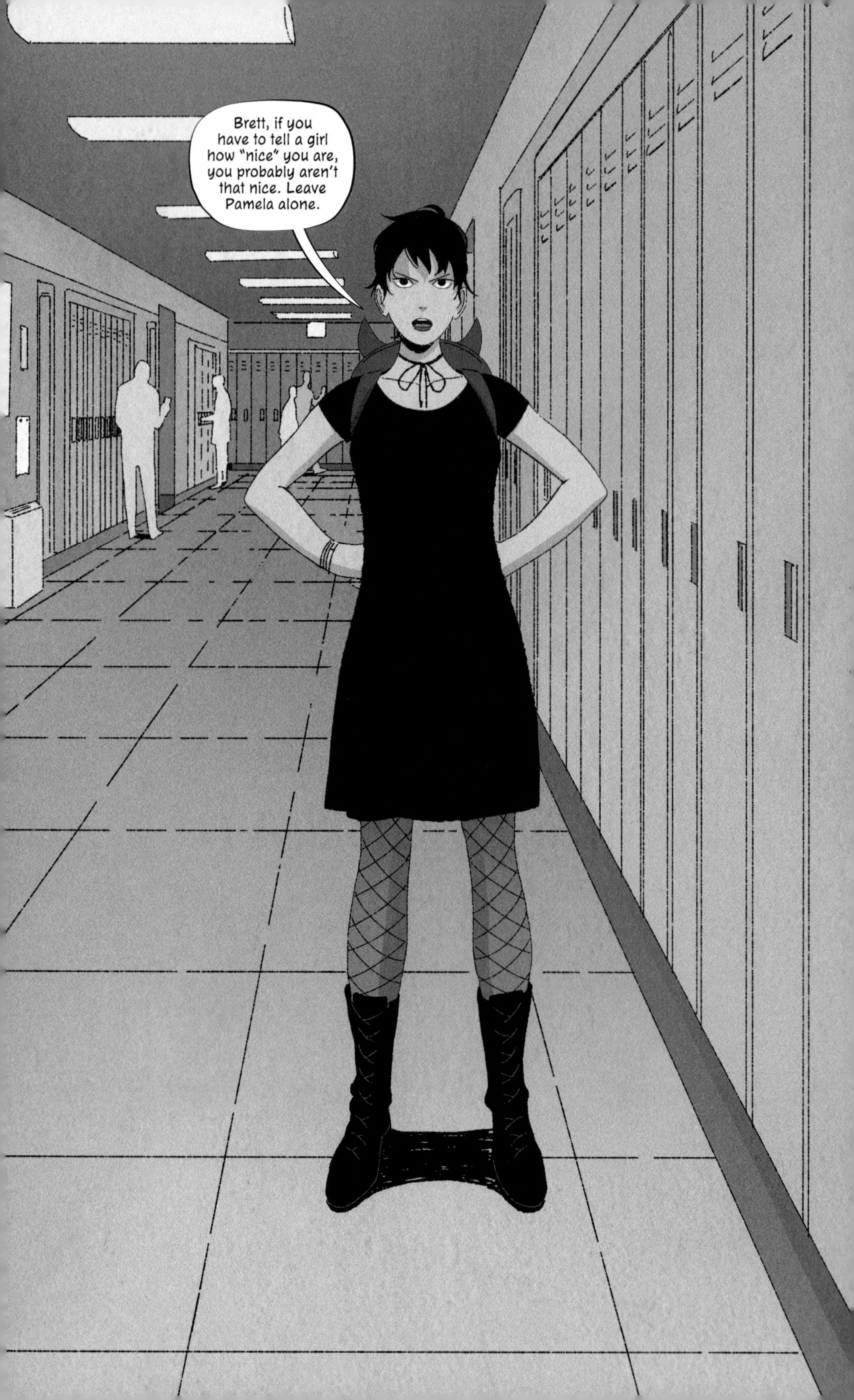
Brett, if you have to tell a girl how "nice" you are, you probably aren't that nice. Leave Pamela alone.

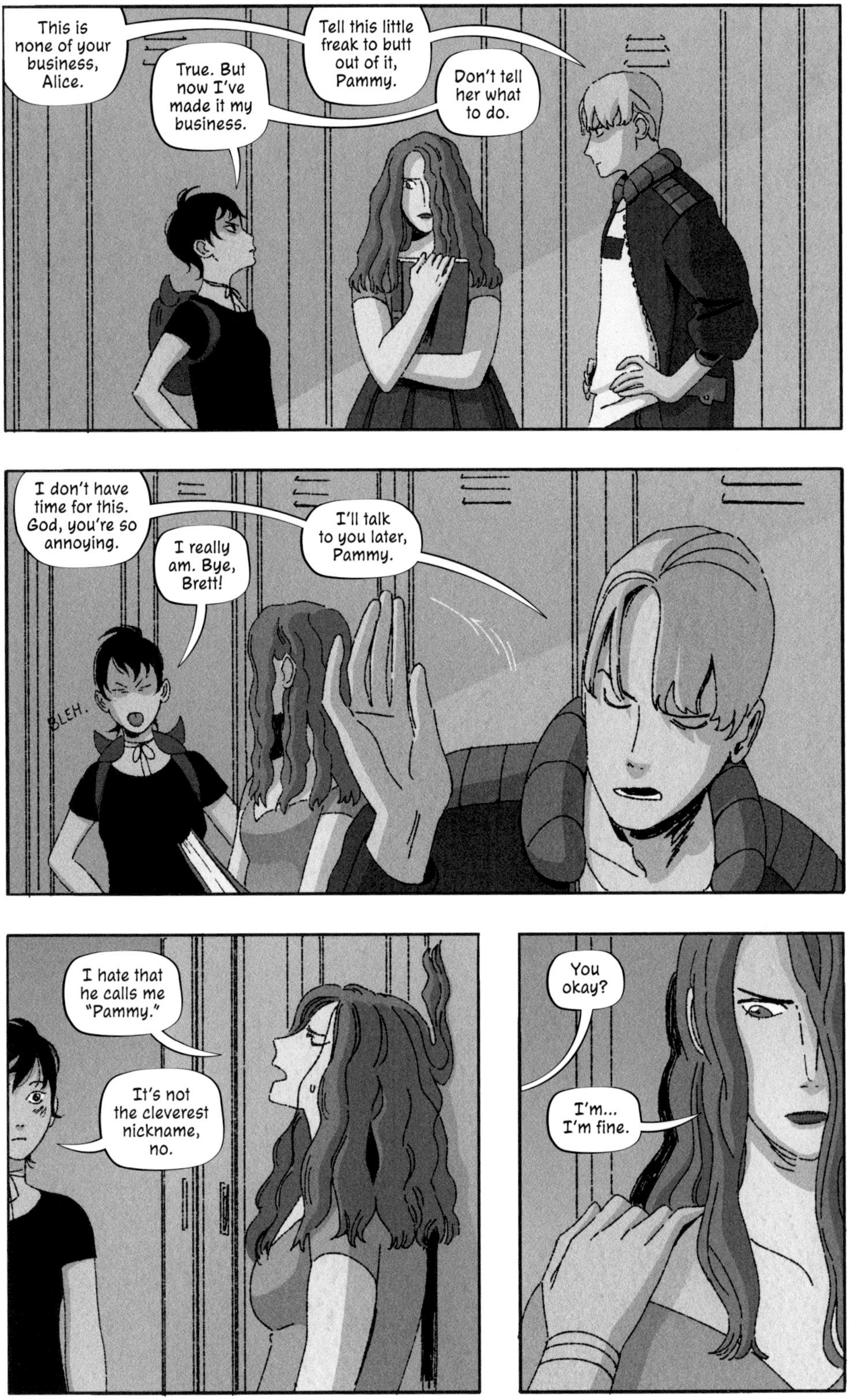
This is none of your business, Alice.
Tell this little freak to butt out of it, Pammy.
True. But now I've made it my business.
Don't tell her what to do.
I don't have time for this. God, you're so annoying.
I really am. Bye, Brett!
BLEH.
I'll talk to you later, Pammy.
I hate that he calls me "Pammy."
It's not the cleverest nickname, no.
You okay?
I'm... I'm fine.

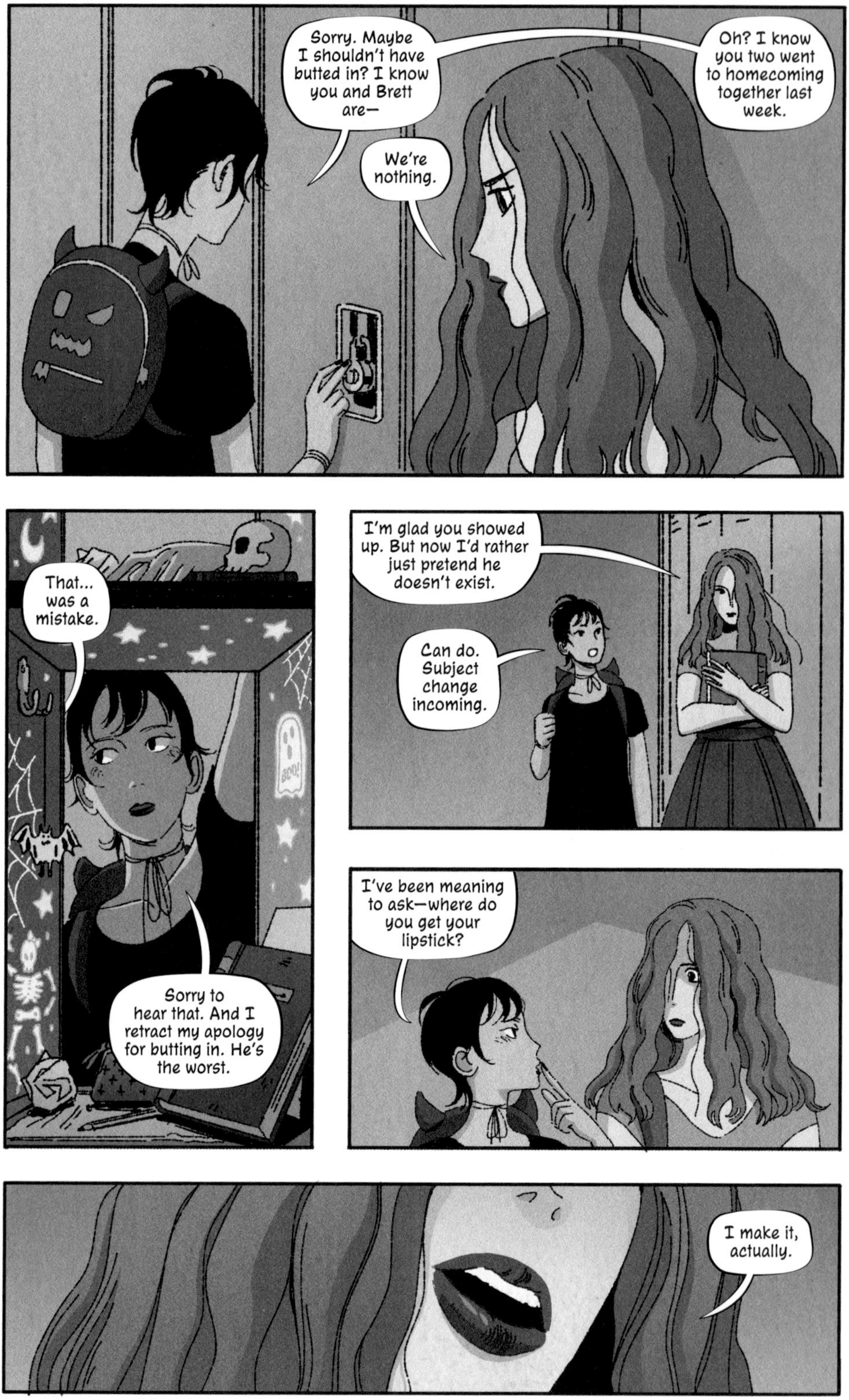

Sorry. Maybe I shouldn't have butted in? I know you and Brett are—
Oh? I know you two went to homecoming together last week.
We're nothing.
That... was a mistake.
Sorry to hear that. And I retract my apology for butting in. He's the worst.
I'm glad you showed up. But now I'd rather just pretend he doesn't exist.
Can do. Subject change incoming.
BOO!
I've been meaning to ask—where do you get your lipstick?
I make it, actually.

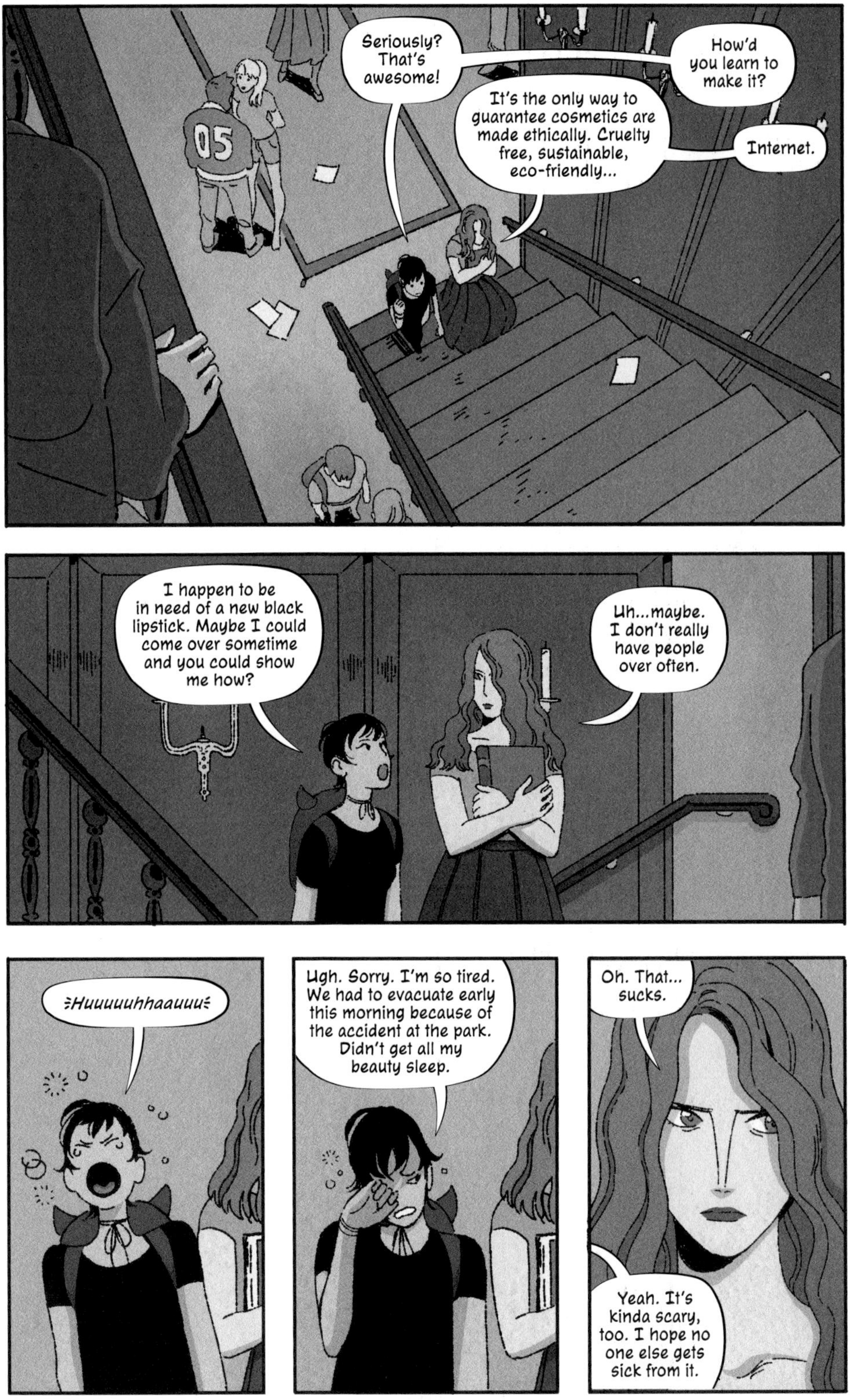
Seriously? That's awesome!
How'd you learn to make it?
It's the only way to guarantee cosmetics are made ethically. Cruelty free, sustainable, eco-friendly...
Internet.
I happen to be in need of a new black lipstick. Maybe I could come over sometime and you could show me how?
Uh...maybe. I don't really have people over often.
Huuuuuhhaauuu
Ugh. Sorry. I'm so tired. We had to evacuate early this morning because of the accident at the park. Didn't get all my beauty sleep.
Oh. That... sucks.
Yeah. It's kinda scary, too. I hope no one else gets sick from it.

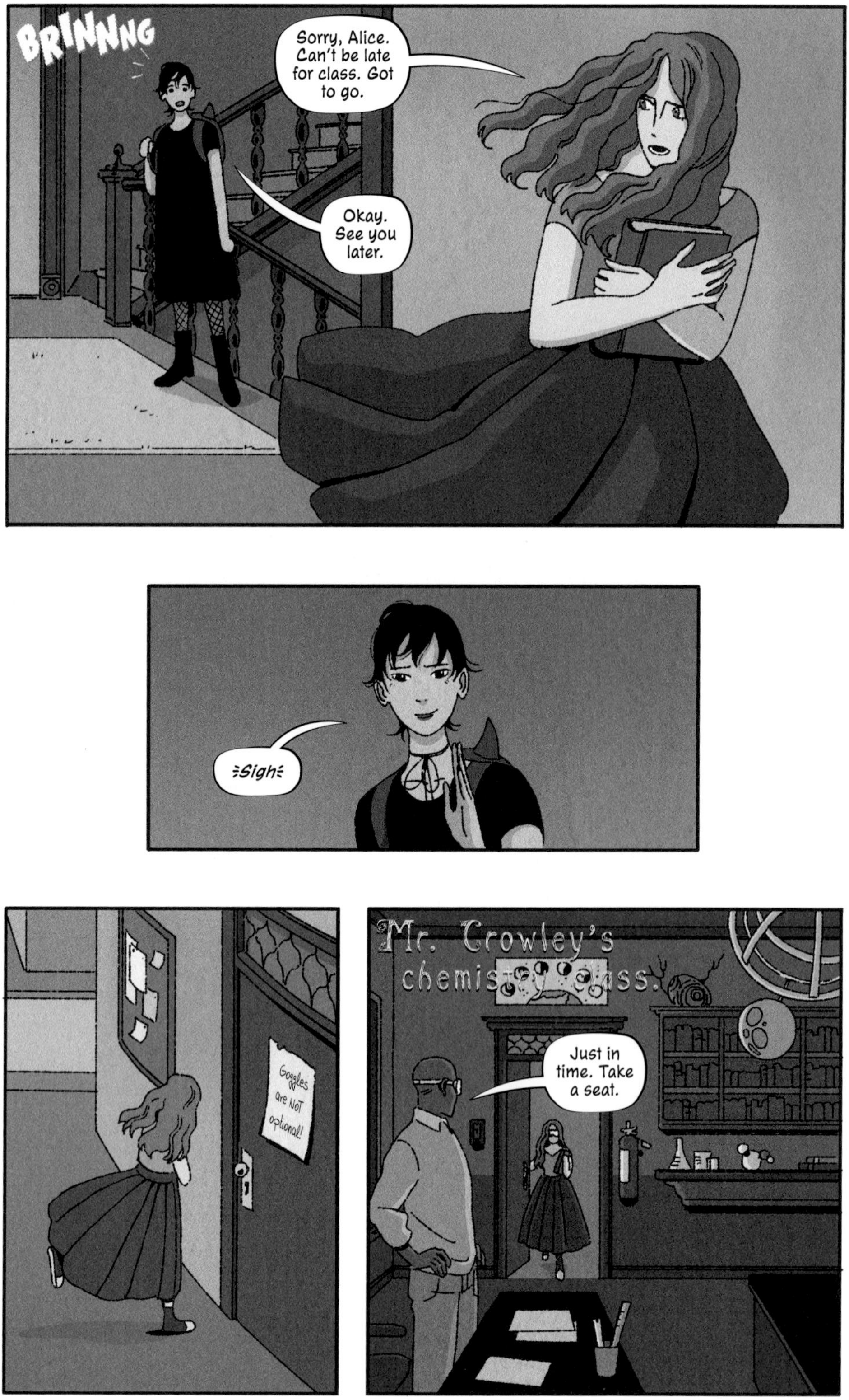
BRINNNG
Sorry, Alice. Can't be late for class. Got to go.
Okay. See you later.
Sigh
Goggles are NOT optional!
Mr. Crowley's chemistry class.
Just in time. Take a seat.

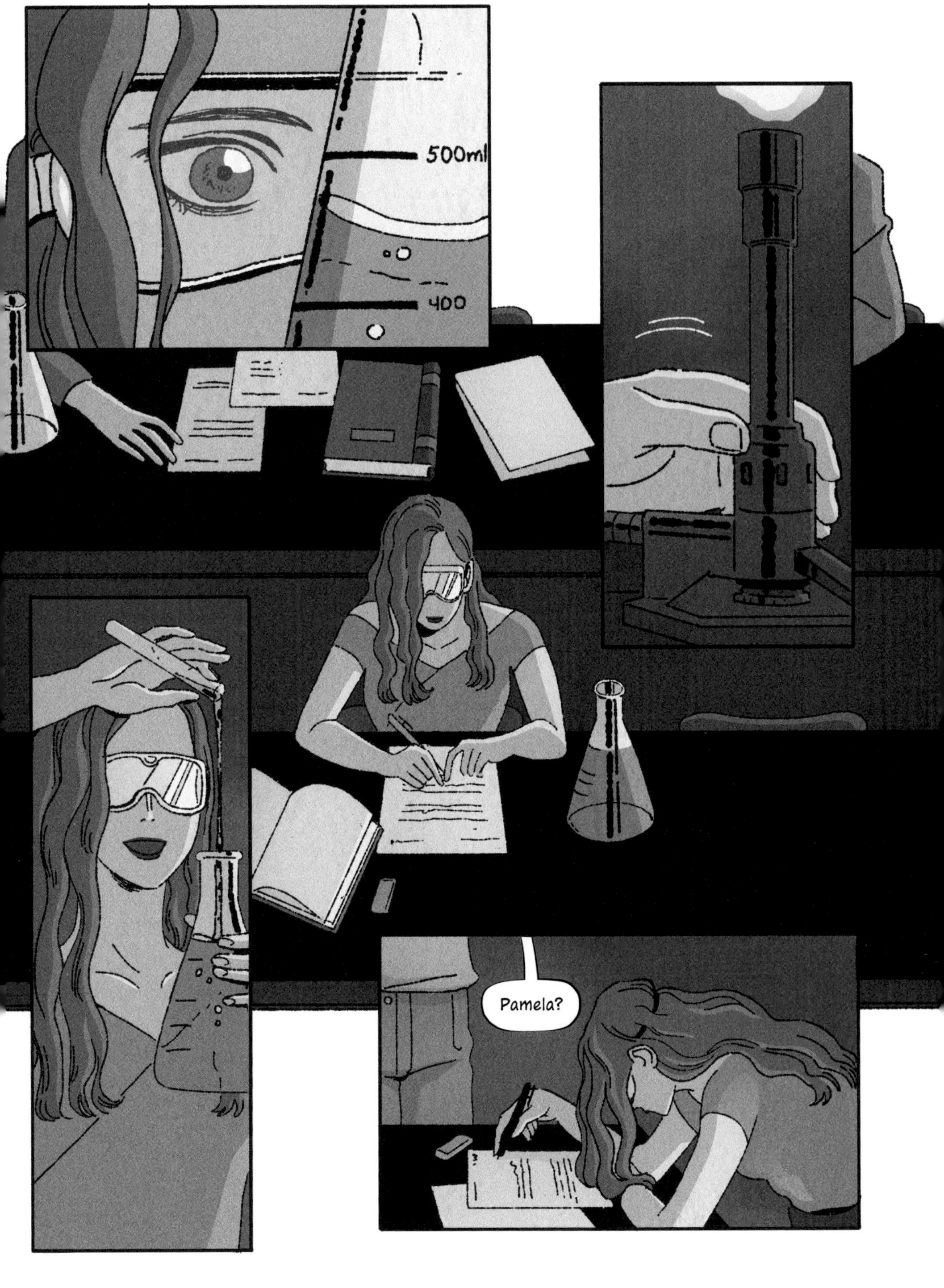
500ml
400
Pamela?

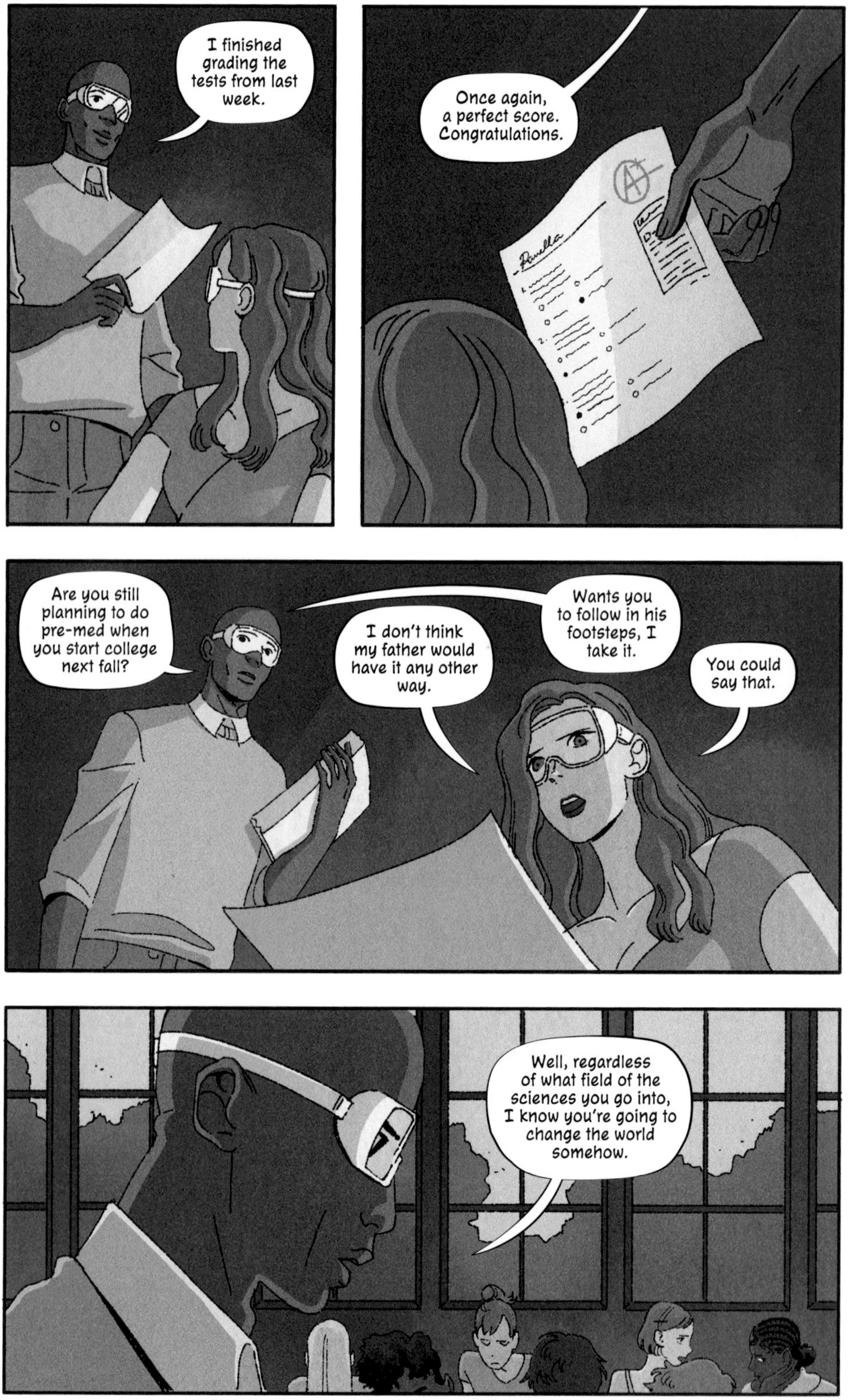
I finished grading the tests from last week.
Once again, a perfect score. Congratulations.
Are you still planning to do pre-med when you start college next fall?
I don't think my father would have it any other way.
Wants you to follow in his footsteps, I take it.
You could say that.
Well, regardless of what field of the sciences you go into, I know you're going to change the world somehow.

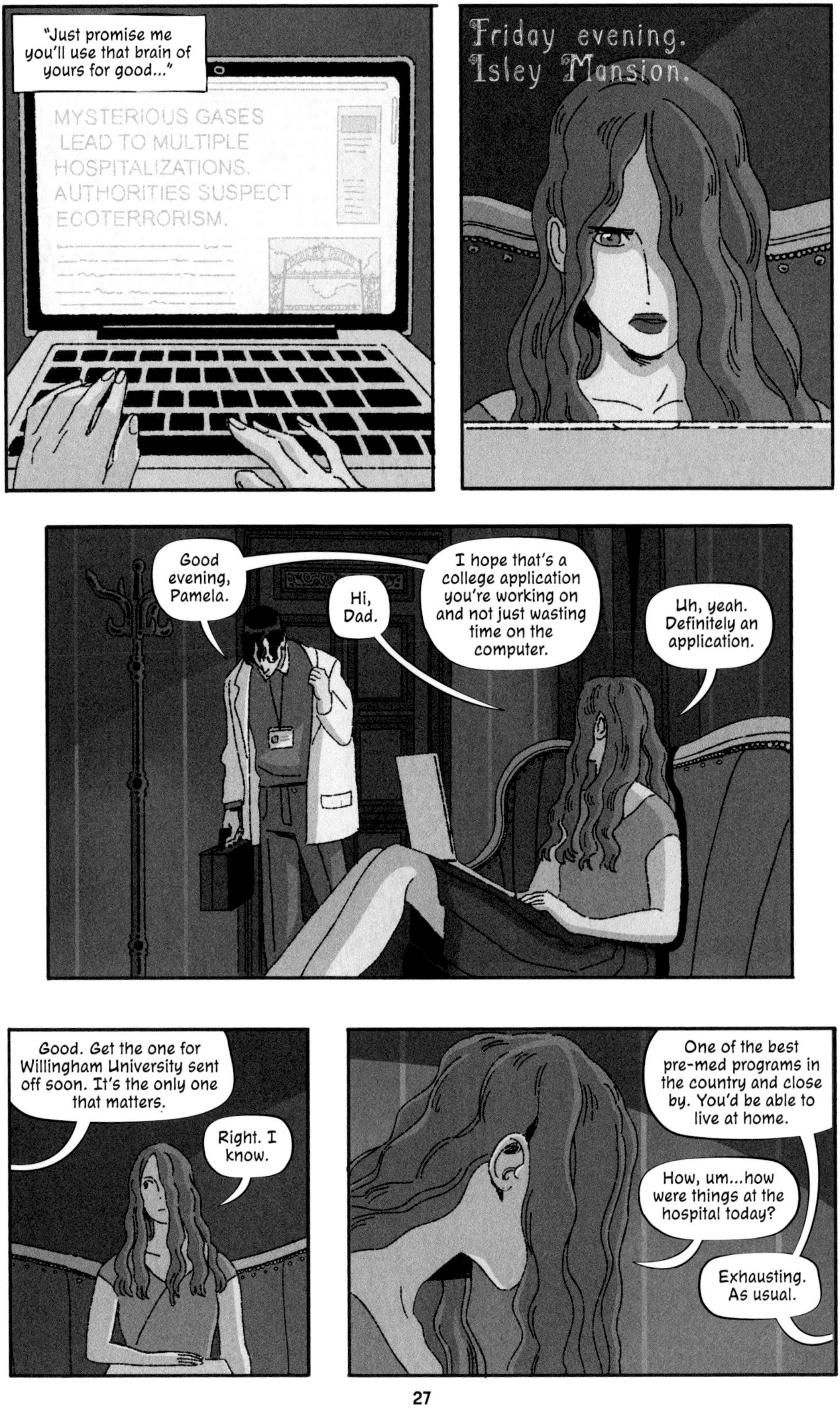

"Just promise me you'll use that brain of yours for good..."
MYSTERIOUS GASES LEAD TO MULTIPLE HOSPITALIZATIONS. AUTHORITIES SUSPECT ECOTERRORISM.
Friday evening. Isley Mansion.
Good evening, Pamela.
Hi, Dad.
I hope that's a college application you're working on and not just wasting time on the computer.
Uh, yeah. Definitely an application.
Good. Get the one for Willingham University sent off soon. It's the only one that matters.
Right. I know.
One of the best pre-med programs in the country and close by. You'd be able to live at home.
How, um...how were things at the hospital today?
Exhausting. As usual.

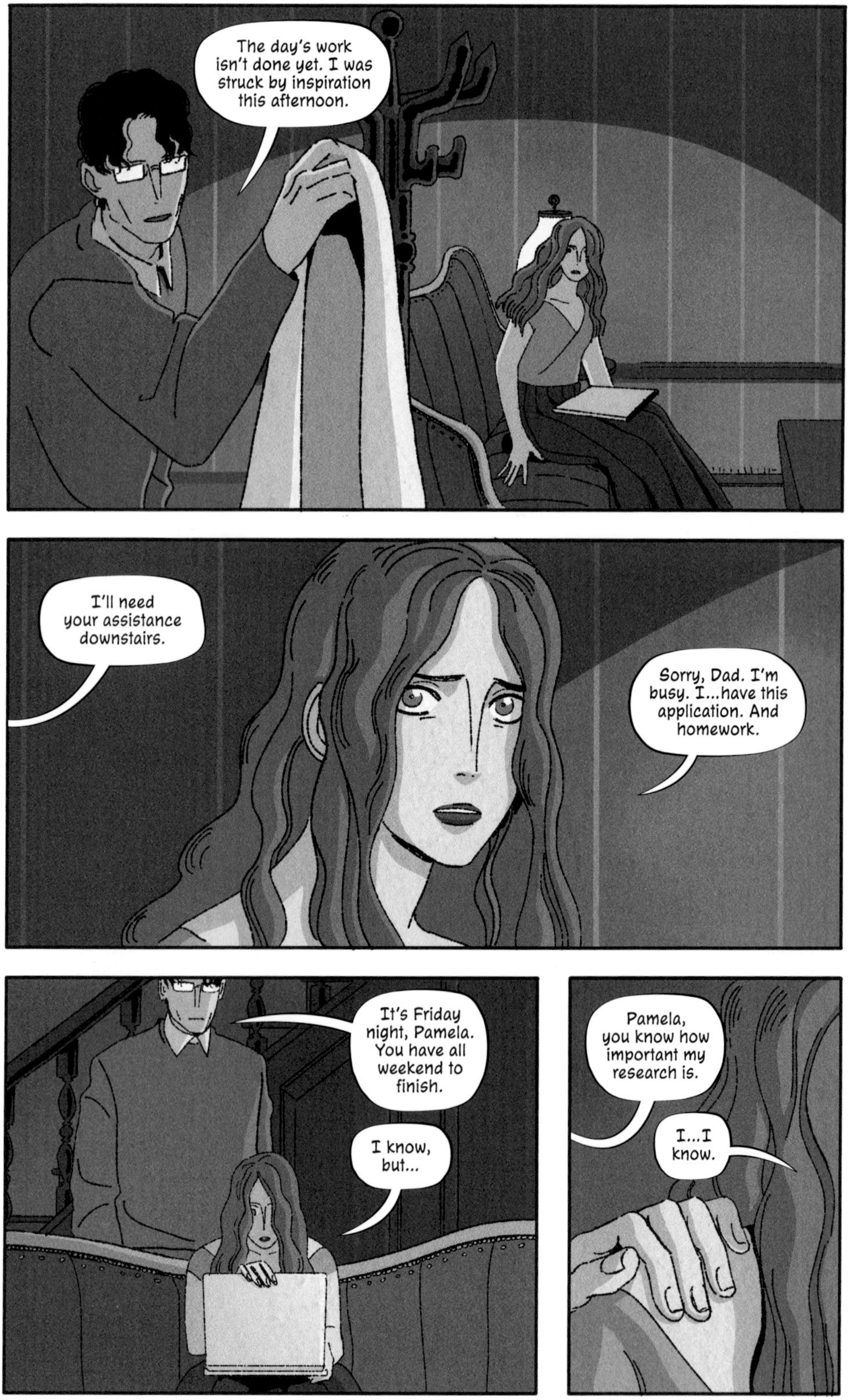
The day's work isn't done yet. I was struck by inspiration this afternoon.
I'll need your assistance downstairs.
Sorry, Dad. I'm busy. I...have this application. And homework.
It's Friday night, Pamela. You have all weekend to finish.
I know, but...
Pamela, you know how important my research is.
I...I know.

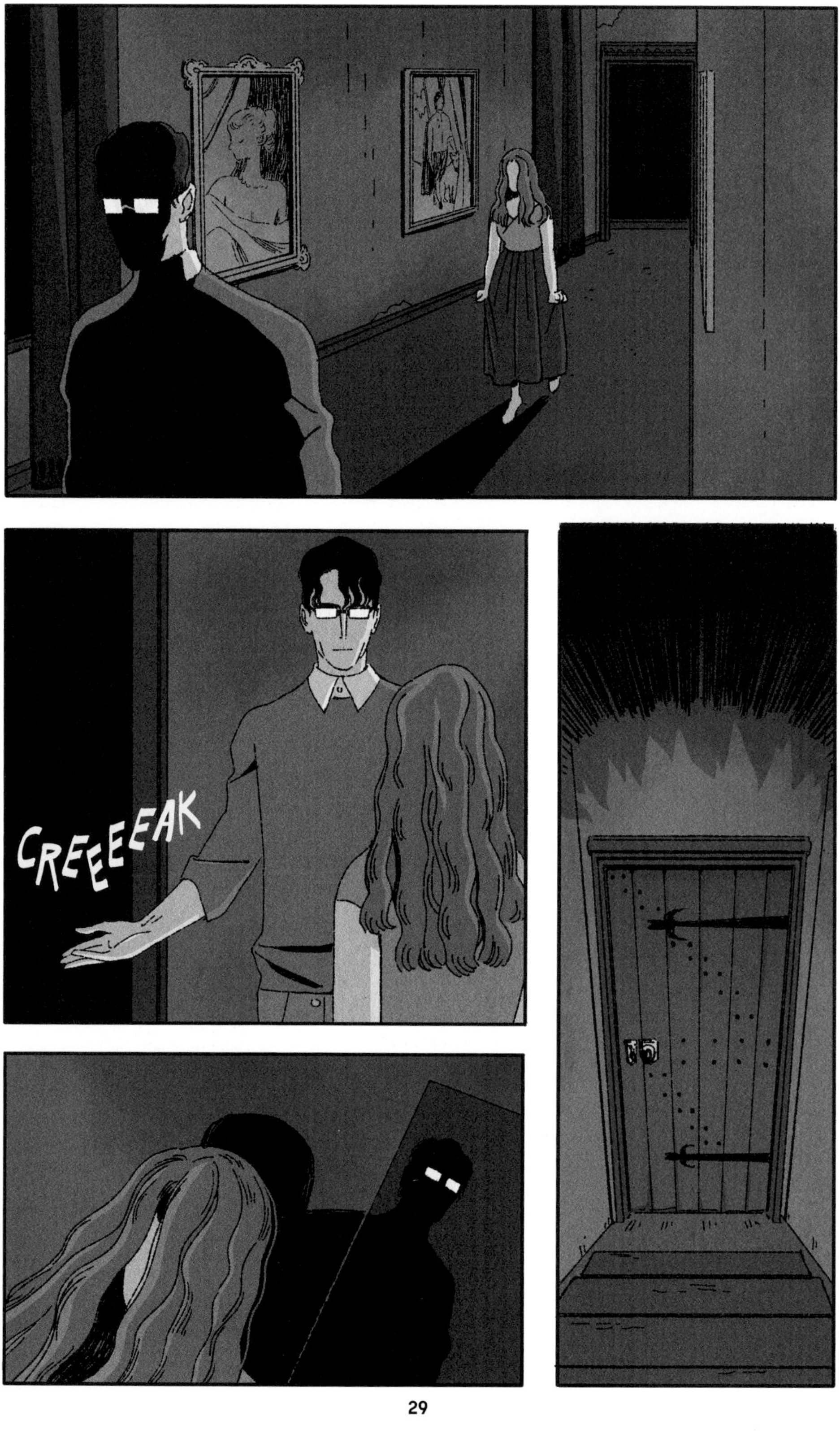
CREEEEAK

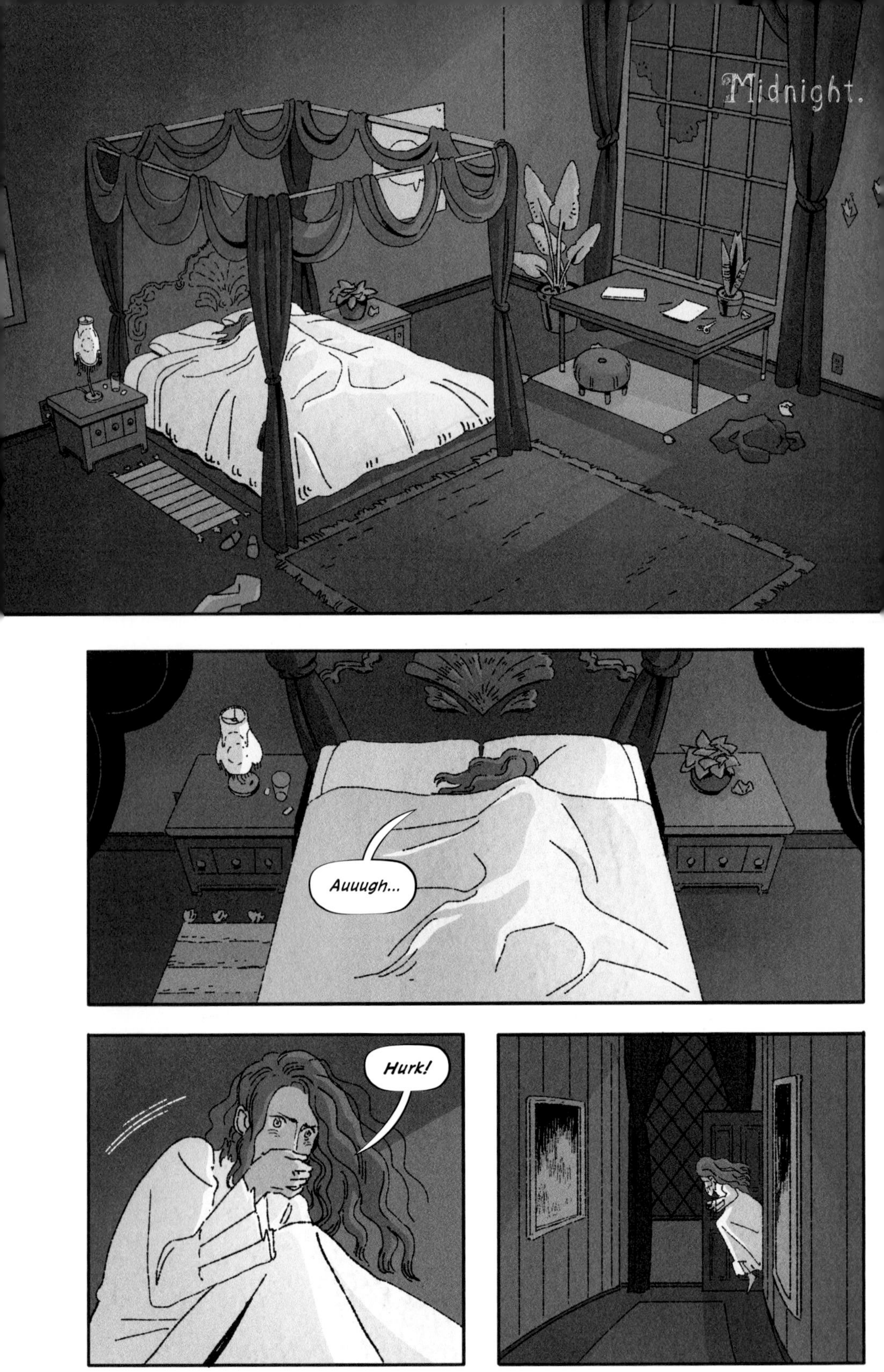
Midnight.
Auuugh...
Hurk!

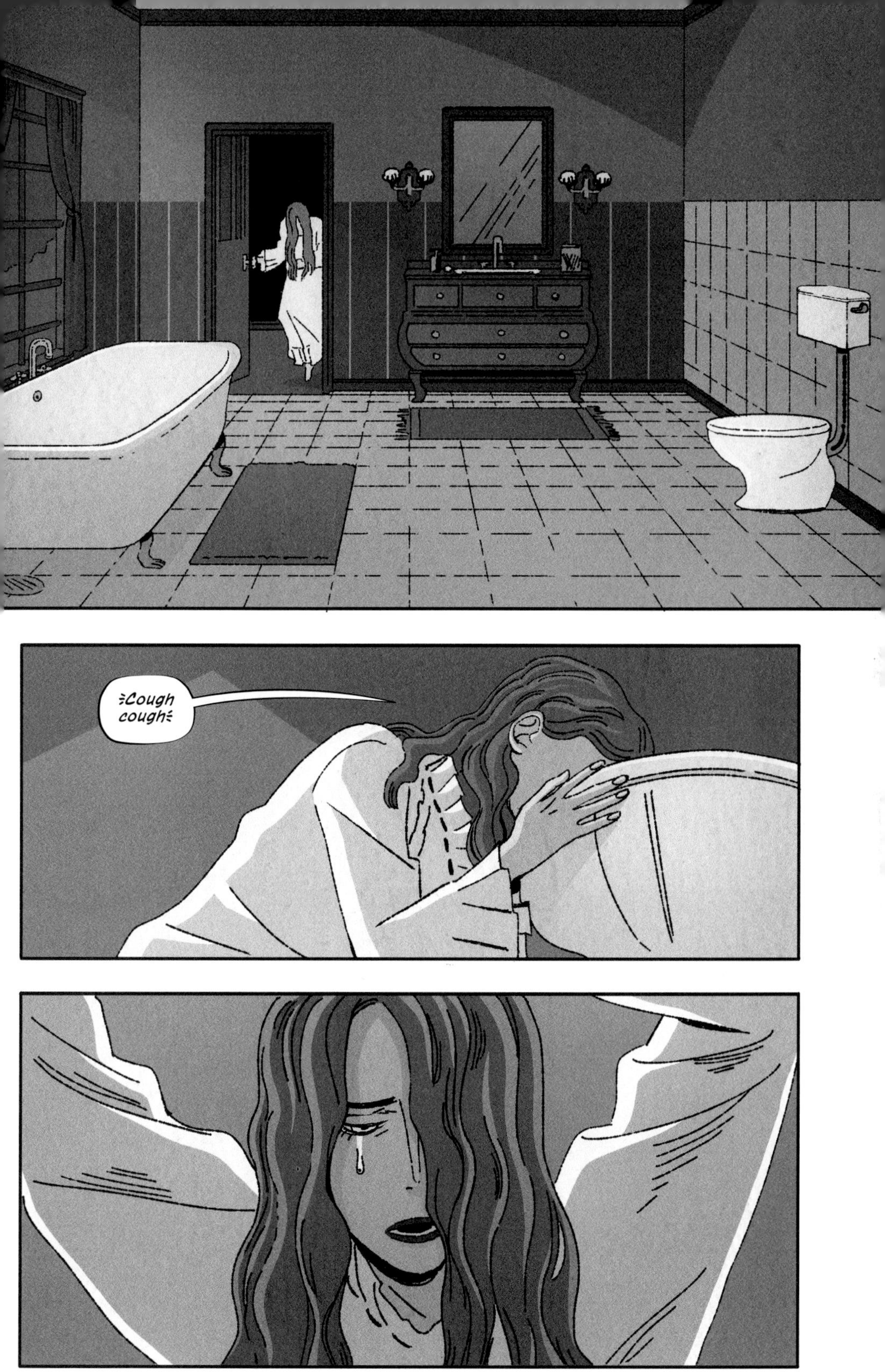
Cough cough

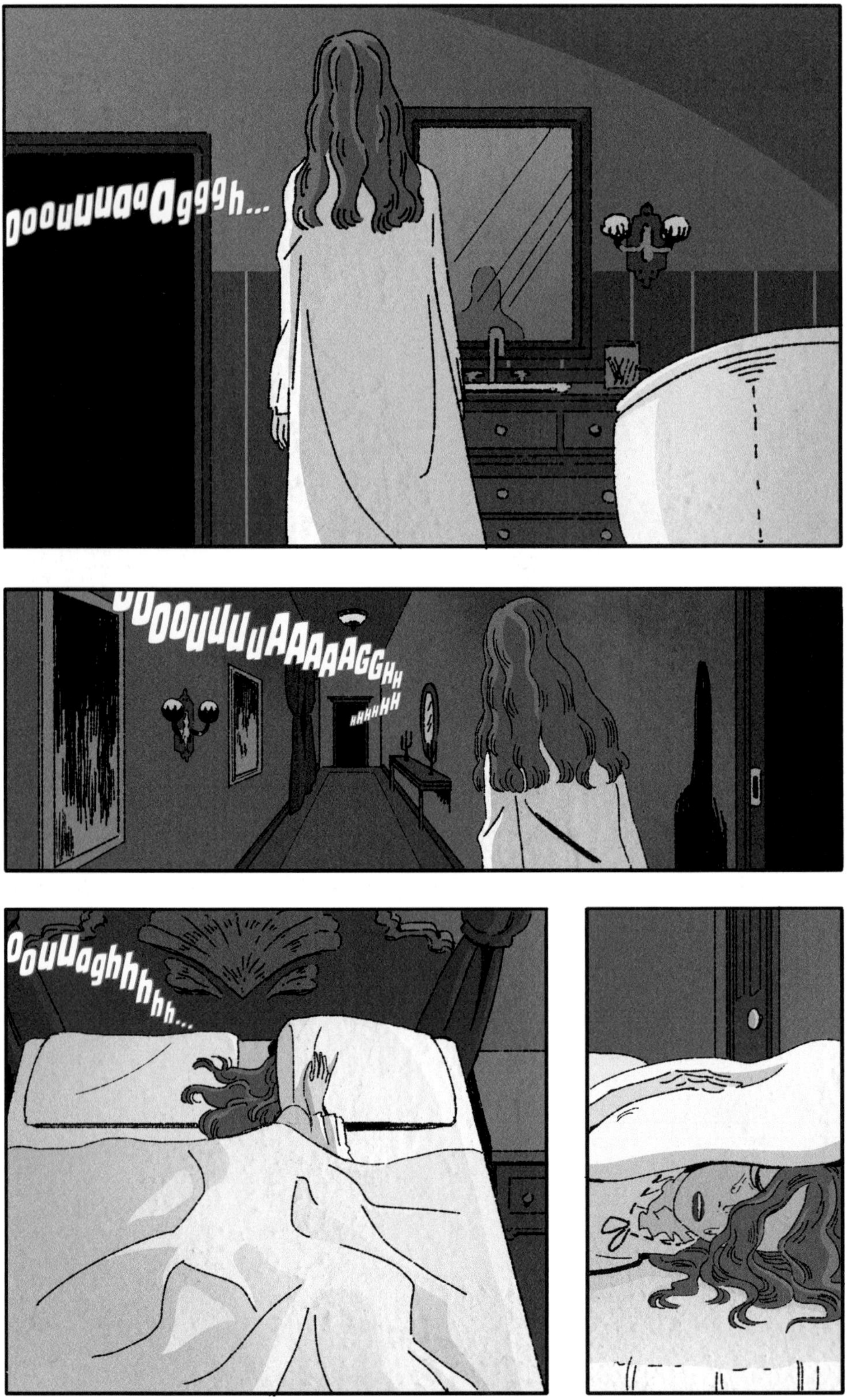
Doouuuaaaggggh...
DOOOUUUUAAAAAGGHHHHHHHH
Oouuaghhhhhh...

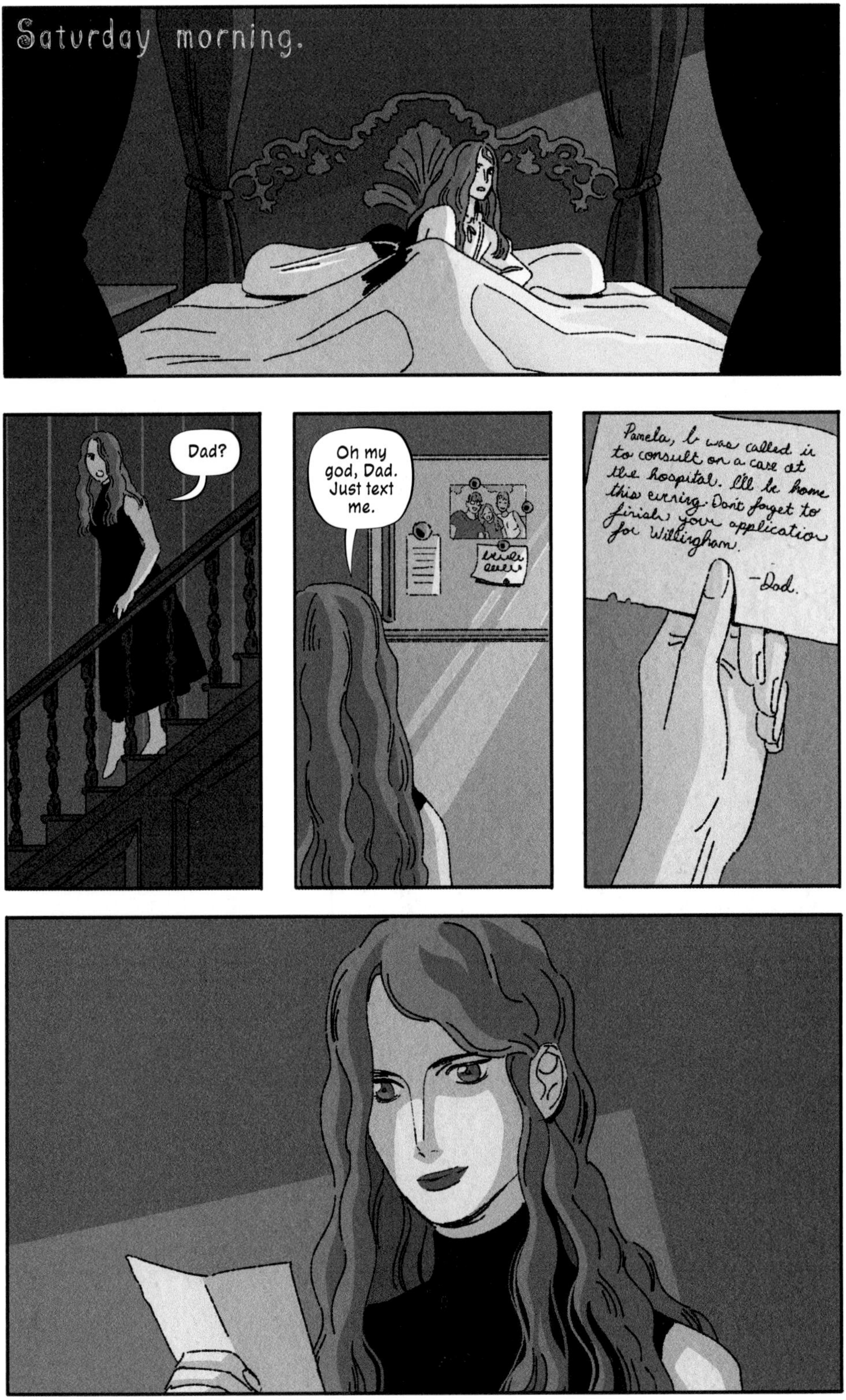
Saturday morning.
Dad?
Oh my god, Dad. Just text me.
Pamela, I was called in to consult on a case at the hospital. I'll be home this evening. Don't forget to finish your application for Willingham.
-Dad.

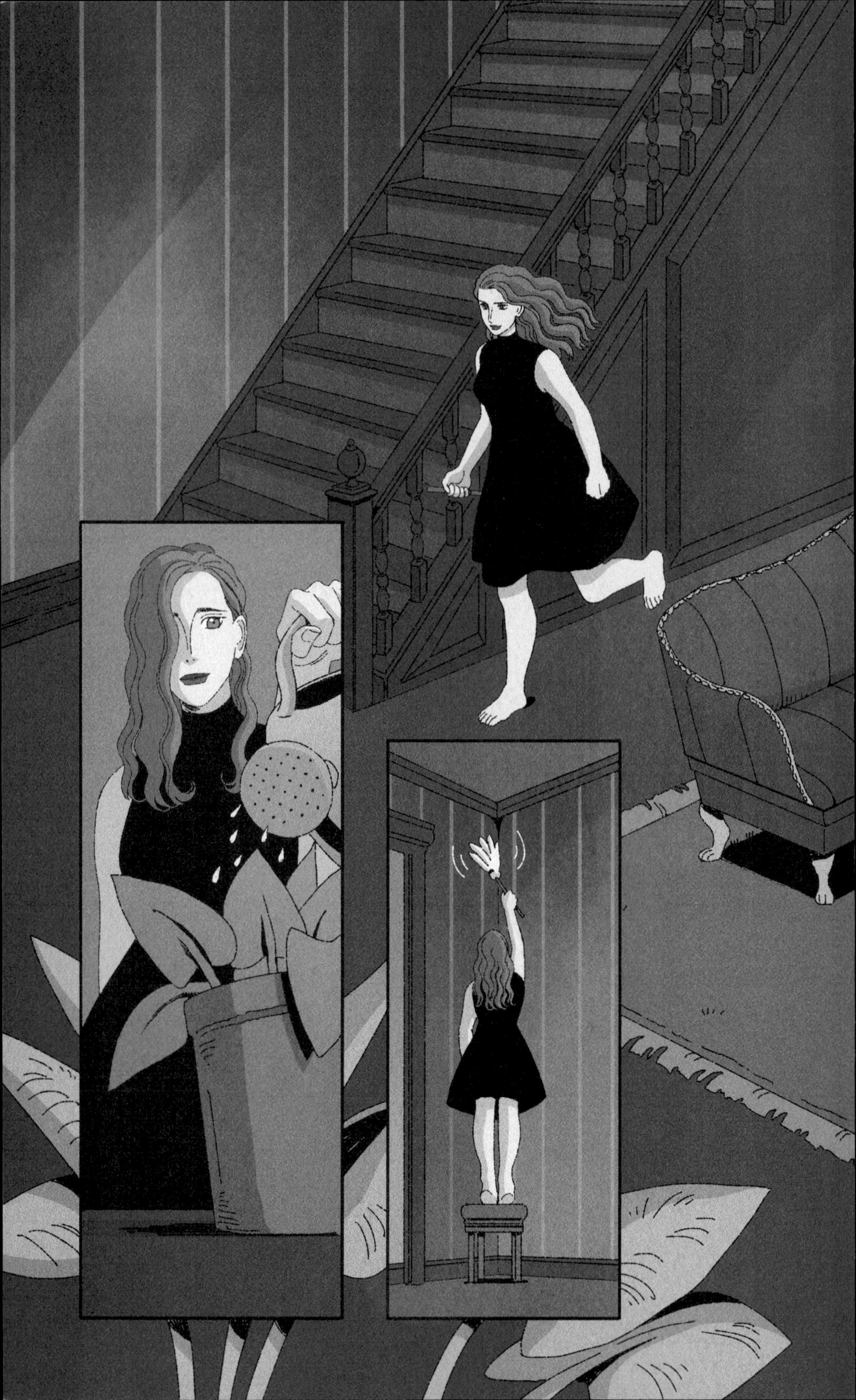

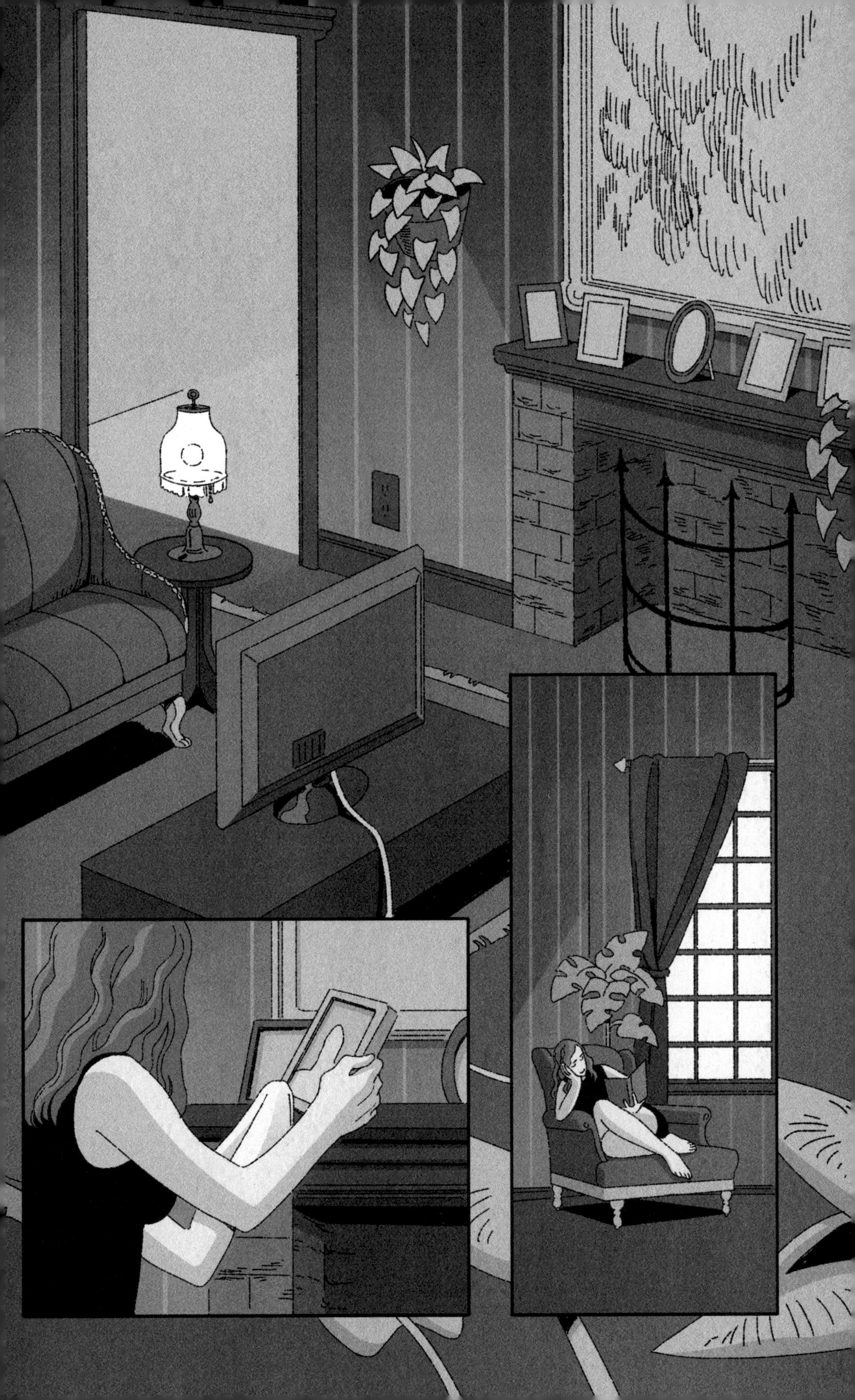

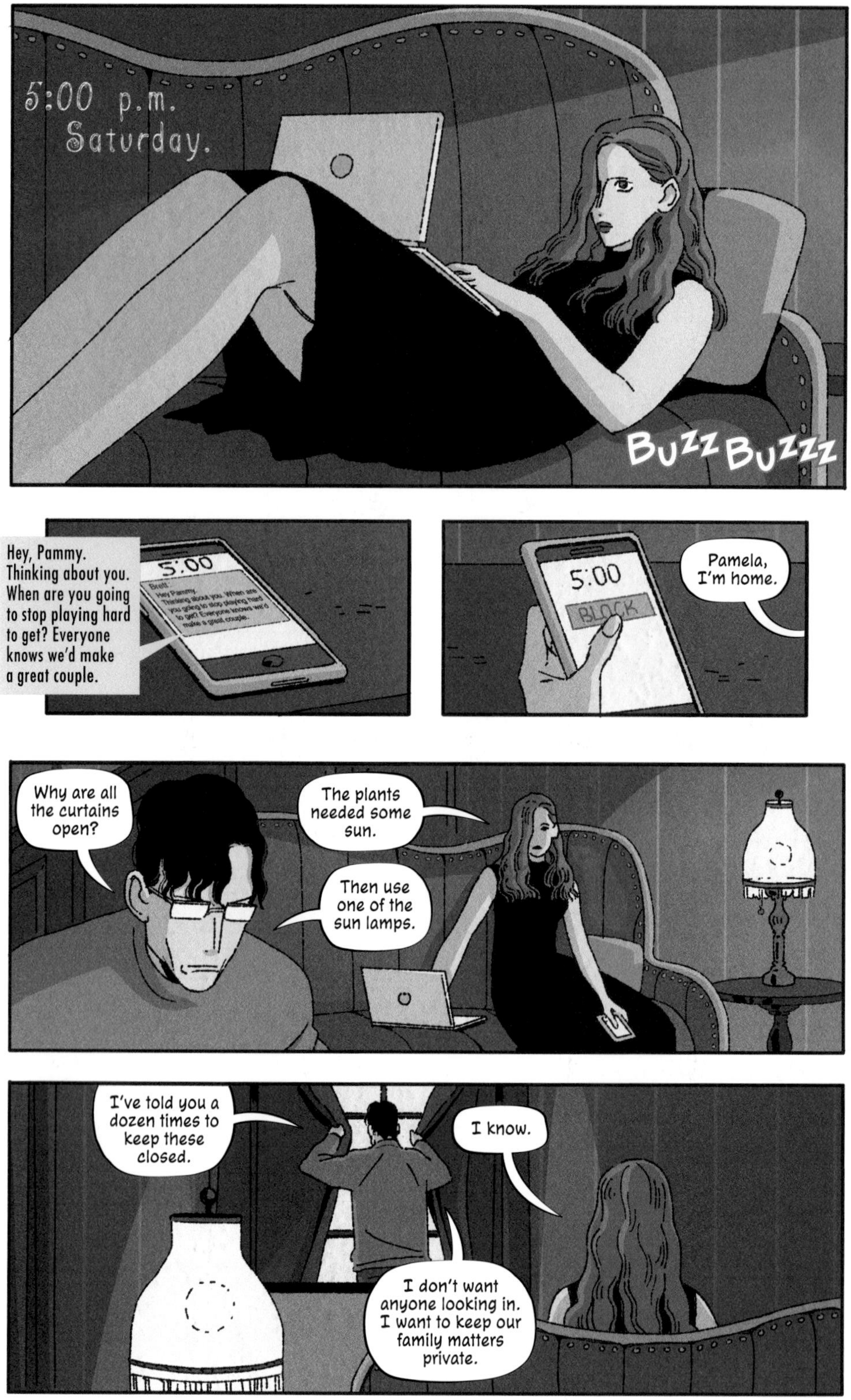
5:00 p.m.
Saturday.
BUZZ BUZZZ
5:00
Hey, Pammy. Thinking about you. When are you going to stop playing hard to get? Everyone knows we'd make a great couple.
5:00
BLOCK
Pamela, I'm home.
Why are all the curtains open?
The plants needed some sun.
Then use one of the sun lamps.
I've told you a dozen times to keep these closed.
I know.
I don't want anyone looking in. I want to keep our family matters private.

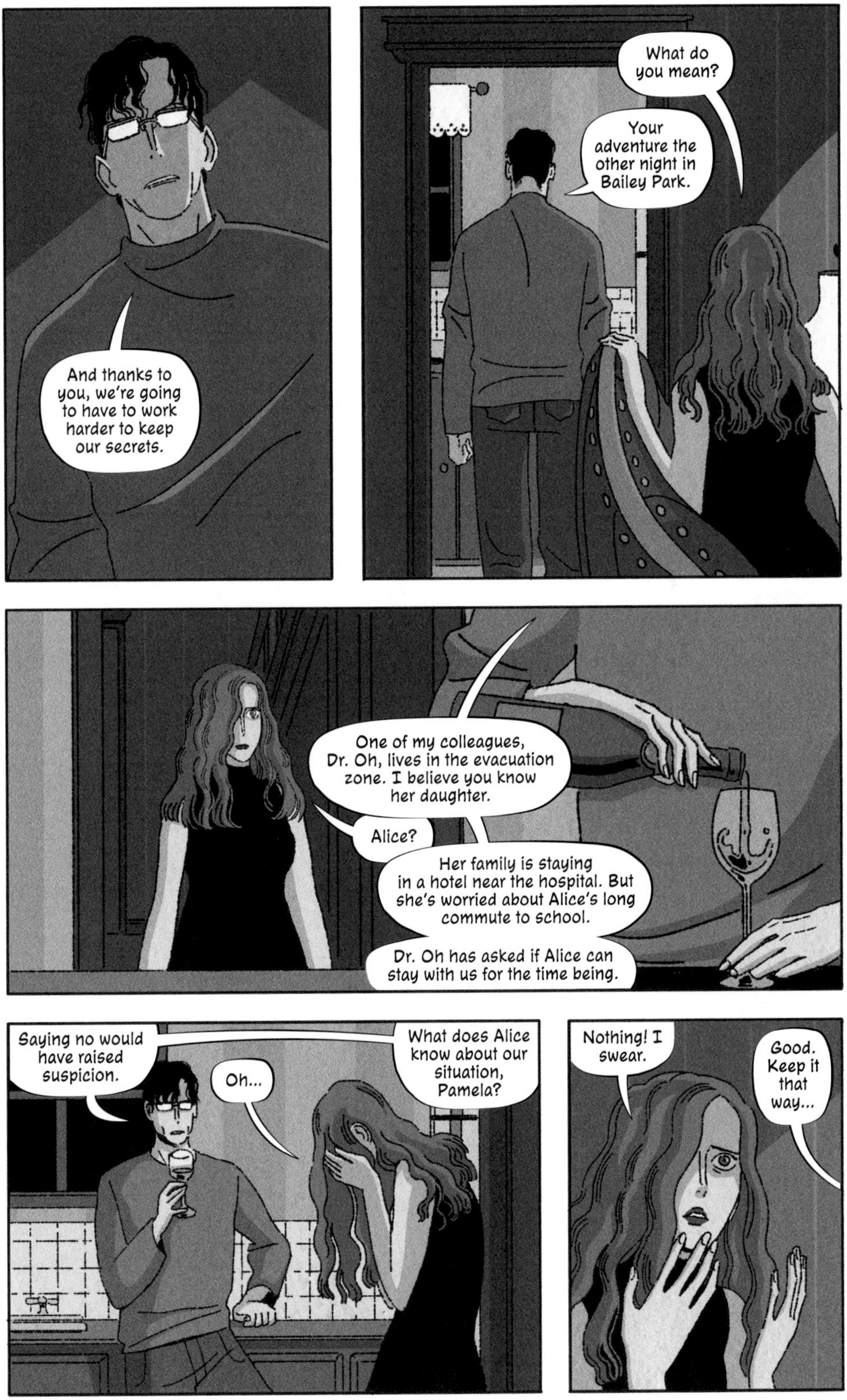
And thanks to you, we're going to have to work harder to keep our secrets.
What do you mean?
Your adventure the other night in Bailey Park.
One of my colleagues, Dr. Oh, lives in the evacuation zone. I believe you know her daughter.
Alice?
Her family is staying in a hotel near the hospital. But she's worried about Alice's long commute to school.
Dr. Oh has asked if Alice can stay with us for the time being.
Saying no would have raised suspicion.
Oh...
What does Alice know about our situation, Pamela?
Nothing! I swear.
Good. Keep it that way...

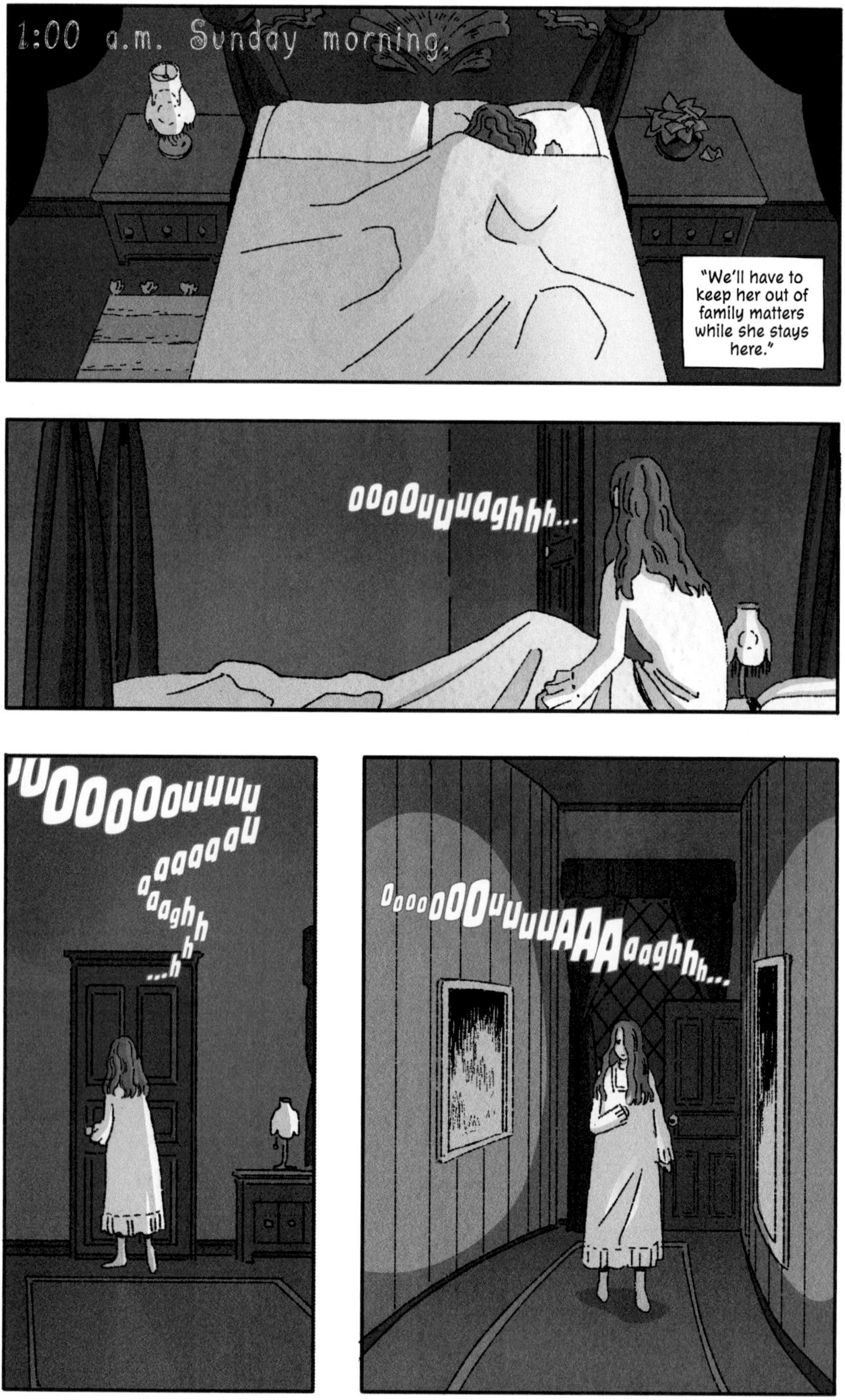
1:00 a.m. Sunday morning.
"We'll have to keep her out of family matters while she stays here."
oooOuuuaghhh...
UOOOOOouuuu
aaaaaau
aaaghhh
...h
ooooOOOuuuuAAAaaghhhh...

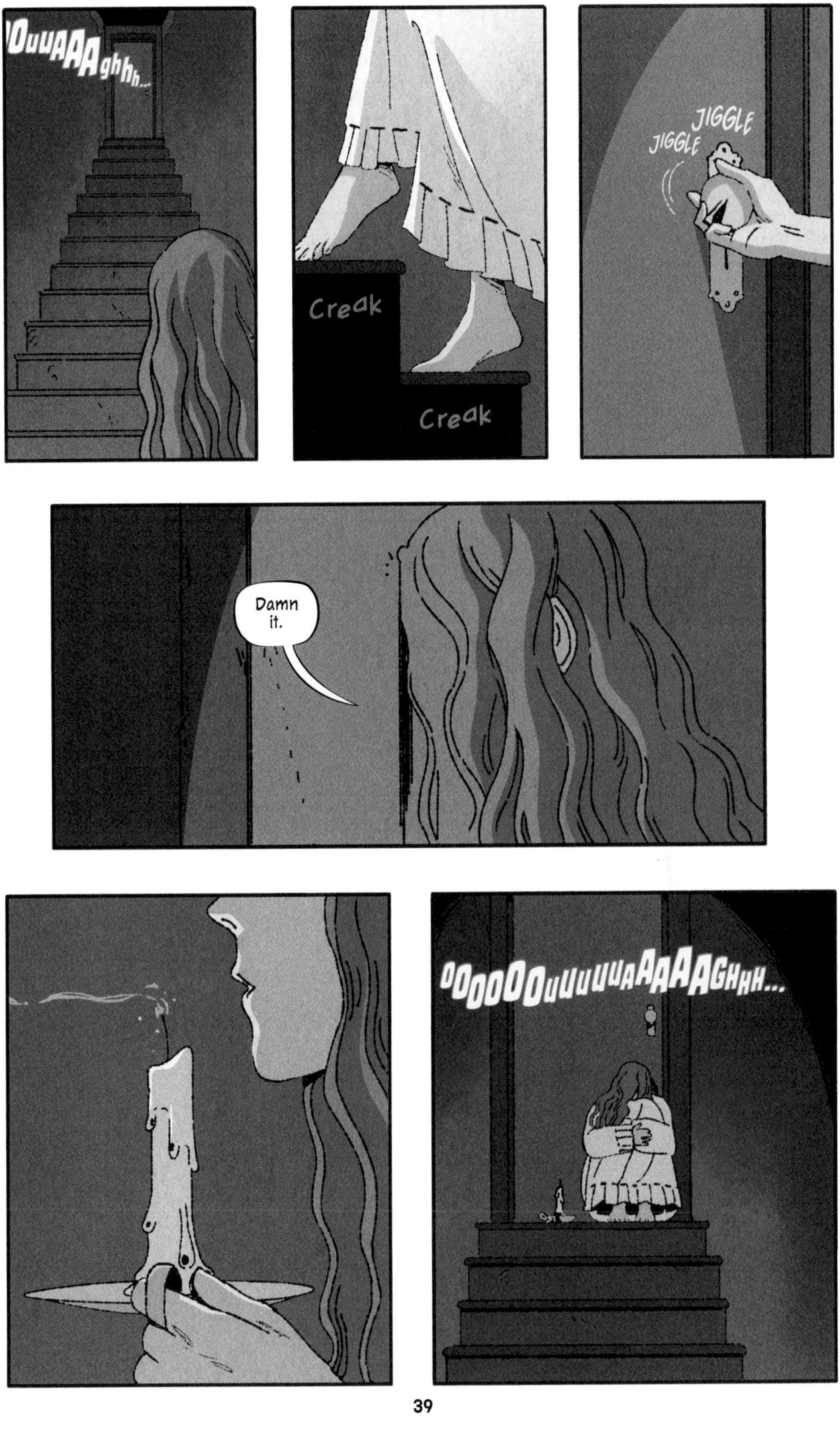
OuuAAAghhh...
Creak
Creak
JIGGLE
JIGGLE
Damn it.
OOOOOOuuuuuAAAAGhhh...

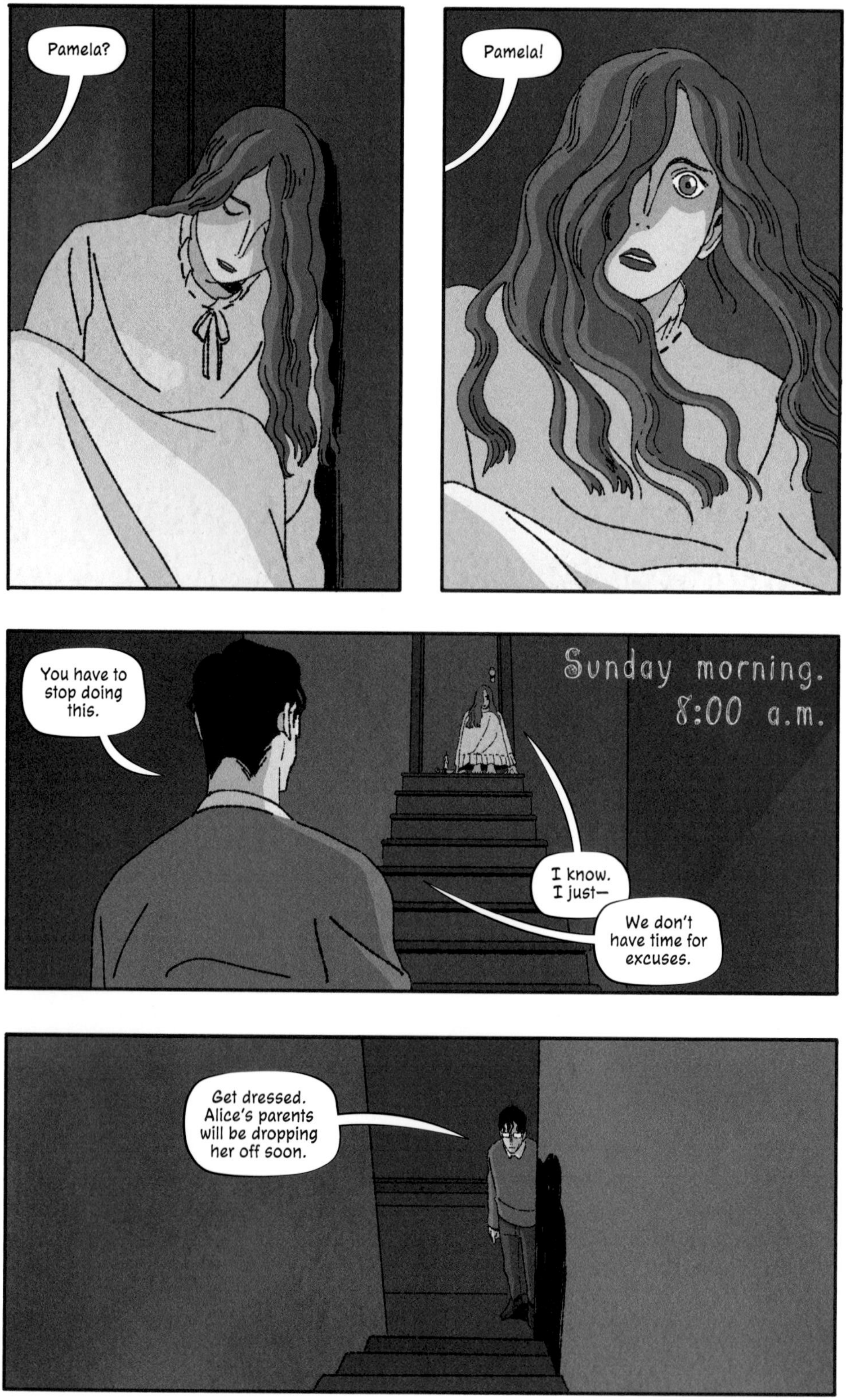
Pamela?
Pamela!
Sunday morning. 8:00 a.m.
You have to stop doing this.
I know. I just—
We don't have time for excuses.
Get dressed. Alice's parents will be dropping her off soon.

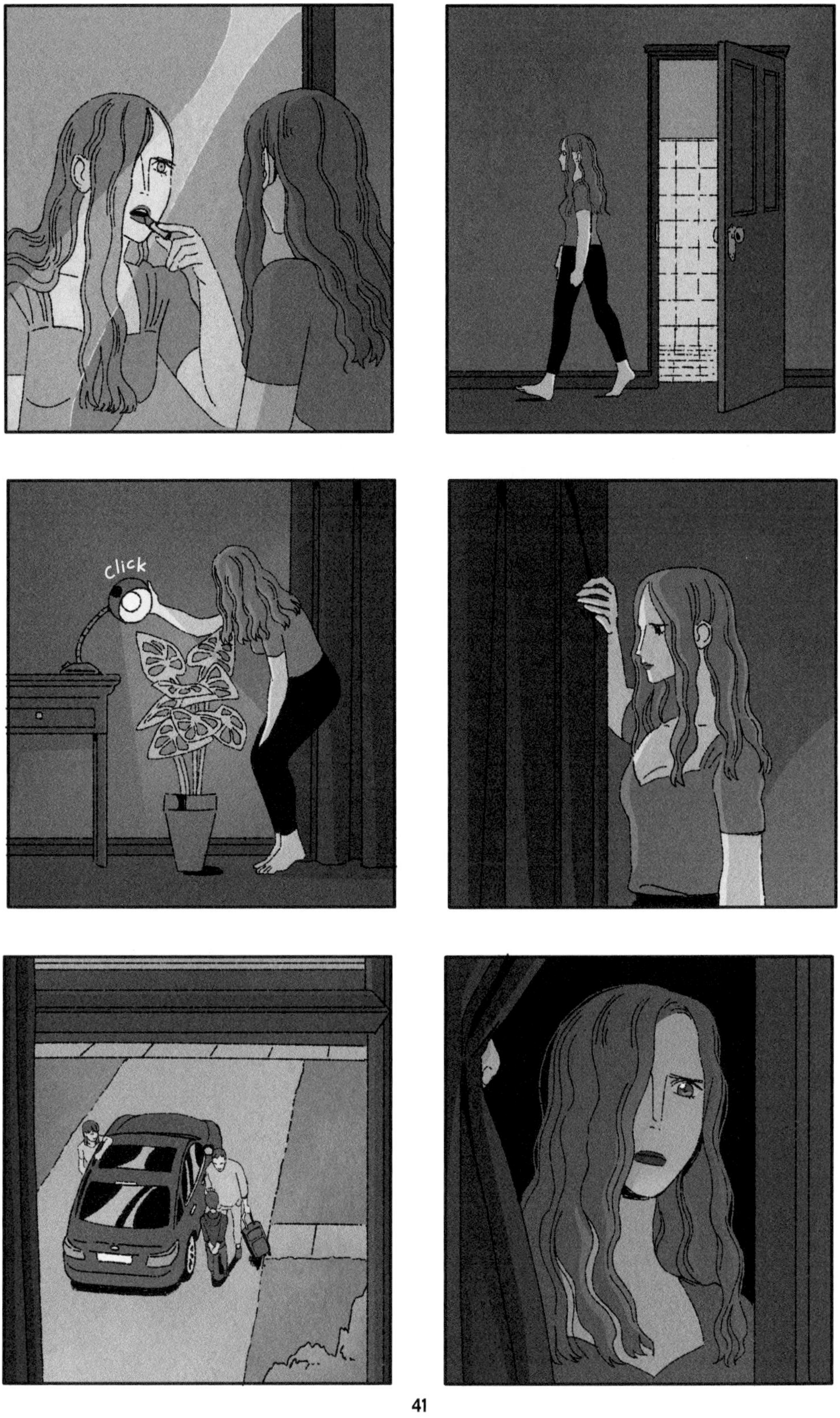
Click

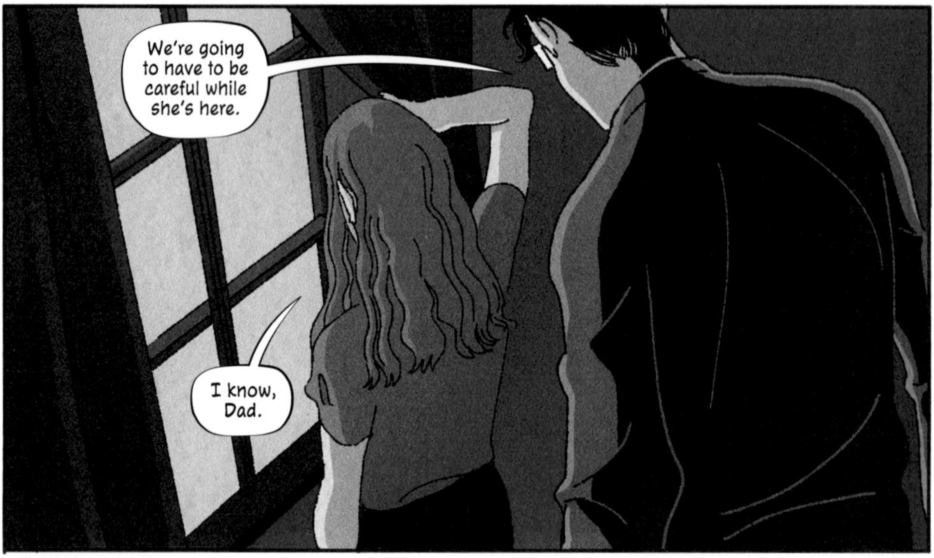
We're going to have to be careful while she's here.
I know, Dad.

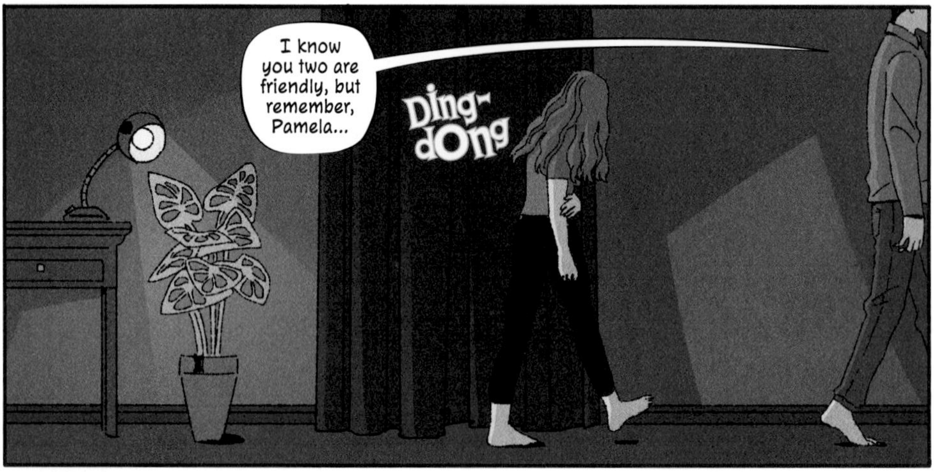
I know you two are friendly, but remember, Pamela...
Ding-dOng

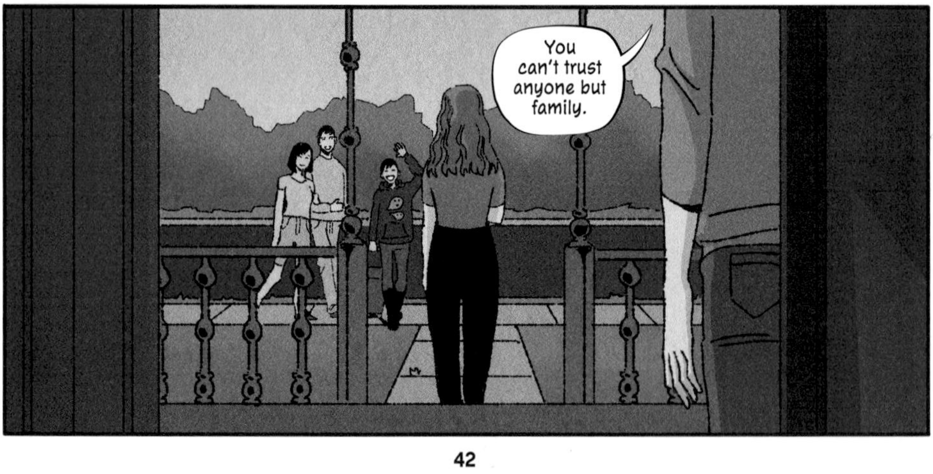
You can't trust anyone but family.

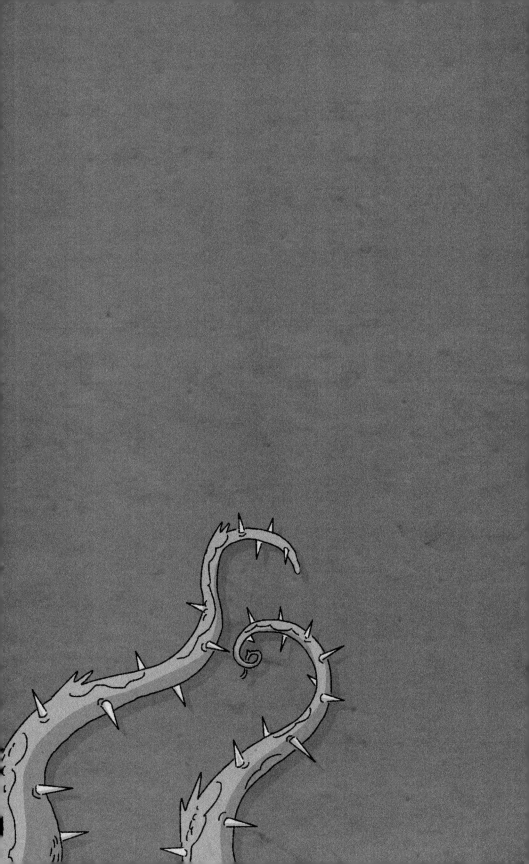

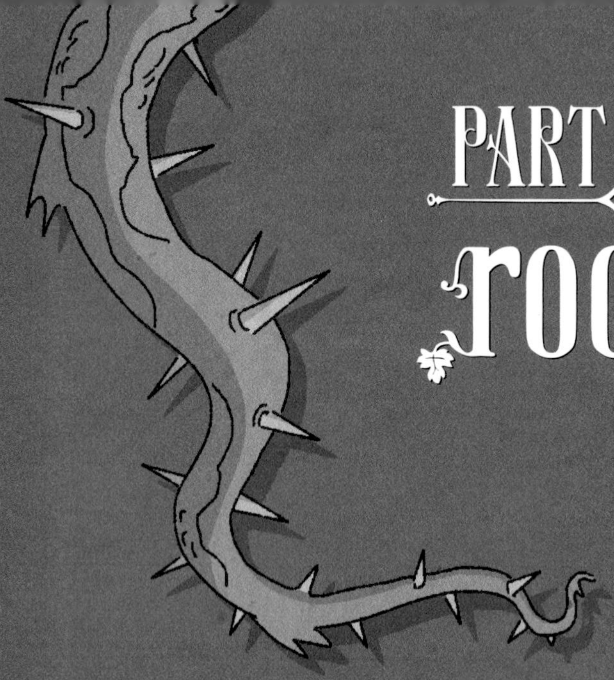

# PART TWO
# roots

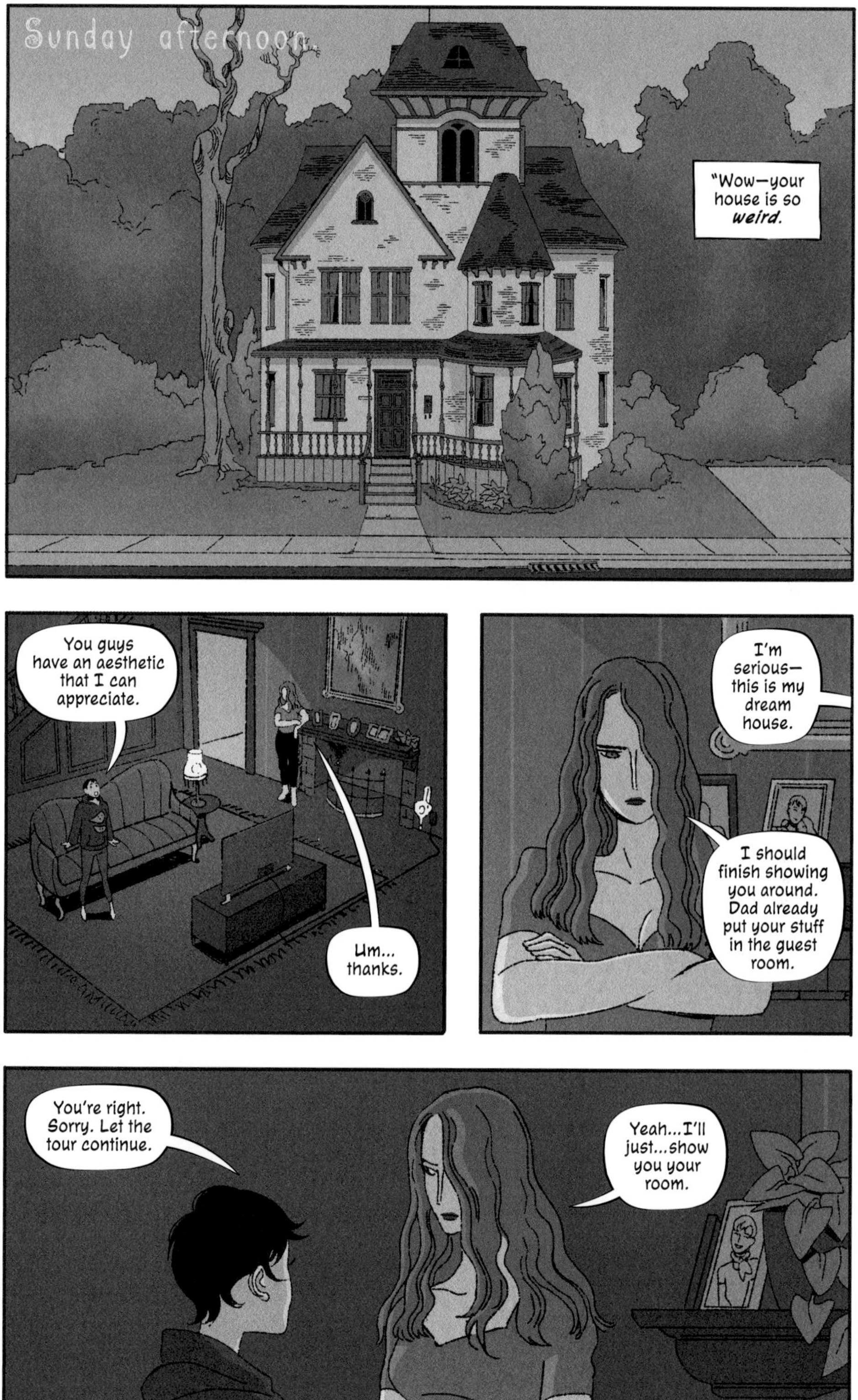
Sunday afternoon...
"Wow—your house is so *weird*.
You guys have an aesthetic that I can appreciate.
Um... thanks.
I'm serious—this is my dream house.
I should finish showing you around. Dad already put your stuff in the guest room.
You're right. Sorry. Let the tour continue.
Yeah...I'll just...show you your room.

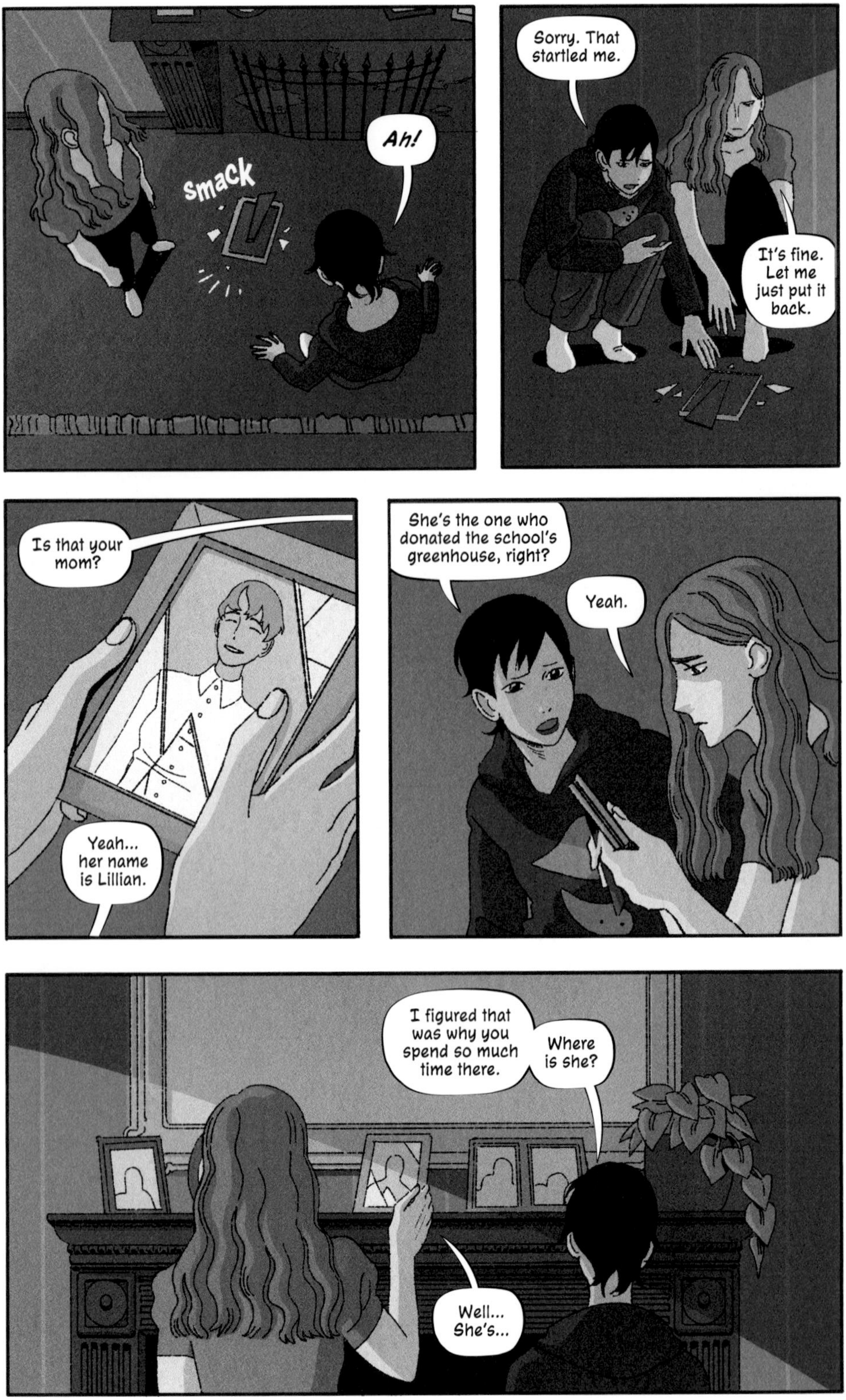
Smack
Ah!
Sorry. That startled me.
It's fine. Let me just put it back.
Is that your mom?
Yeah... her name is Lillian.
She's the one who donated the school's greenhouse, right?
Yeah.
I figured that was why you spend so much time there.
Where is she?
Well... She's...

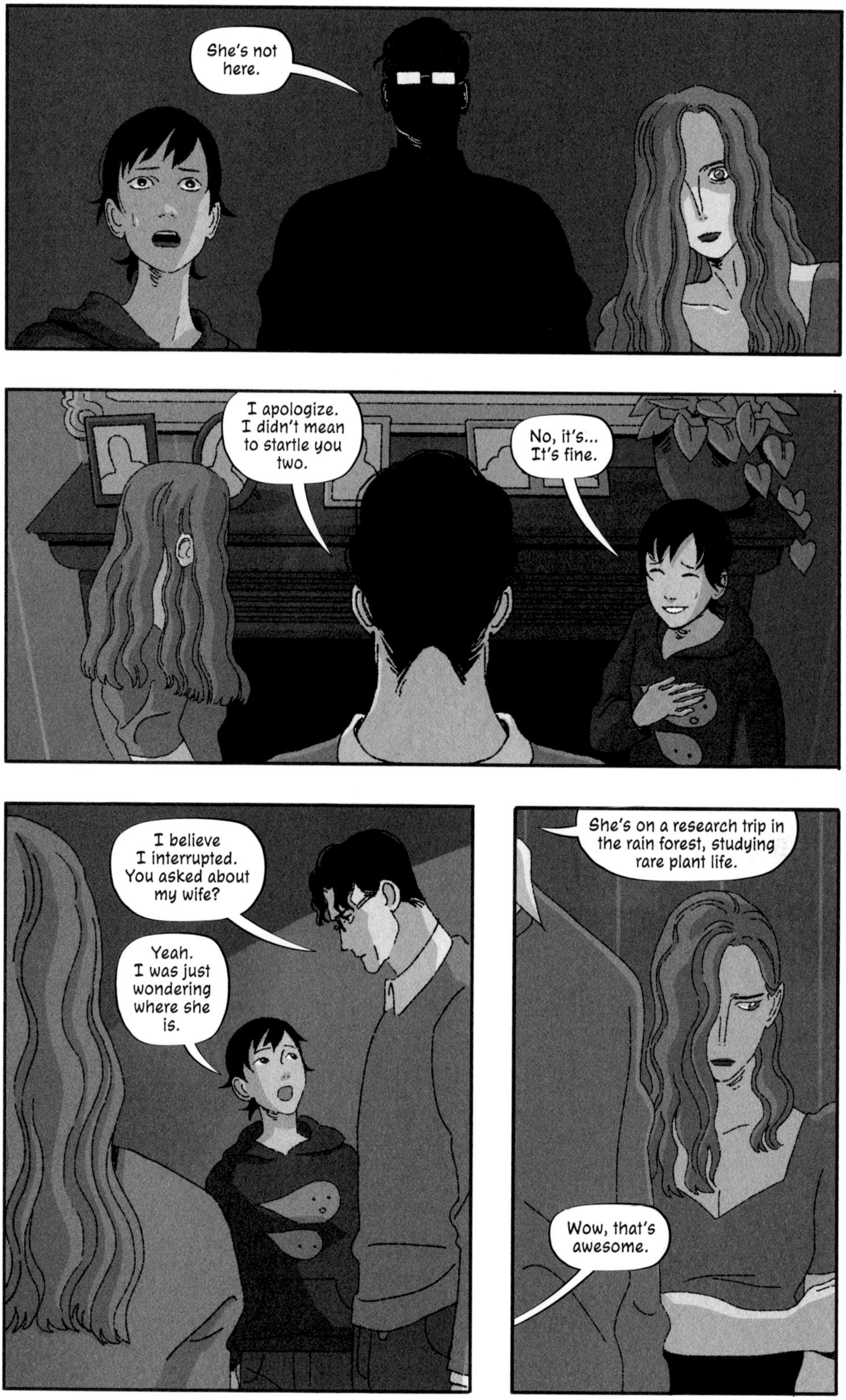
She's not here.
I apologize. I didn't mean to startle you two.
No, it's... It's fine.
I believe I interrupted. You asked about my wife?
Yeah. I was just wondering where she is.
She's on a research trip in the rain forest, studying rare plant life.
Wow, that's awesome.

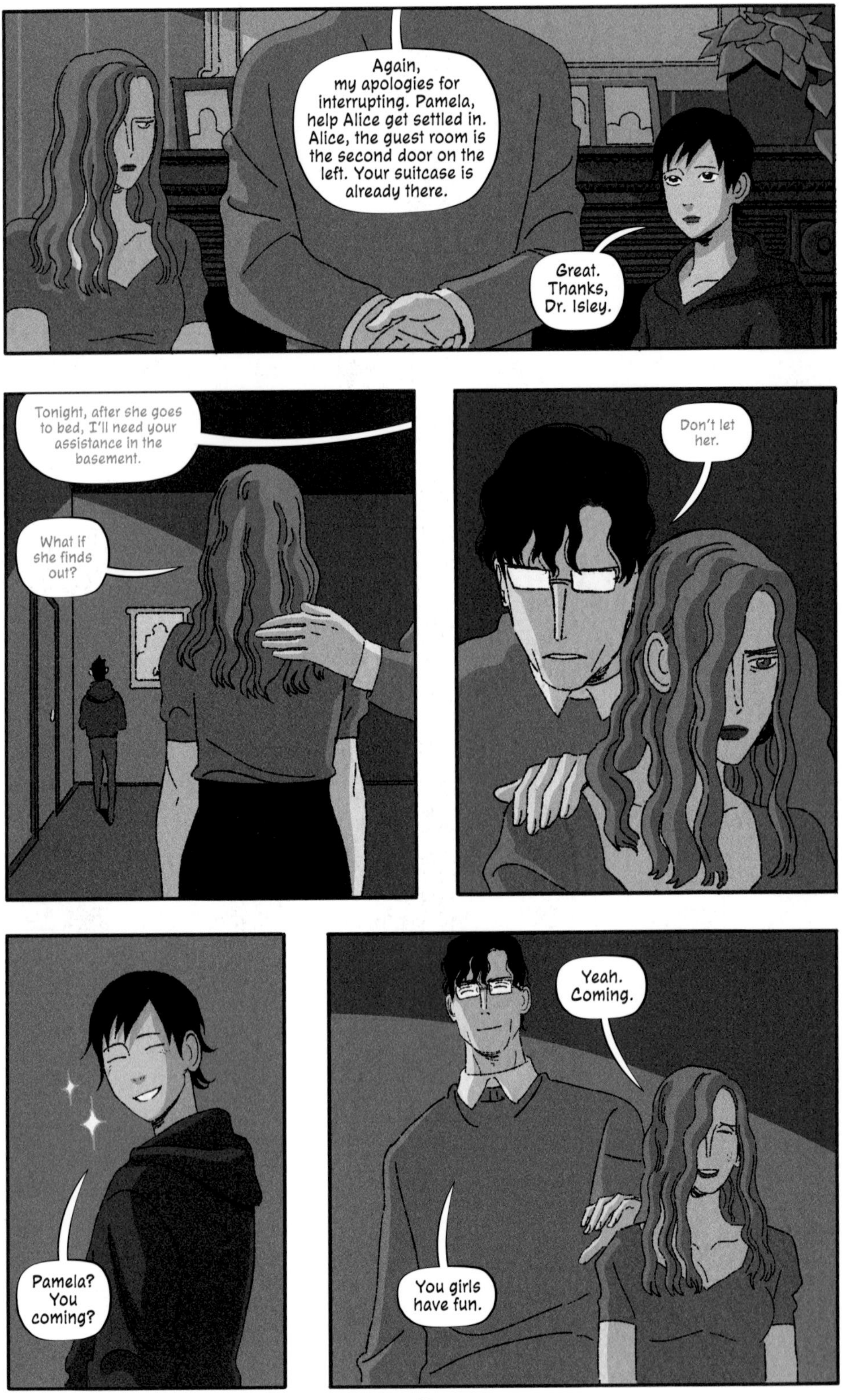
Again, my apologies for interrupting. Pamela, help Alice get settled in. Alice, the guest room is the second door on the left. Your suitcase is already there.
Great. Thanks, Dr. Isley.
Tonight, after she goes to bed, I'll need your assistance in the basement.
What if she finds out?
Don't let her.
Pamela? You coming?
Yeah. Coming.
You girls have fun.

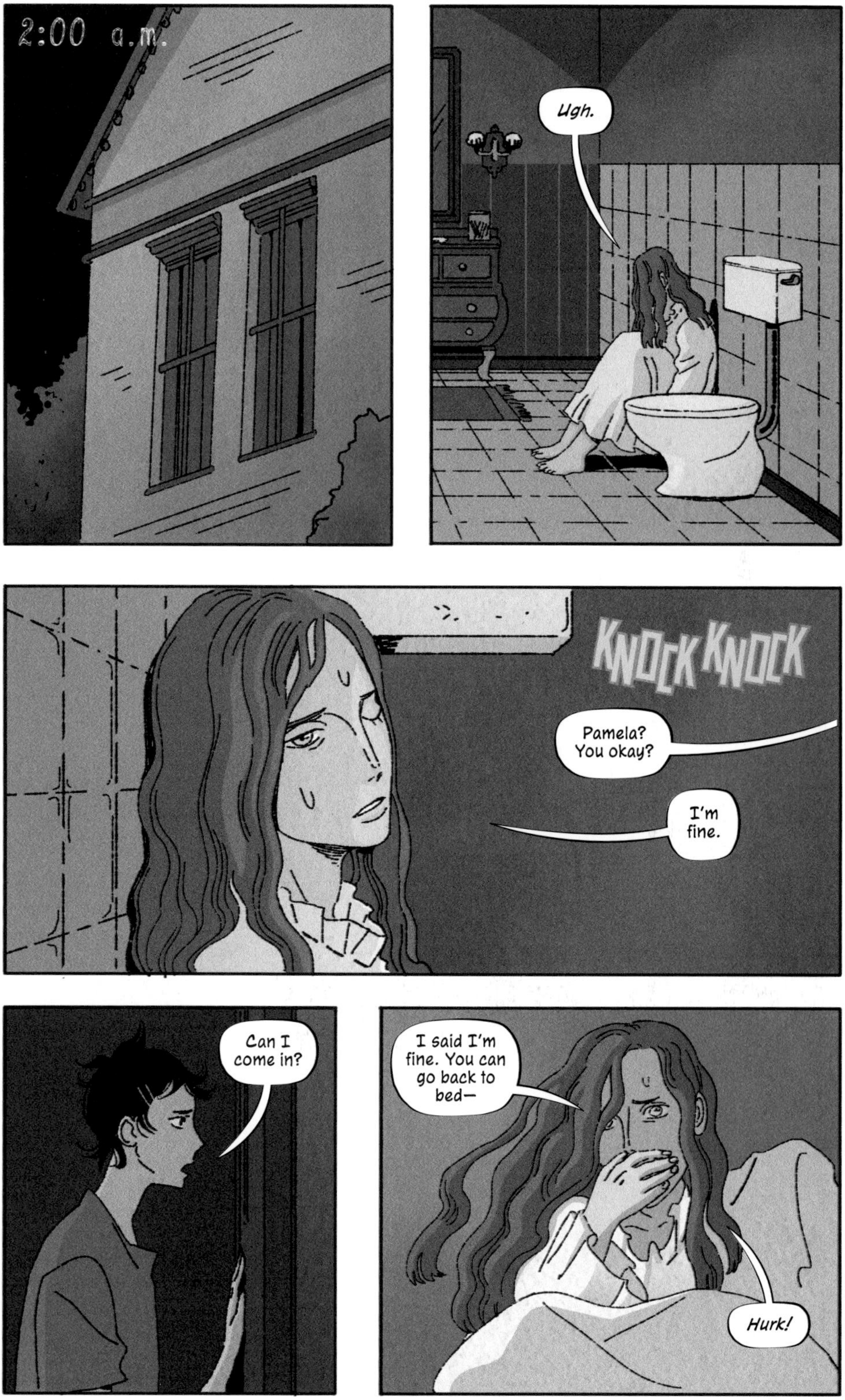
2:00 a.m.
Ugh.
KNOCK KNOCK
Pamela? You okay?
I'm fine.
Can I come in?
I said I'm fine. You can go back to bed—
Hurk!

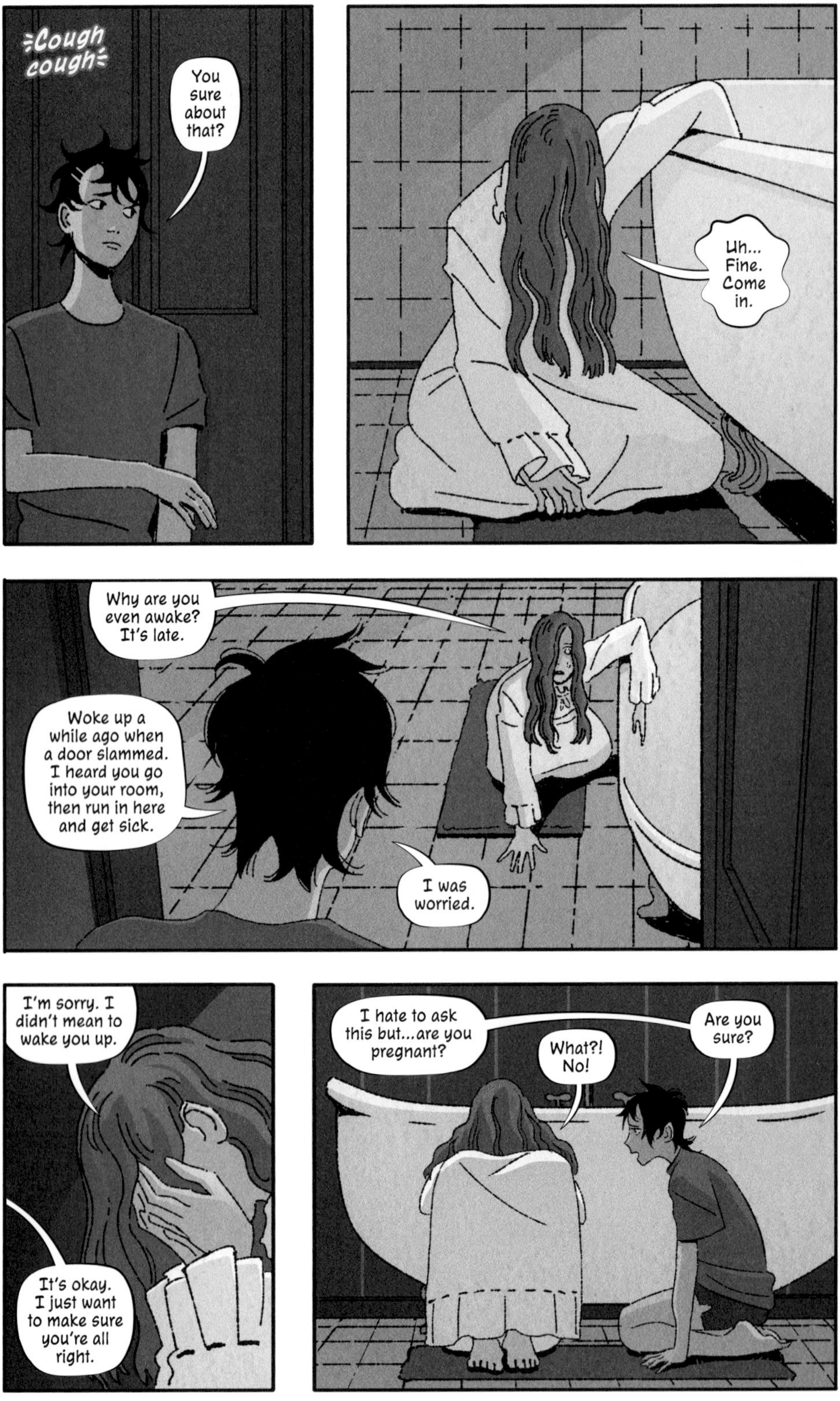
Cough cough
You sure about that?
Uh... Fine. Come in.
Why are you even awake? It's late.
Woke up a while ago when a door slammed. I heard you go into your room, then run in here and get sick.
I was worried.
I'm sorry. I didn't mean to wake you up.
It's okay. I just want to make sure you're all right.
I hate to ask this but...are you pregnant?
What?! No!
Are you sure?

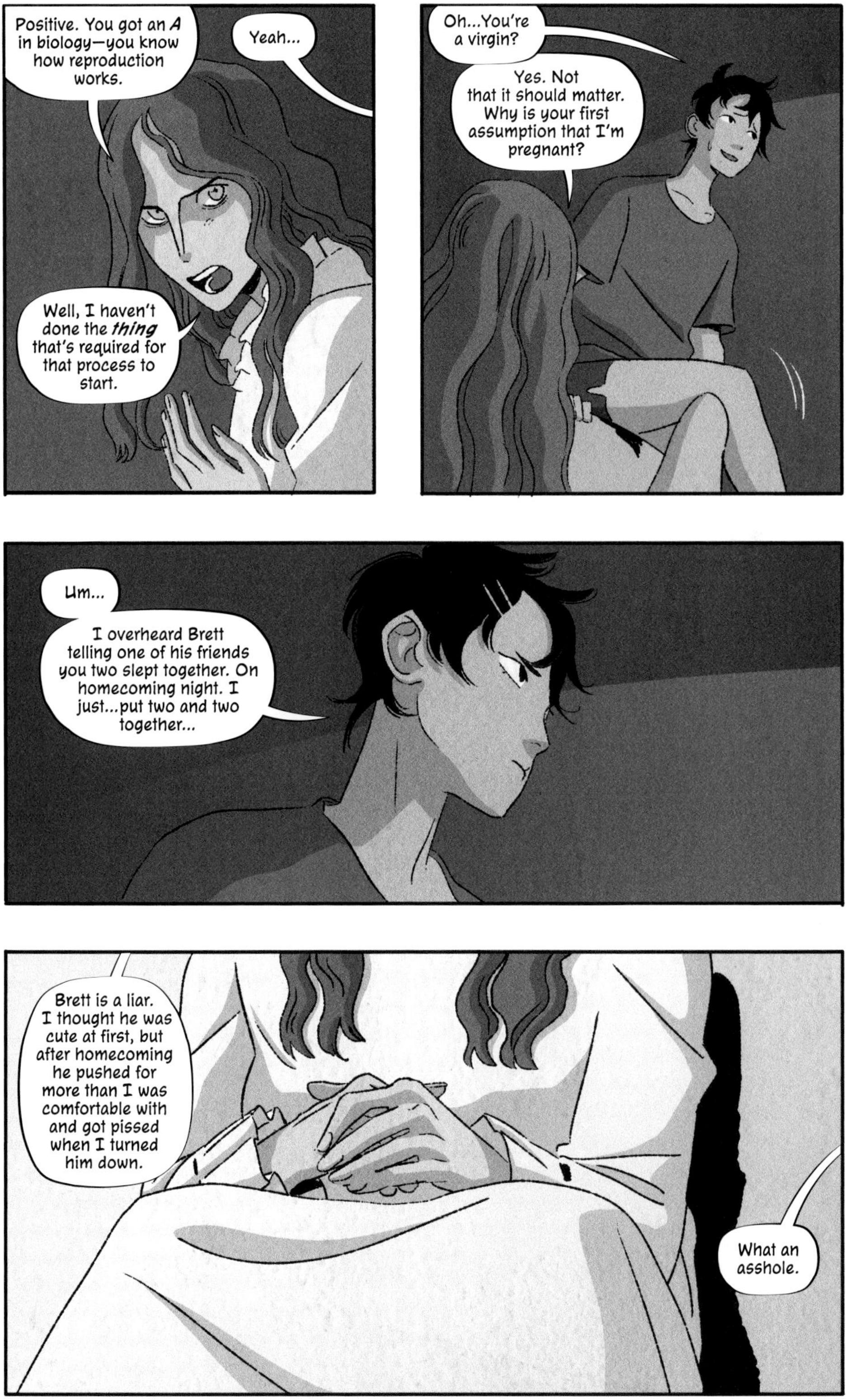
Positive. You got an *A* in biology—you know how reproduction works.
Yeah...
Well, I haven't done the *thing* that's required for that process to start.
Oh...You're a virgin?
Yes. Not that it should matter. Why is your first assumption that I'm pregnant?
Um...
I overheard Brett telling one of his friends you two slept together. On homecoming night. I just...put two and two together...
Brett is a liar. I thought he was cute at first, but after homecoming he pushed for more than I was comfortable with and got pissed when I turned him down.
What an asshole.

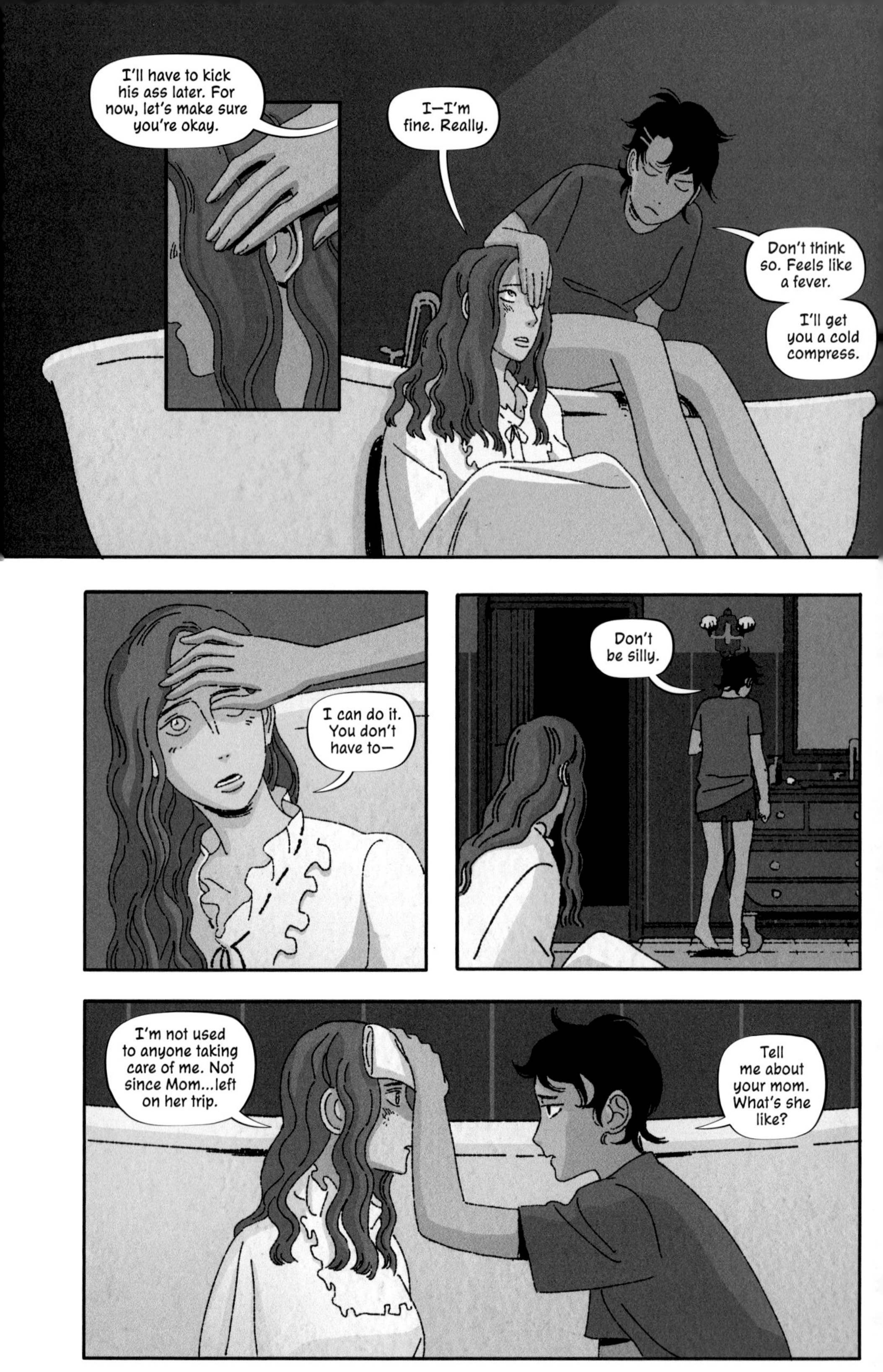
I'll have to kick his ass later. For now, let's make sure you're okay.
I—I'm fine. Really.
Don't think so. Feels like a fever.
I'll get you a cold compress.
I can do it. You don't have to—
Don't be silly.
I'm not used to anyone taking care of me. Not since Mom...left on her trip.
Tell me about your mom. What's she like?

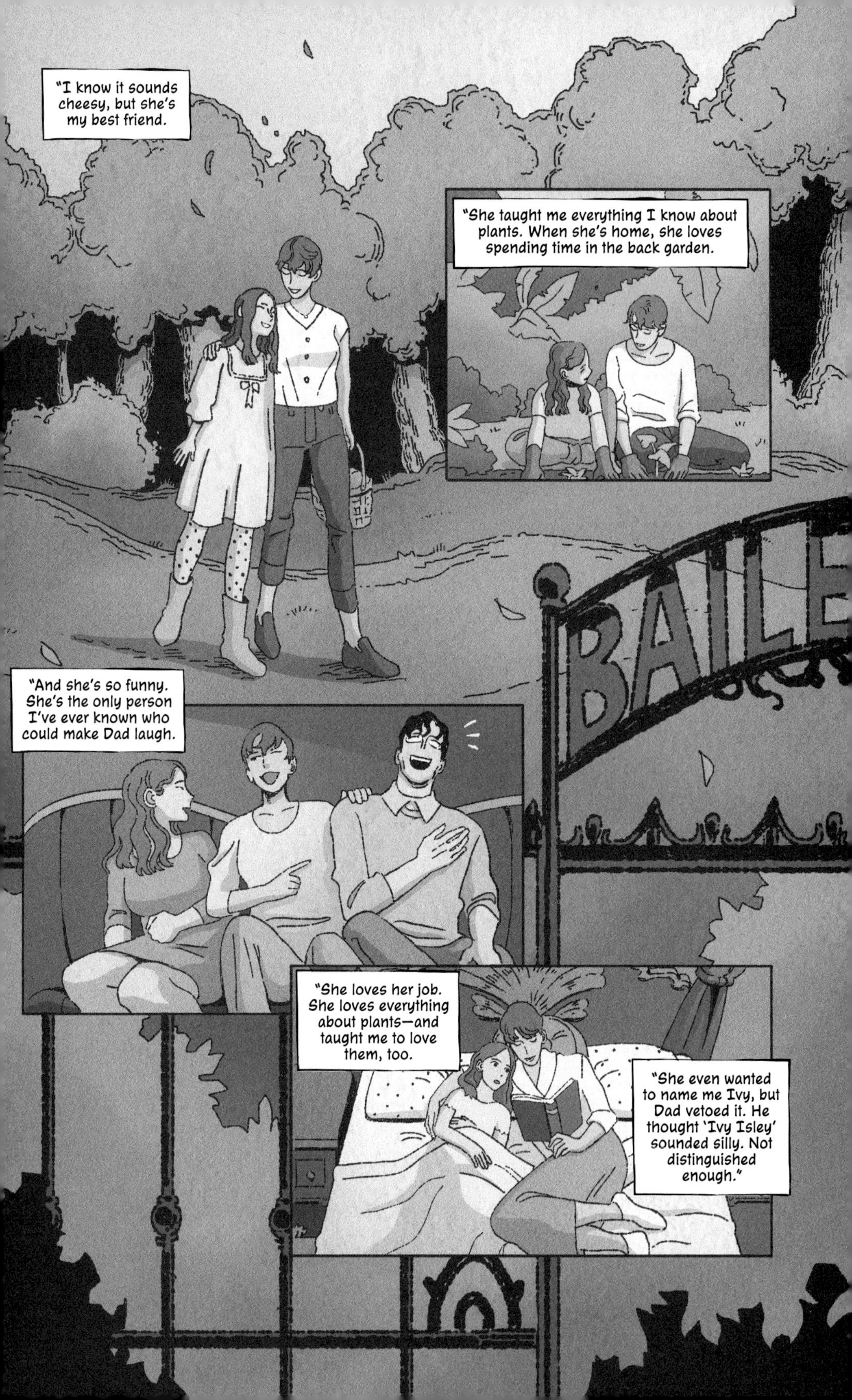
"I know it sounds cheesy, but she's my best friend.
"She taught me everything I know about plants. When she's home, she loves spending time in the back garden.
BAILE
"And she's so funny. She's the only person I've ever known who could make Dad laugh.
"She loves her job. She loves everything about plants—and taught me to love them, too.
"She even wanted to name me Ivy, but Dad vetoed it. He thought 'Ivy Isley' sounded silly. Not distinguished enough."

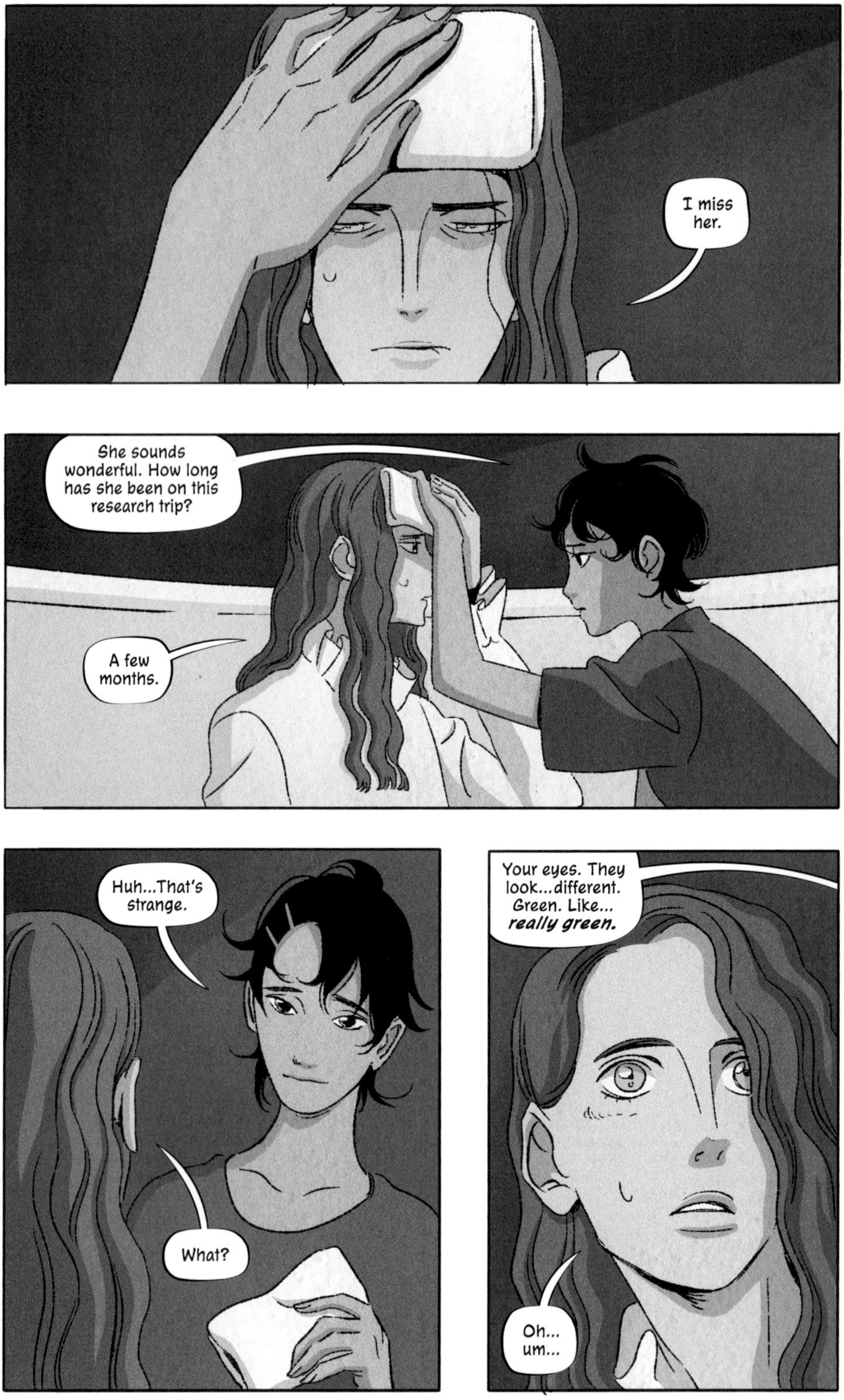
I miss her.
She sounds wonderful. How long has she been on this research trip?
A few months.
Huh...That's strange.
What?
Your eyes. They look...different. Green. Like... **really green.**
Oh... um...

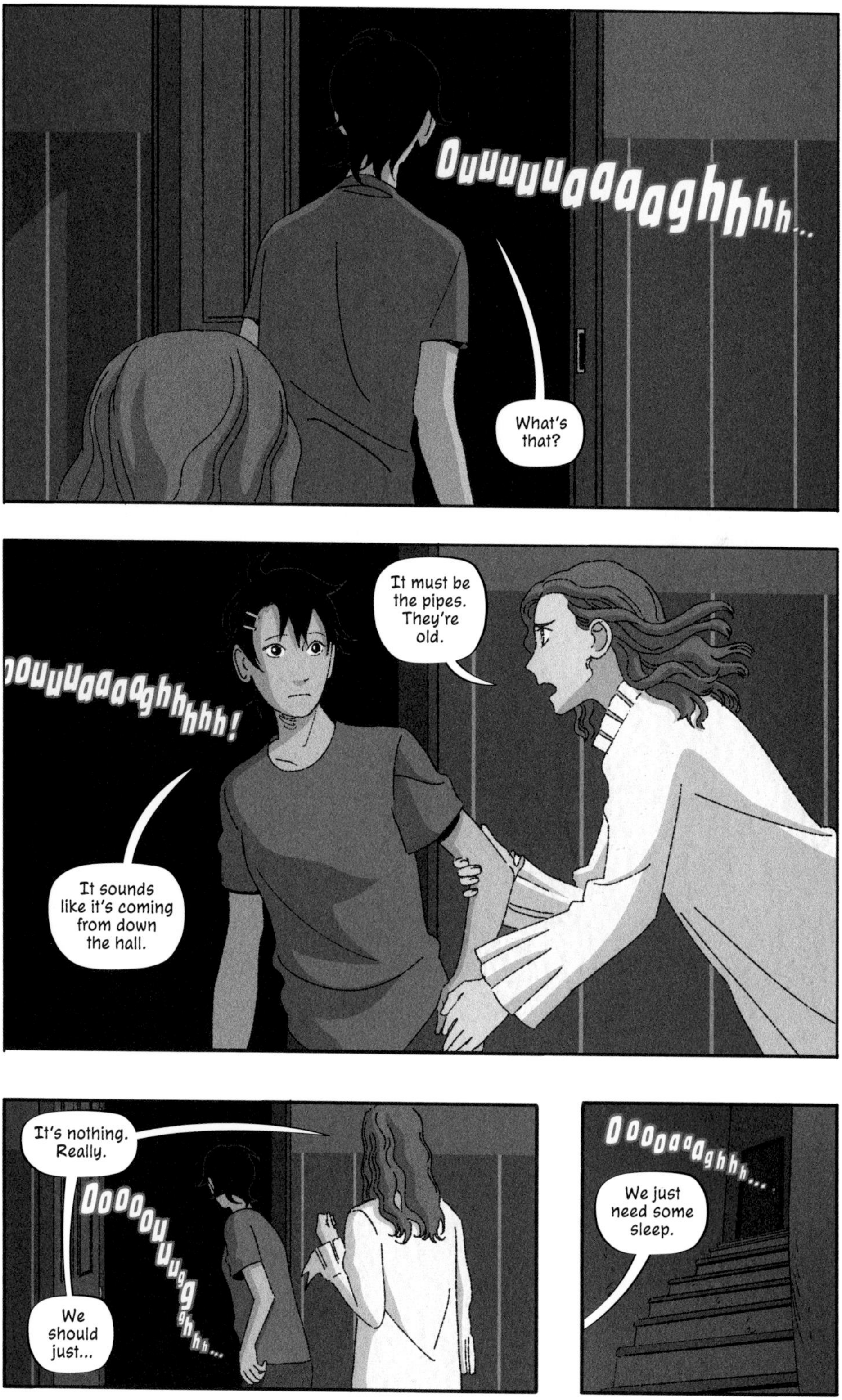
Ouuuuuaaaaghhhh...
What's that?
oouuuaaaaghhhhh!
It must be the pipes. They're old.
It sounds like it's coming from down the hall.
It's nothing. Really.
Ooooouuuggghhh...
We should just...
Ooooaaaghhh...
We just need some sleep.

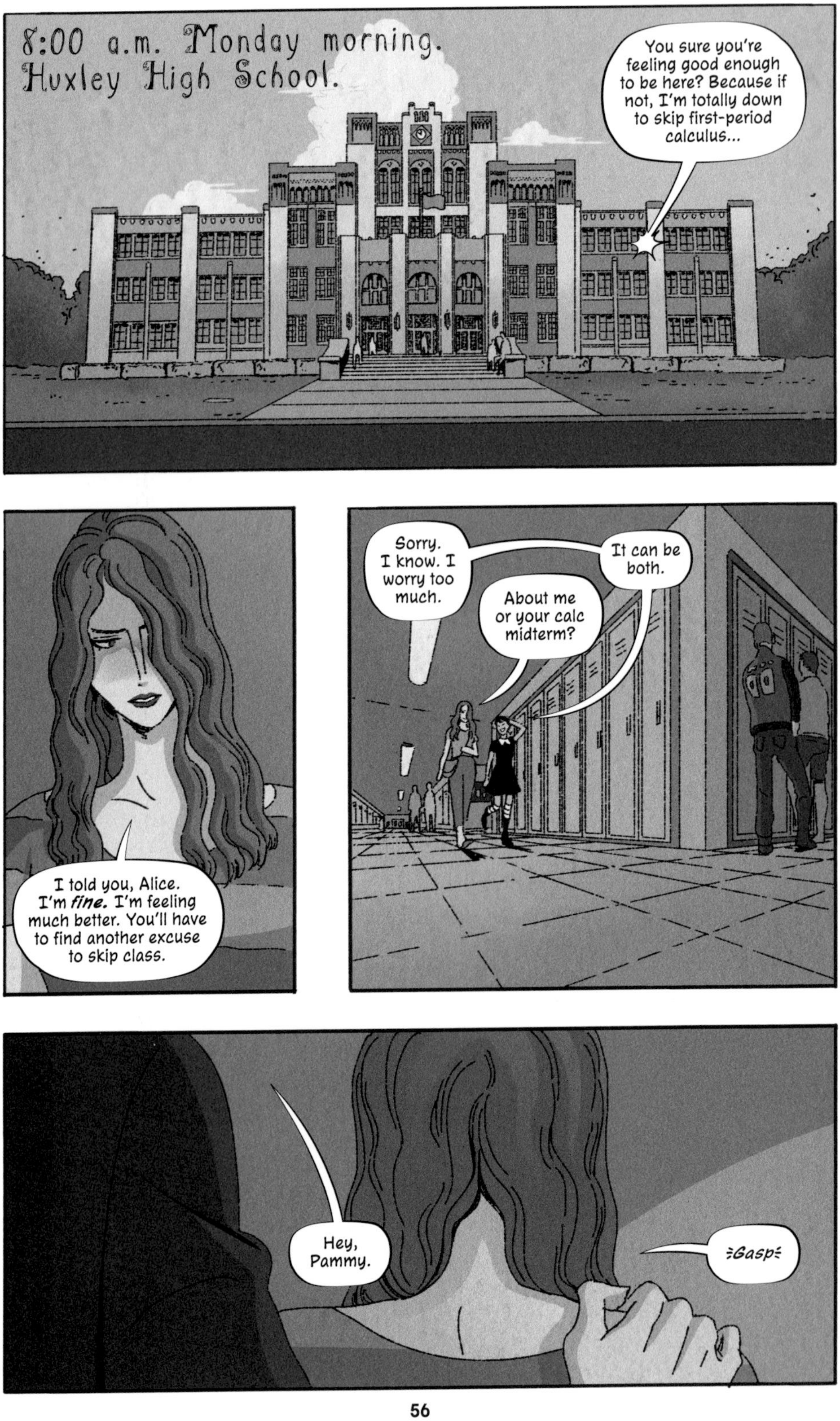
8:00 a.m. Monday morning. Huxley High School.
You sure you're feeling good enough to be here? Because if not, I'm totally down to skip first-period calculus...
I told you, Alice. I'm *fine.* I'm feeling much better. You'll have to find another excuse to skip class.
Sorry. I know. I worry too much.
It can be both.
About me or your calc midterm?
Hey, Pammy.
Gasp

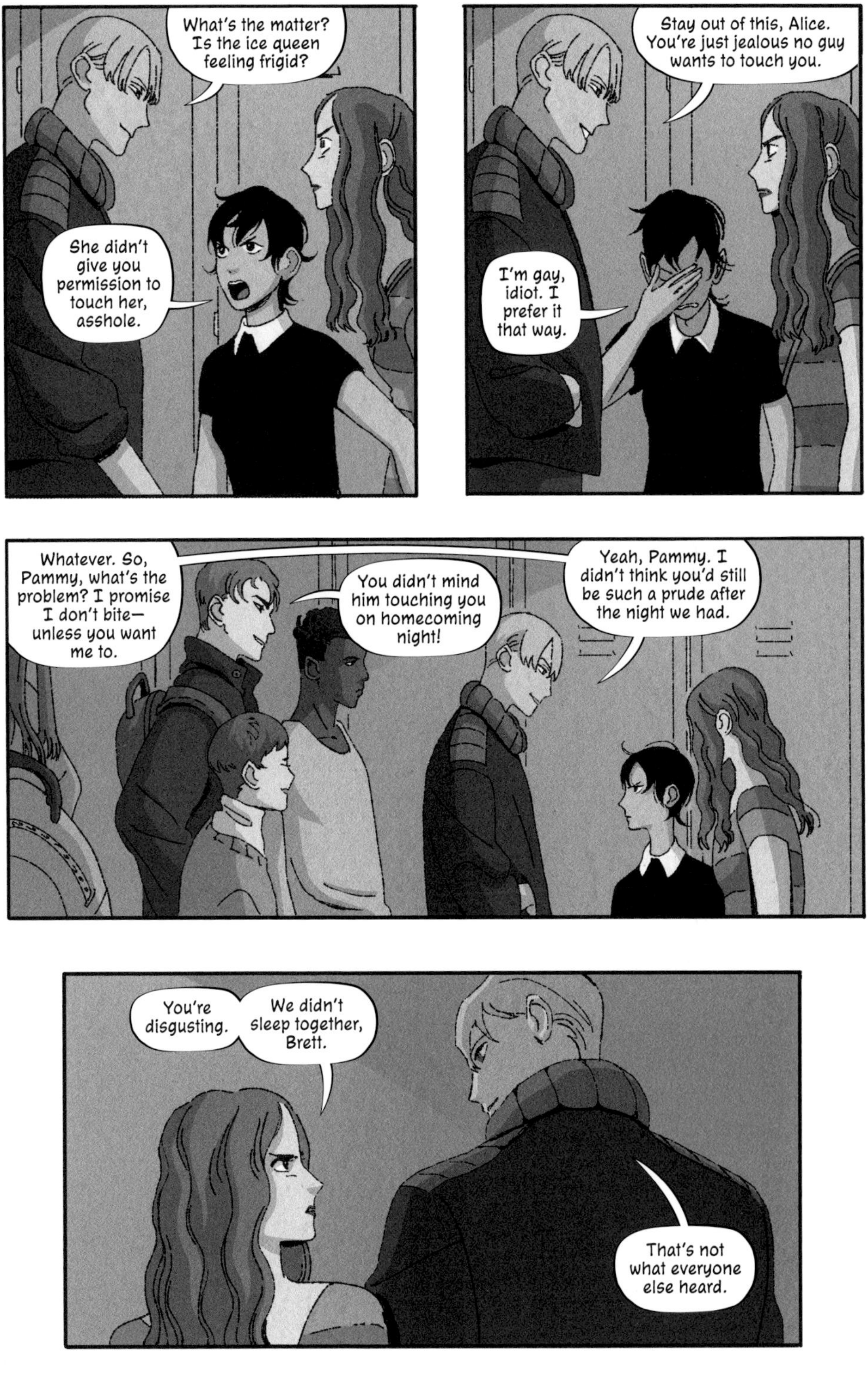
What's the matter? Is the ice queen feeling frigid?
She didn't give you permission to touch her, asshole.
Stay out of this, Alice. You're just jealous no guy wants to touch you.
I'm gay, idiot. I prefer it that way.
Whatever. So, Pammy, what's the problem? I promise I don't bite— unless you want me to.
You didn't mind him touching you on homecoming night!
Yeah, Pammy. I didn't think you'd still be such a prude after the night we had.
You're disgusting.
We didn't sleep together, Brett.
That's not what everyone else heard.

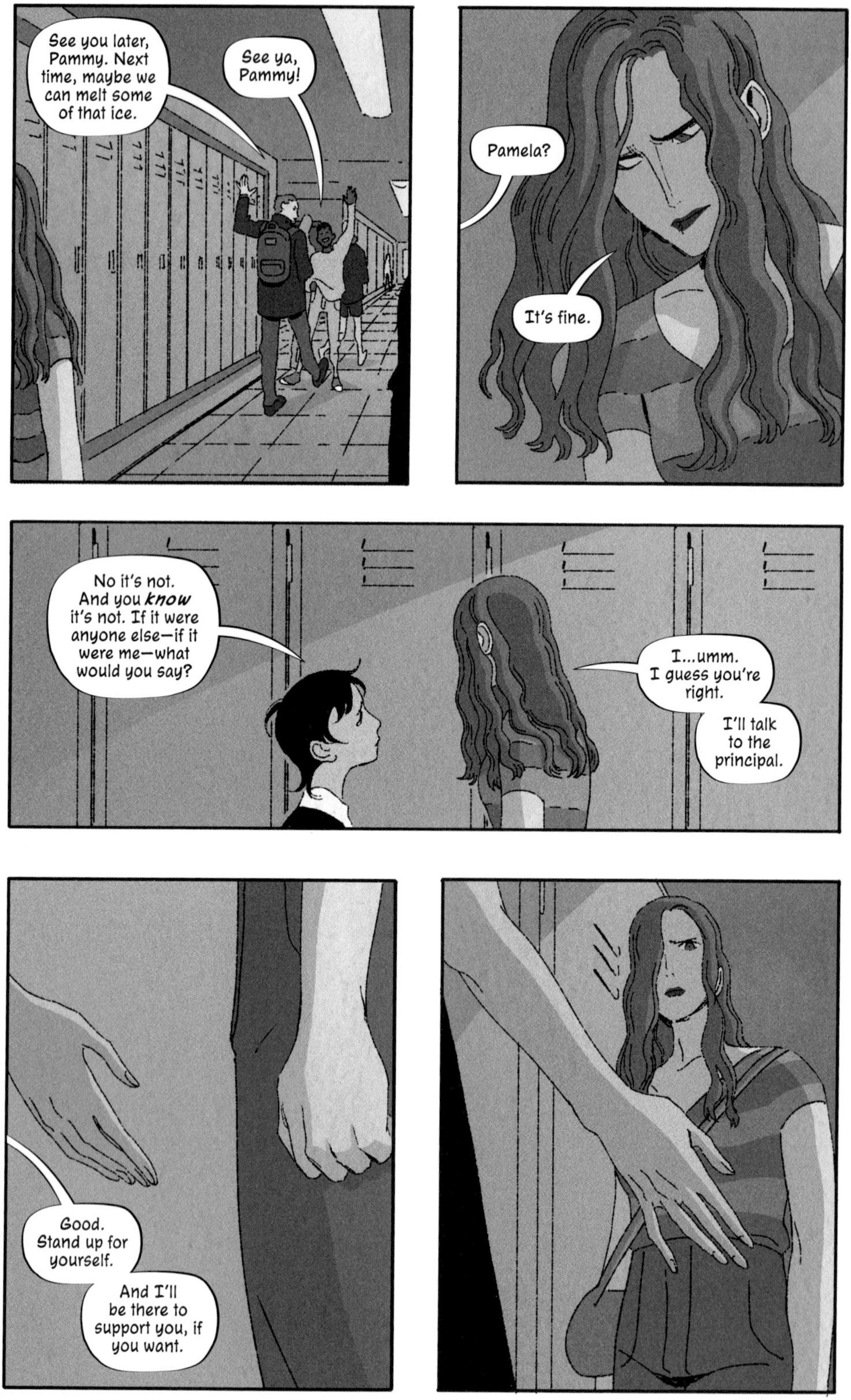
See you later, Pammy. Next time, maybe we can melt some of that ice.
See ya, Pammy!
Pamela?
It's fine.
No it's not. And you *know* it's not. If it were anyone else—if it were me—what would you say?
I...umm. I guess you're right.
I'll talk to the principal.
Good. Stand up for yourself.
And I'll be there to support you, if you want.

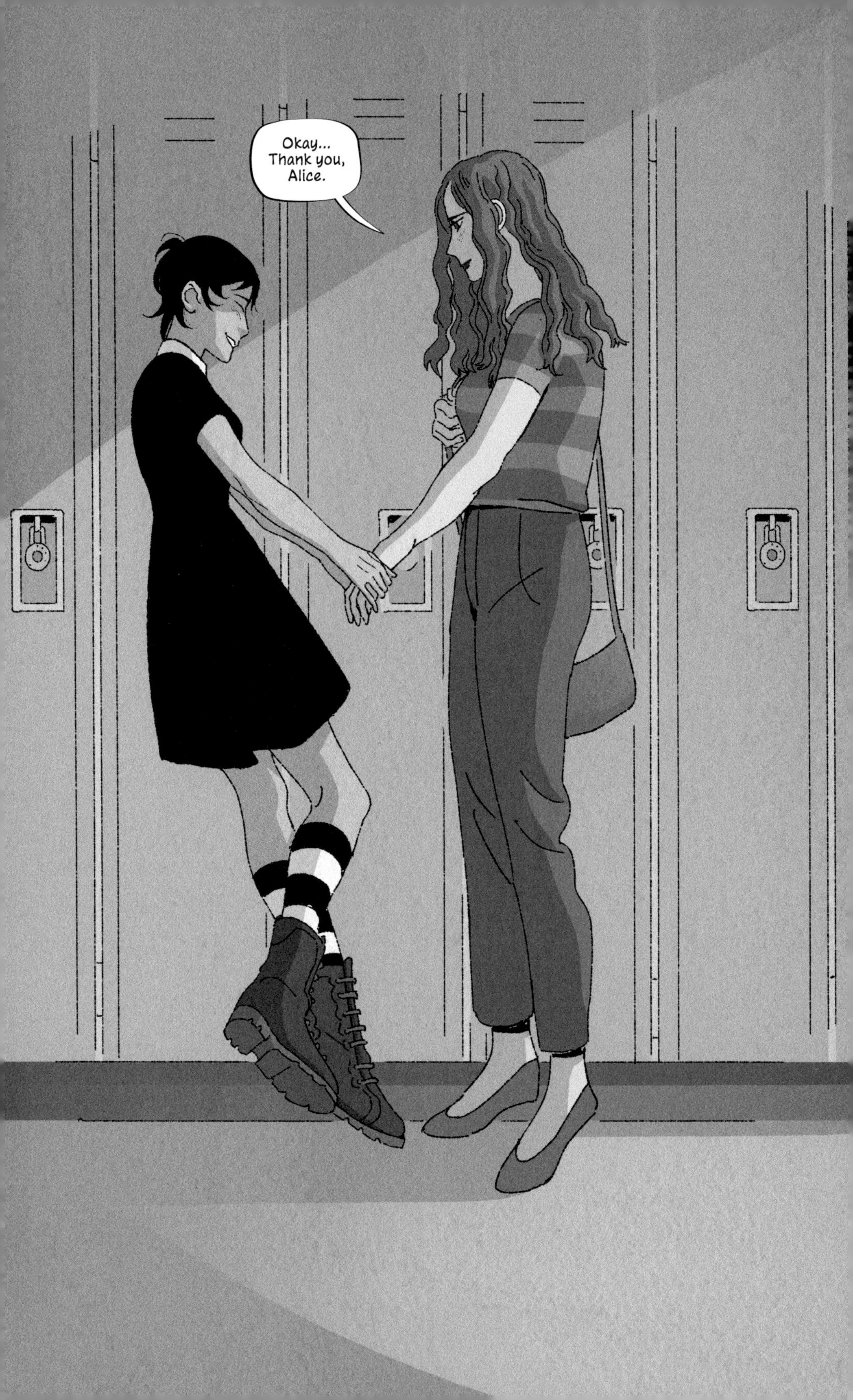
Okay... Thank you, Alice.

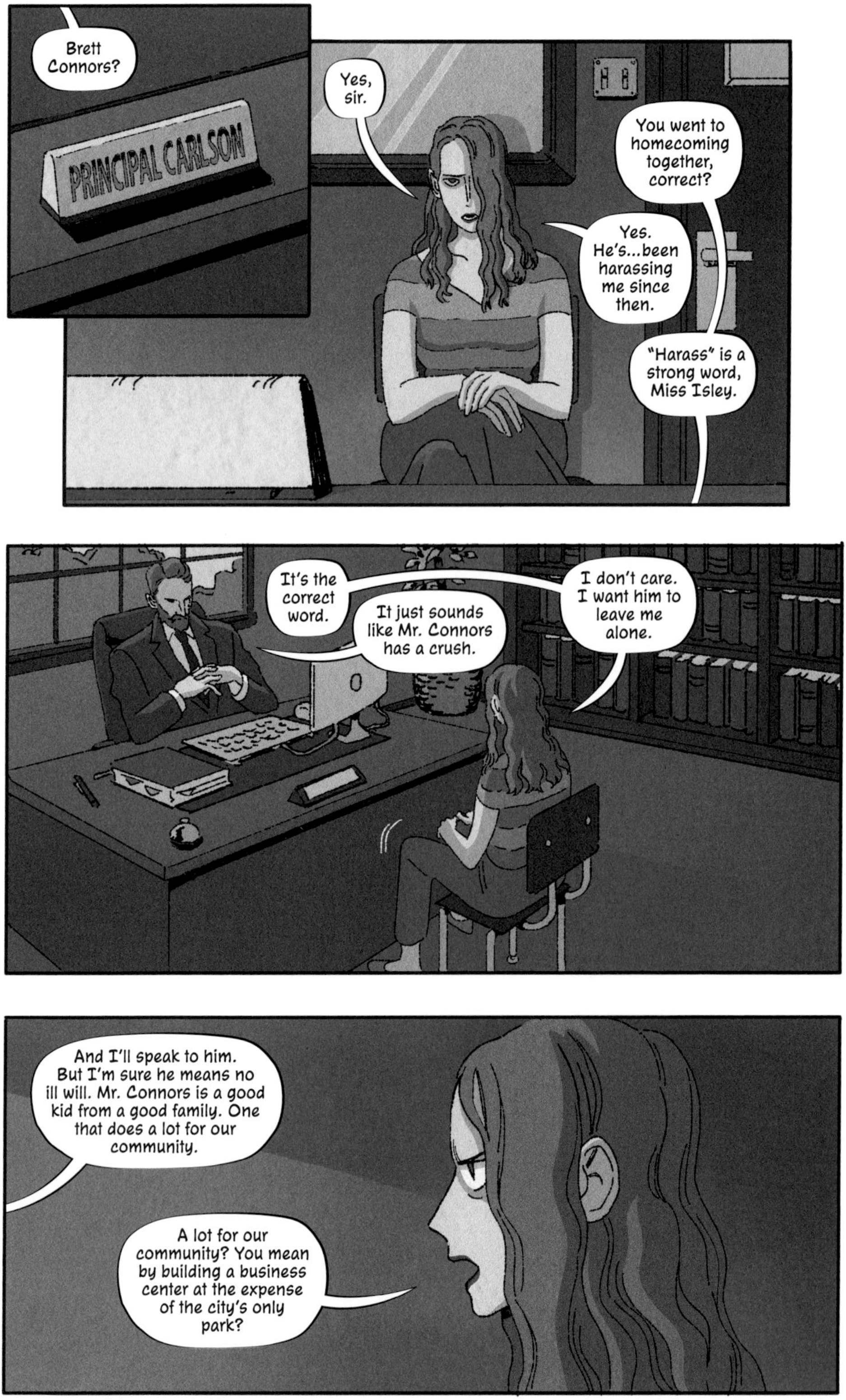
Brett Connors?
PRINCIPAL CARLSON
Yes, sir.
You went to homecoming together, correct?
Yes. He's...been harassing me since then.
"Harass" is a strong word, Miss Isley.
It's the correct word.
It just sounds like Mr. Connors has a crush.
I don't care. I want him to leave me alone.
And I'll speak to him. But I'm sure he means no ill will. Mr. Connors is a good kid from a good family. One that does a lot for our community.
A lot for our community? You mean by building a business center at the expense of the city's only park?

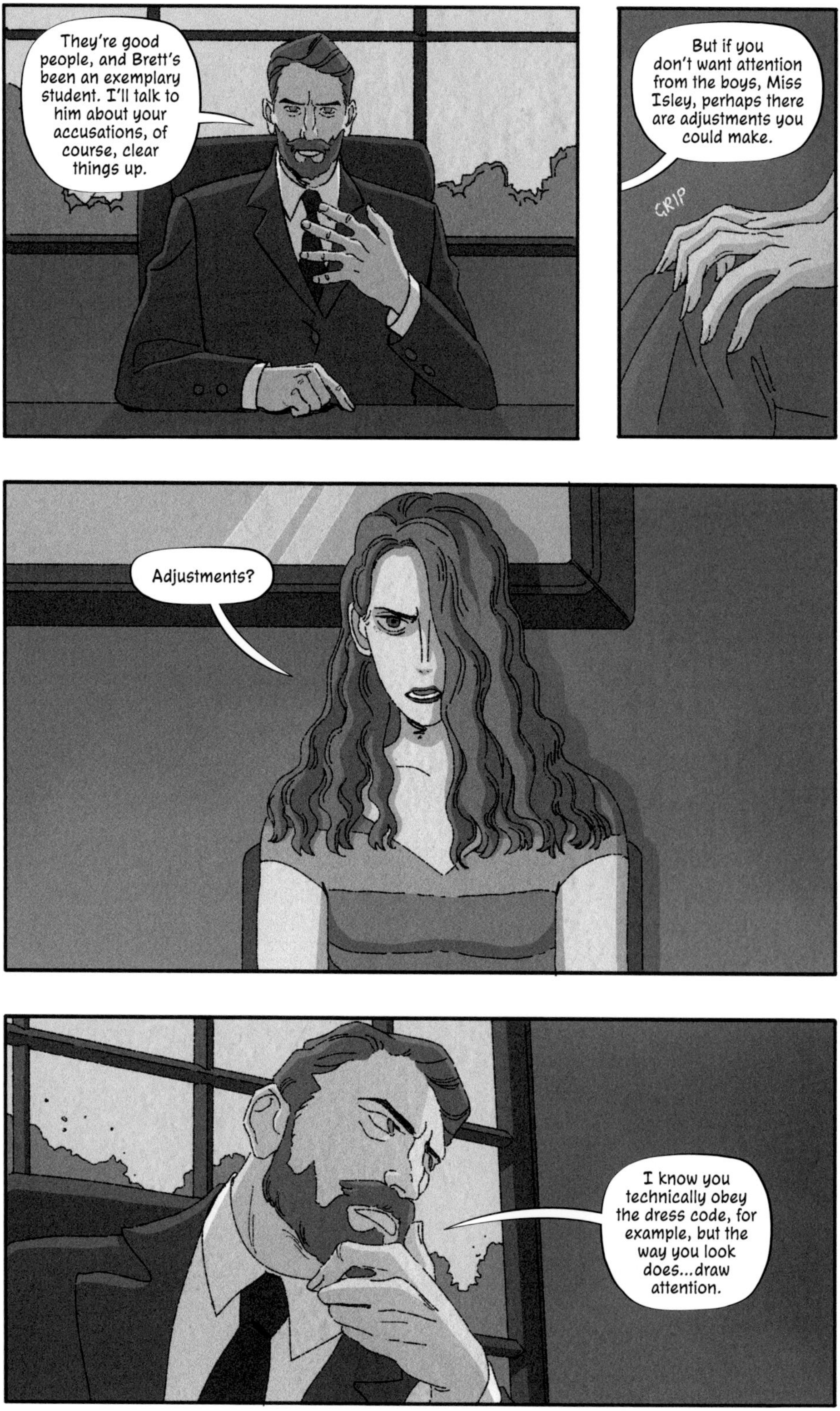
They're good people, and Brett's been an exemplary student. I'll talk to him about your accusations, of course, clear things up.
But if you don't want attention from the boys, Miss Isley, perhaps there are adjustments you could make.
GRIP
Adjustments?
I know you technically obey the dress code, for example, but the way you look does...draw attention.

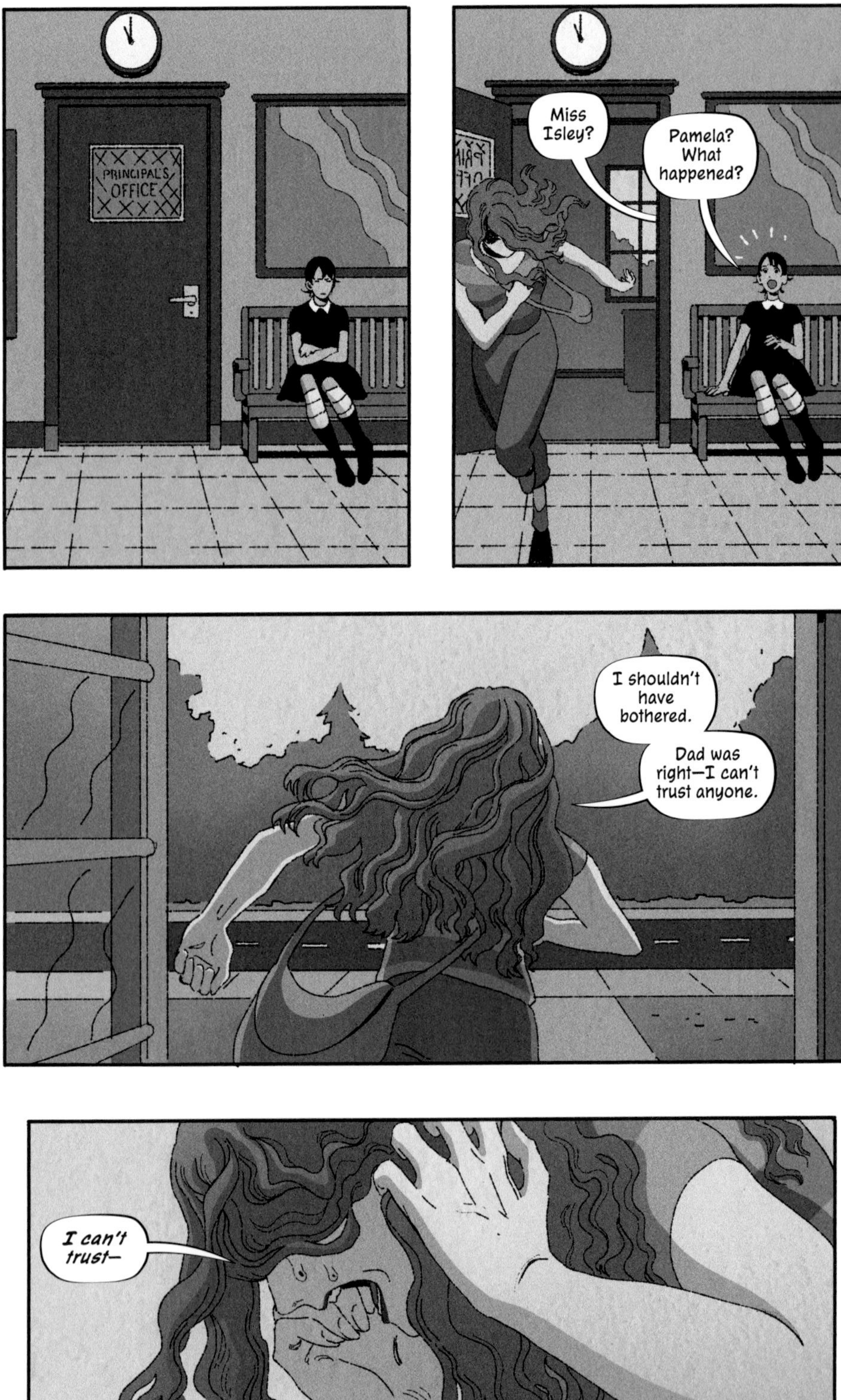
PRINCIPAL'S OFFICE
Miss Isley?
Pamela? What happened?
I shouldn't have bothered.
Dad was right—I can't trust anyone.
*I can't trust—*

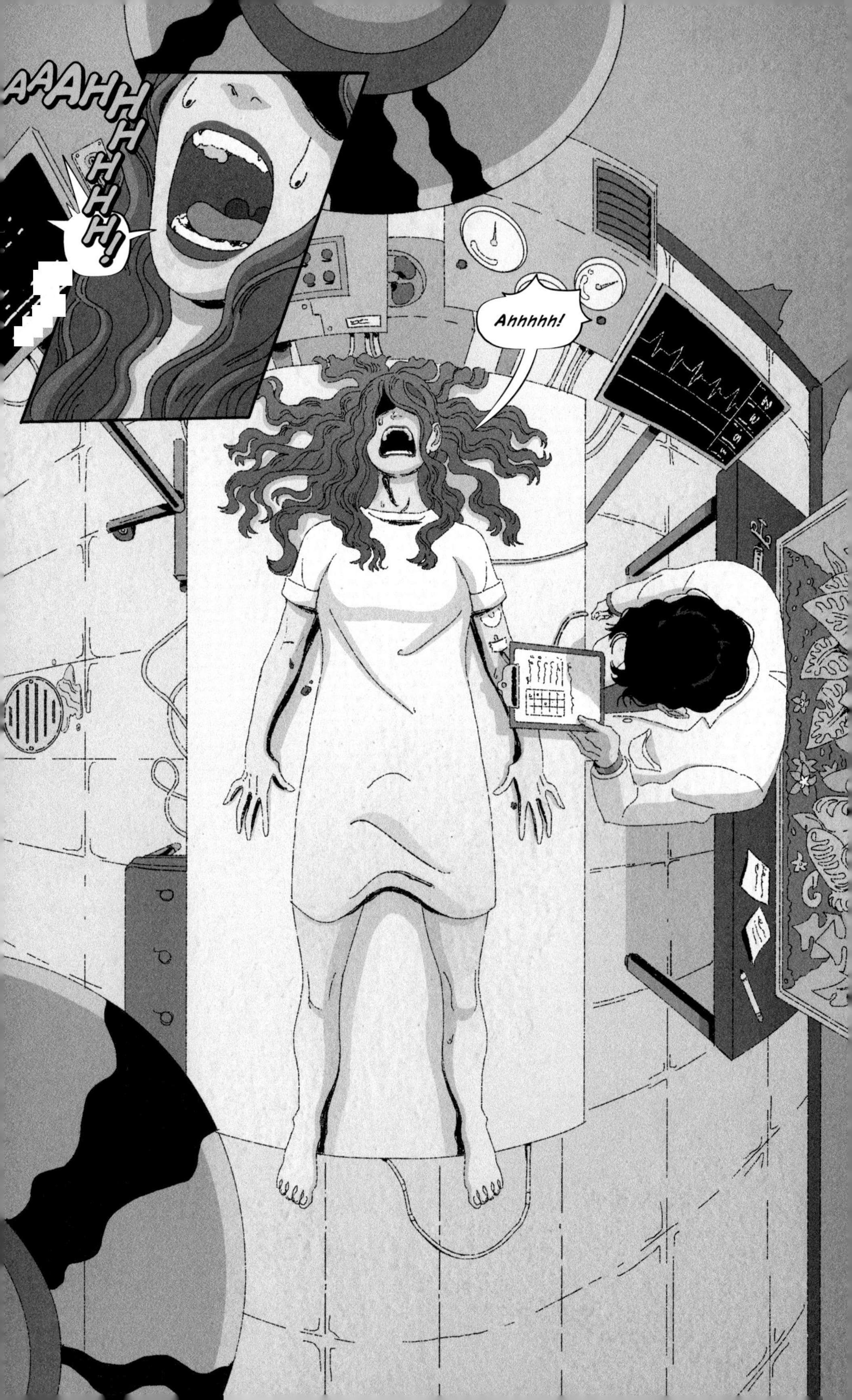
AAAHHHHHH!
Ahhhhh!

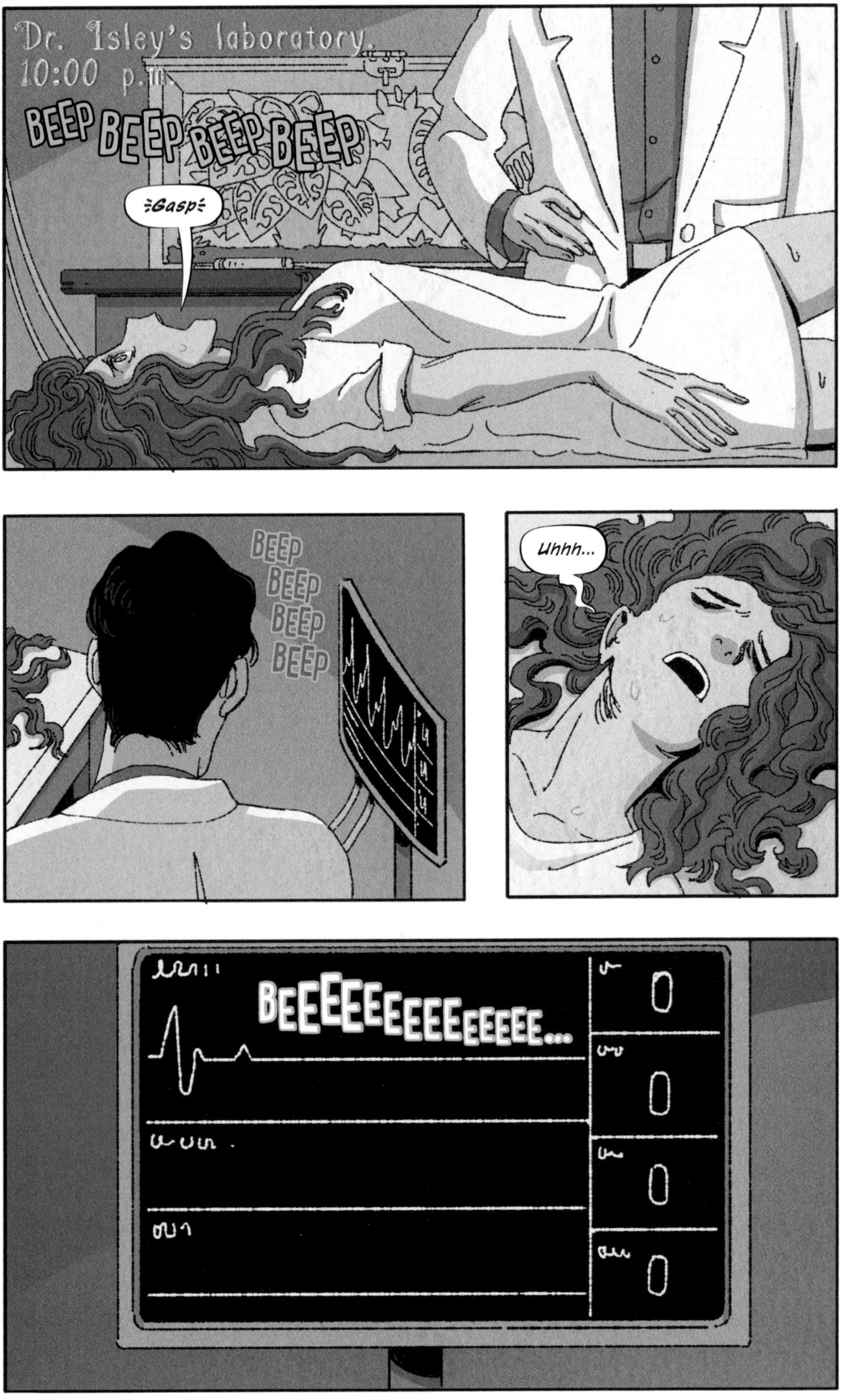
Dr. Isley's laboratory.
10:00 p.m.
BEEP BEEP BEEP BEEP
Gasp
BEEP
BEEP
BEEP
BEEP
Uhhh...
BEEEEEEEEEEEEEE...

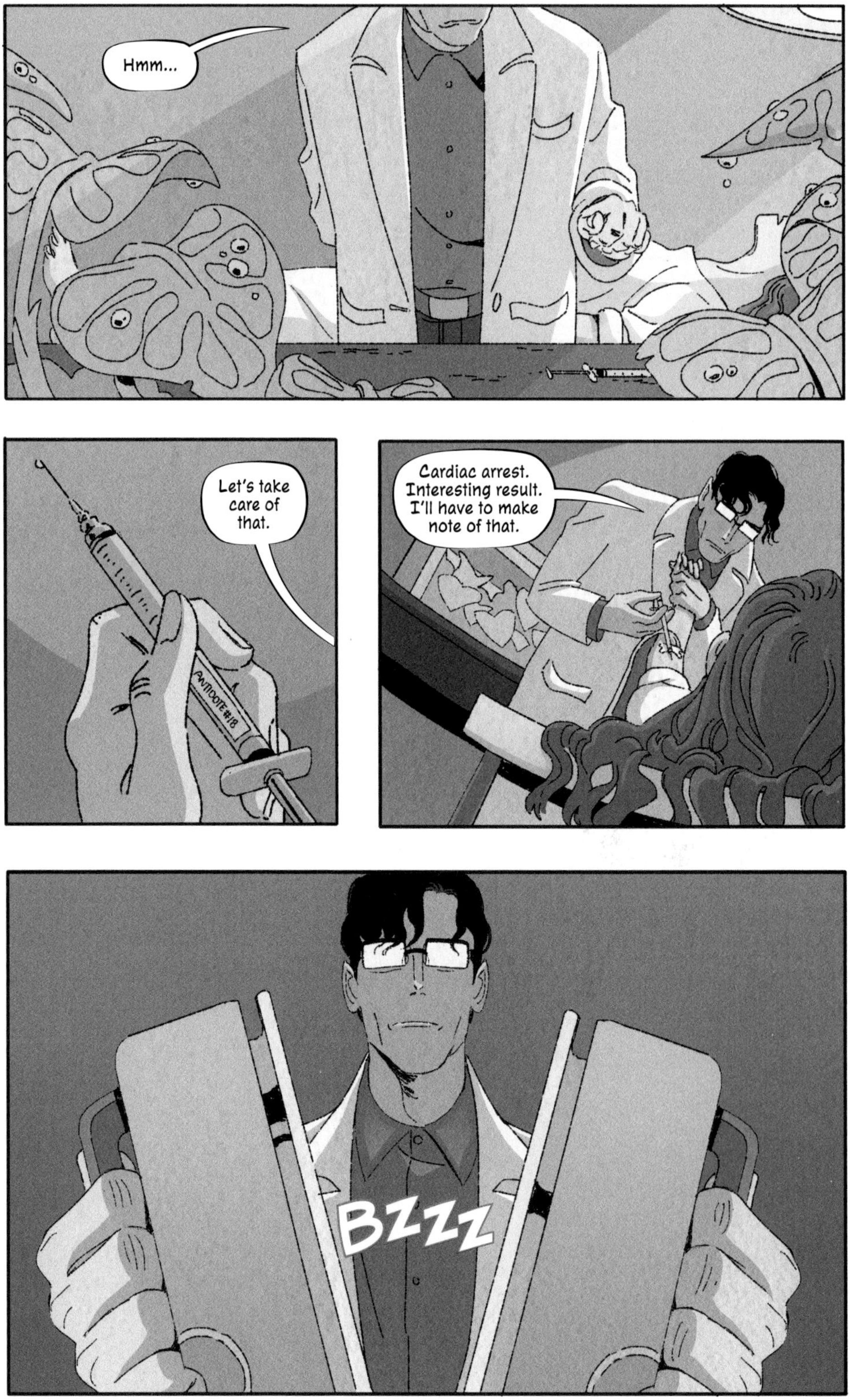
Hmm...
Let's take care of that.
ANTIDOTE #18
Cardiac arrest. Interesting result. I'll have to make note of that.
BZZZ

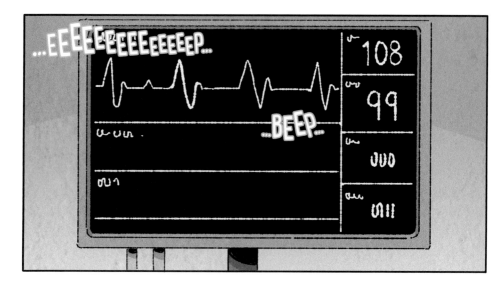

...EEEEEEEEEEEEEEP...

...BEEP...

108

99

≥GASP≥

Clearly attempt number eighteen was a failure, but I think we're getting closer.

Dad...

I don't think I can do this anymore.

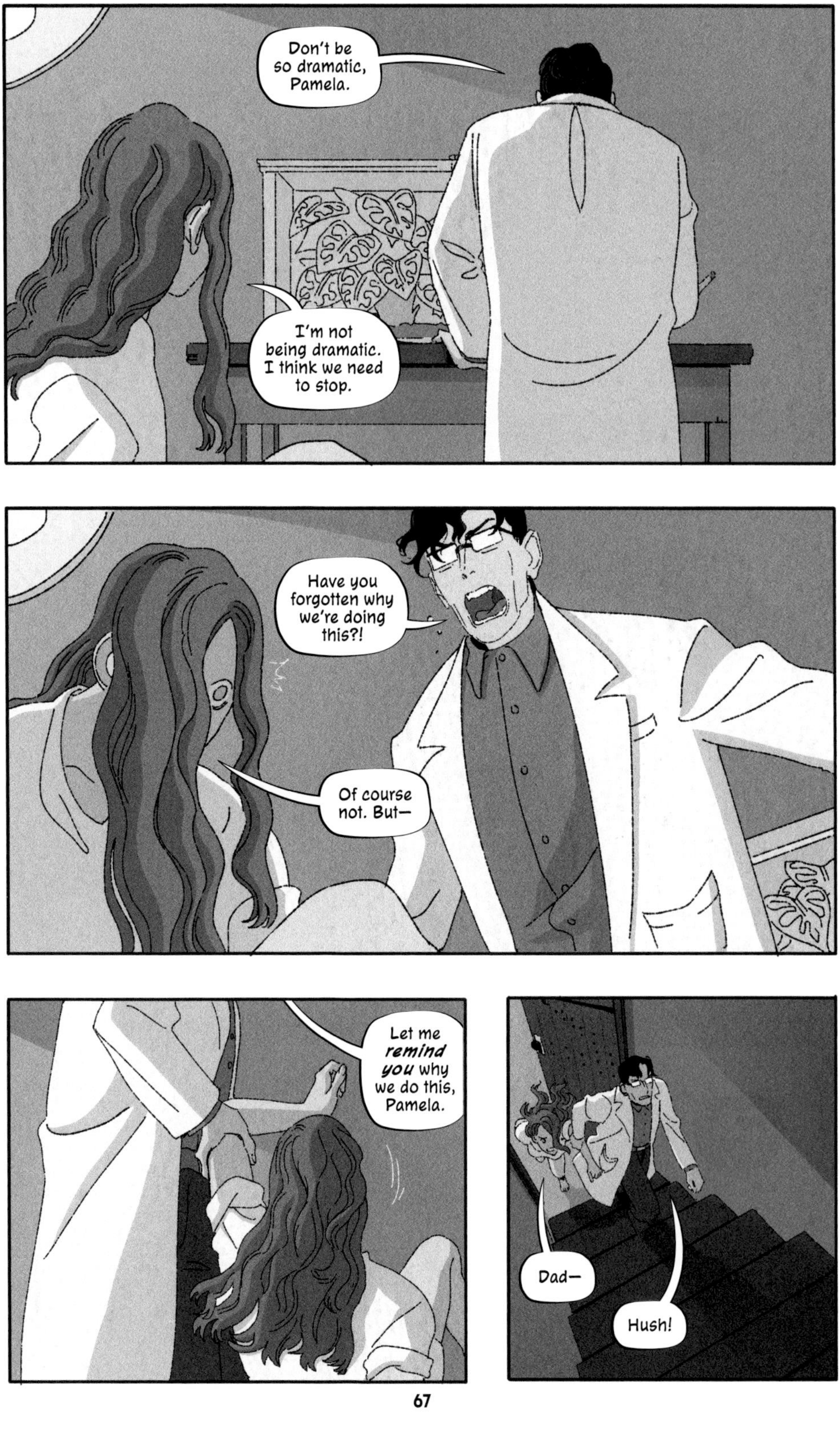
Don't be so dramatic, Pamela.
I'm not being dramatic. I think we need to stop.
Have you forgotten why we're doing this?!
Of course not. But—
Let me *remind you* why we do this, Pamela.
Dad—
Hush!

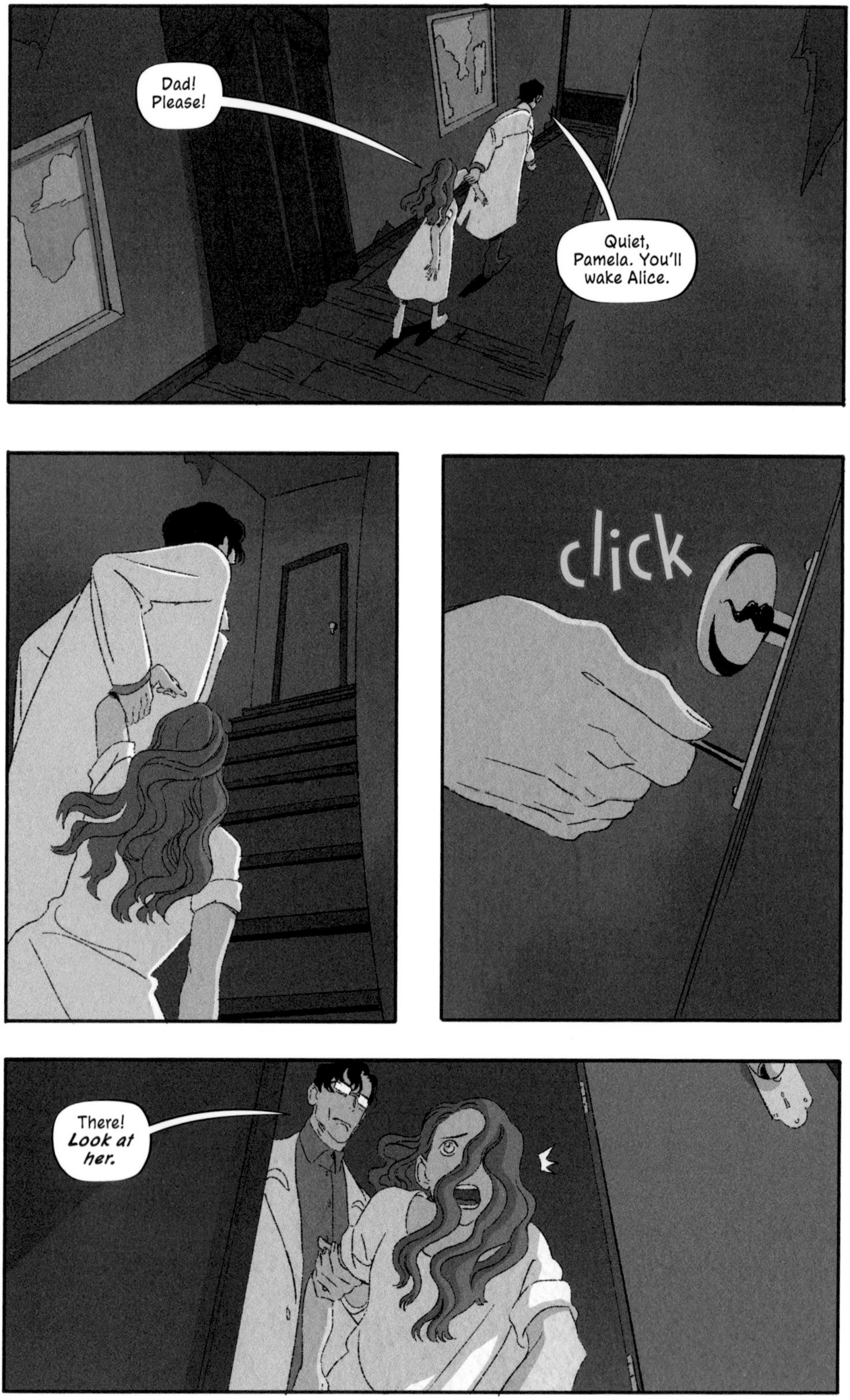
Dad! Please!
Quiet, Pamela. You'll wake Alice.
click
There! *Look at her.*

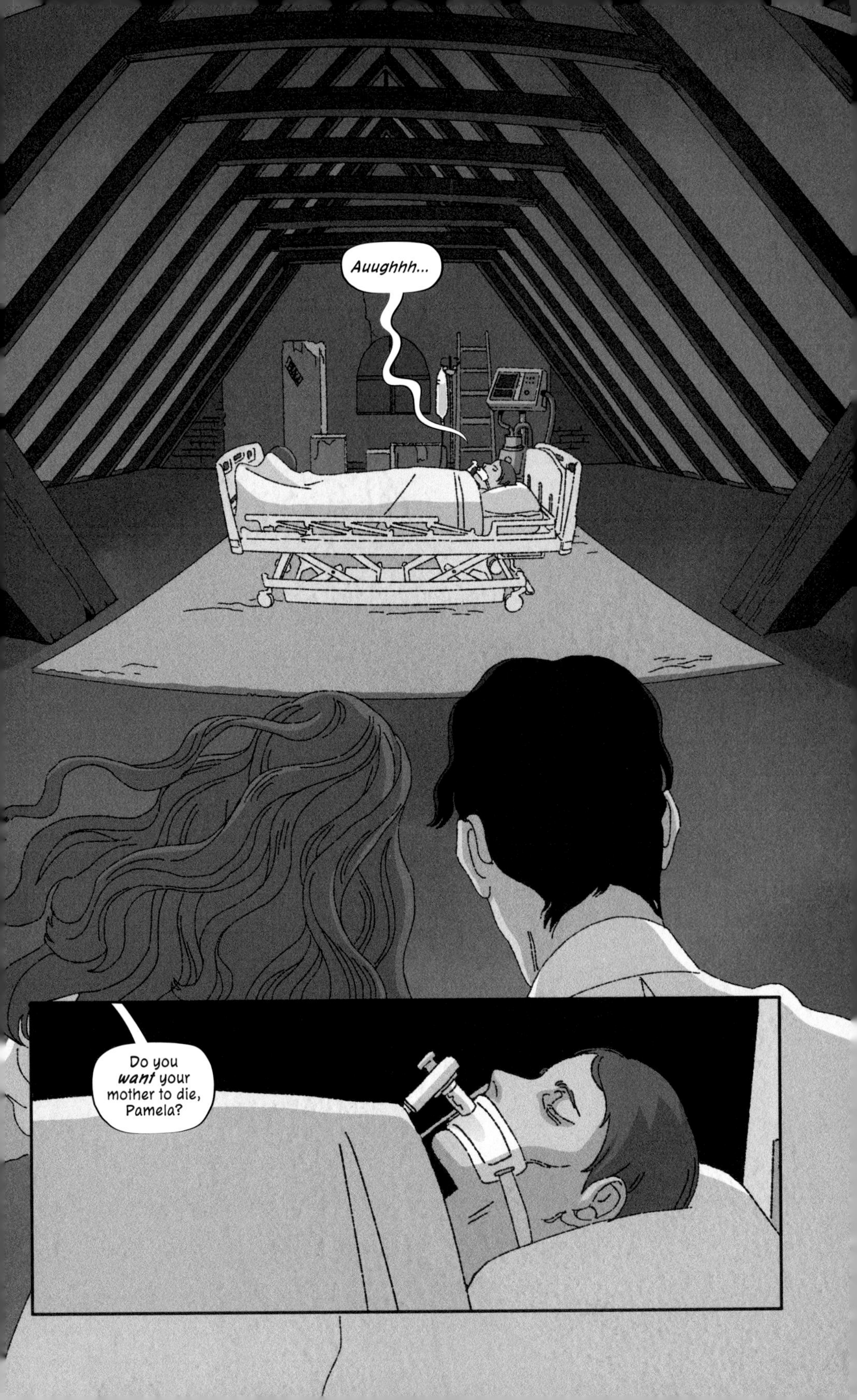
Auughhh...
Do you *want* your mother to die, Pamela?

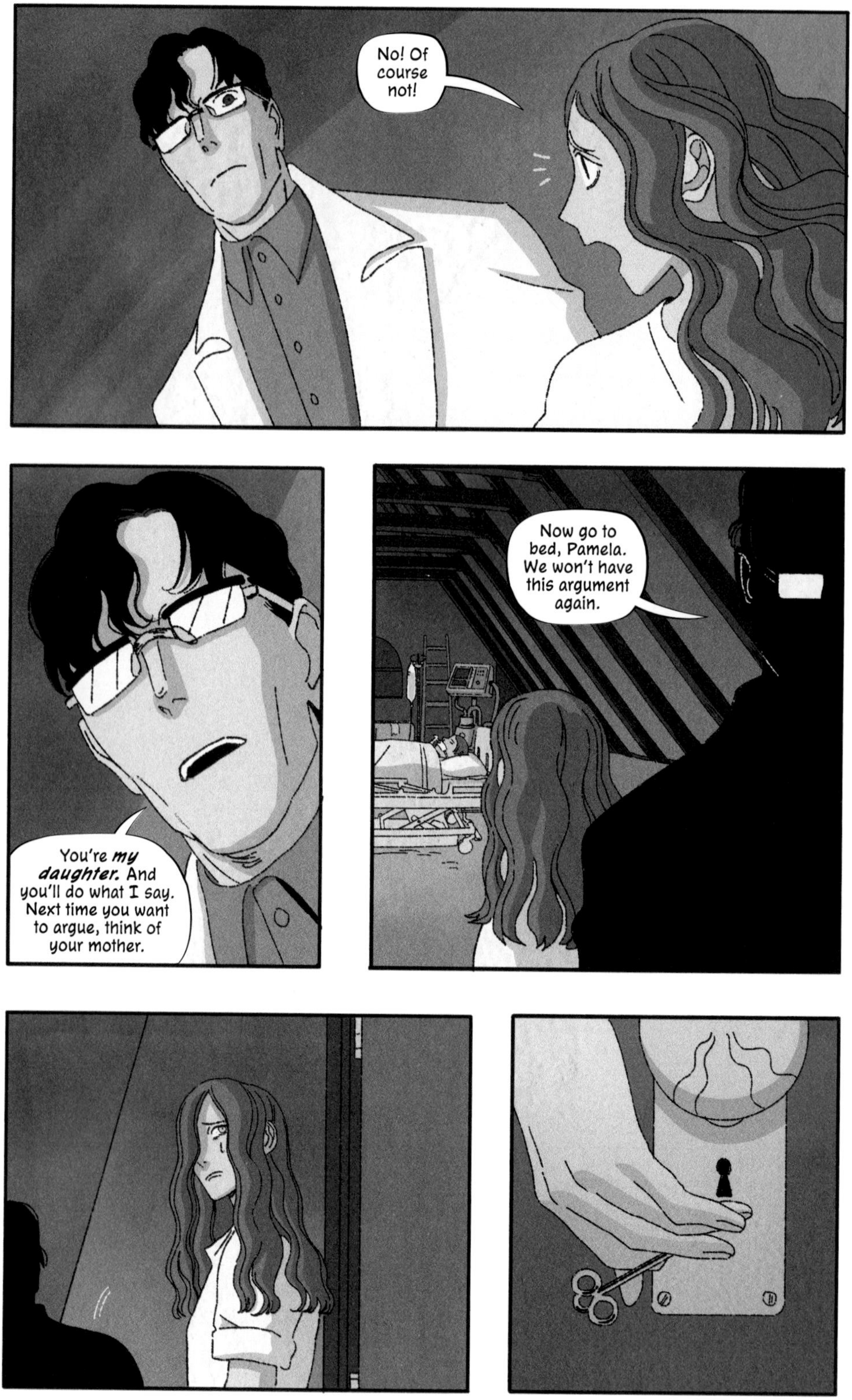
No! Of course not!
You're *my* ***daughter.*** And you'll do what I say. Next time you want to argue, think of your mother.
Now go to bed, Pamela. We won't have this argument again.

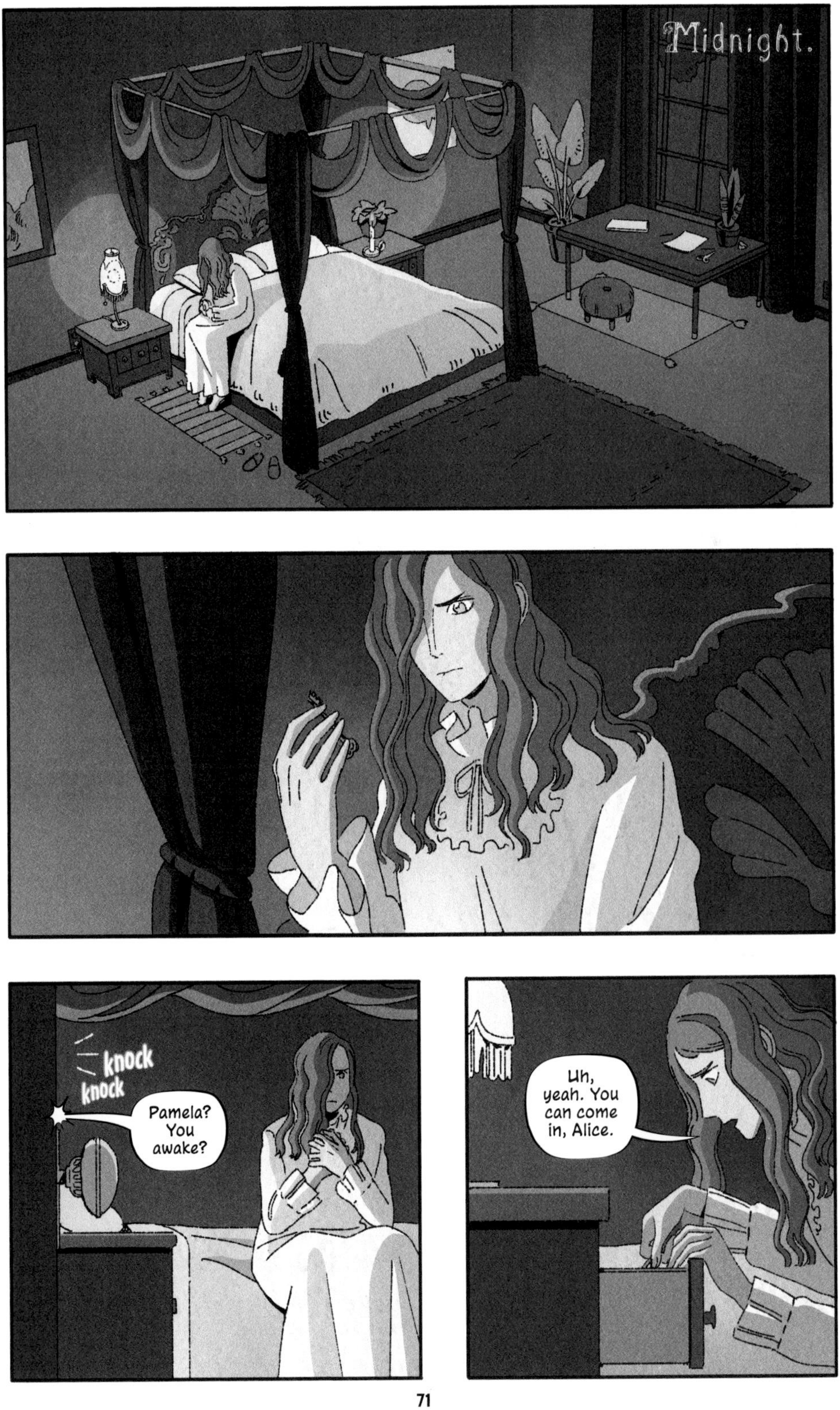
Midnight.
knock
knock
Pamela? You awake?
Uh, yeah. You can come in, Alice.

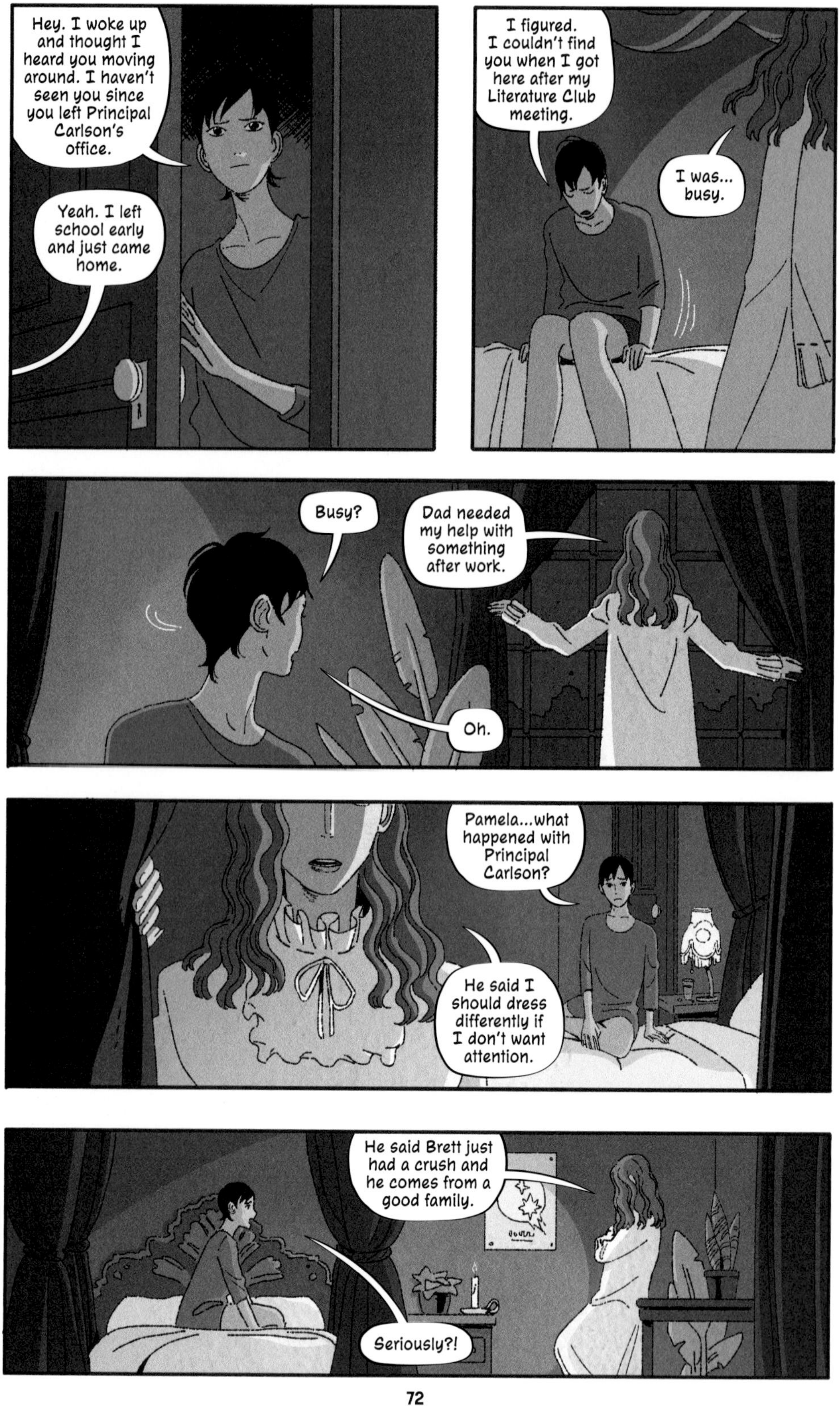
Hey. I woke up and thought I heard you moving around. I haven't seen you since you left Principal Carlson's office.
Yeah. I left school early and just came home.
I figured. I couldn't find you when I got here after my Literature Club meeting.
I was... busy.
Busy?
Dad needed my help with something after work.
Oh.
Pamela...what happened with Principal Carlson?
He said I should dress differently if I don't want attention.
He said Brett just had a crush and he comes from a good family.
Seriously?!

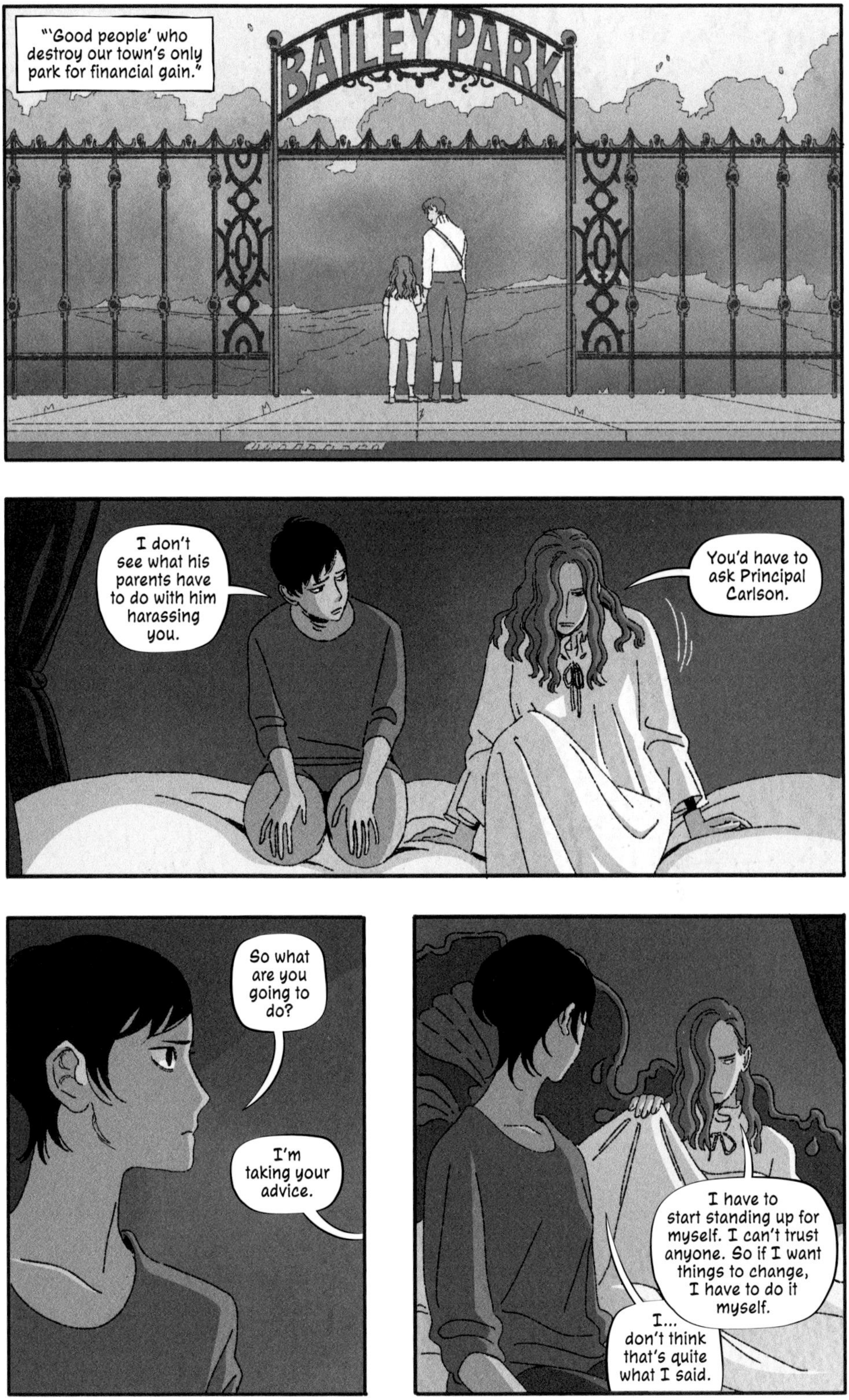
"'Good people' who destroy our town's only park for financial gain."
BAILEY PARK
I don't see what his parents have to do with him harassing you.
You'd have to ask Principal Carlson.
So what are you going to do?
I'm taking your advice.
I have to start standing up for myself. I can't trust anyone. So if I want things to change, I have to do it myself.
I... don't think that's quite what I said.

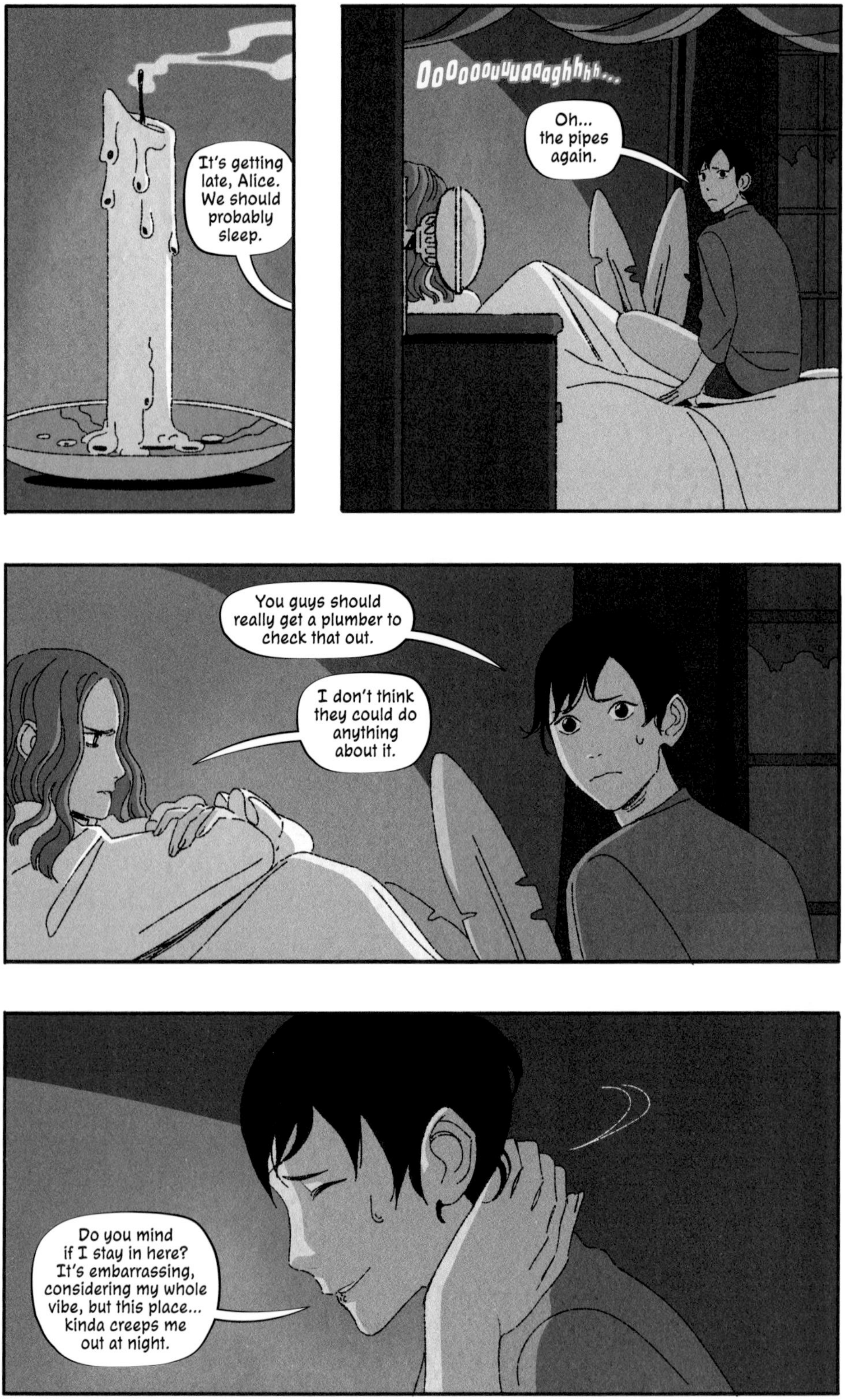
It's getting late, Alice. We should probably sleep.
Ooooooouuuaaaghhhh...
Oh... the pipes again.
You guys should really get a plumber to check that out.
I don't think they could do anything about it.
Do you mind if I stay in here? It's embarrassing, considering my whole vibe, but this place... kinda creeps me out at night.

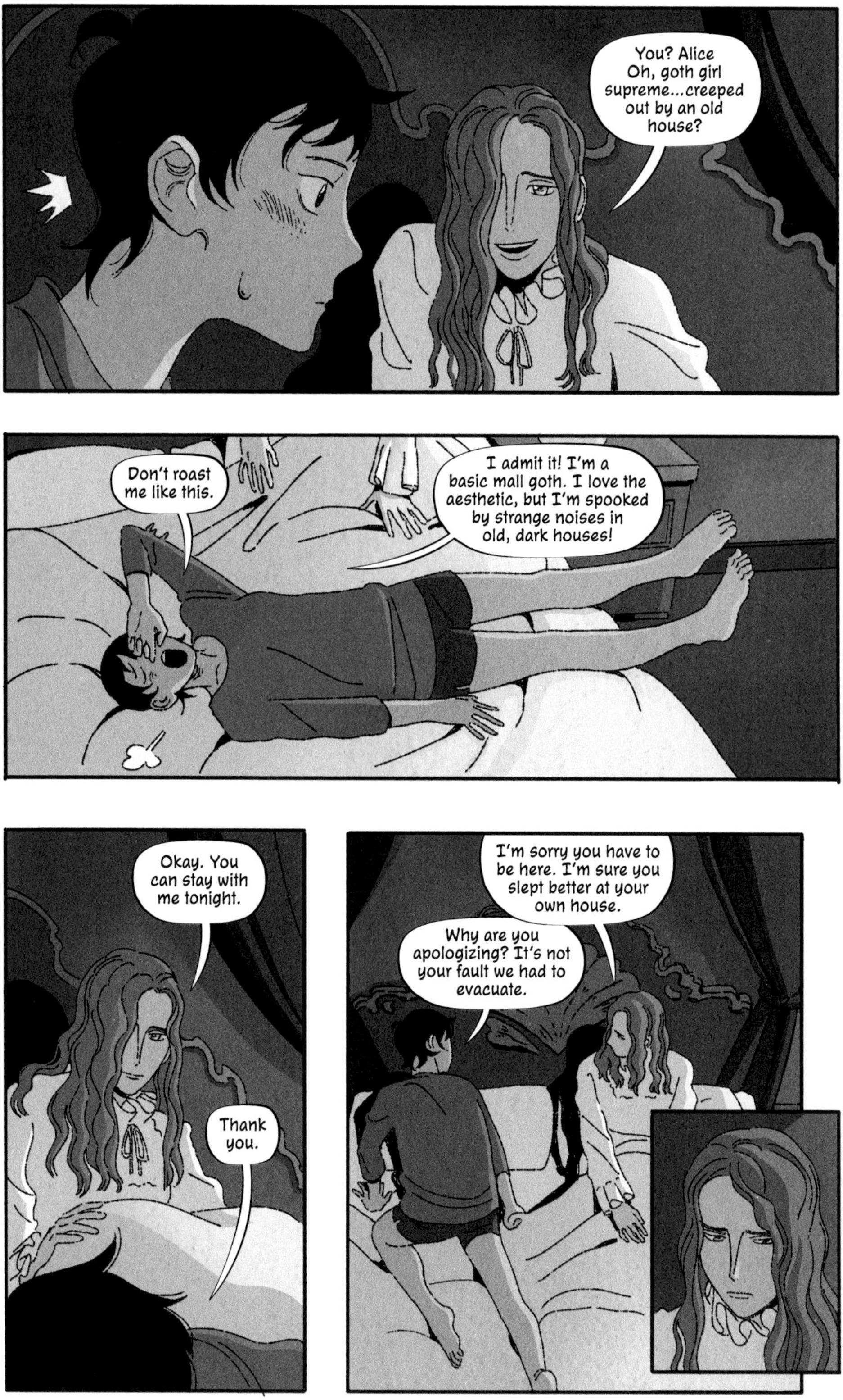
You? Alice
Oh, goth girl supreme...creeped out by an old house?
Don't roast me like this.
I admit it! I'm a basic mall goth. I love the aesthetic, but I'm spooked by strange noises in old, dark houses!
Okay. You can stay with me tonight.
Thank you.
I'm sorry you have to be here. I'm sure you slept better at your own house.
Why are you apologizing? It's not your fault we had to evacuate.

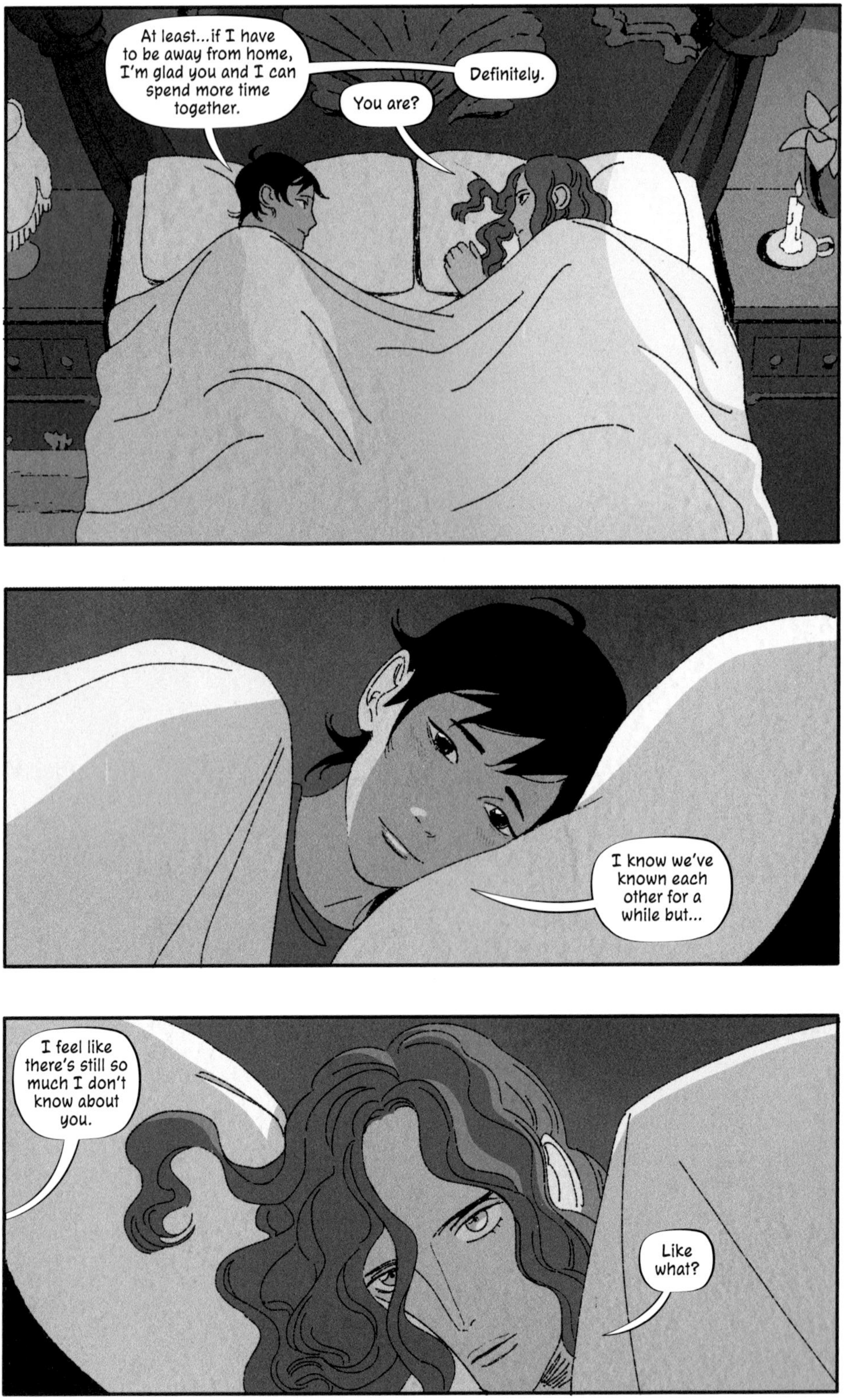
At least...if I have to be away from home, I'm glad you and I can spend more time together.
You are?
Definitely.
I know we've known each other for a while but...
I feel like there's still so much I don't know about you.
Like what?

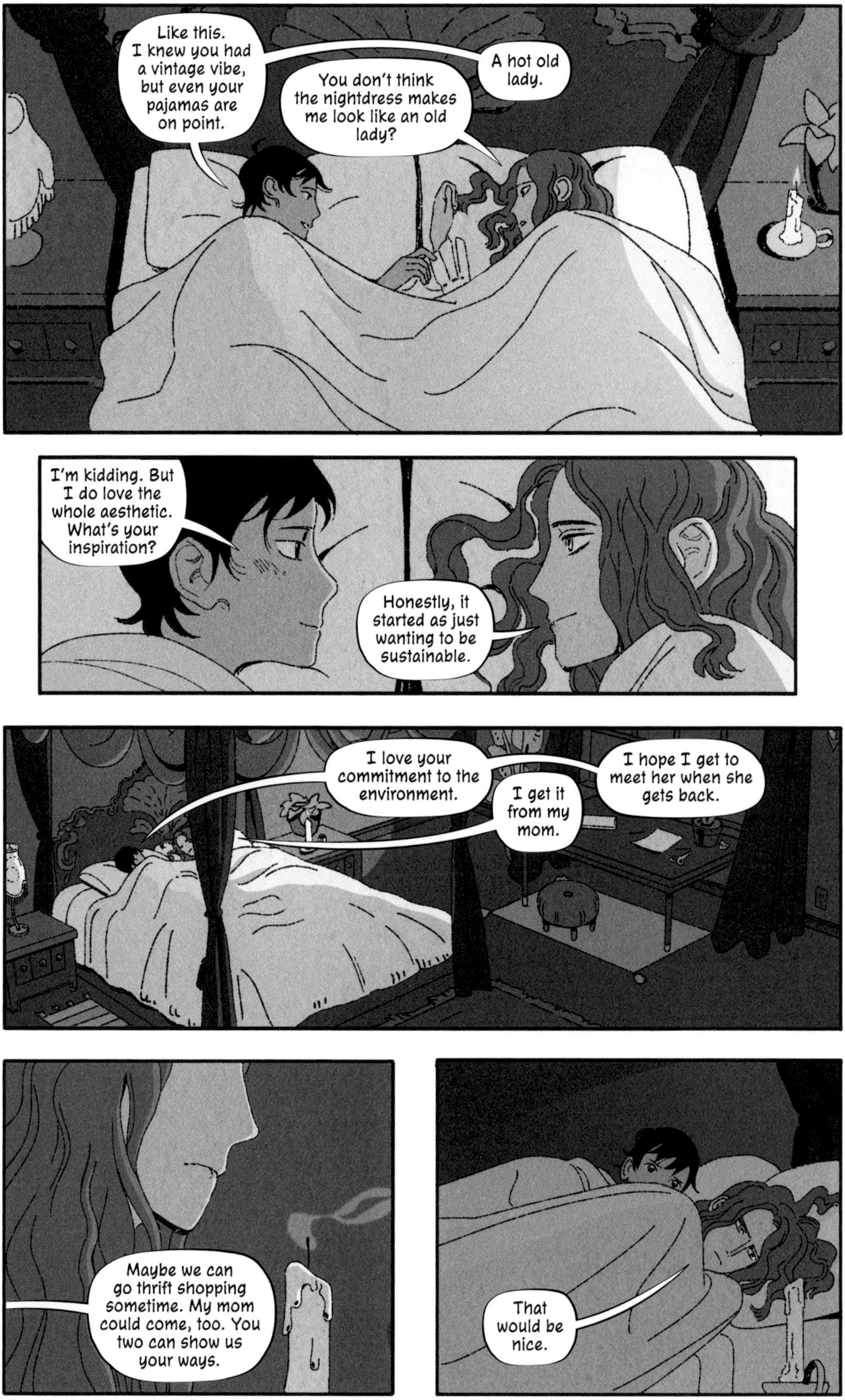
Like this. I knew you had a vintage vibe, but even your pajamas are on point.
You don't think the nightdress makes me look like an old lady?
A hot old lady.
I'm kidding. But I do love the whole aesthetic. What's your inspiration?
Honestly, it started as just wanting to be sustainable.
I love your commitment to the environment.
I get it from my mom.
I hope I get to meet her when she gets back.
Maybe we can go thrift shopping sometime. My mom could come, too. You two can show us your ways.
That would be nice.

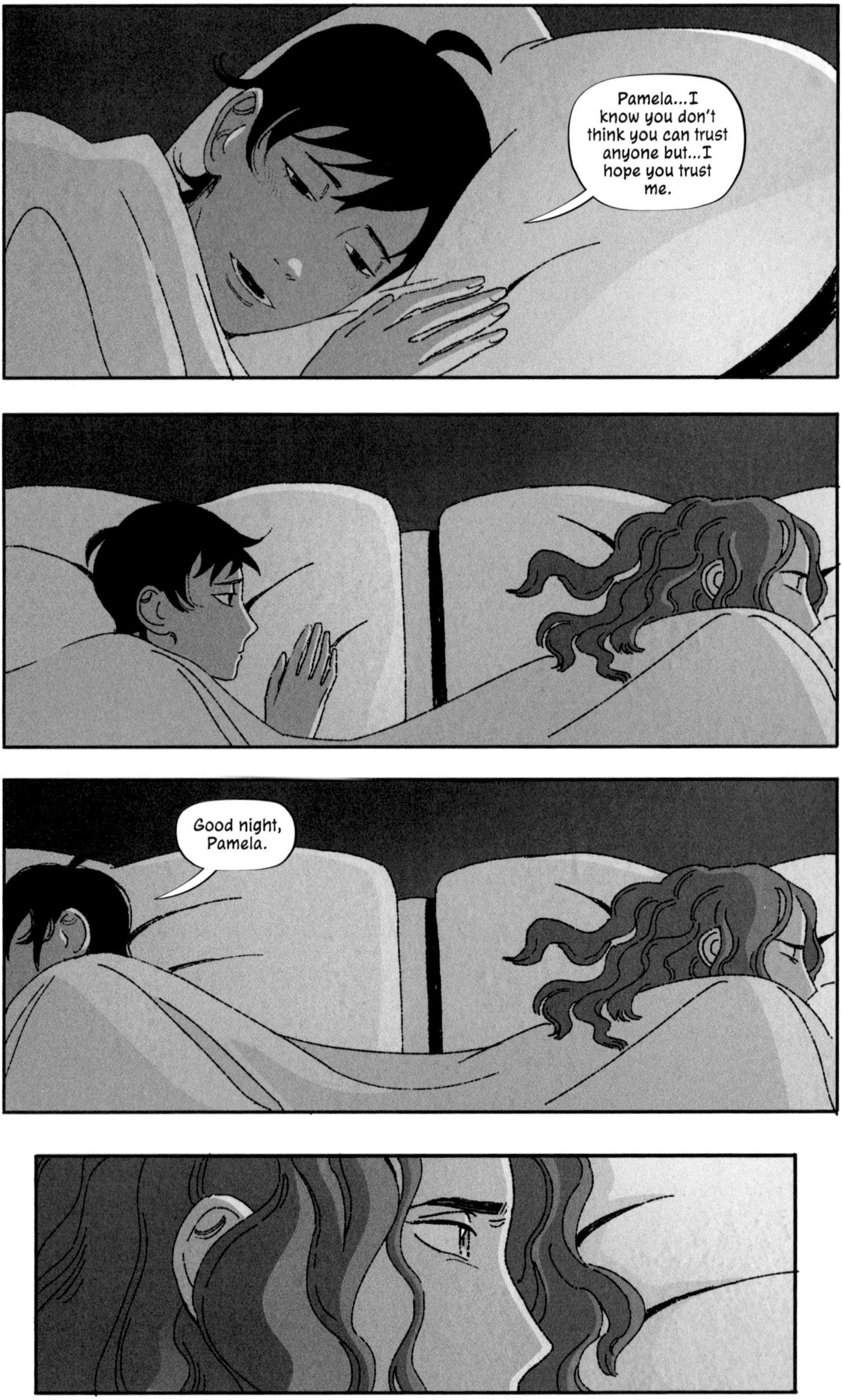
Pamela...I know you don't think you can trust anyone but...I hope you trust me.
Good night, Pamela.

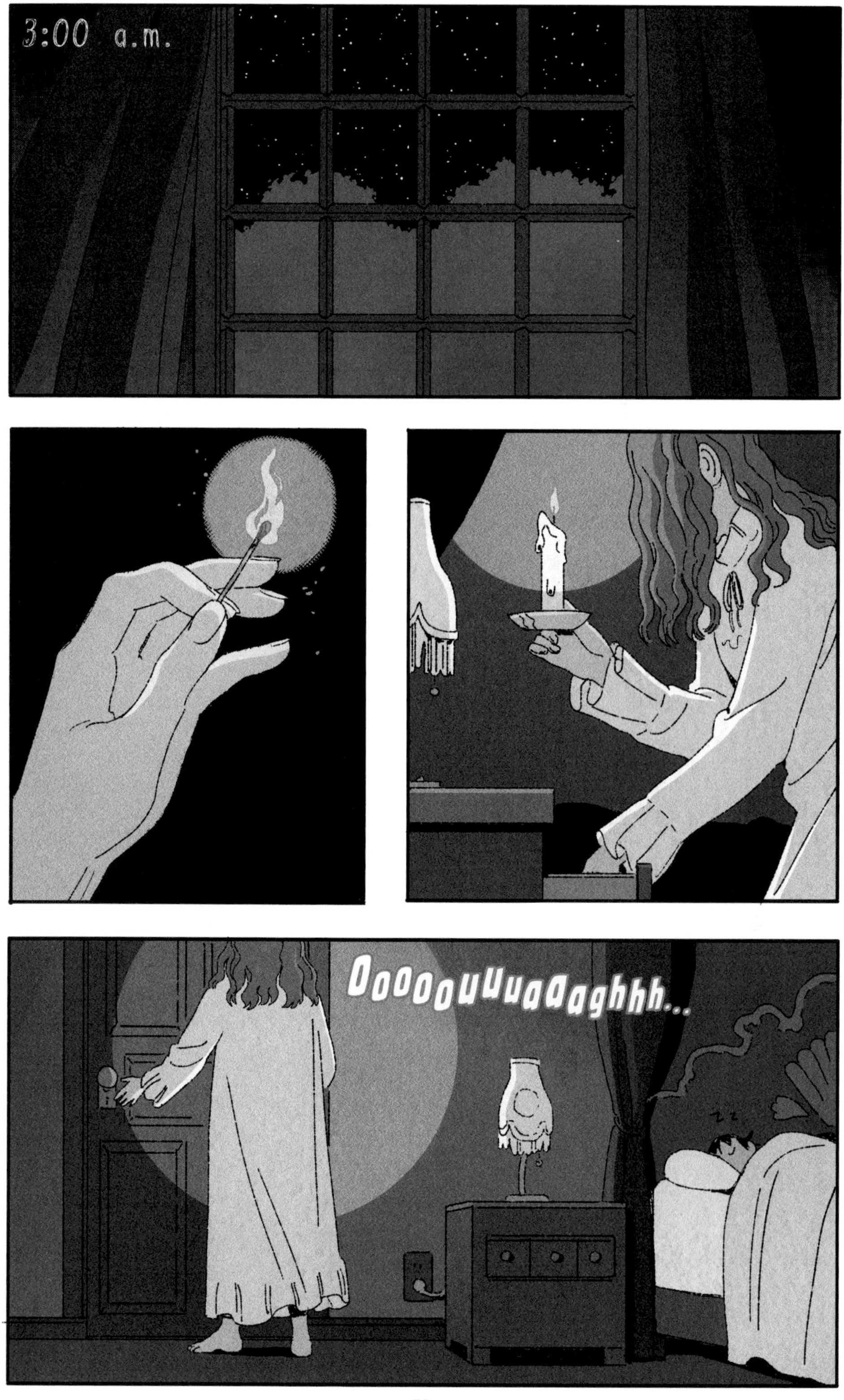
3:00 a.m.
Oooooouuuaaaghhh...

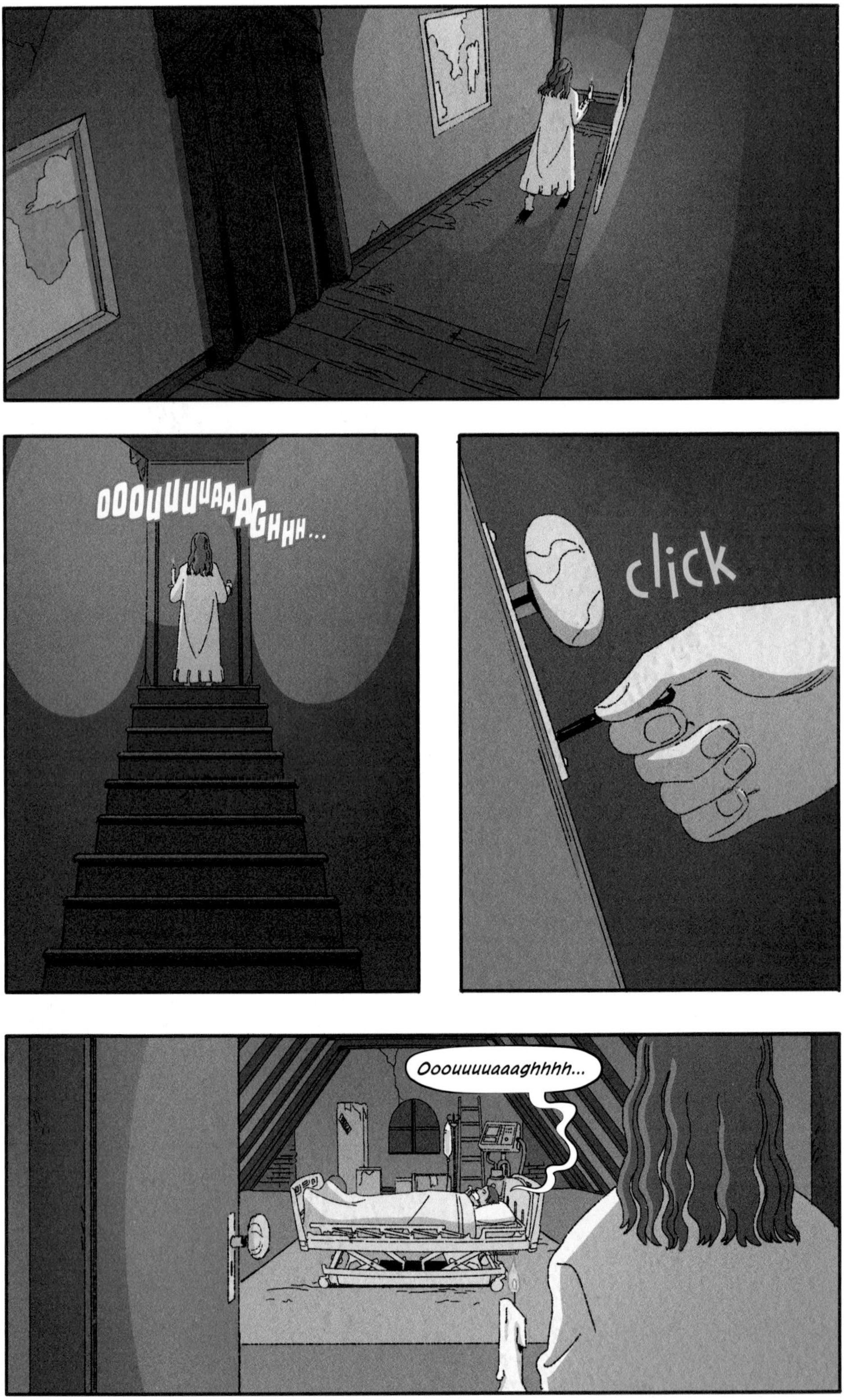
OOOUUUUUAAAGHHH...
click
Ooouuuuaaaghhhh...

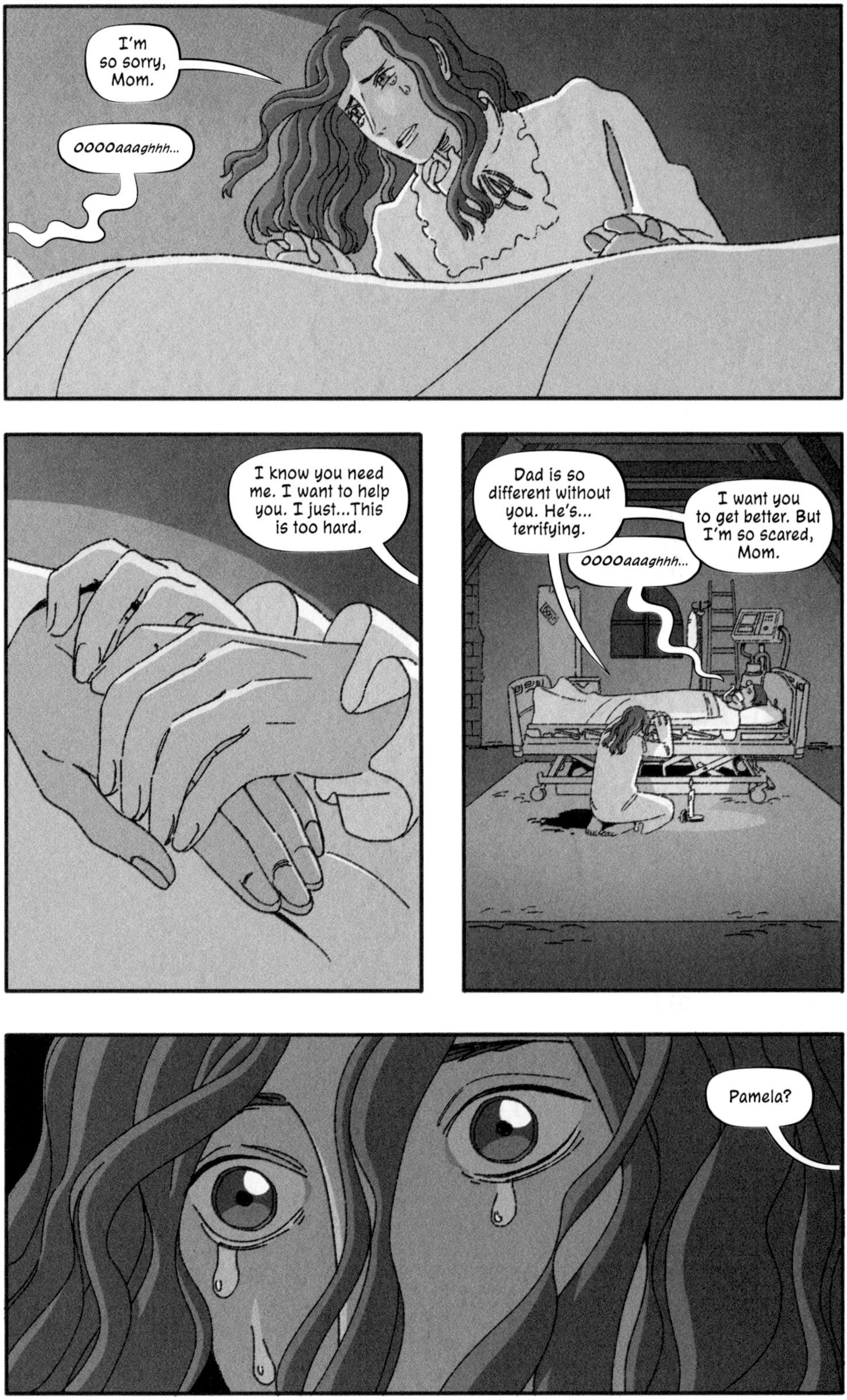
I'm so sorry, Mom.
OOOOaaaghhh...
I know you need me. I want to help you. I just...This is too hard.
Dad is so different without you. He's... terrifying.
I want you to get better. But I'm so scared, Mom.
OOOOaaaghhh...
Pamela?

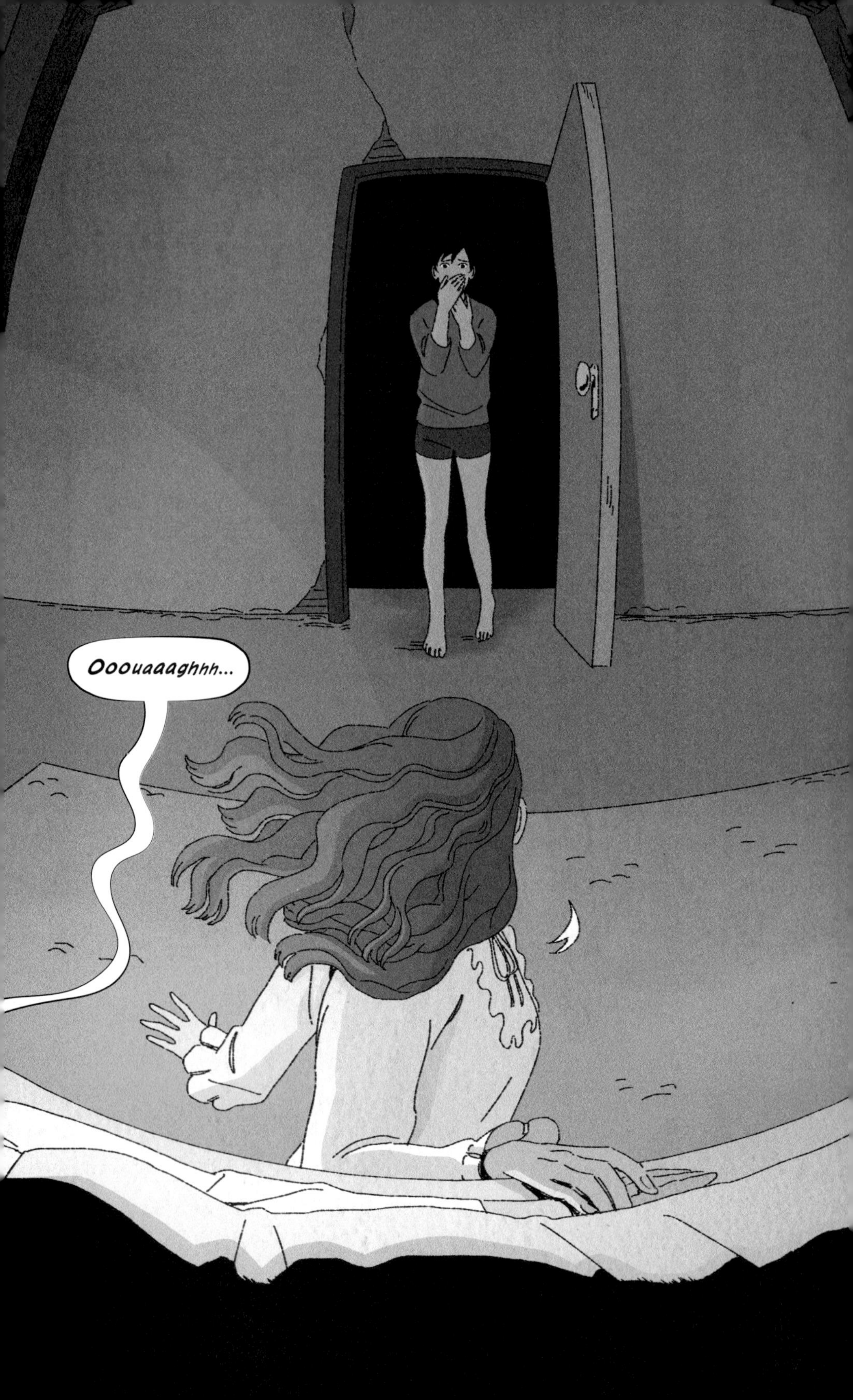
Ooouaaaghhh...

# PART THREE

# bloom

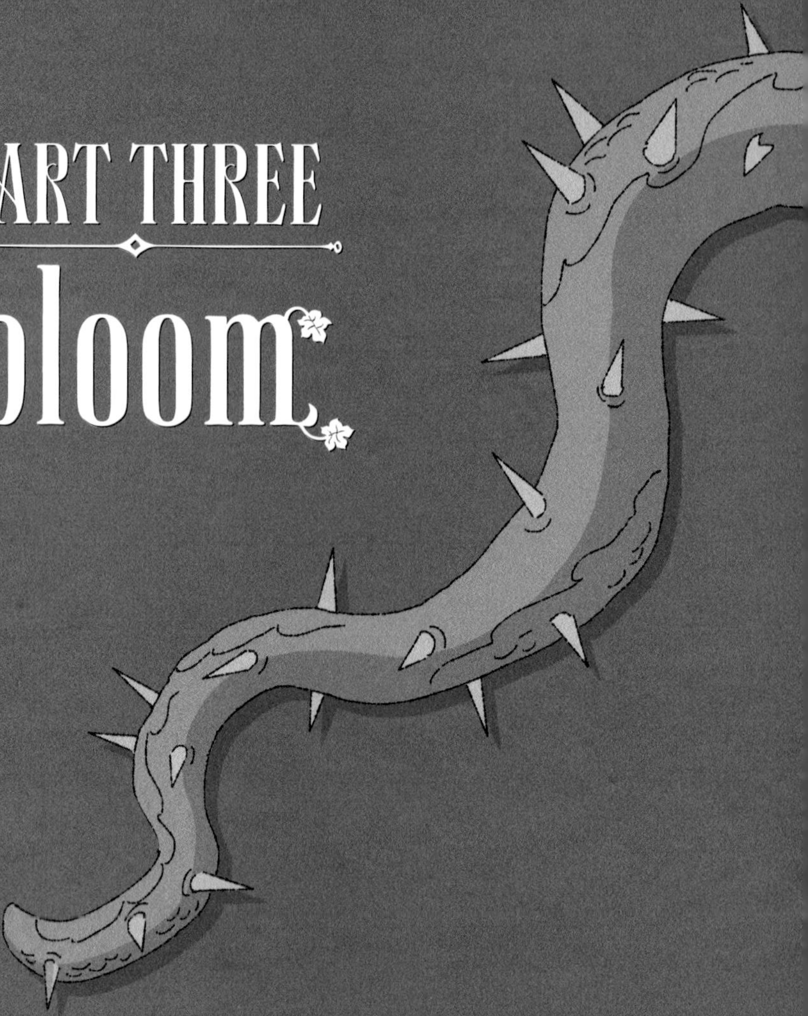

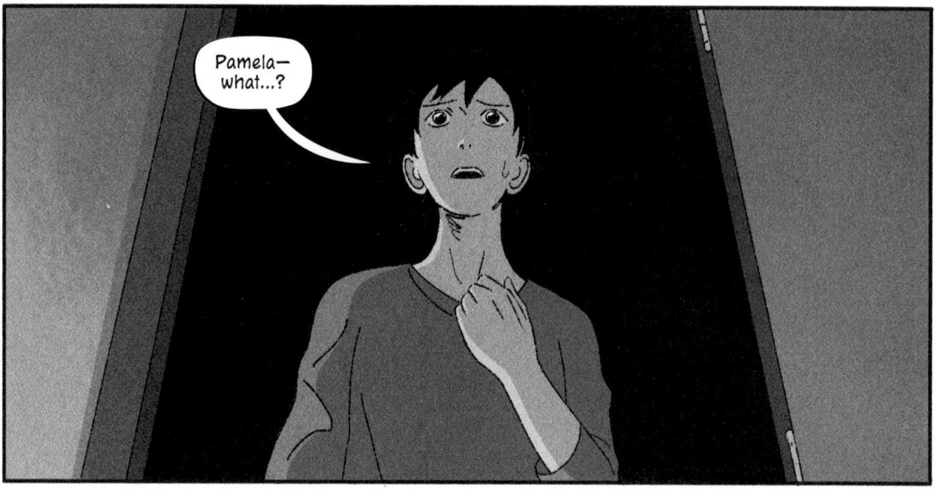
Pamela—
what...?

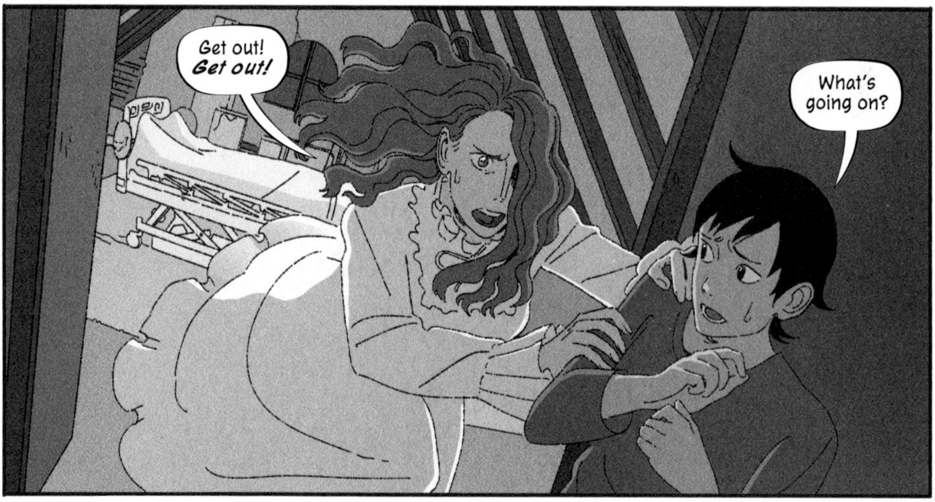
Get out!
*Get out!*
What's going on?

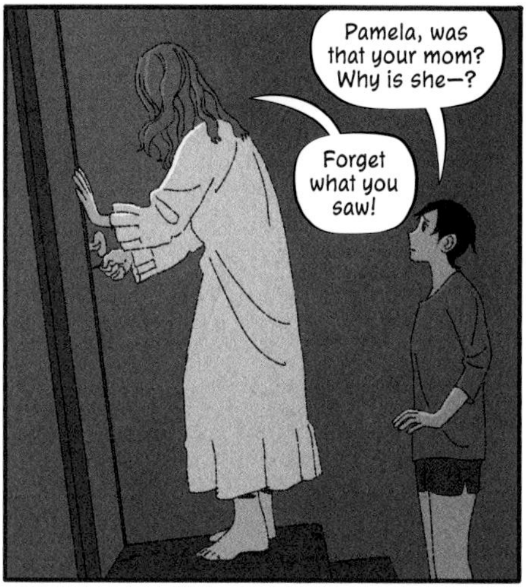
Pamela, was that your mom? Why is she—?
Forget what you saw!

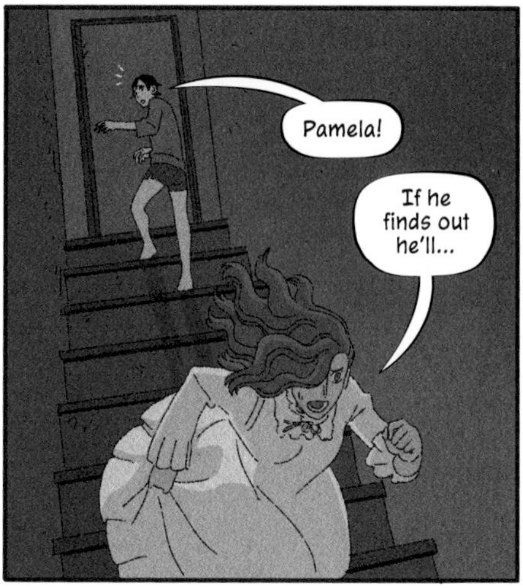
Pamela!
If he finds out he'll...

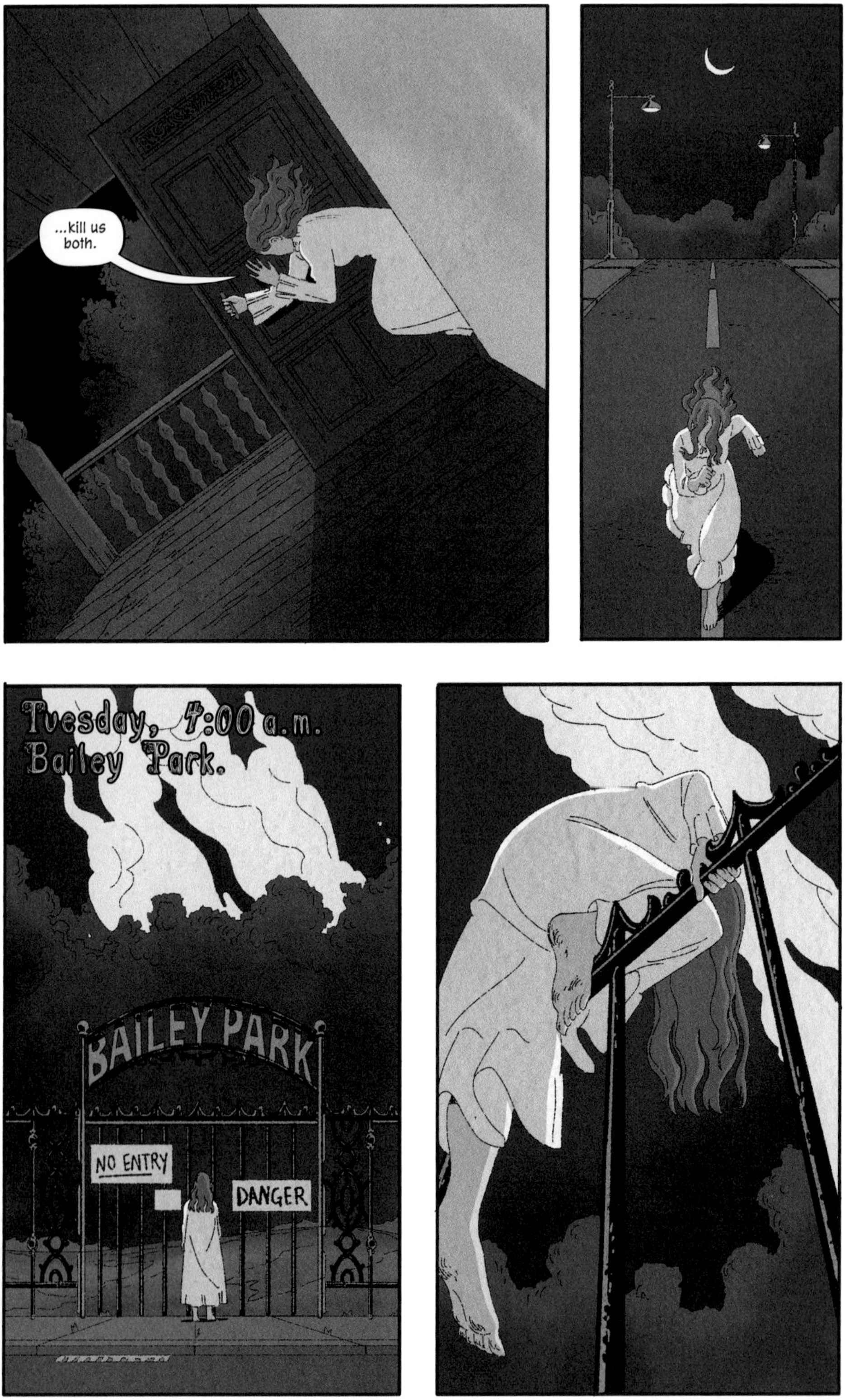
...kill us both.
Tuesday, 4:00 a.m. Bailey Park.
BAILEY PARK
NO ENTRY
DANGER

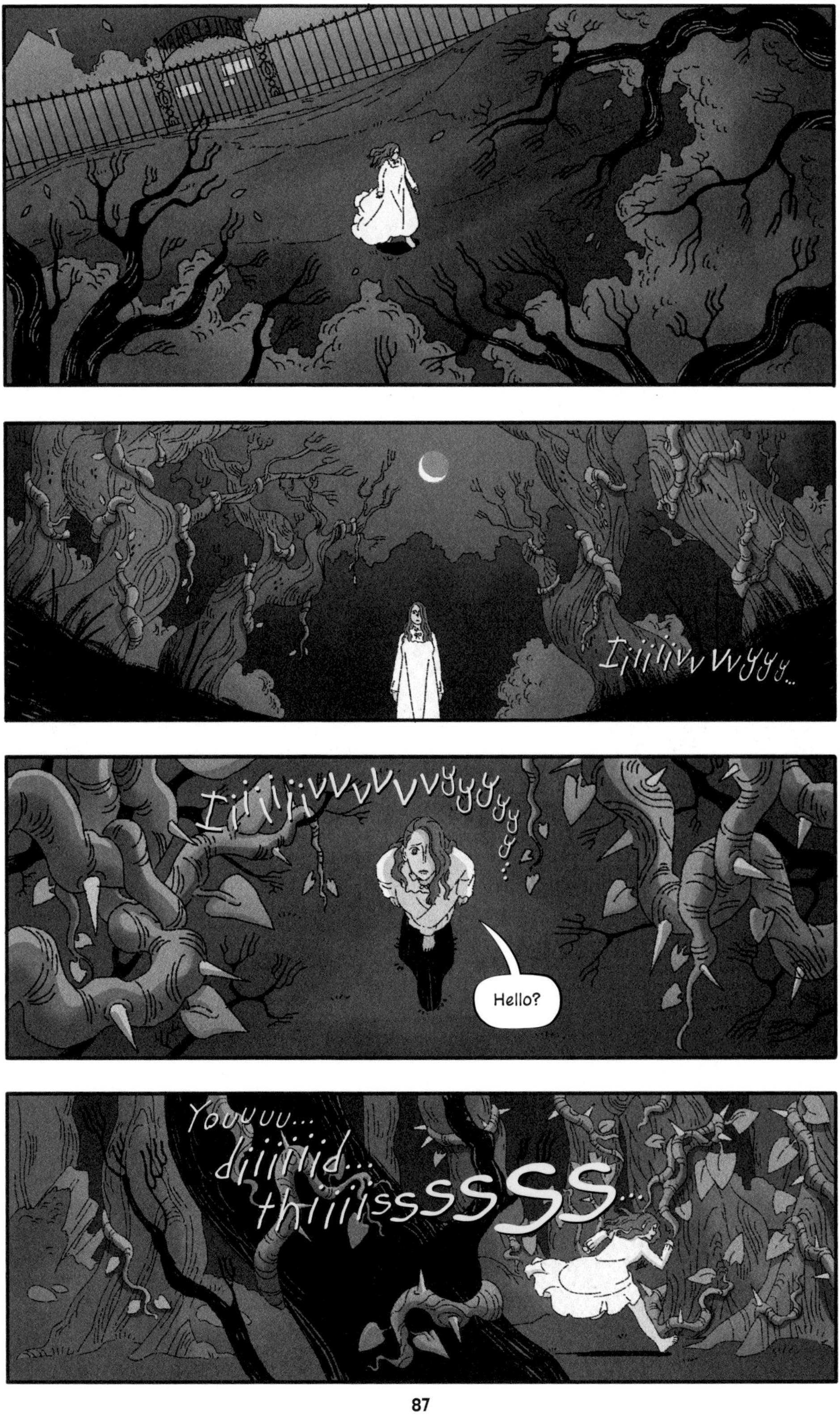

BAILEY PARK
Iiiiiivvvvyyyy...
Iiiiiivvvvvvvyyyyyyy...
Hello?
Youuuu...
diiiiid...
thiiiissssSSS...

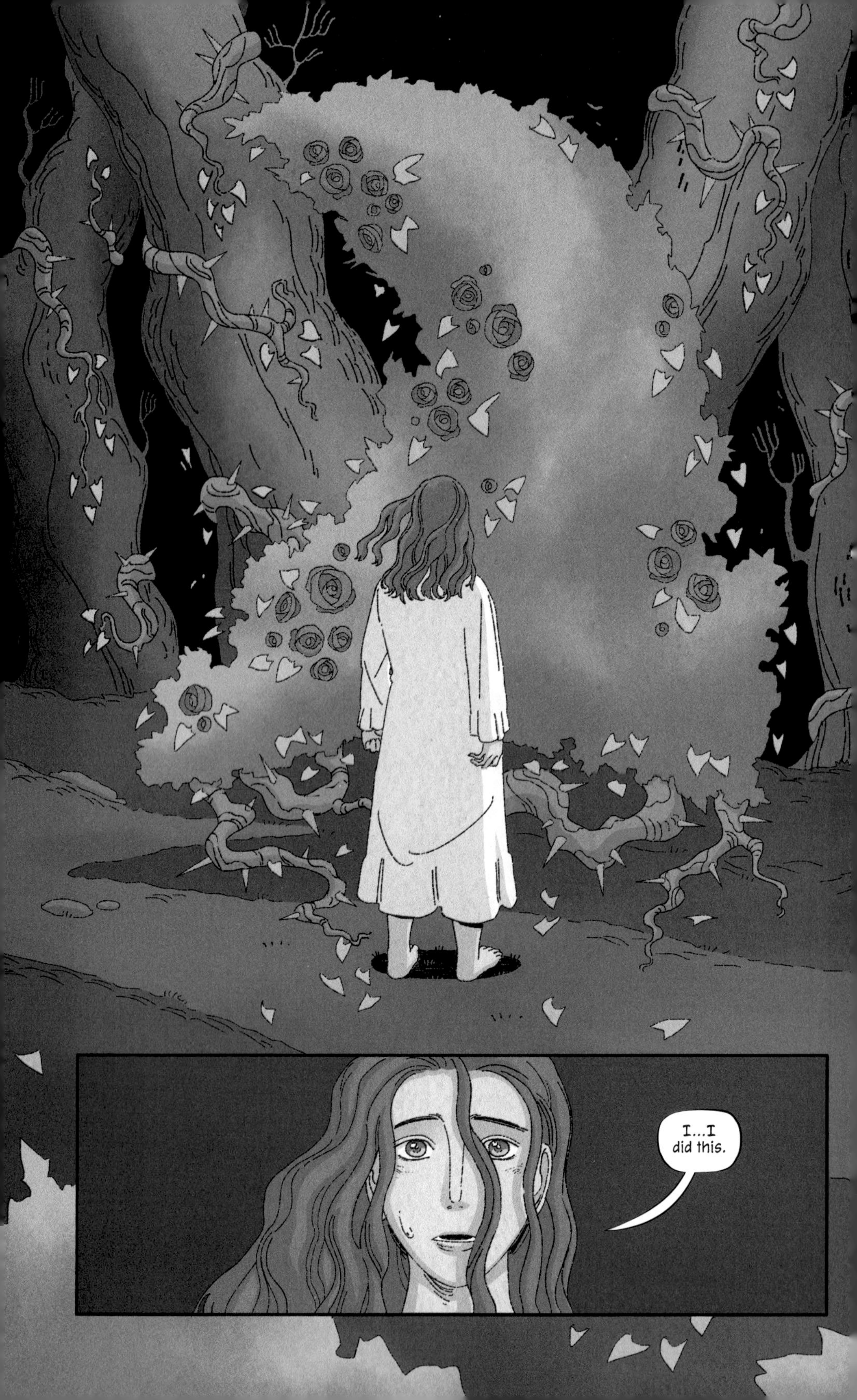
I...I did this.

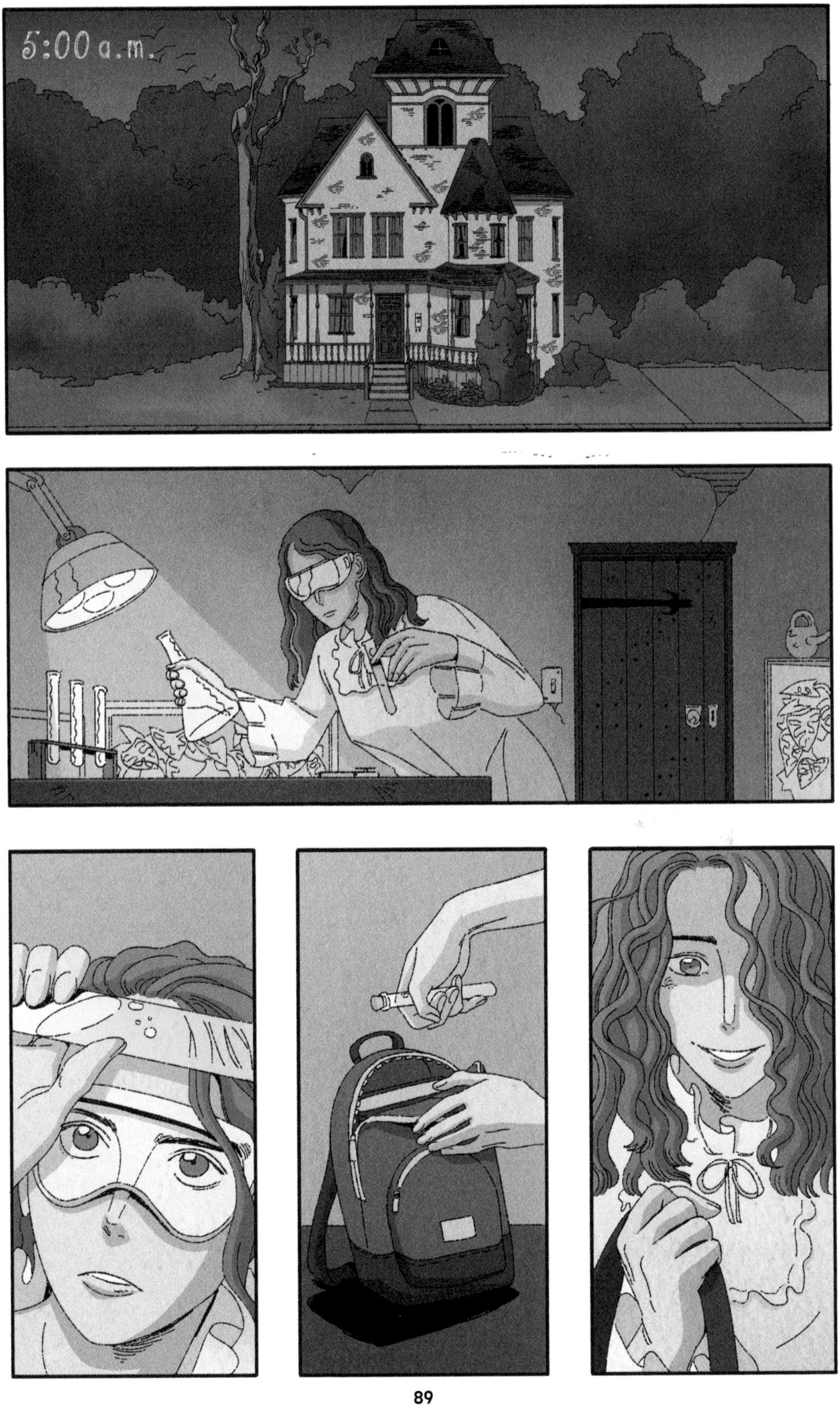
5:00 a.m.

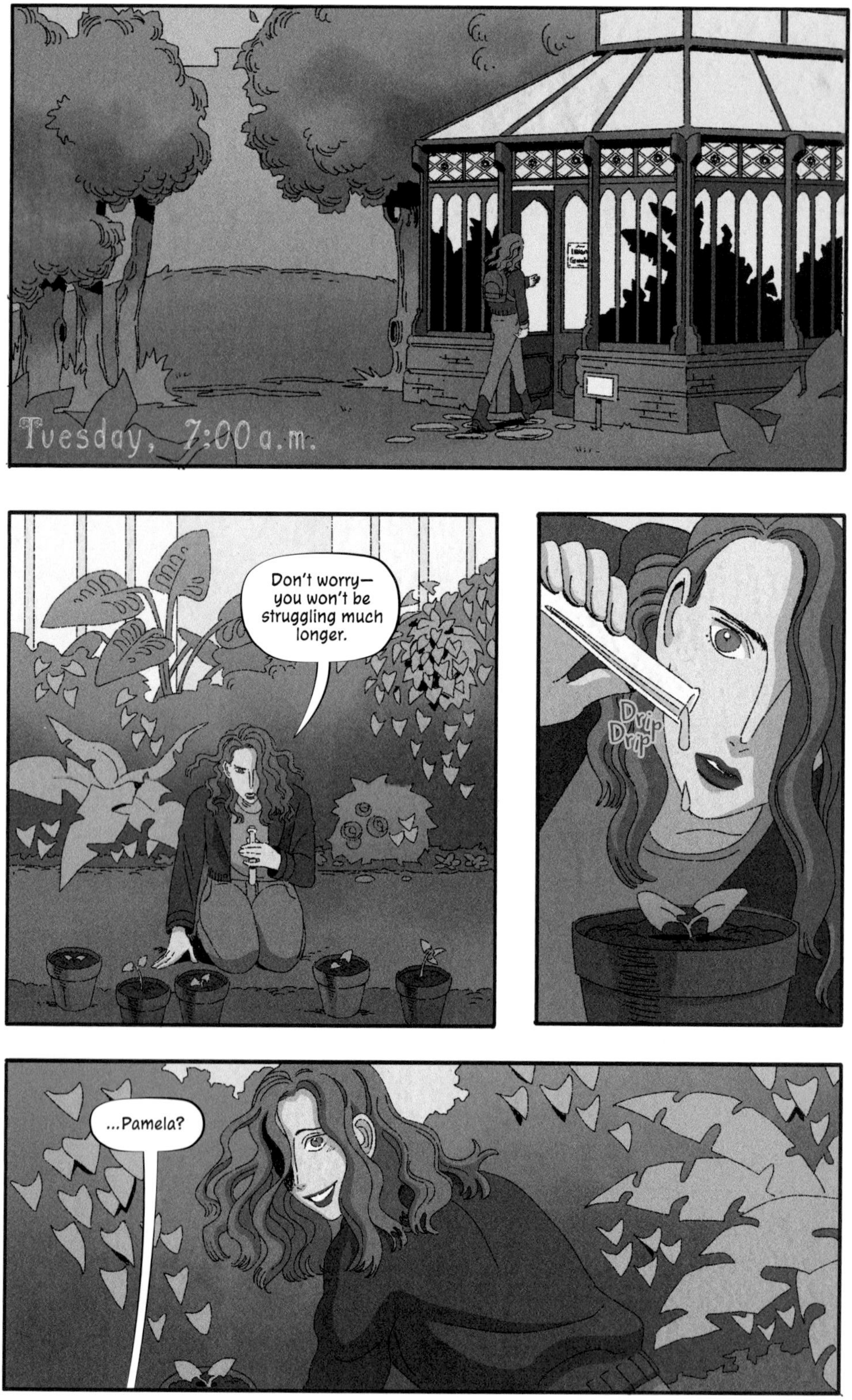
Tuesday, 7:00 a.m.
Don't worry—you won't be struggling much longer.
Drip Drip
...Pamela?

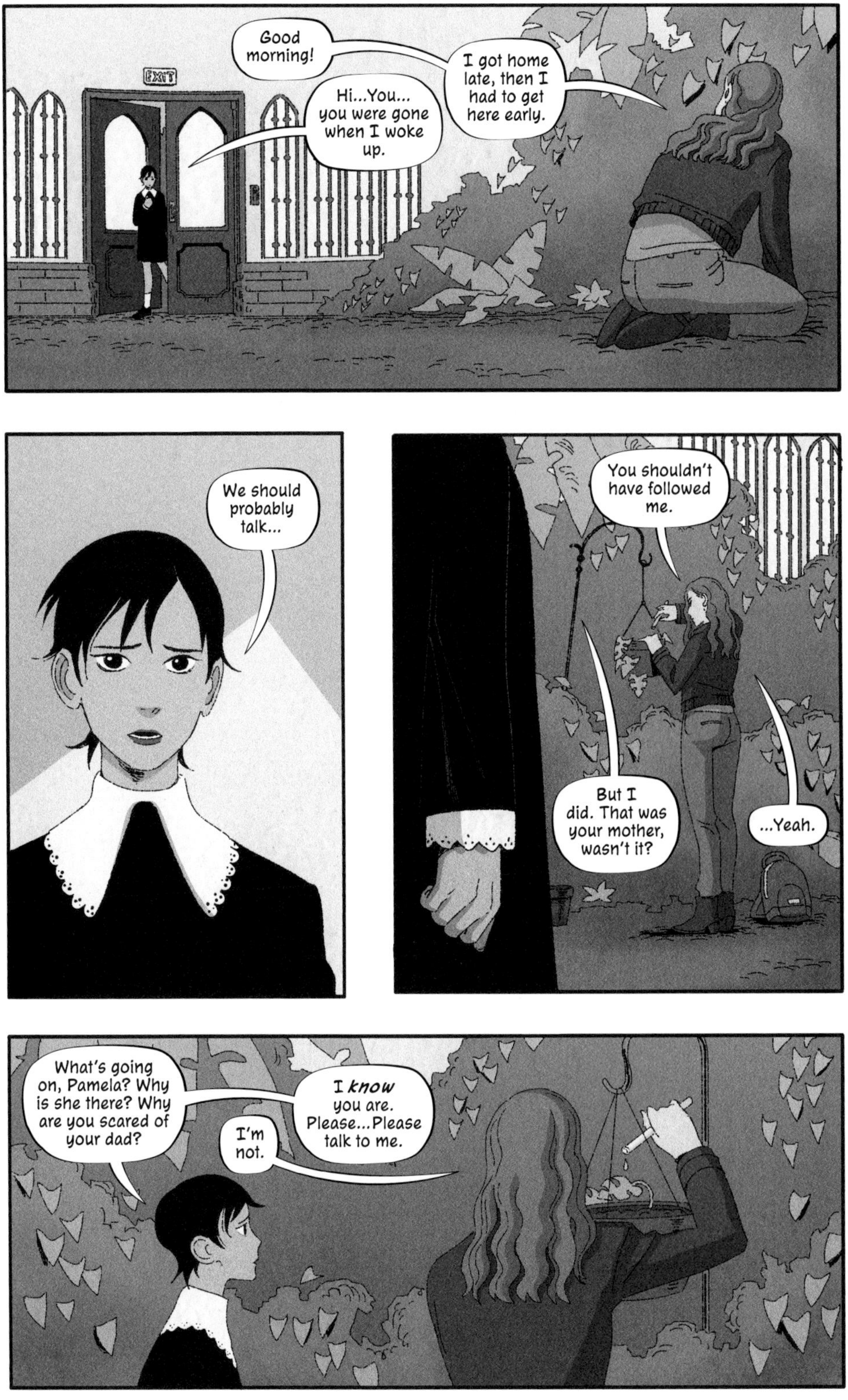

Good morning!
Hi...You... you were gone when I woke up.
I got home late, then I had to get here early.
EXIT
We should probably talk...
You shouldn't have followed me.
But I did. That was your mother, wasn't it?
...Yeah.
What's going on, Pamela? Why is she there? Why are you scared of your dad?
I'm not.
I *know* you are. Please...Please talk to me.

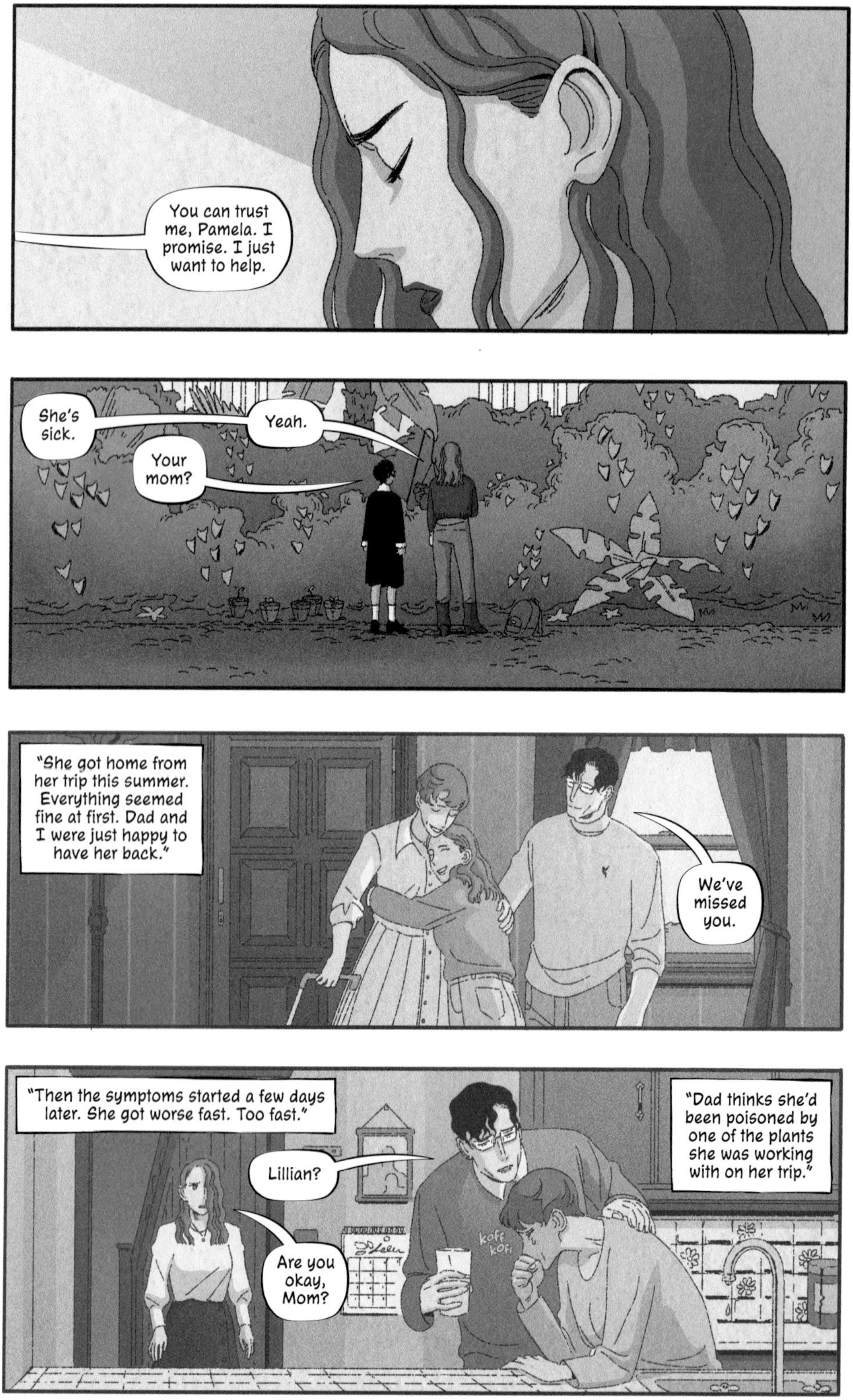
You can trust me, Pamela. I promise. I just want to help.
She's sick.
Your mom?
Yeah.
"She got home from her trip this summer. Everything seemed fine at first. Dad and I were just happy to have her back."
We've missed you.
"Then the symptoms started a few days later. She got worse fast. Too fast."
Lillian?
koff koff
Are you okay, Mom?
"Dad thinks she'd been poisoned by one of the plants she was working with on her trip."

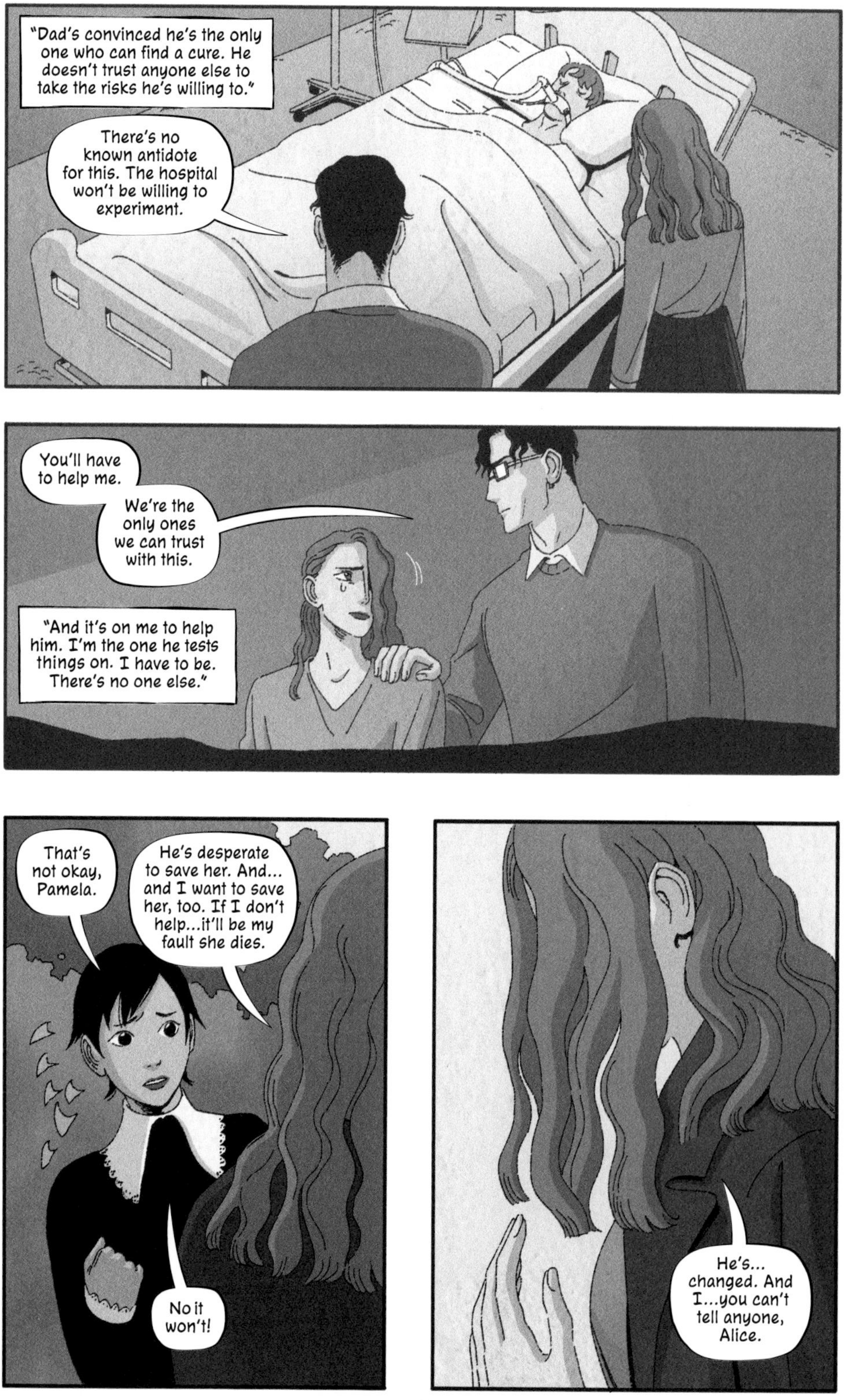
"Dad's convinced he's the only one who can find a cure. He doesn't trust anyone else to take the risks he's willing to."
There's no known antidote for this. The hospital won't be willing to experiment.
You'll have to help me.
We're the only ones we can trust with this.
"And it's on me to help him. I'm the one he tests things on. I have to be. There's no one else."
That's not okay, Pamela.
He's desperate to save her. And... and I want to save her, too. If I don't help...it'll be my fault she dies.
No it won't!
He's... changed. And I...you can't tell anyone, Alice.

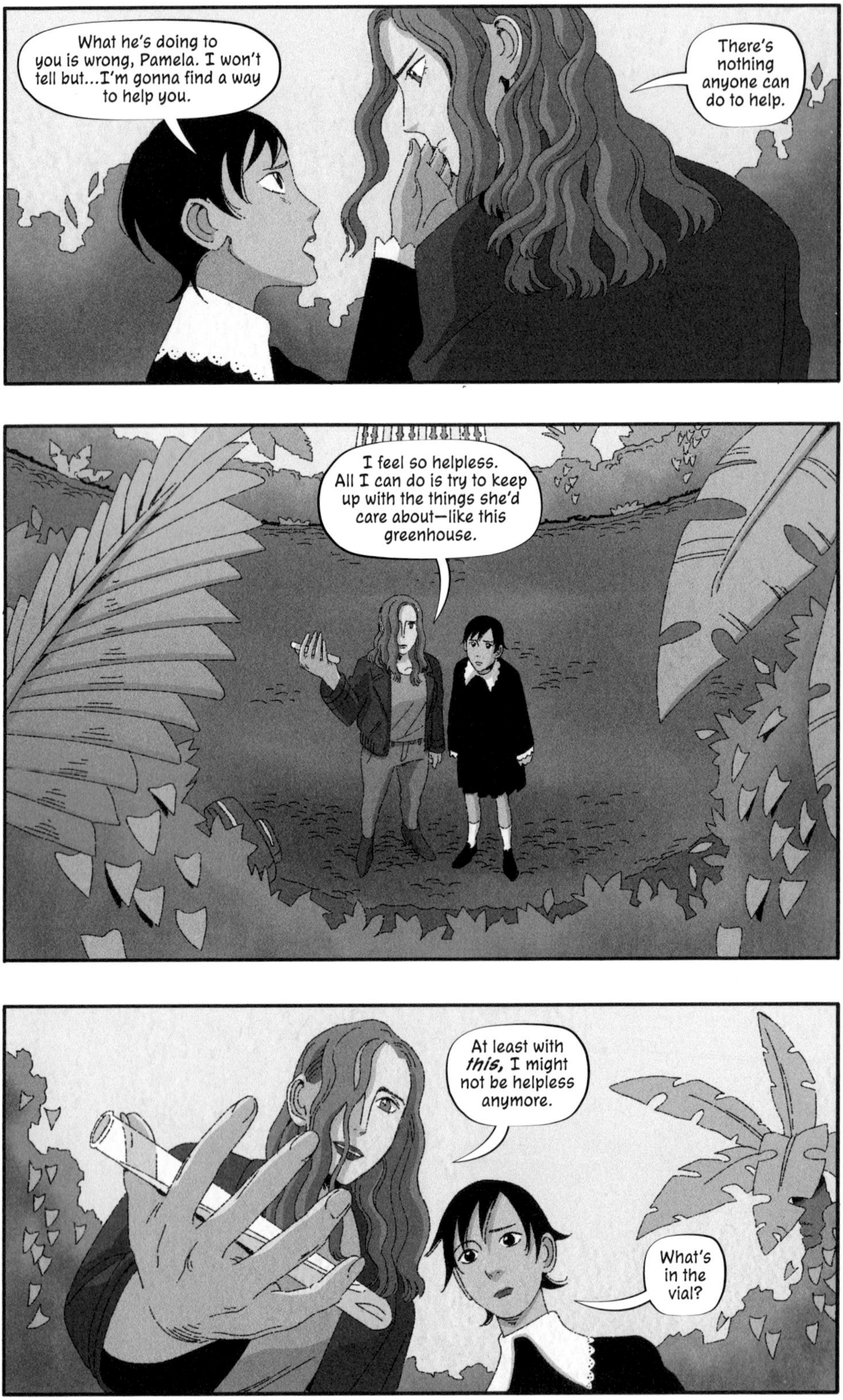
What he's doing to you is wrong, Pamela. I won't tell but...I'm gonna find a way to help you.
There's nothing anyone can do to help.
I feel so helpless. All I can do is try to keep up with the things she'd care about—like this greenhouse.
At least with *this,* I might not be helpless anymore.
What's in the vial?

Alice, I think I made something—something *amazing.*

The stuff in this vial will make the plants grow—grow big and fast! The plants will be so much stronger. I can save them!

That's great, but how do you know?

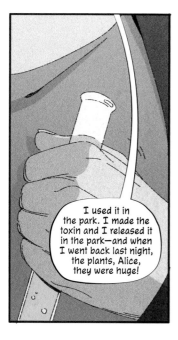

I used it in the park. I made the toxin and I released it in the park—and when I went back last night, the plants, Alice, they were huge!

Wait... the park? A toxin? It...you did that? The poisonous gas?

95

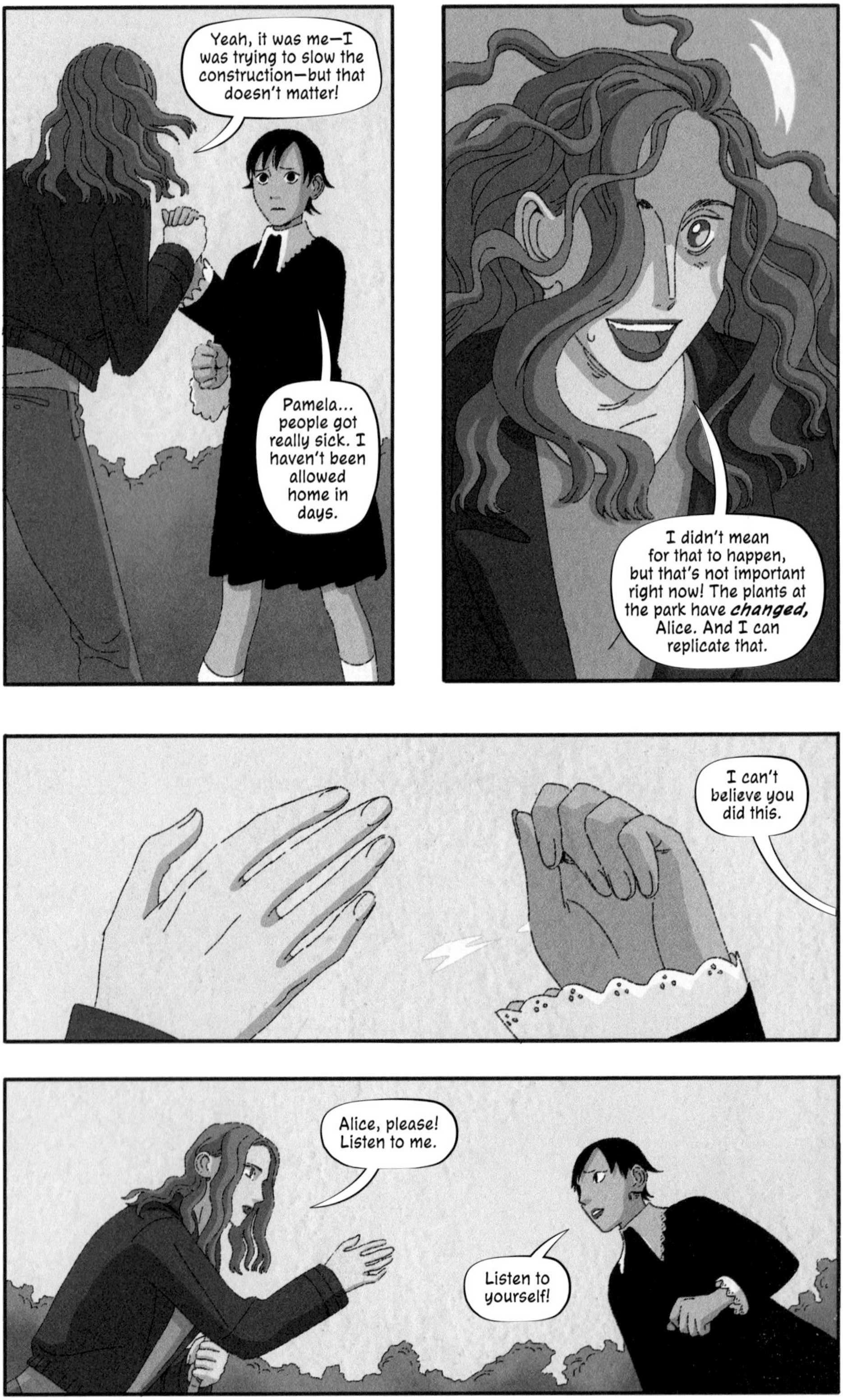

Yeah, it was me—I was trying to slow the construction—but that doesn't matter!
Pamela... people got really sick. I haven't been allowed home in days.
I didn't mean for that to happen, but that's not important right now! The plants at the park have ***changed,*** Alice. And I can replicate that.
I can't believe you did this.
Alice, please! Listen to me.
Listen to yourself!

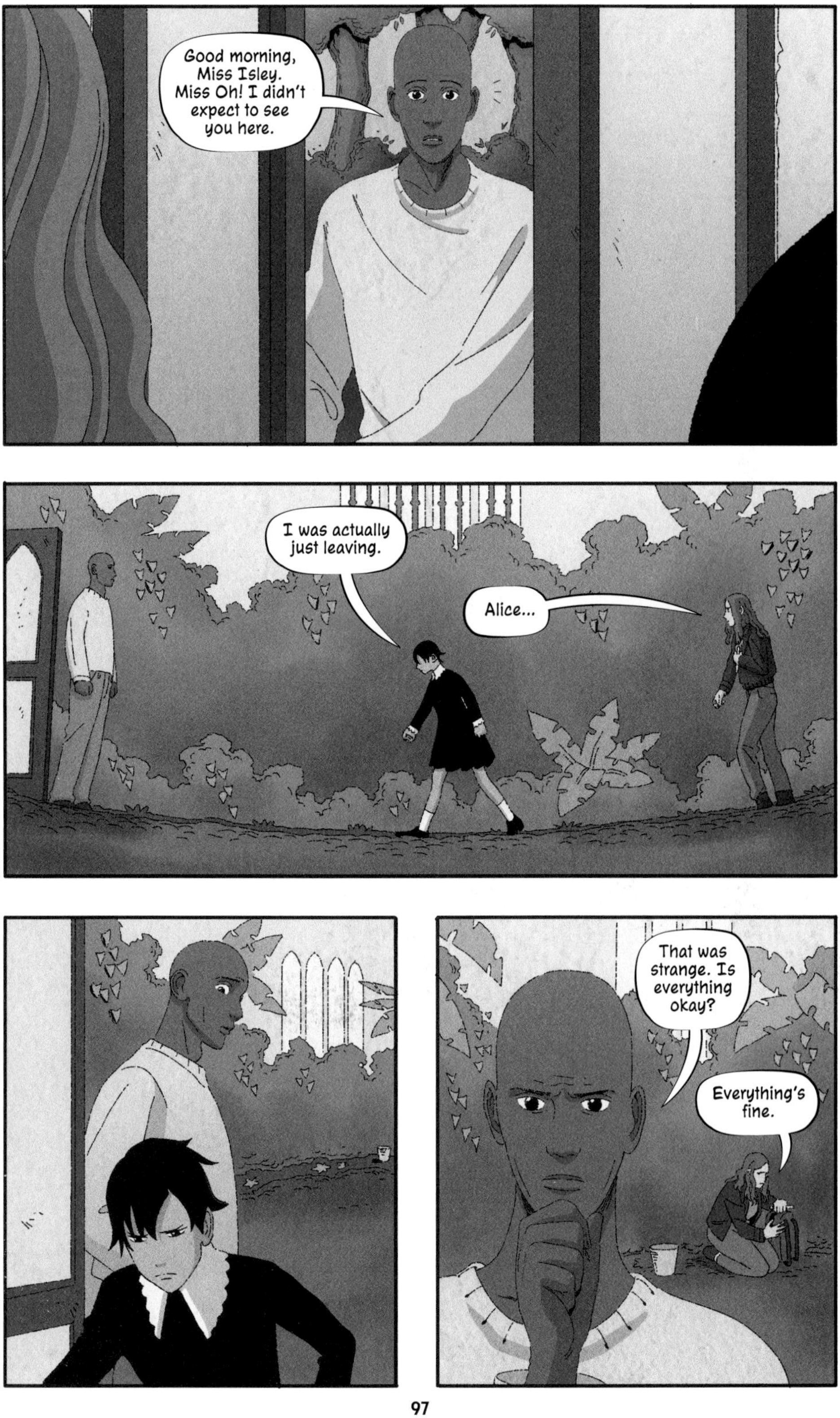
Good morning, Miss Isley. Miss Oh! I didn't expect to see you here.
I was actually just leaving.
Alice...
That was strange. Is everything okay?
Everything's fine.

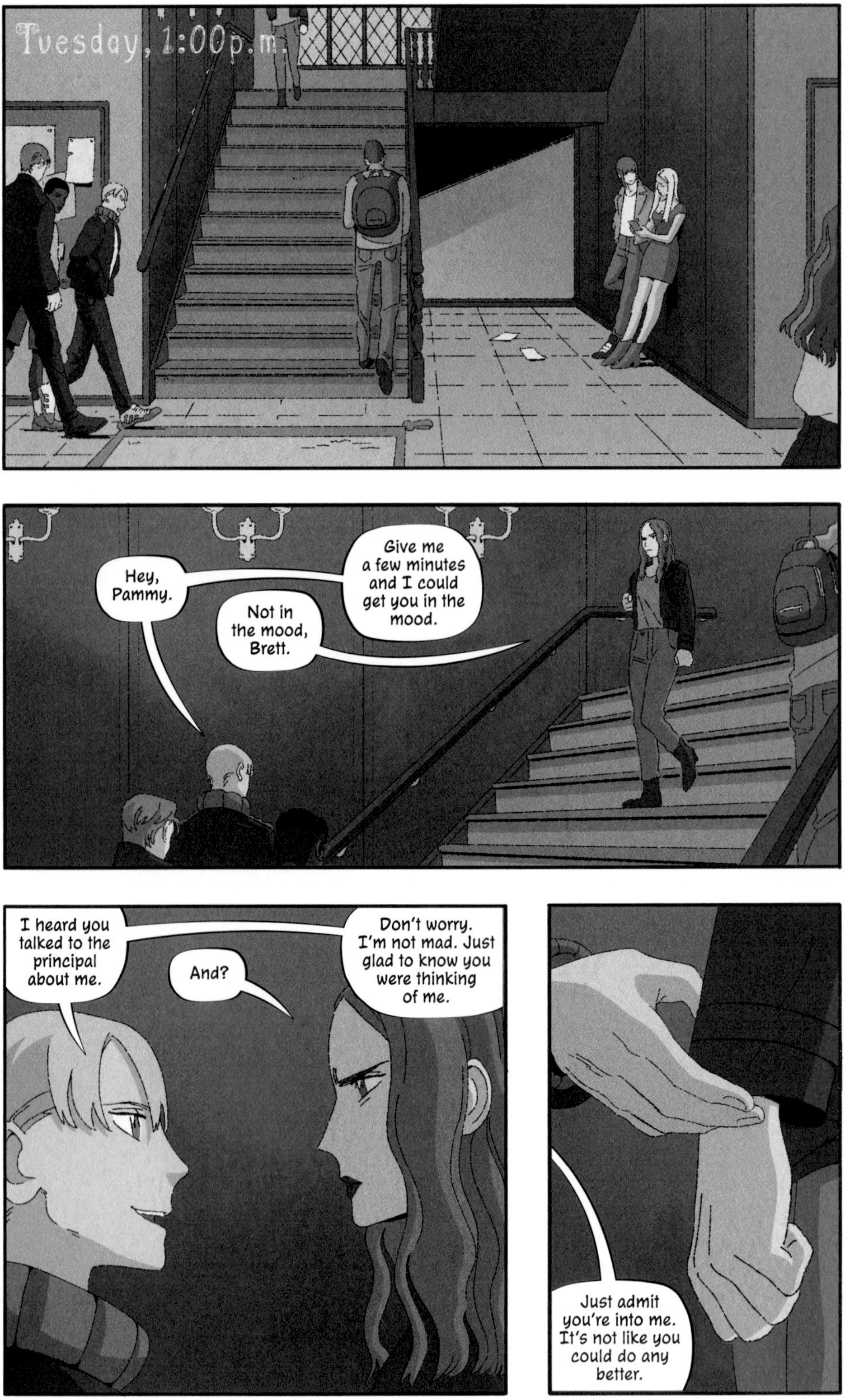
Tuesday, 1:00p.m.
Hey, Pammy.
Give me a few minutes and I could get you in the mood.
Not in the mood, Brett.
I heard you talked to the principal about me.
And?
Don't worry. I'm not mad. Just glad to know you were thinking of me.
Just admit you're into me. It's not like you could do any better.

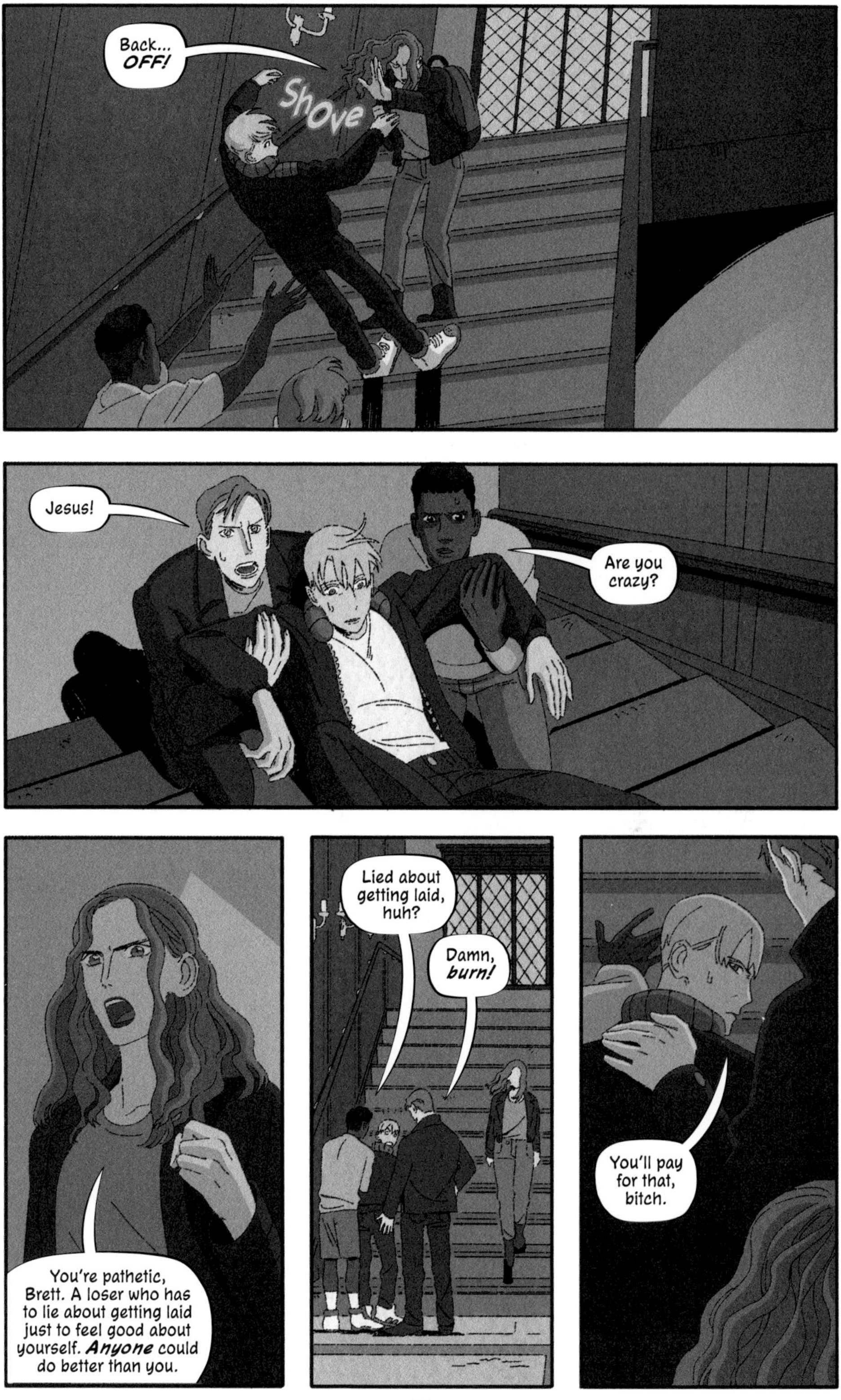
Back... *OFF!*
Shove
Jesus!
Are you crazy?
You're pathetic, Brett. A loser who has to lie about getting laid just to feel good about yourself. *Anyone* could do better than you.
Lied about getting laid, huh?
Damn, *burn!*
You'll pay for that, bitch.

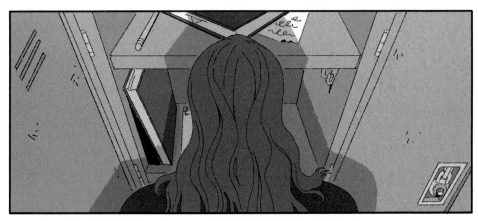

Miss Isley?

Oh, sorry! I didn't mean to startle you. I just wanted to check in. You've seemed a little off today.

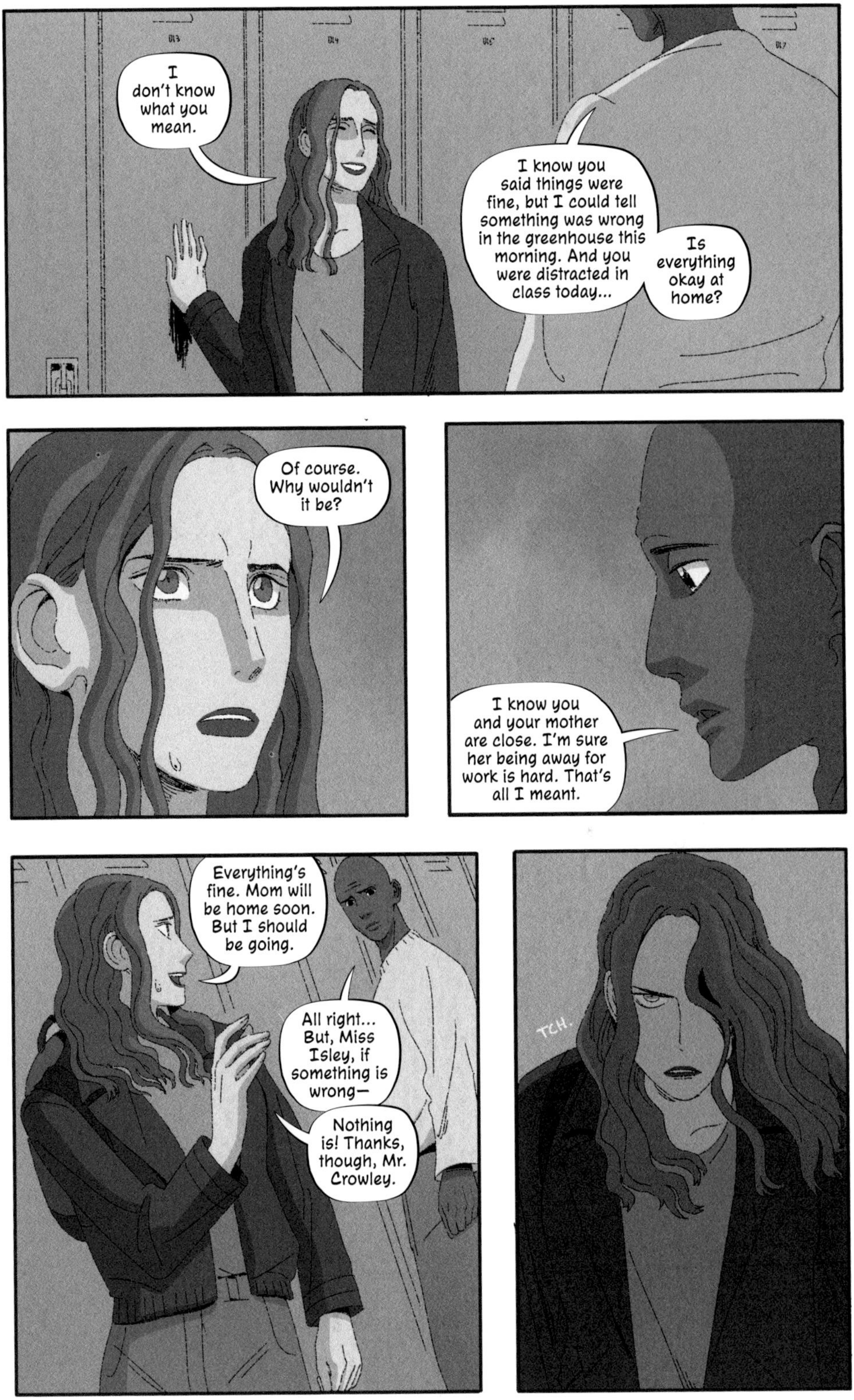
I don't know what you mean.
I know you said things were fine, but I could tell something was wrong in the greenhouse this morning. And you were distracted in class today...
Is everything okay at home?
Of course. Why wouldn't it be?
I know you and your mother are close. I'm sure her being away for work is hard. That's all I meant.
Everything's fine. Mom will be home soon. But I should be going.
All right... But, Miss Isley, if something is wrong—
Nothing is! Thanks, though, Mr. Crowley.
TCH.

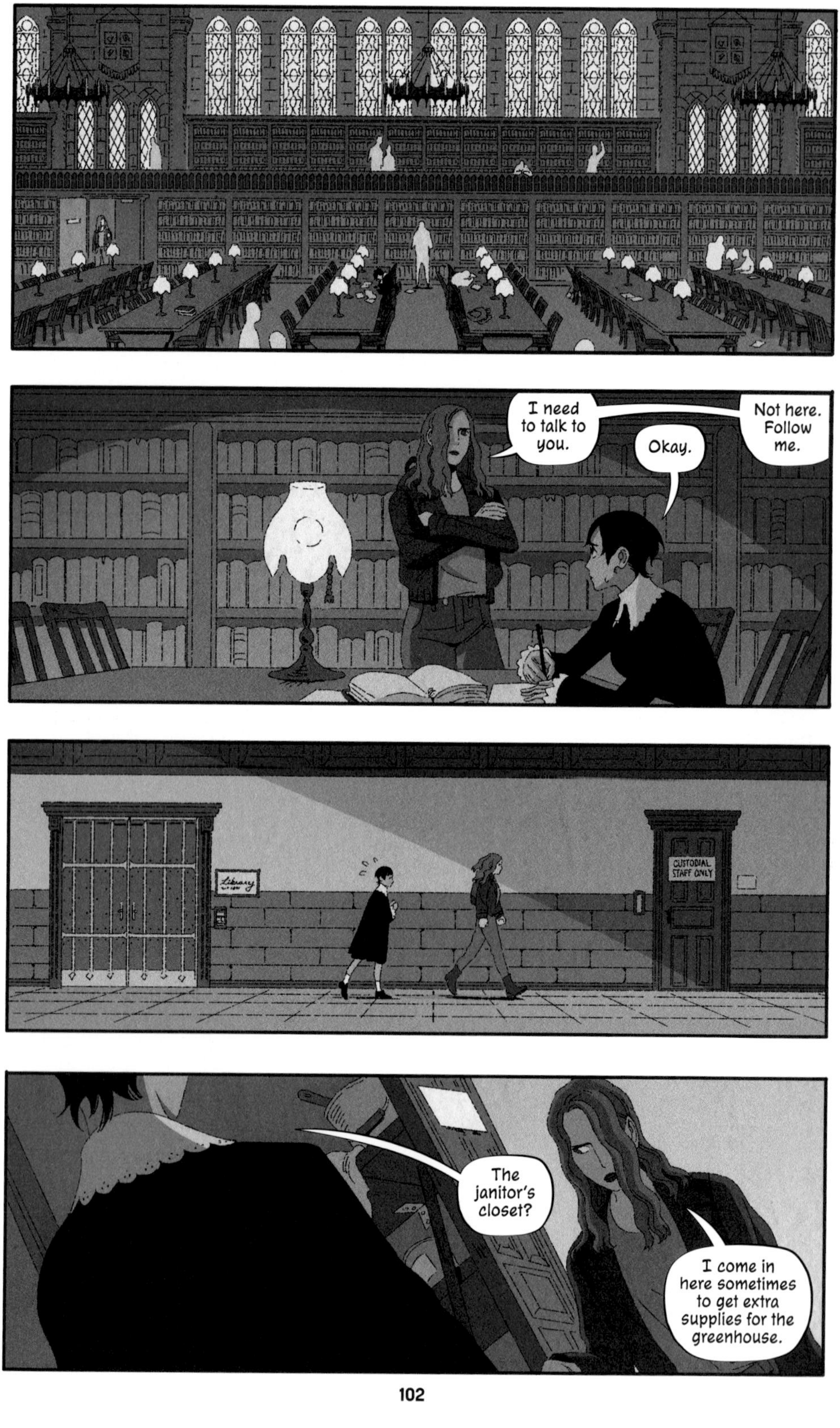
I need to talk to you.
Okay.
Not here. Follow me.
CUSTODIAL STAFF ONLY
The janitor's closet?
I come in here sometimes to get extra supplies for the greenhouse.

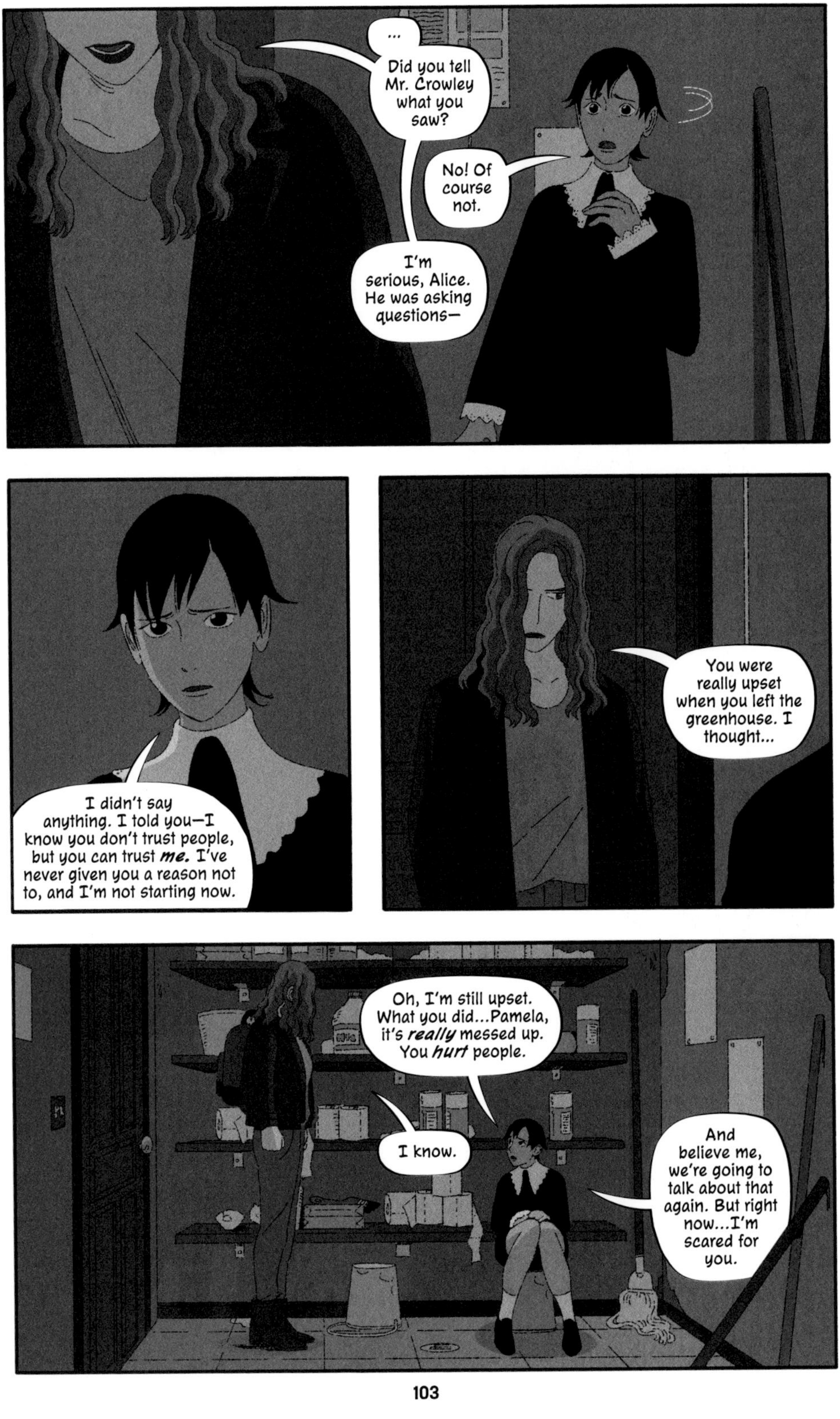
...
Did you tell Mr. Crowley what you saw?
No! Of course not.
I'm serious, Alice. He was asking questions—
I didn't say anything. I told you—I know you don't trust people, but you can trust *me.* I've never given you a reason not to, and I'm not starting now.
You were really upset when you left the greenhouse. I thought...
Oh, I'm still upset. What you did...Pamela, it's *really* messed up. You *hurt* people.
I know.
And believe me, we're going to talk about that again. But right now...I'm scared for you.

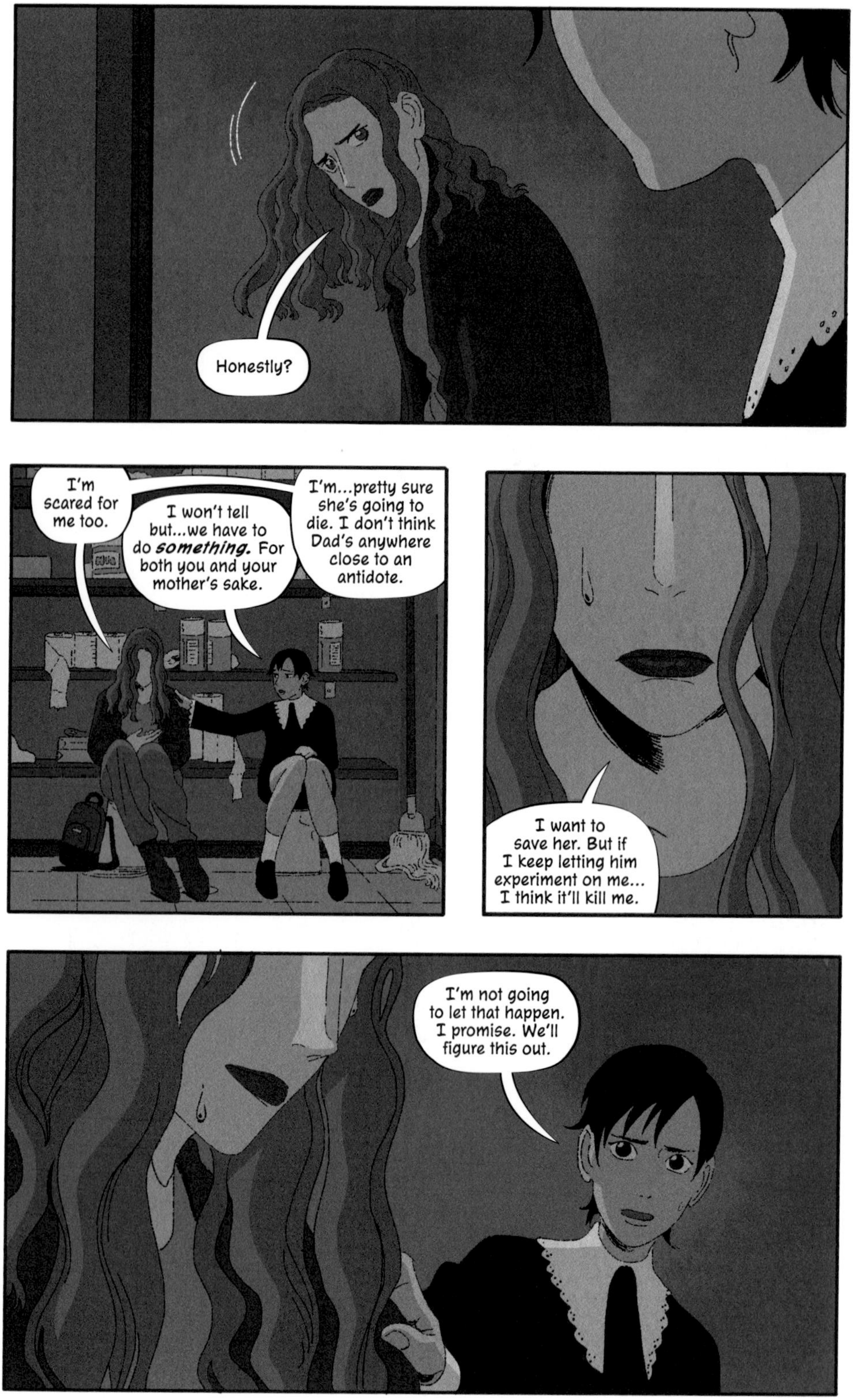
Honestly?
I'm...pretty sure she's going to die. I don't think Dad's anywhere close to an antidote.
I'm scared for me too.
I won't tell but...we have to do *something.* For both you and your mother's sake.
I want to save her. But if I keep letting him experiment on me... I think it'll kill me.
I'm not going to let that happen. I promise. We'll figure this out.

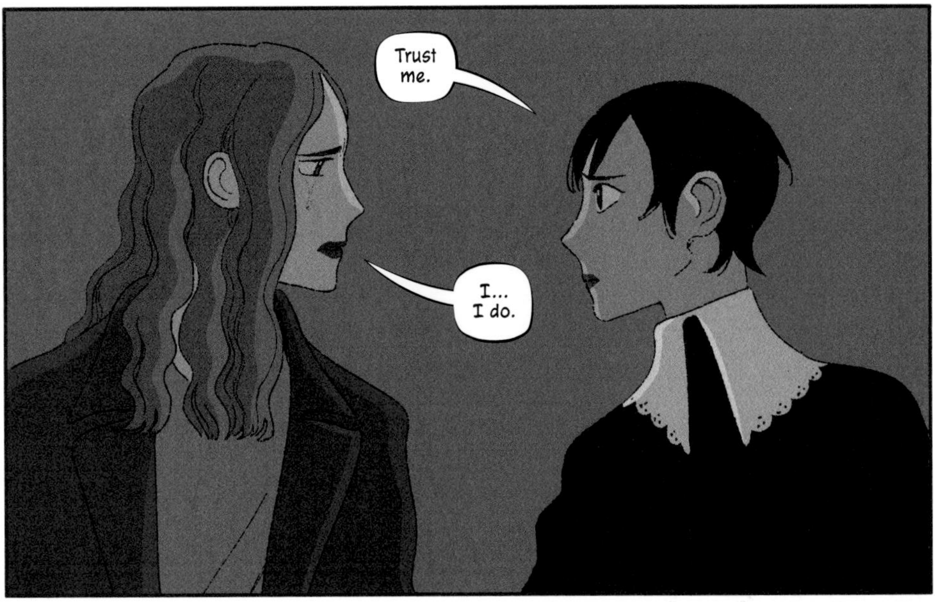
Trust me.
I... I do.

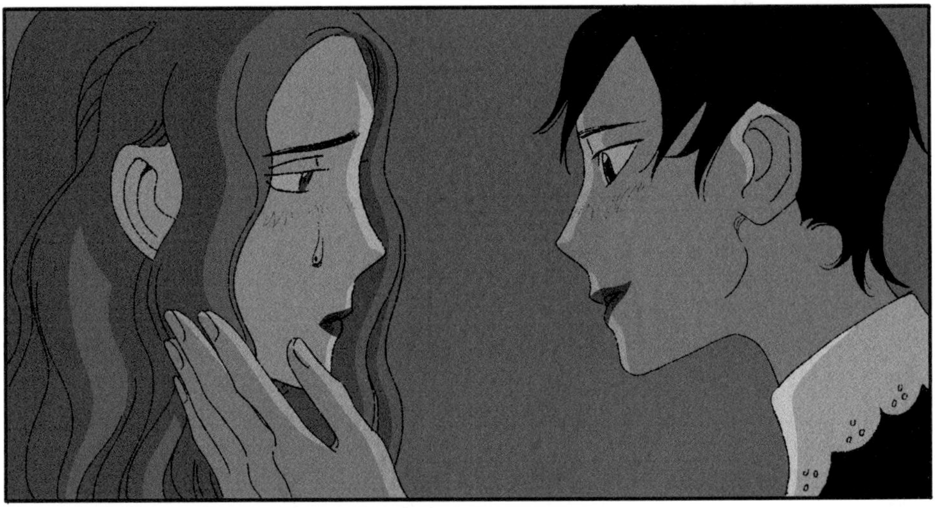

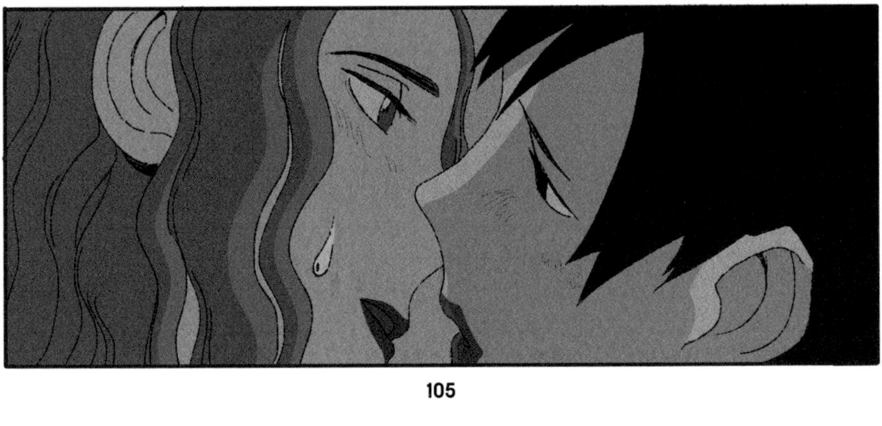

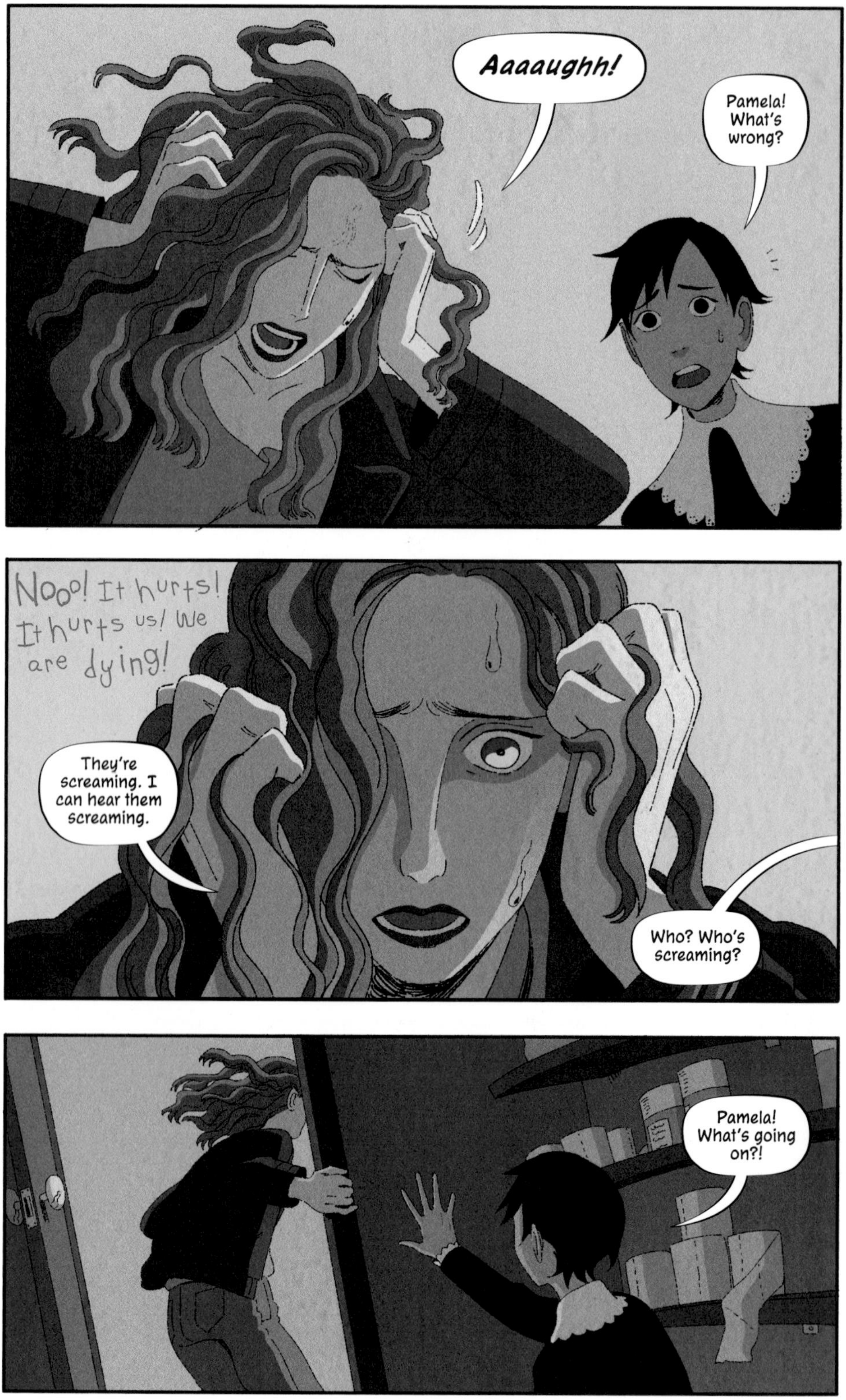
Aaaaughh!
Pamela! What's wrong?
Nooo! It hurts! It hurts us! We are dying!
They're screaming. I can hear them screaming.
Who? Who's screaming?
Pamela! What's going on?!

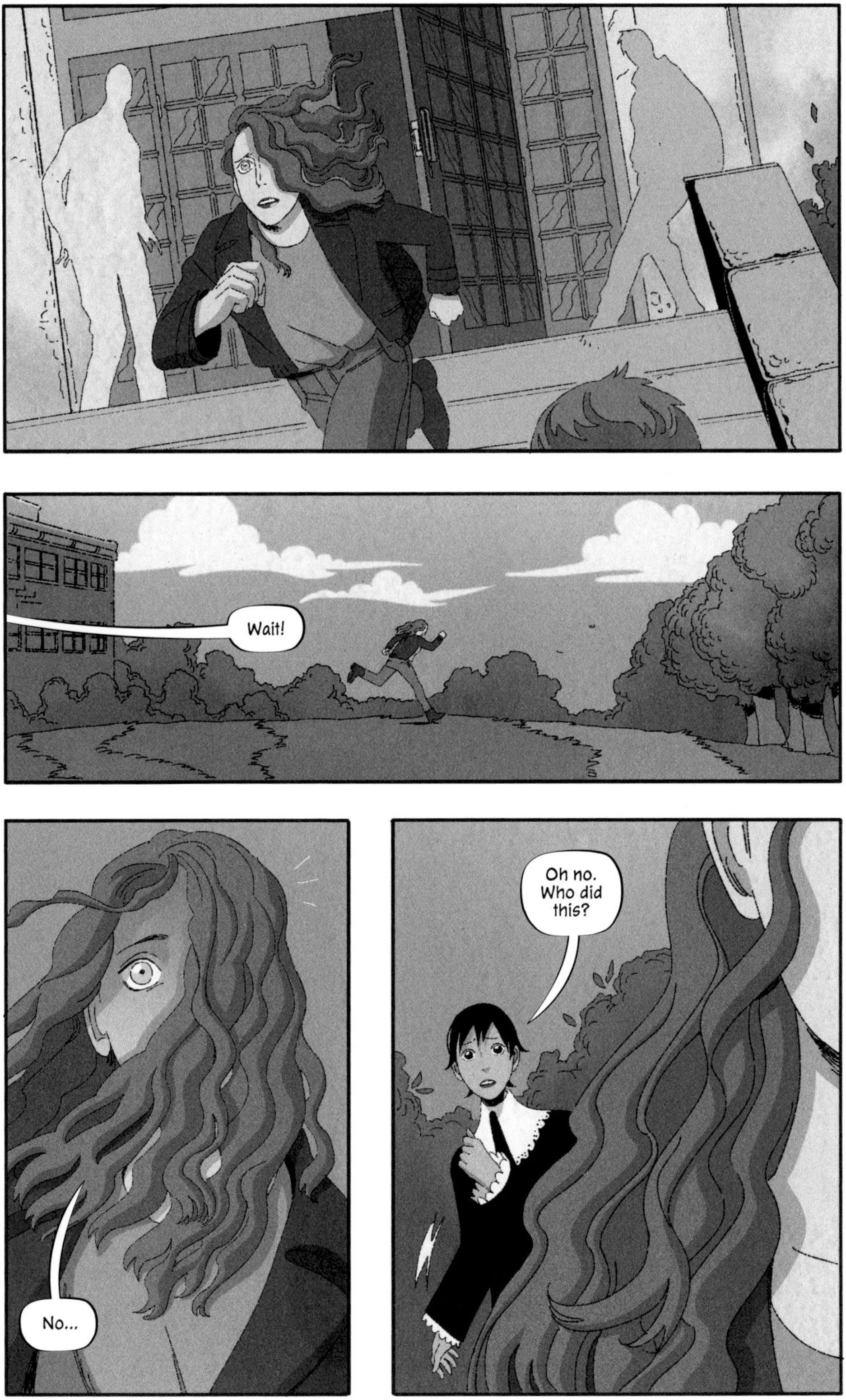
Wait!
No...
Oh no.
Who did
this?

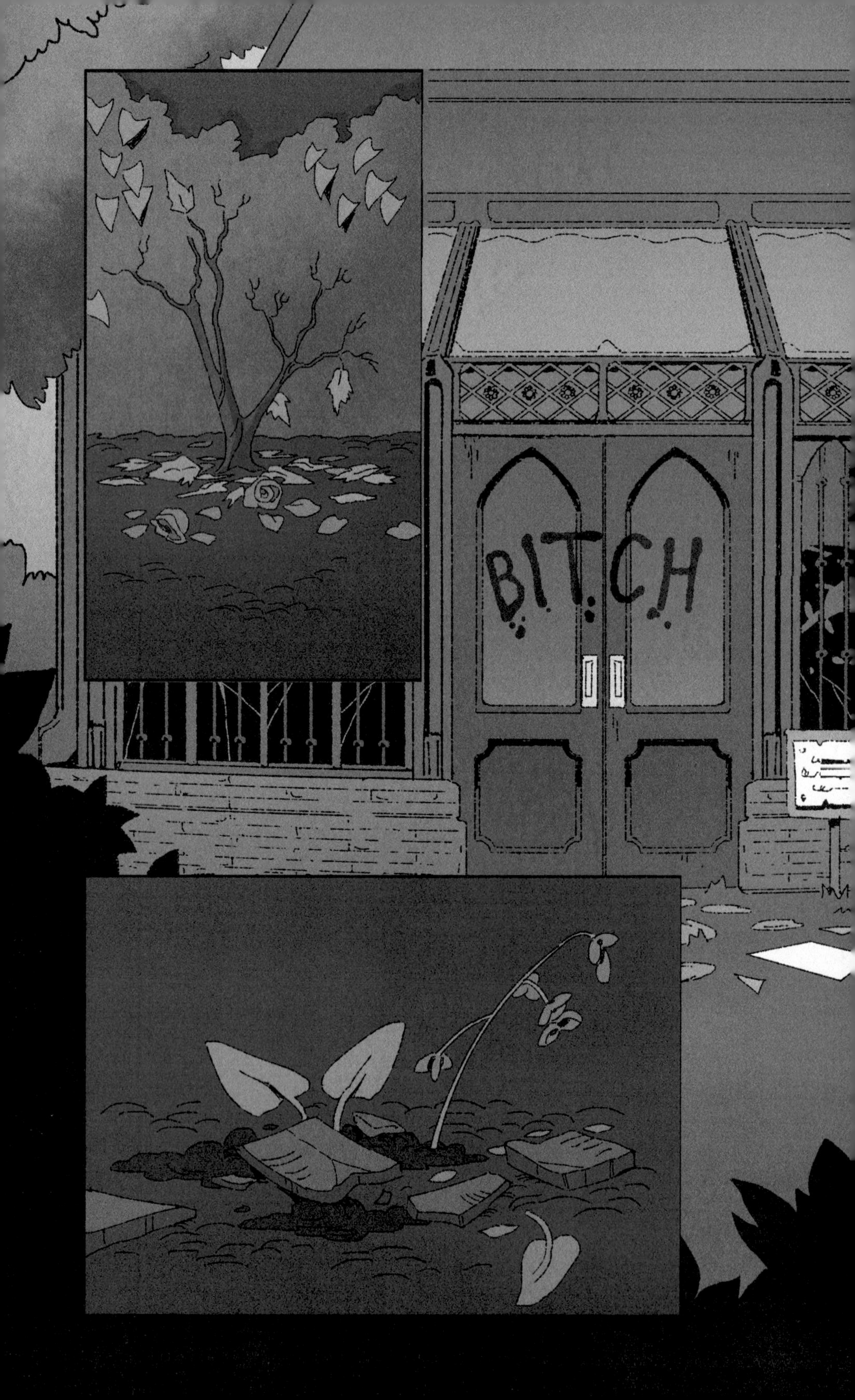
BITCH

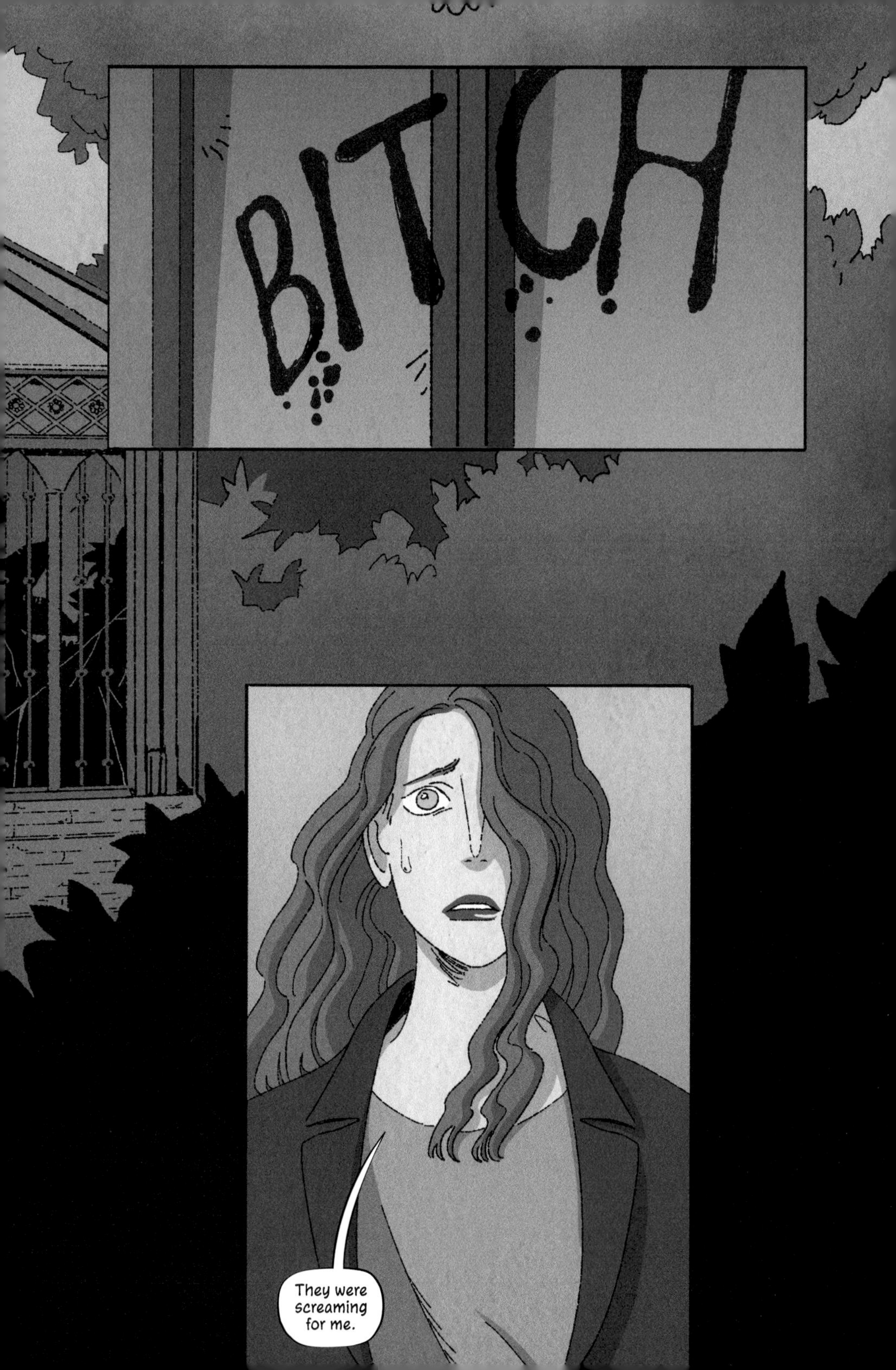
BITCH
They were screaming for me.

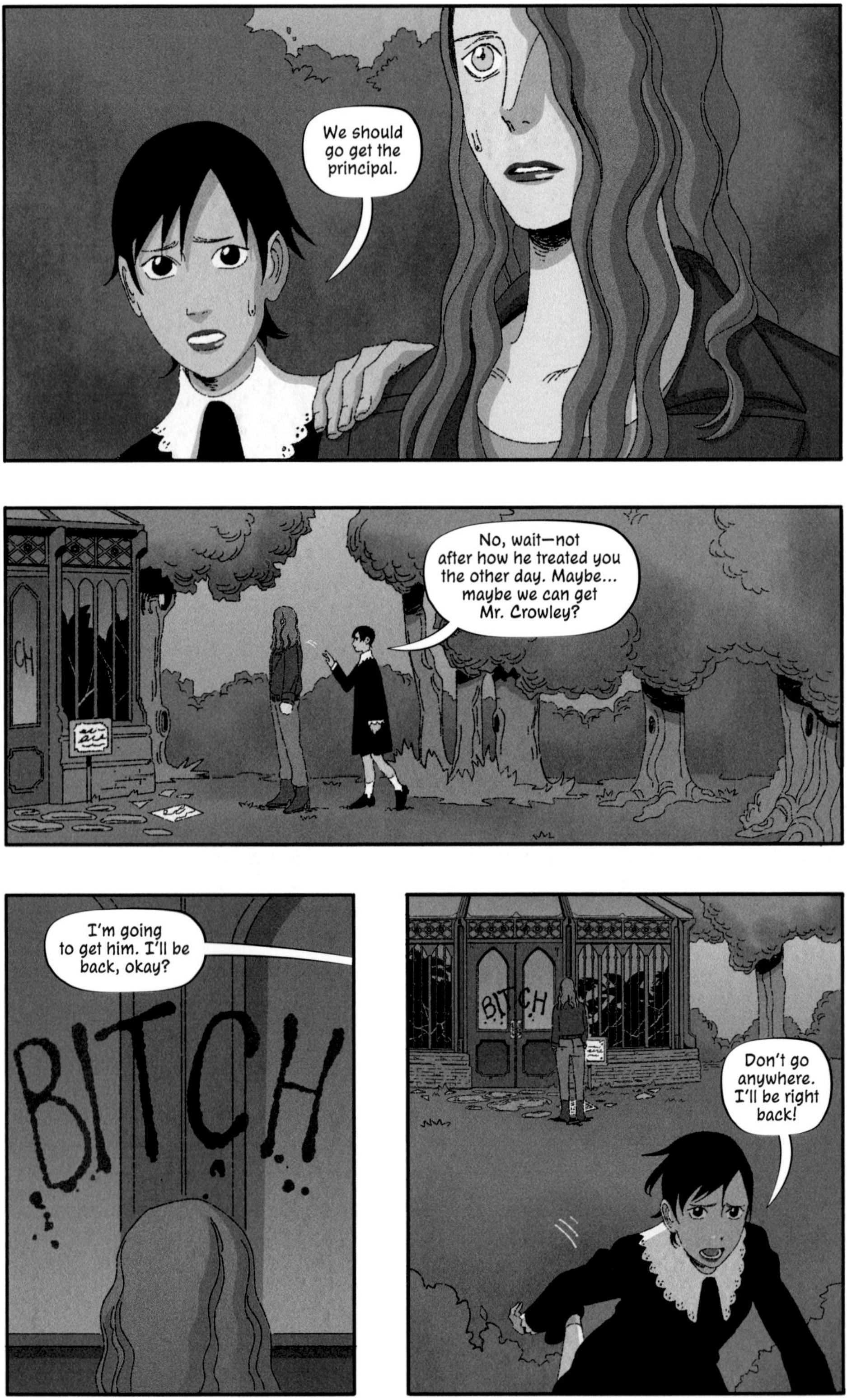
We should go get the principal.
No, wait—not after how he treated you the other day. Maybe... maybe we can get Mr. Crowley?
I'm going to get him. I'll be back, okay?
BITCH
Don't go anywhere. I'll be right back!

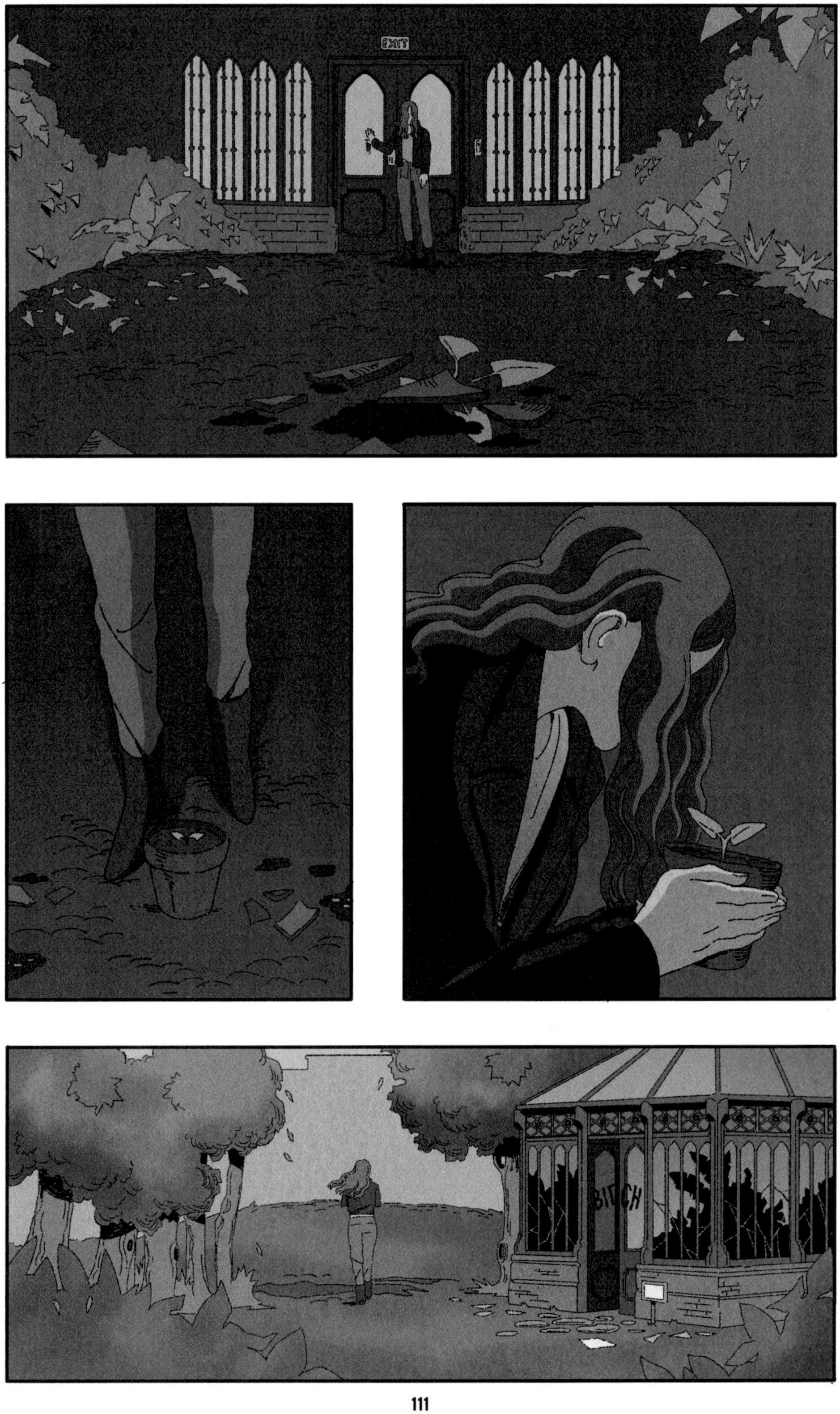
EXIT
BITCH

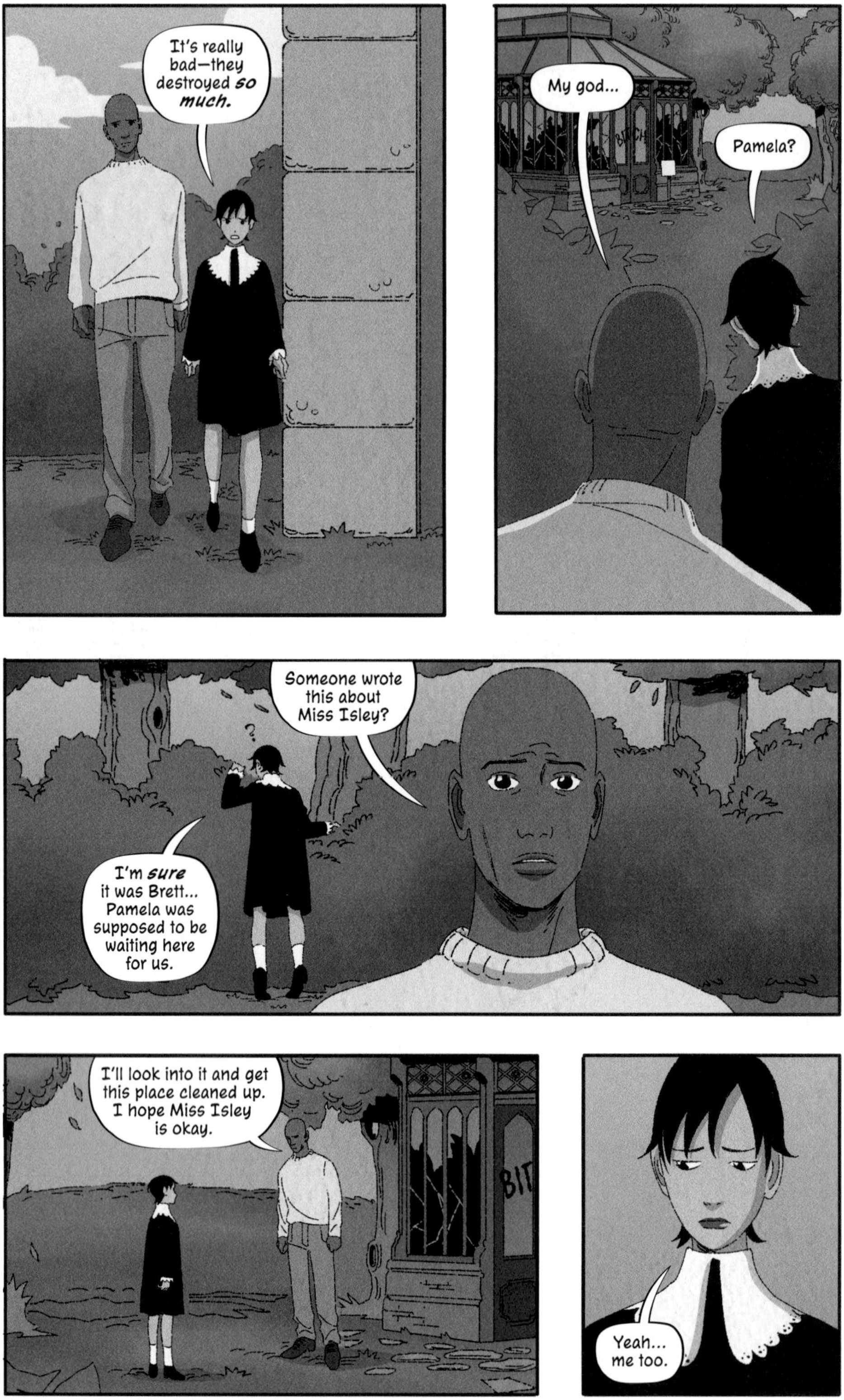
It's really bad—they destroyed *so much.*
My god...
Pamela?
BITCH
Someone wrote this about Miss Isley?
I'm *sure* it was Brett... Pamela was supposed to be waiting here for us.
I'll look into it and get this place cleaned up. I hope Miss Isley is okay.
Yeah... me too.

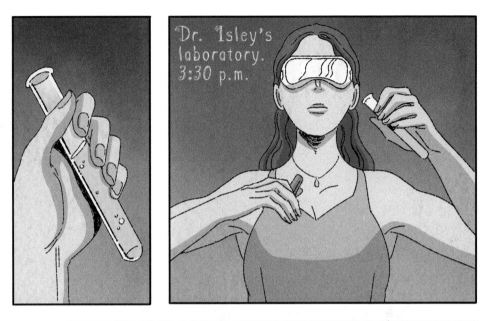

Dr. Isley's laboratory. 3:30 p.m.

Rustle Rustle

Rustle

Swish

Swish

Swish

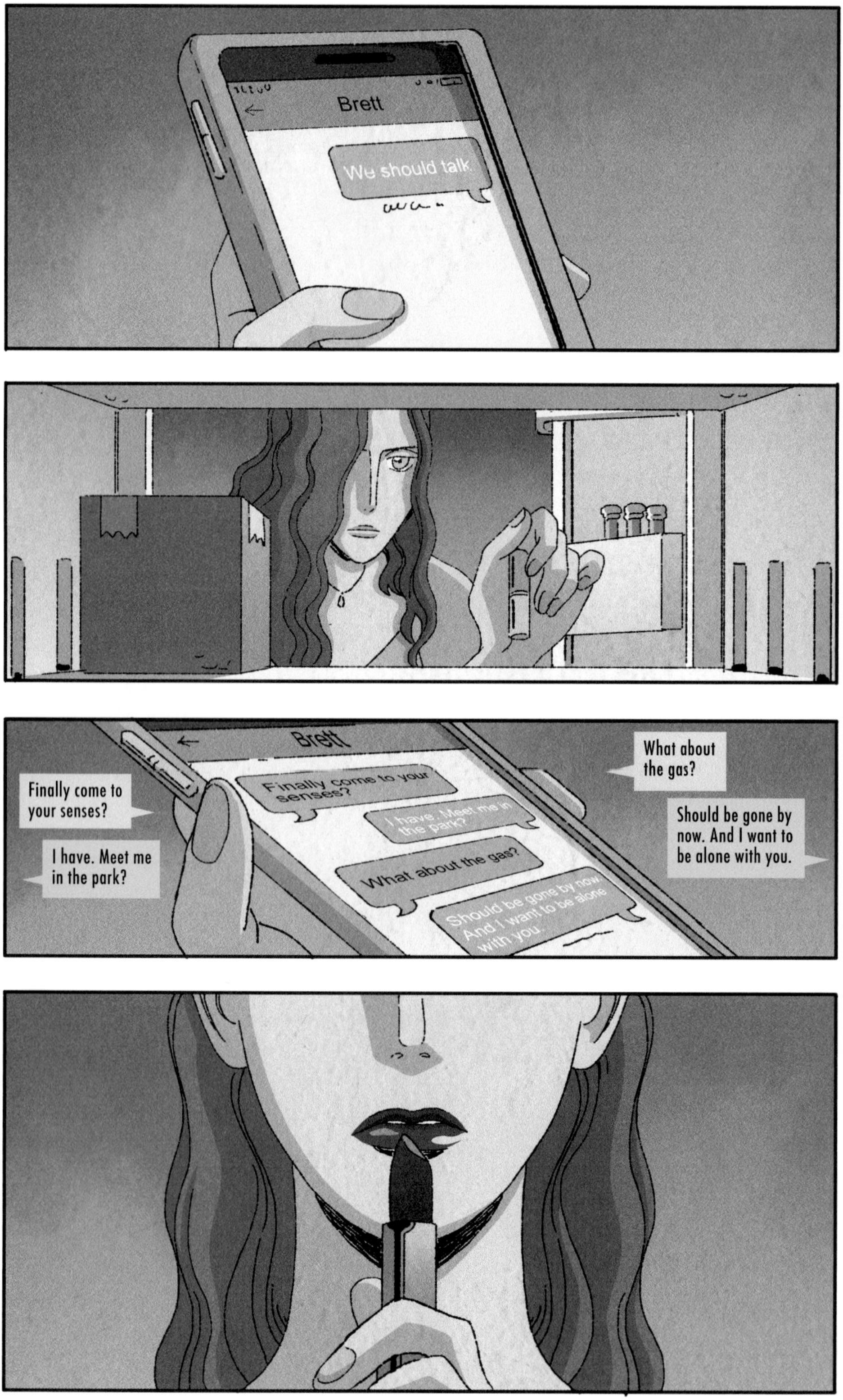
Brett
We should talk.
Brett
Finally come to your senses?
I have. Meet me in the park?
What about the gas?
Should be gone by now. And I want to be alone with you.

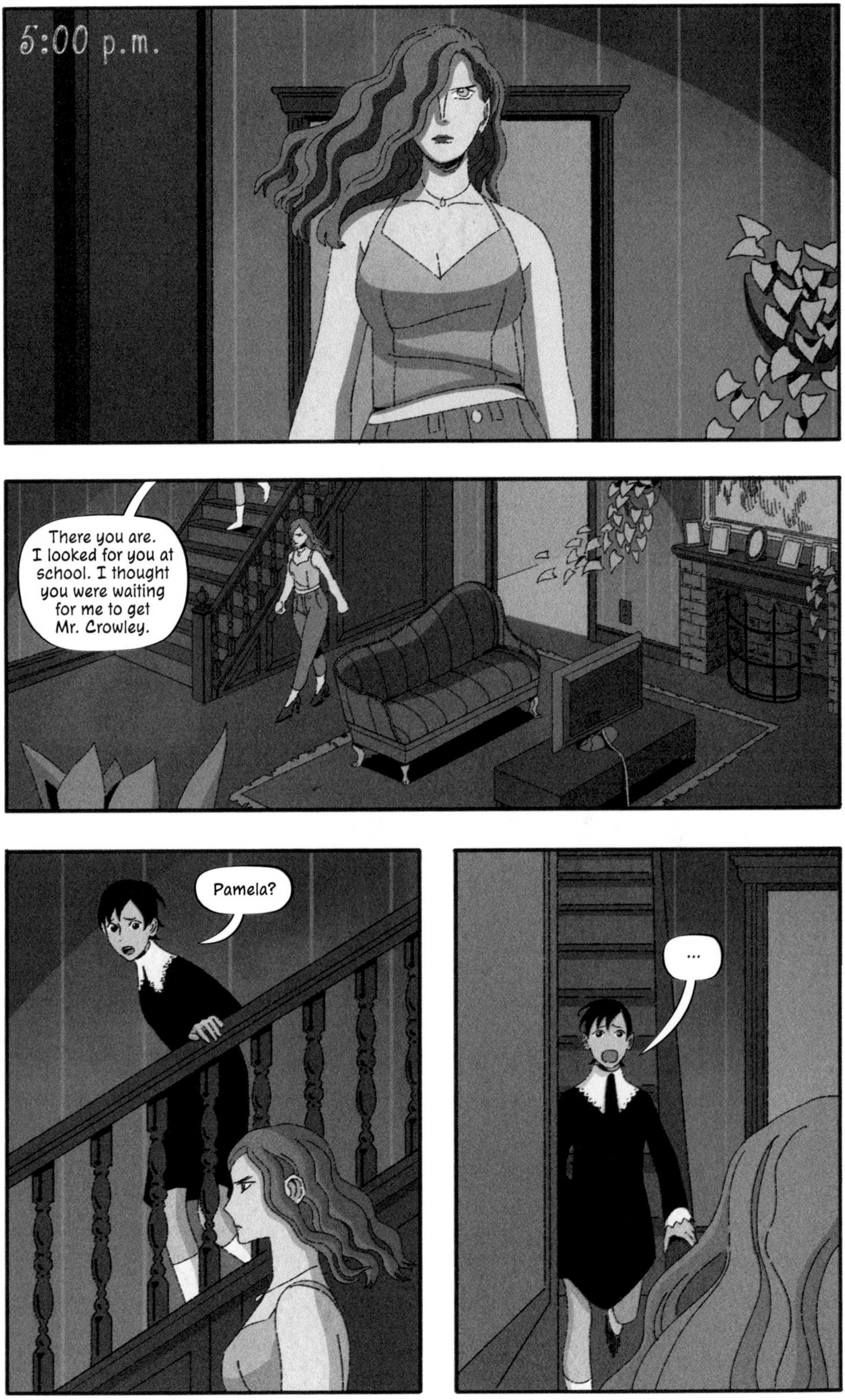
5:00 p.m.
There you are. I looked for you at school. I thought you were waiting for me to get Mr. Crowley.
Pamela?
...

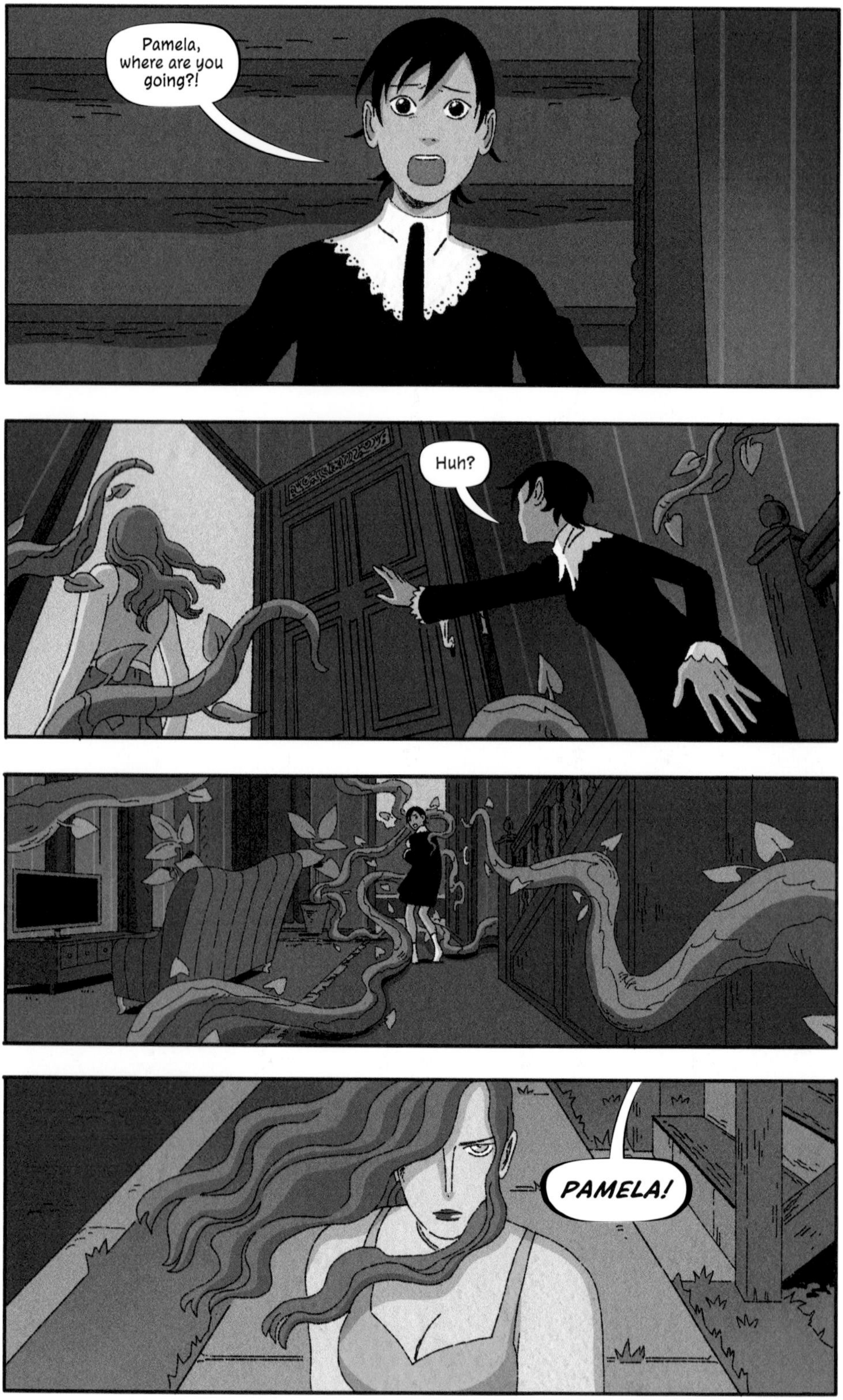
Pamela, where are you going?!
Huh?
PAMELA!

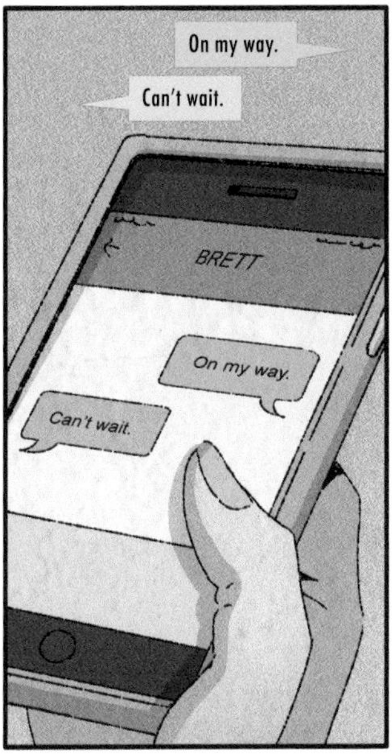
On my way.
Can't wait.
BRETT
On my way.
Can't wait.

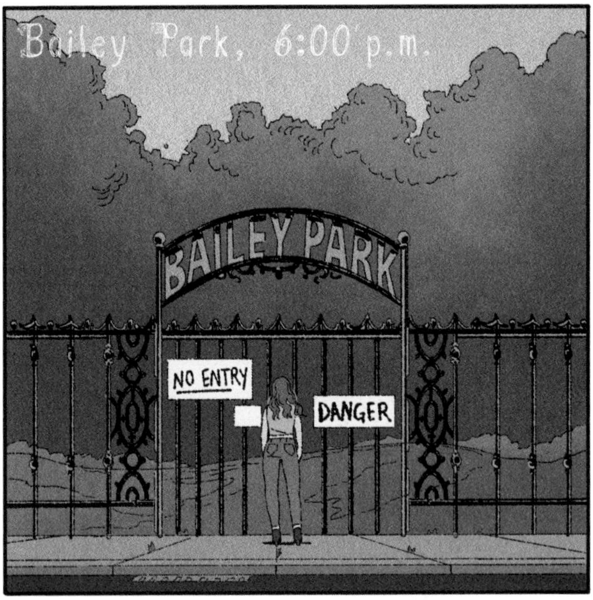
Bailey Park, 6:00 p.m.
BAILEY PARK
NO ENTRY
DANGER

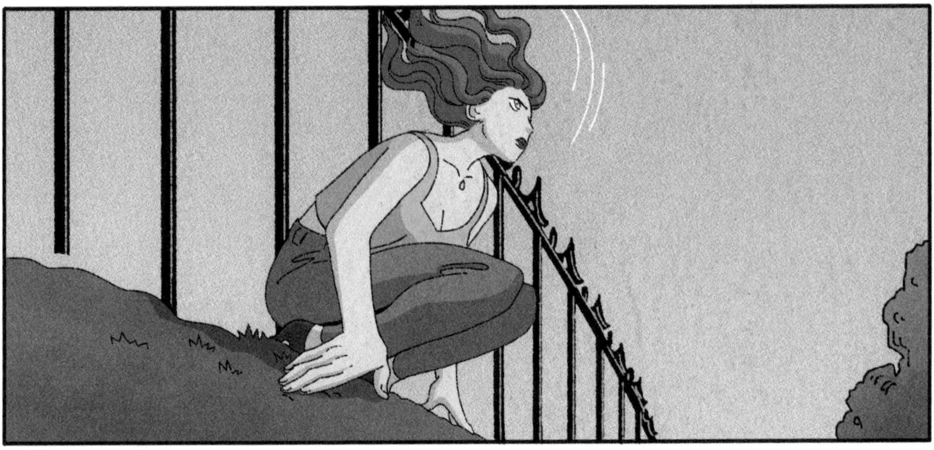

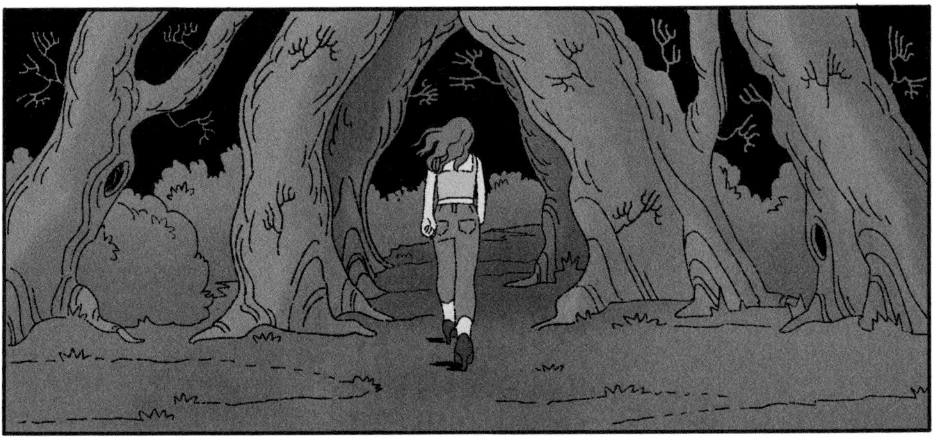

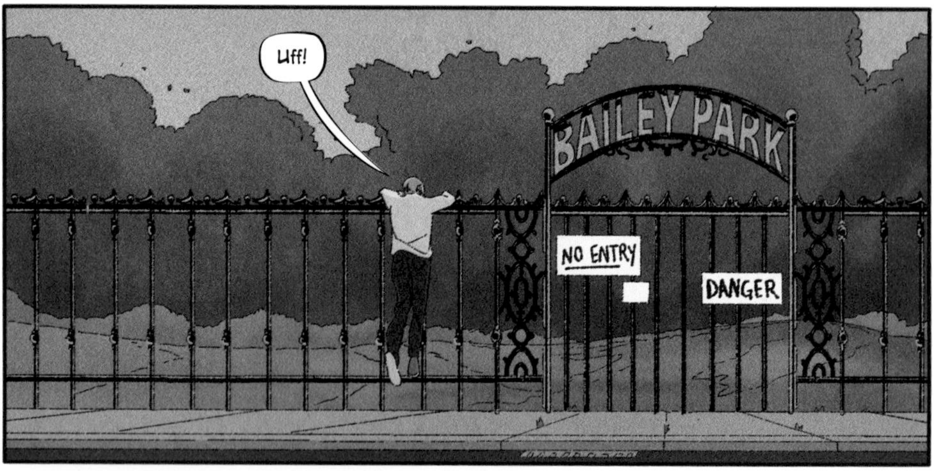
Uff!
BAILEY PARK
NO ENTRY
DANGER

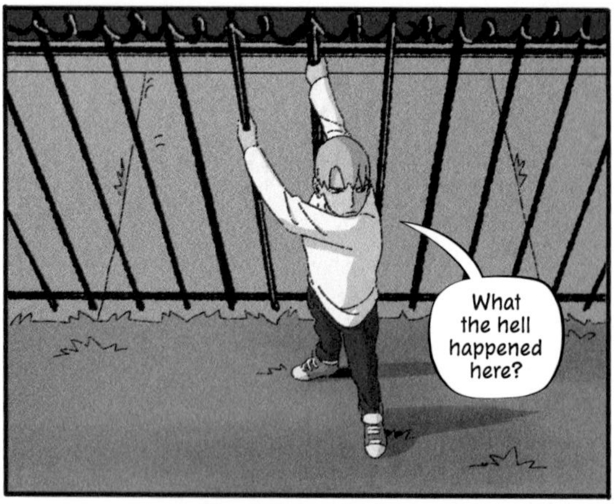
What the hell happened here?

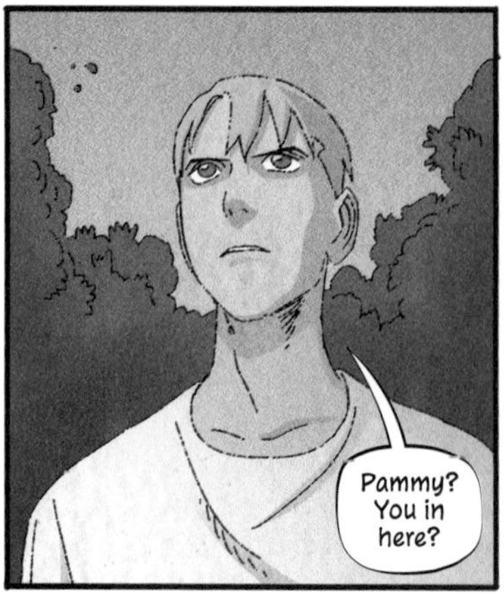
Pammy? You in here?

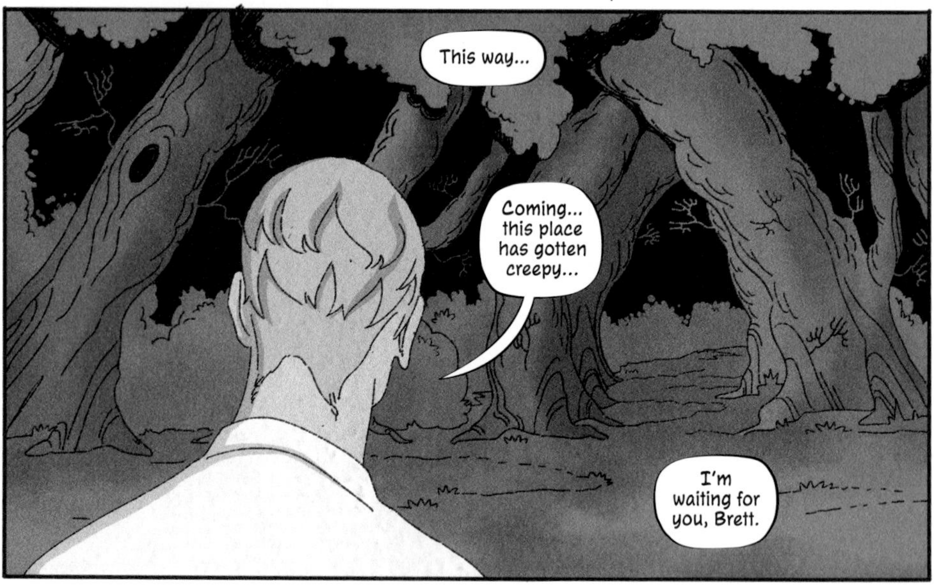
This way...
Coming... this place has gotten creepy...
I'm waiting for you, Brett.

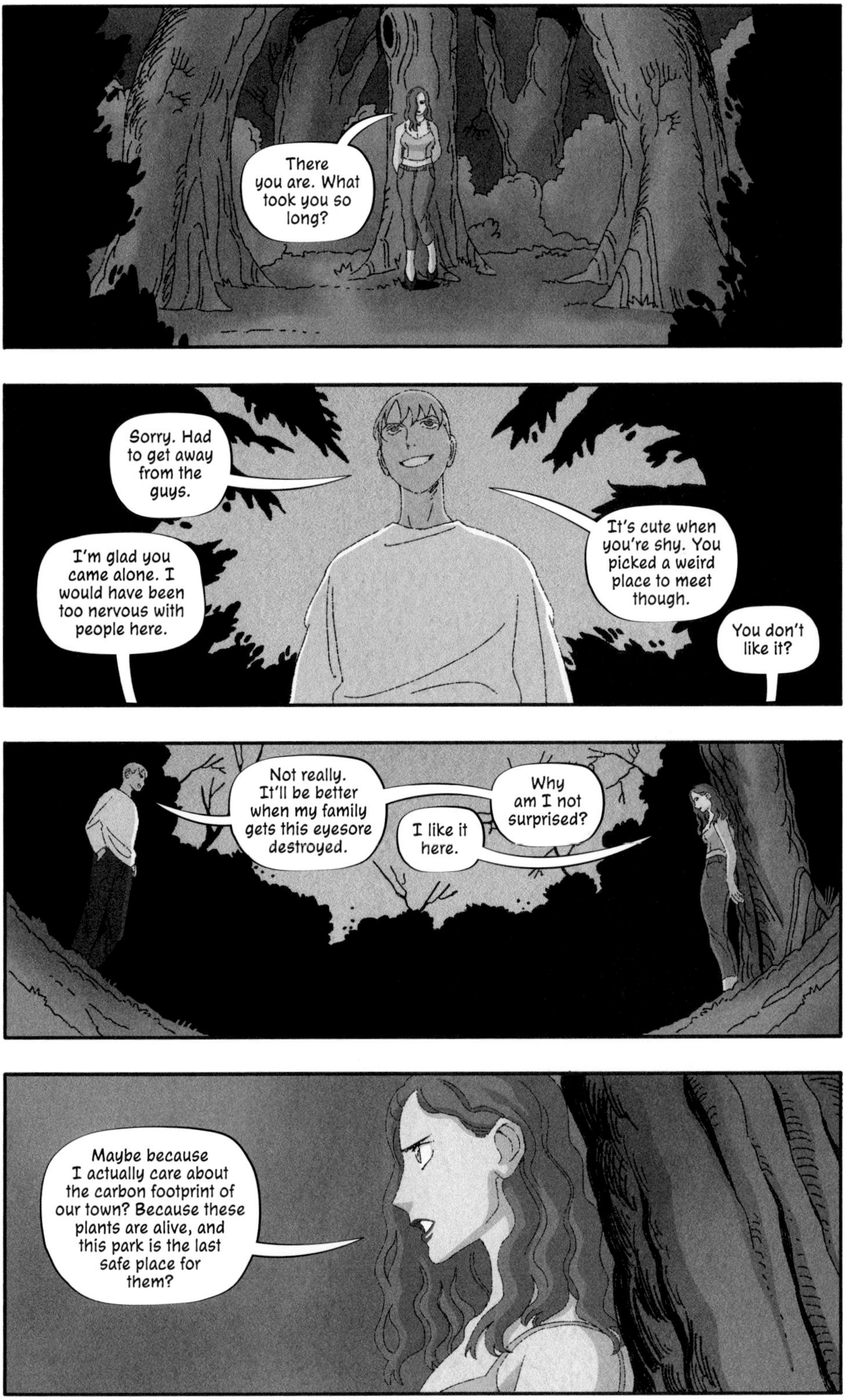
There you are. What took you so long?
Sorry. Had to get away from the guys.
I'm glad you came alone. I would have been too nervous with people here.
It's cute when you're shy. You picked a weird place to meet though.
You don't like it?
Not really. It'll be better when my family gets this eyesore destroyed.
I like it here.
Why am I not surprised?
Maybe because I actually care about the carbon footprint of our town? Because these plants are alive, and this park is the last safe place for them?

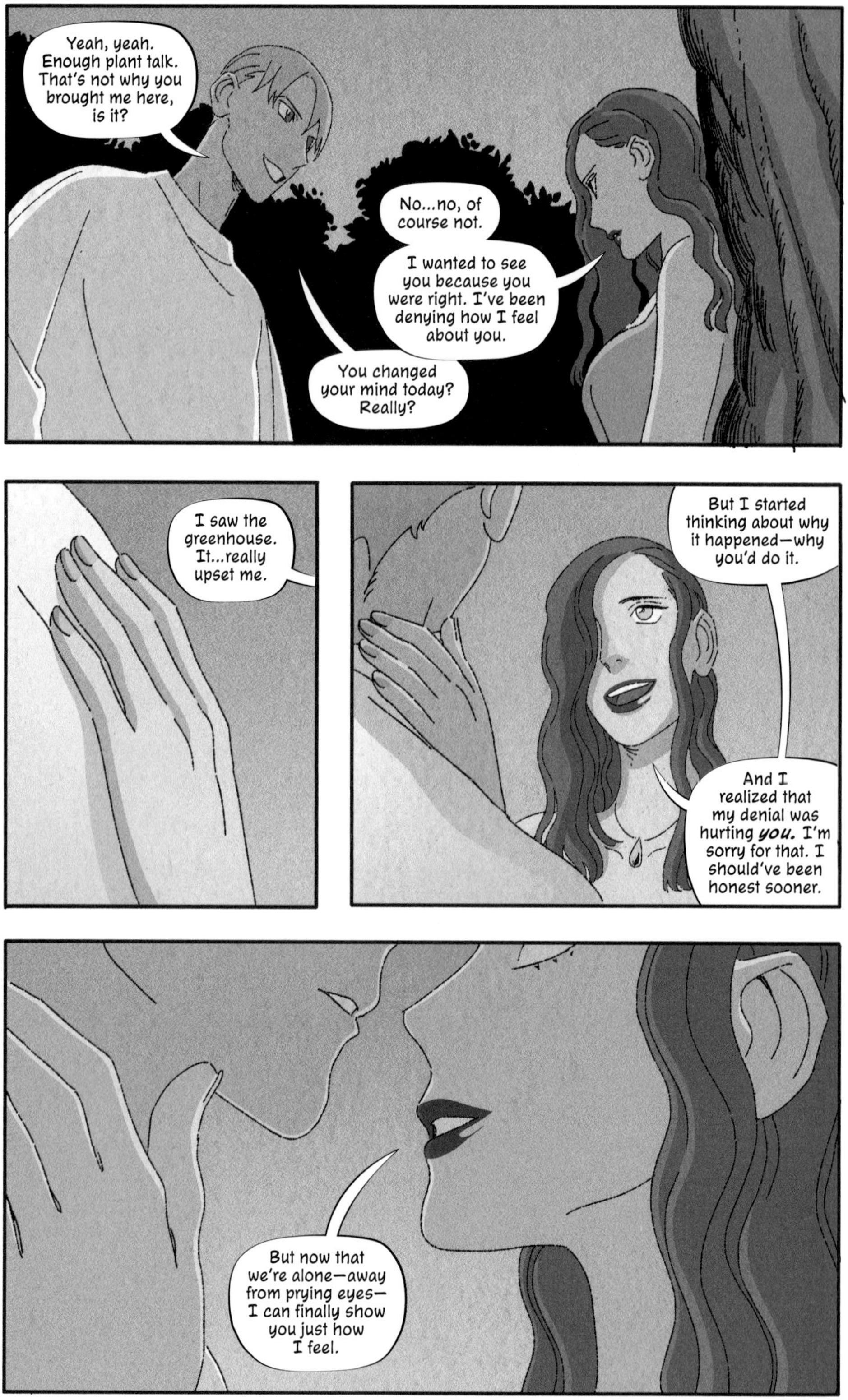
Yeah, yeah. Enough plant talk. That's not why you brought me here, is it?
No...no, of course not.
I wanted to see you because you were right. I've been denying how I feel about you.
You changed your mind today? Really?
I saw the greenhouse. It...really upset me.
But I started thinking about why it happened—why you'd do it.
And I realized that my denial was hurting *you.* I'm sorry for that. I should've been honest sooner.
But now that we're alone—away from prying eyes—I can finally show you just how I feel.

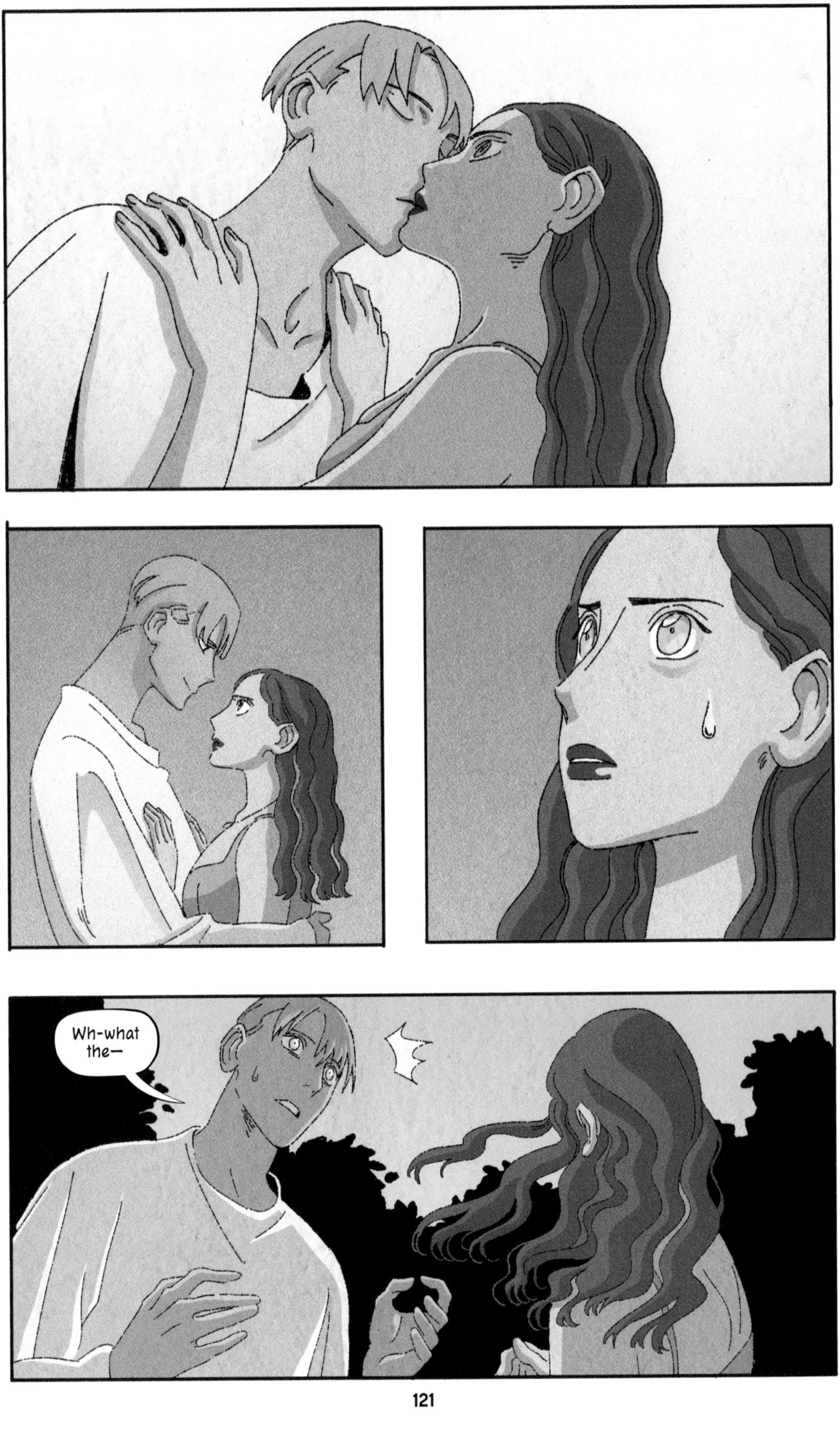
Wh-what the—

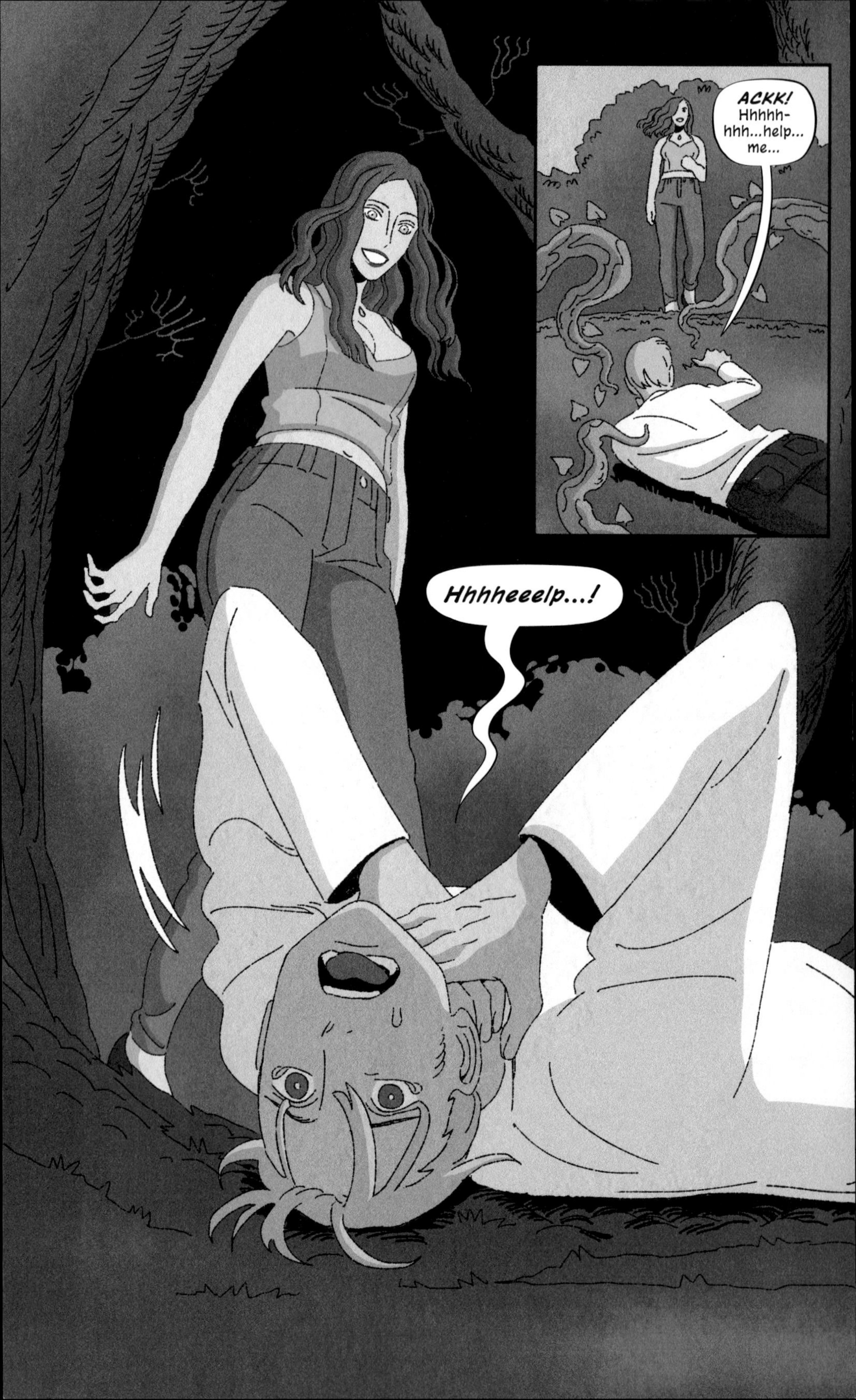
ACKK! Hhhhh-hhh...help... me...
Hhhheeelp...!

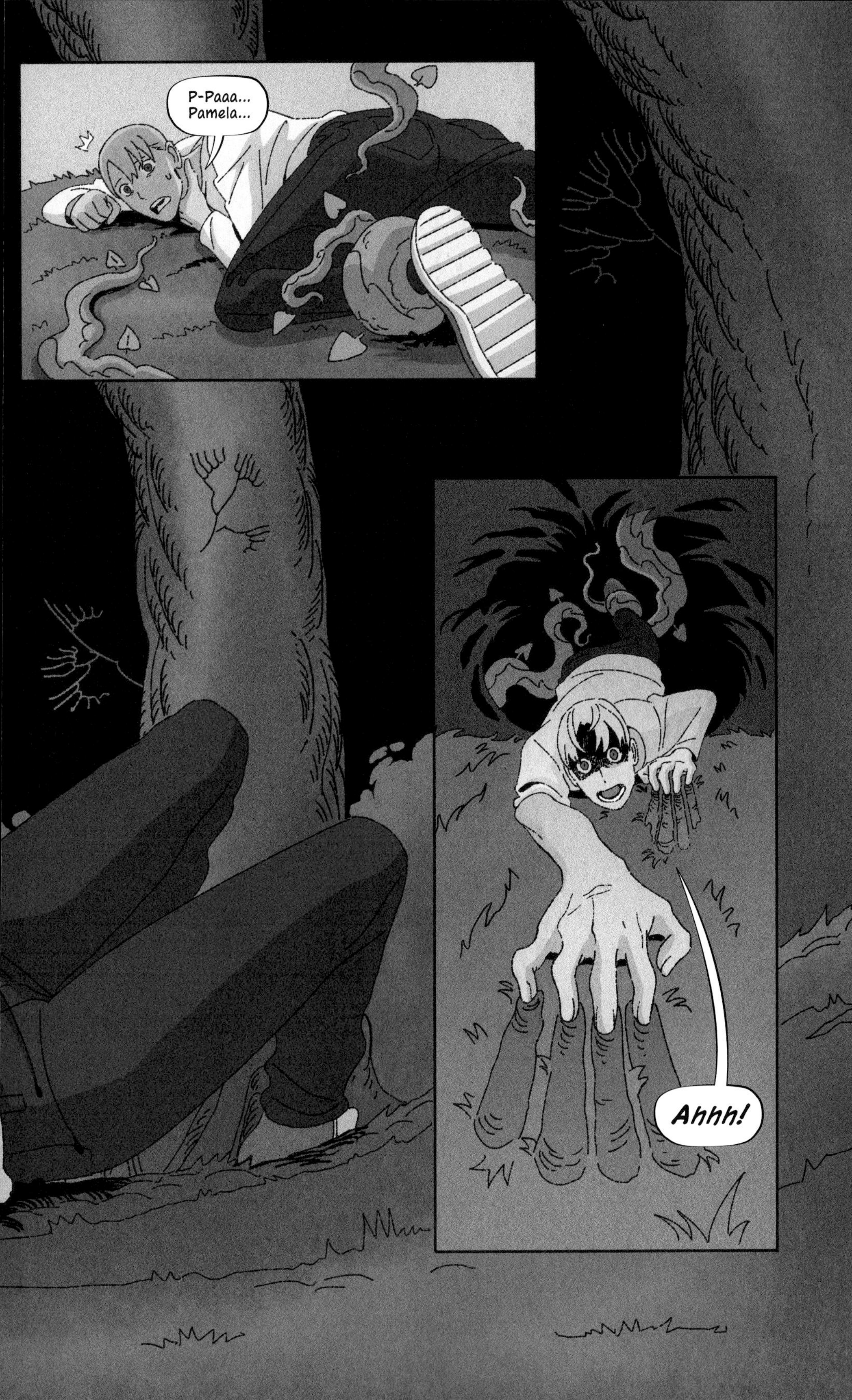
P-Paaa...
Pamela...
Ahhh!

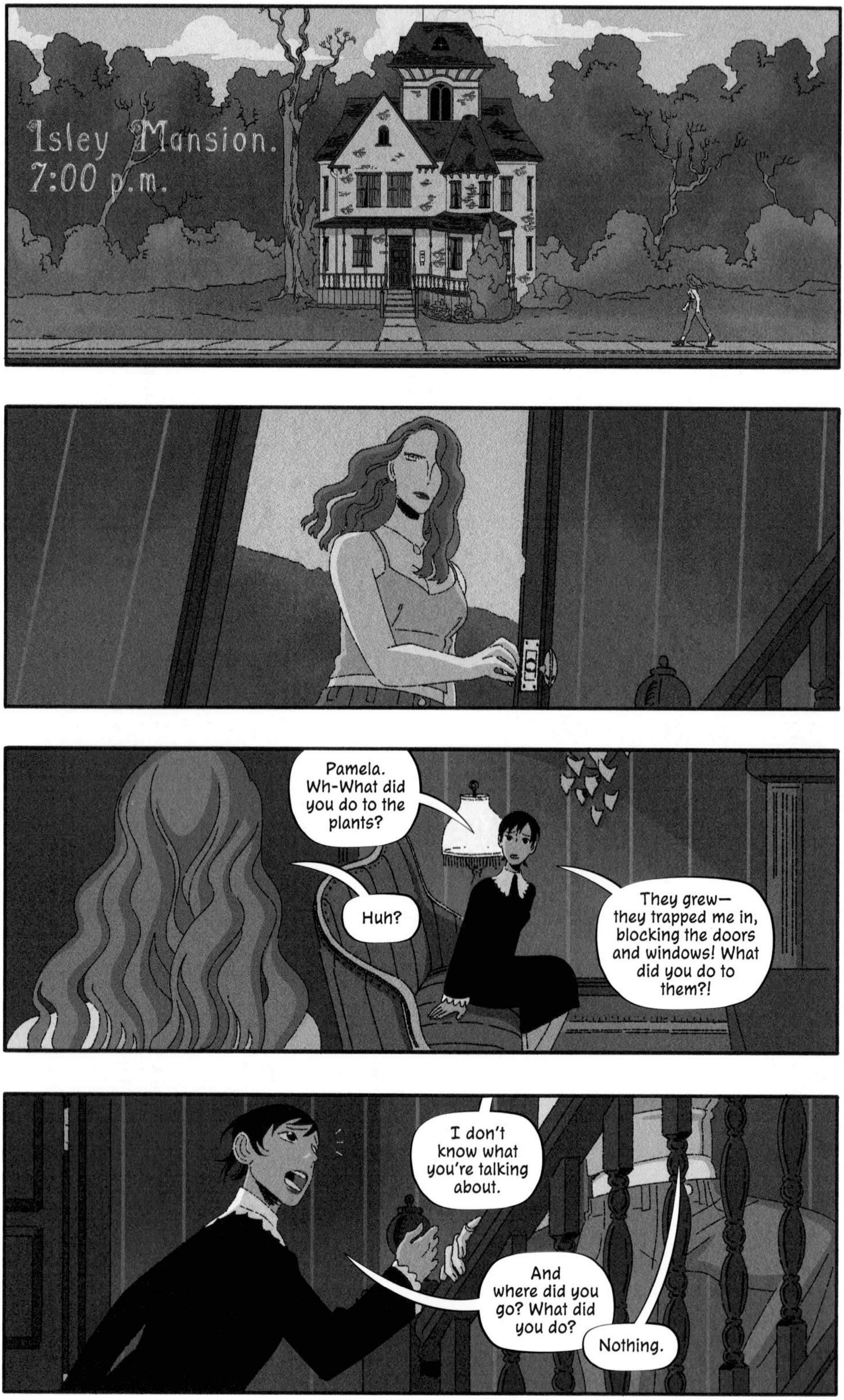
Isley Mansion.
7:00 p.m.
Pamela. Wh-What did you do to the plants?
Huh?
They grew— they trapped me in, blocking the doors and windows! What did you do to them?!
I don't know what you're talking about.
And where did you go? What did you do?
Nothing.

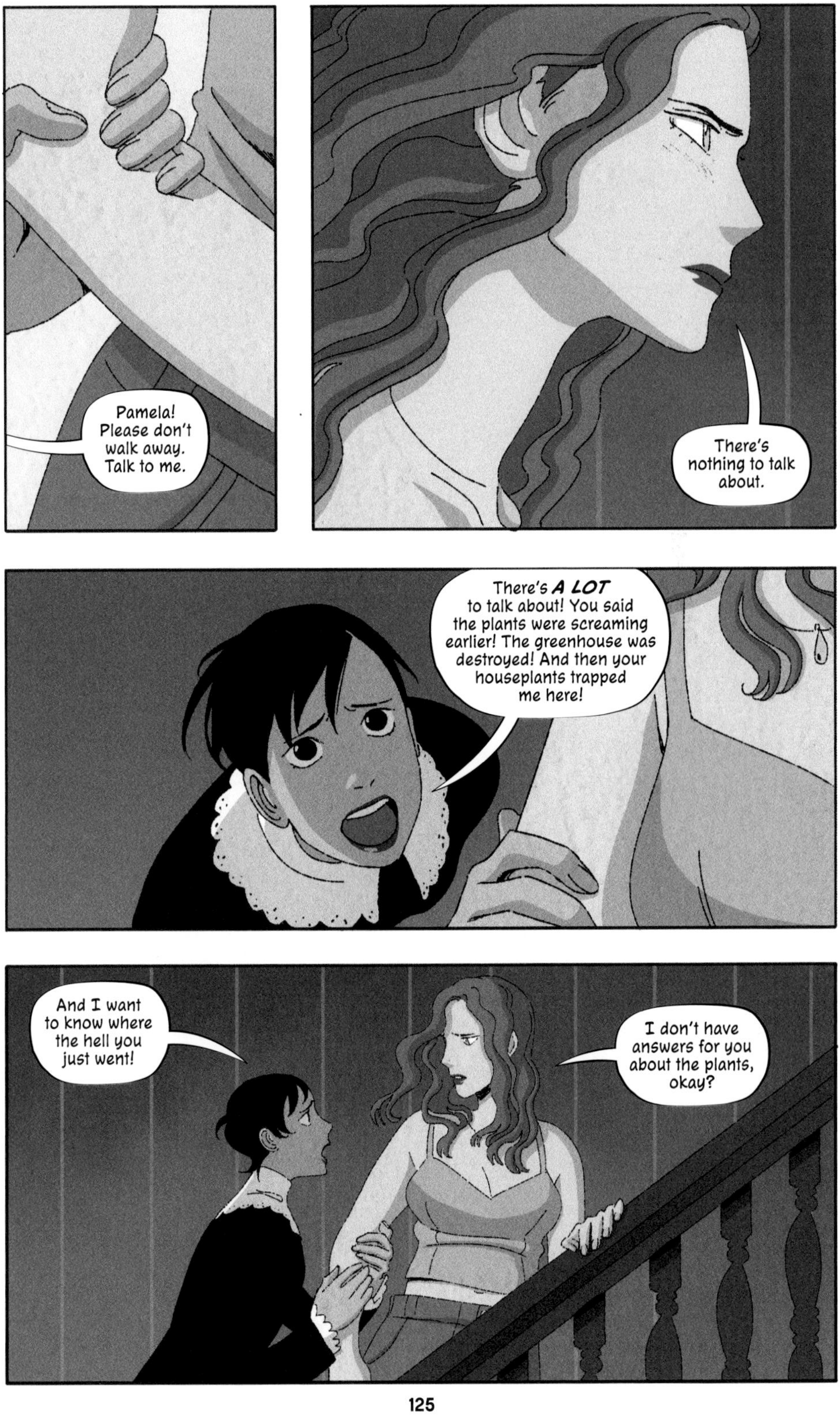
Pamela! Please don't walk away. Talk to me.
There's nothing to talk about.
There's **A LOT** to talk about! You said the plants were screaming earlier! The greenhouse was destroyed! And then your houseplants trapped me here!
And I want to know where the hell you just went!
I don't have answers for you about the plants, okay?

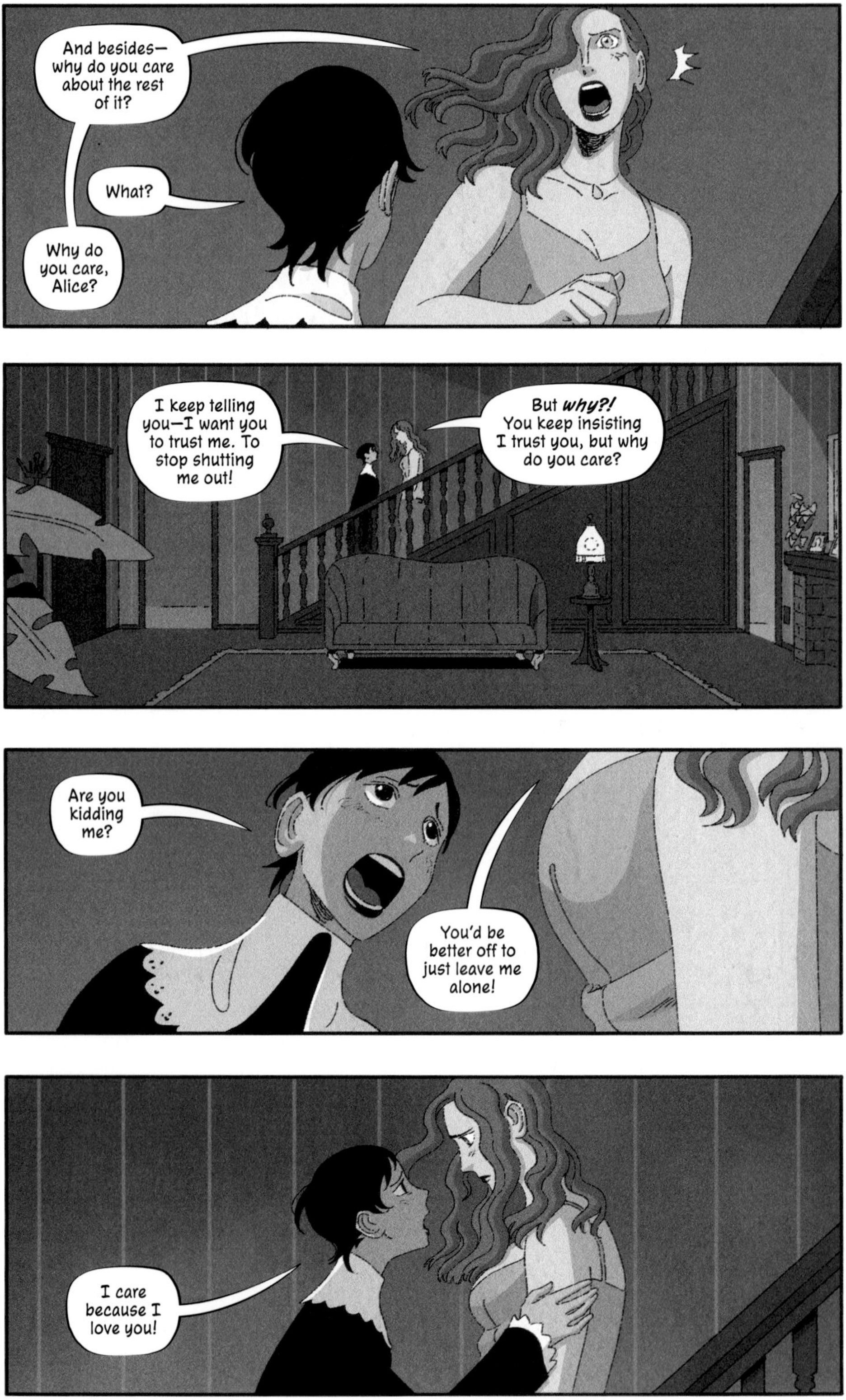
And besides—why do you care about the rest of it?
What?
Why do you care, Alice?
I keep telling you—I want you to trust me. To stop shutting me out!
But *why?!* You keep insisting I trust you, but why do you care?
Are you kidding me?
You'd be better off to just leave me alone!
I care because I love you!

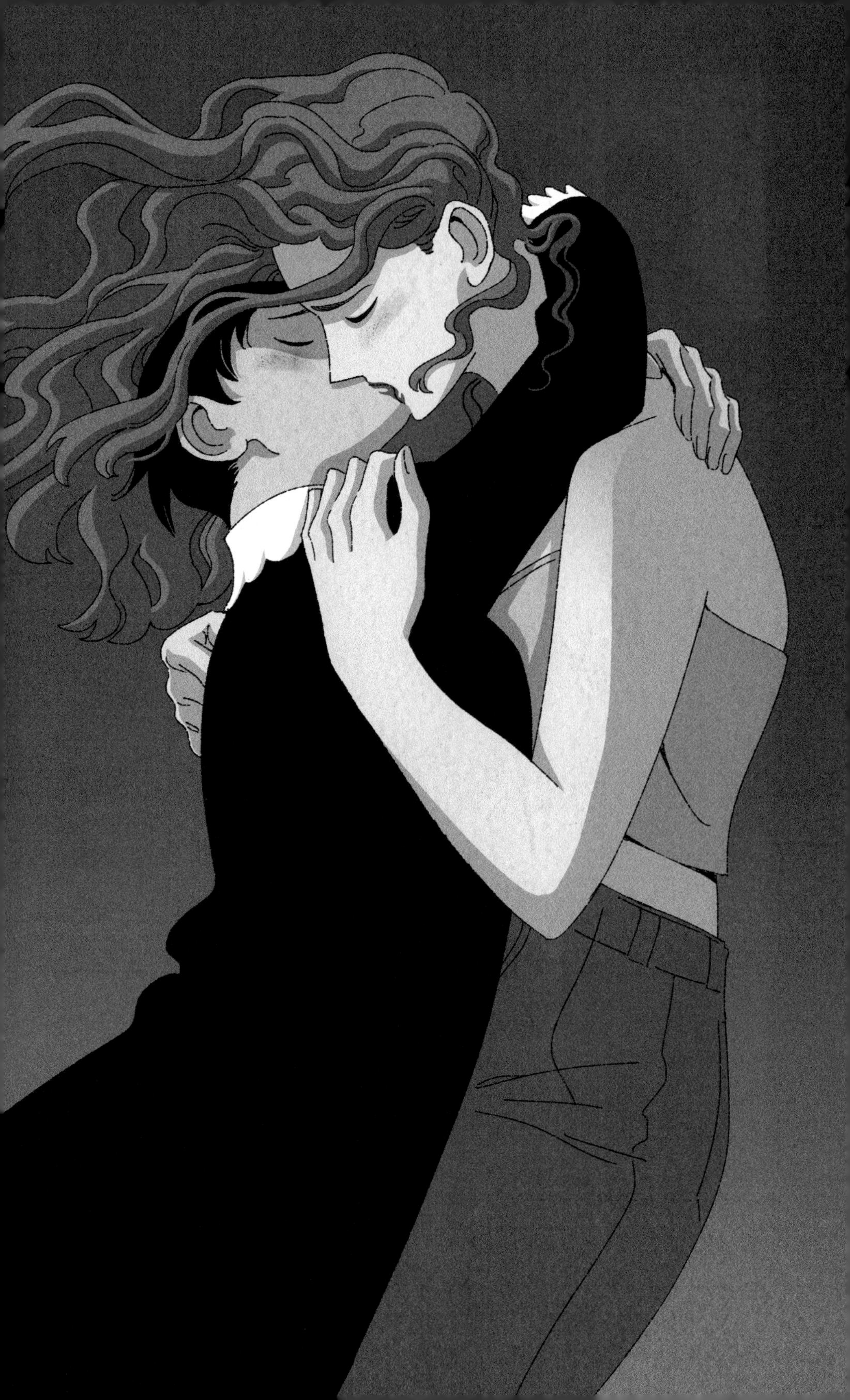

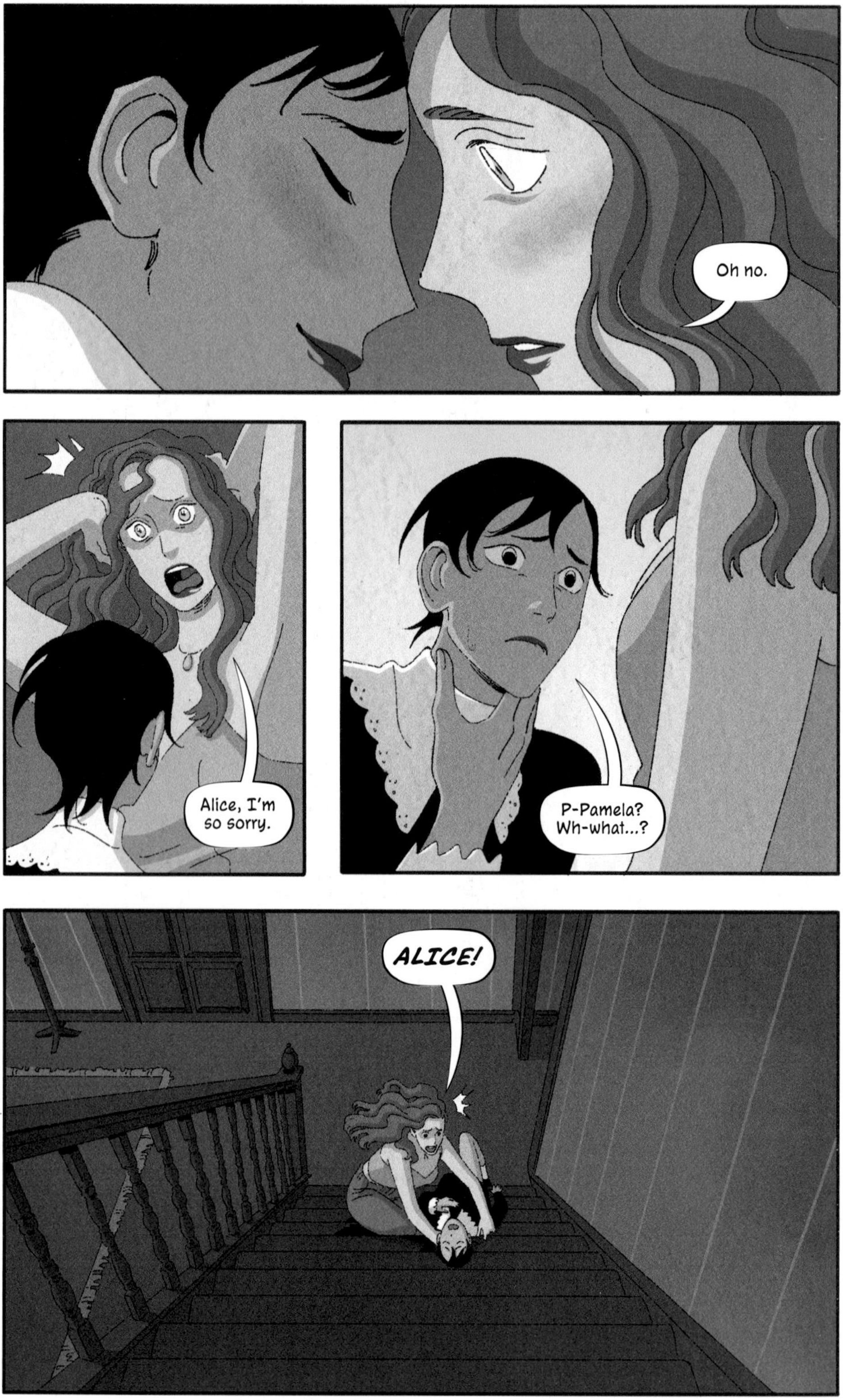
Oh no.
Alice, I'm so sorry.
P-Pamela? Wh-what...?
ALICE!

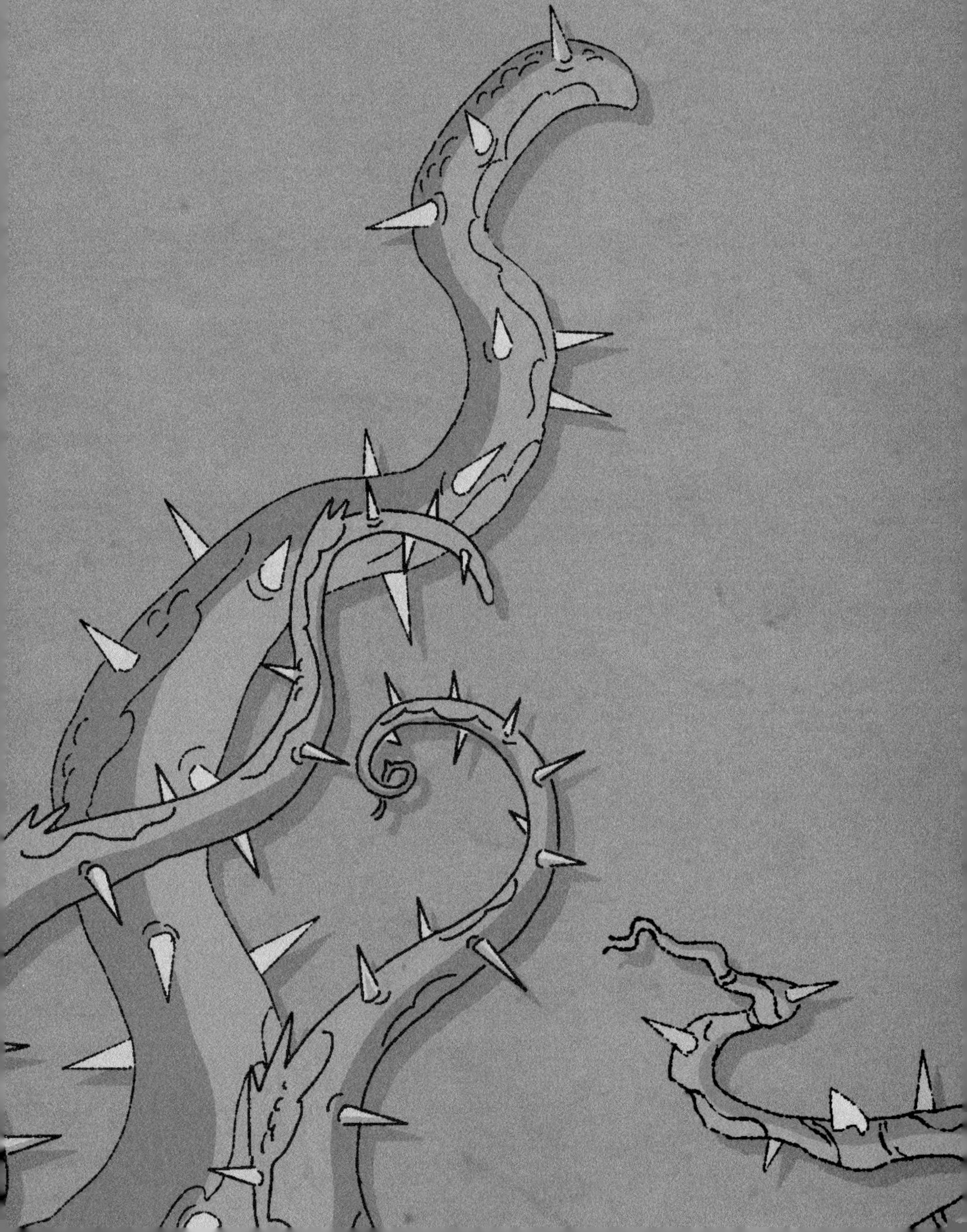

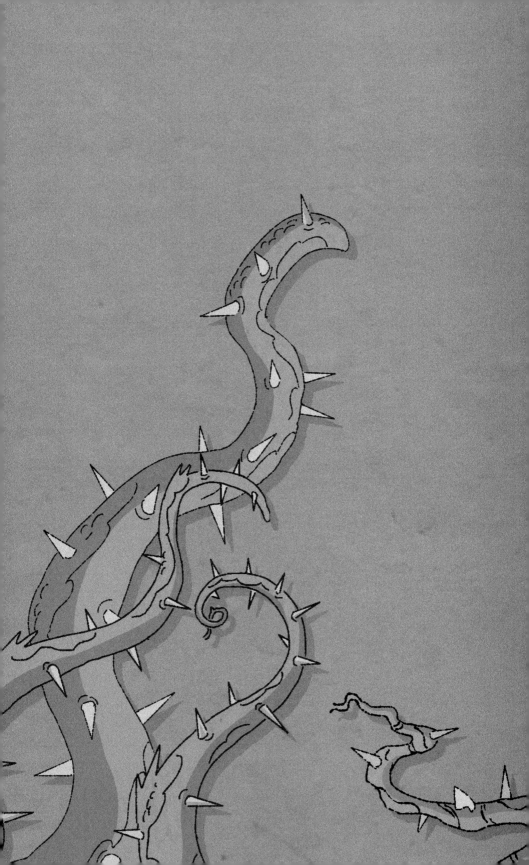

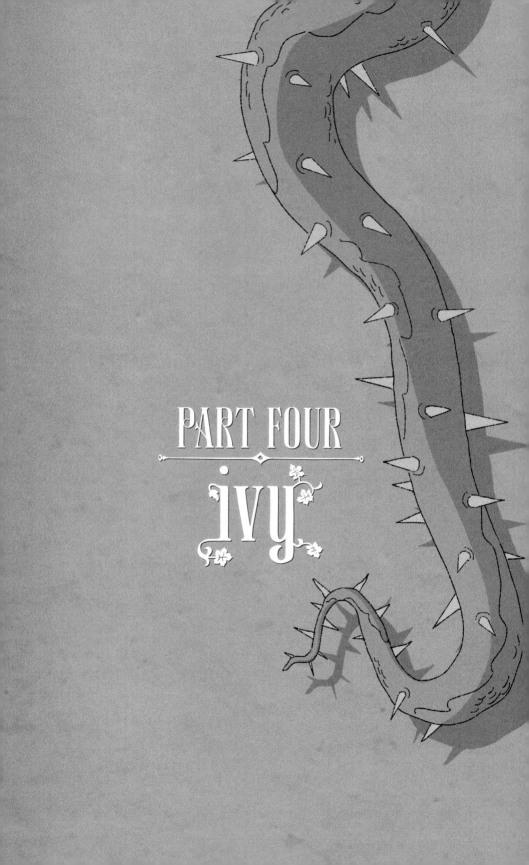

# PART FOUR

## ivy

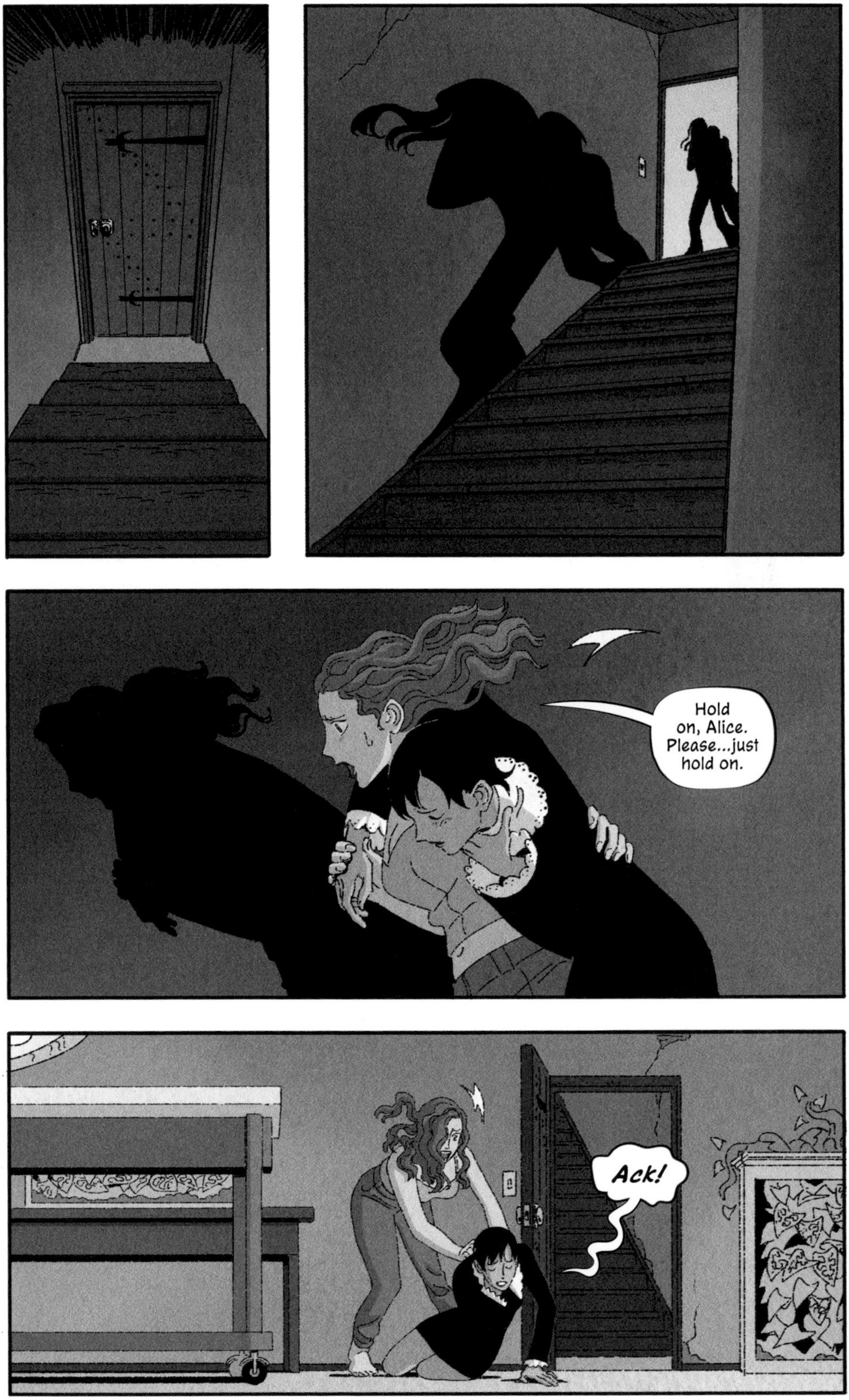
Hold on, Alice. Please...just hold on.
Ack!

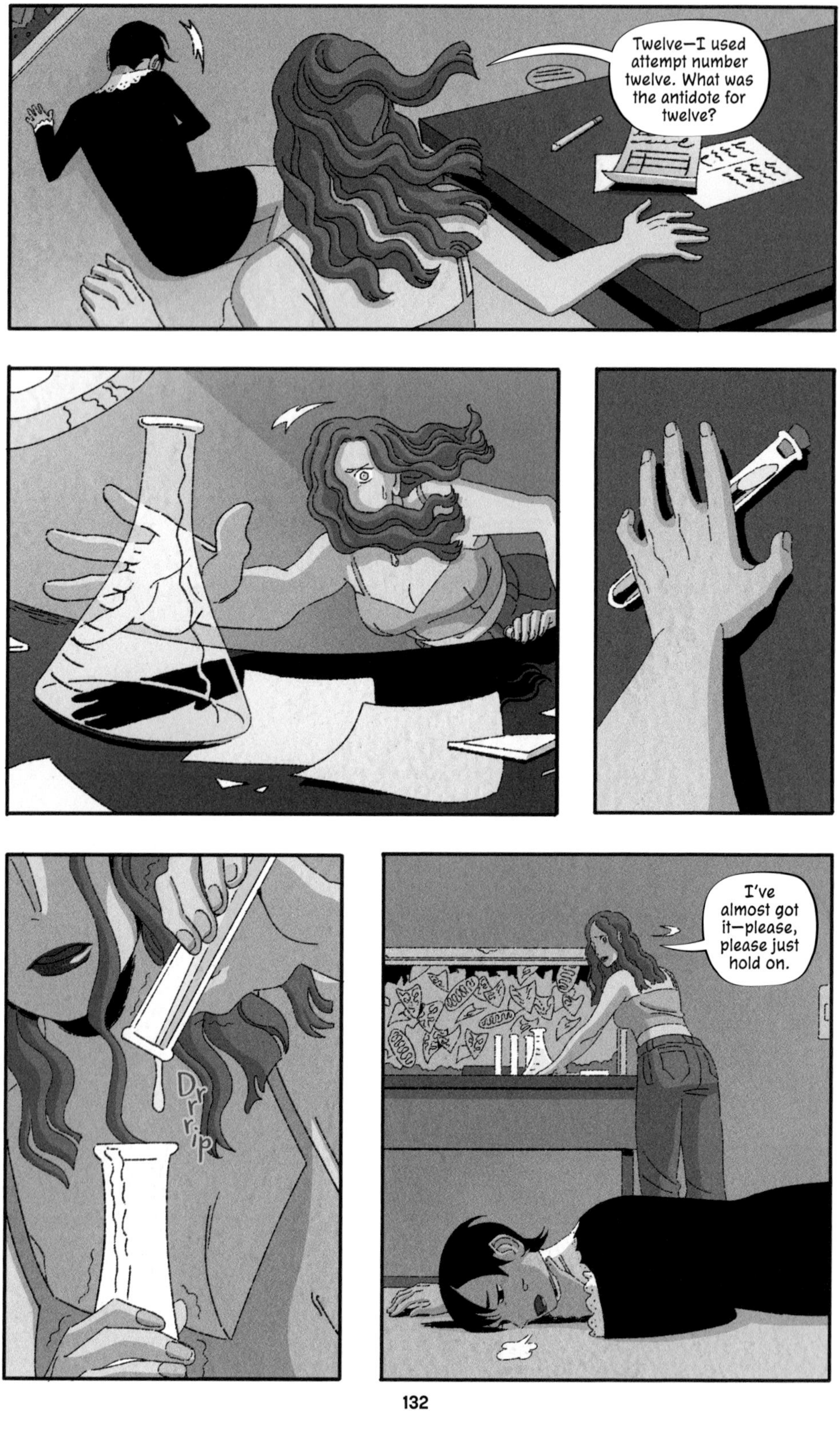
Twelve—I used attempt number twelve. What was the antidote for twelve?
Drrrip
I've almost got it—please, please just hold on.

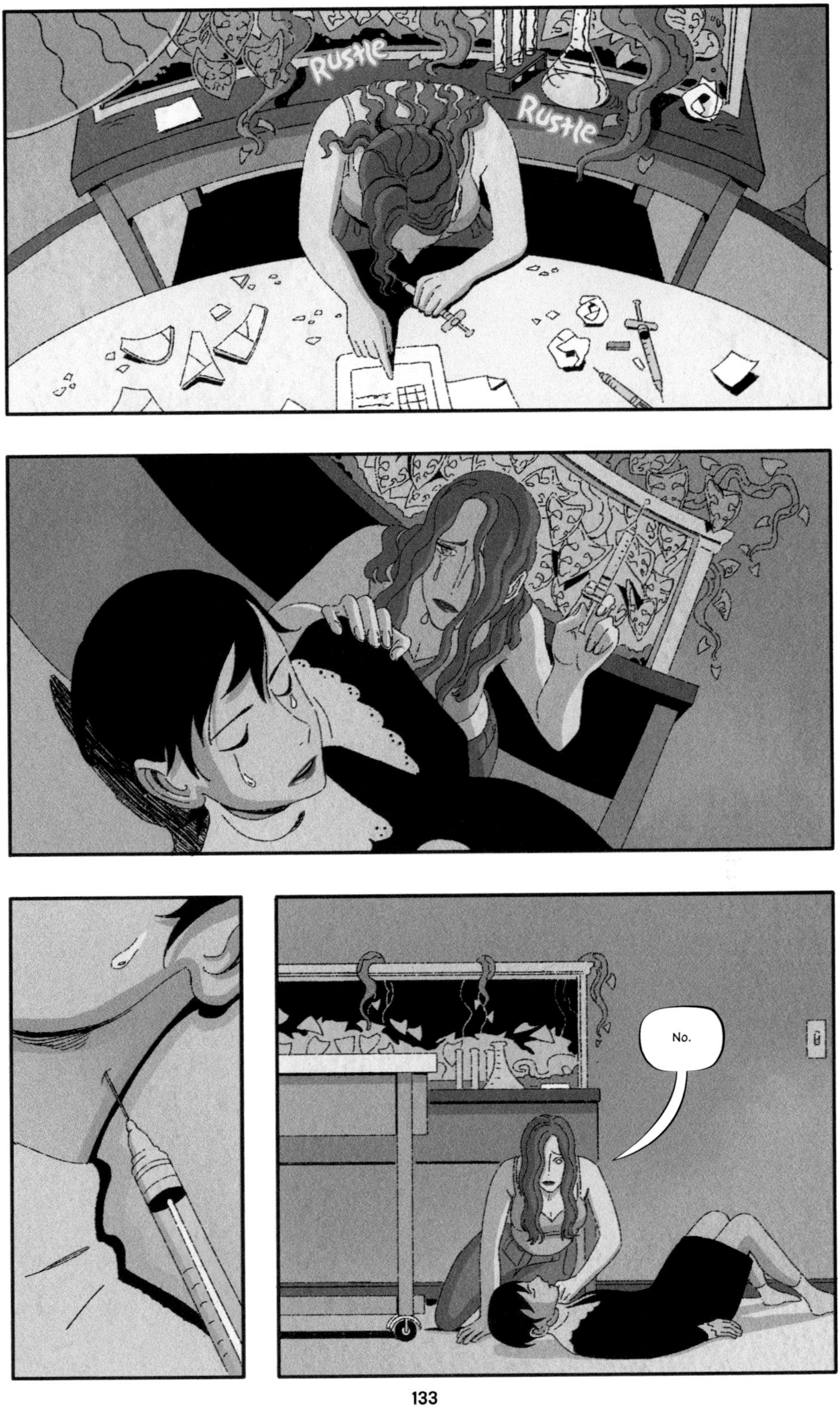
Rustle
Rustle
No.

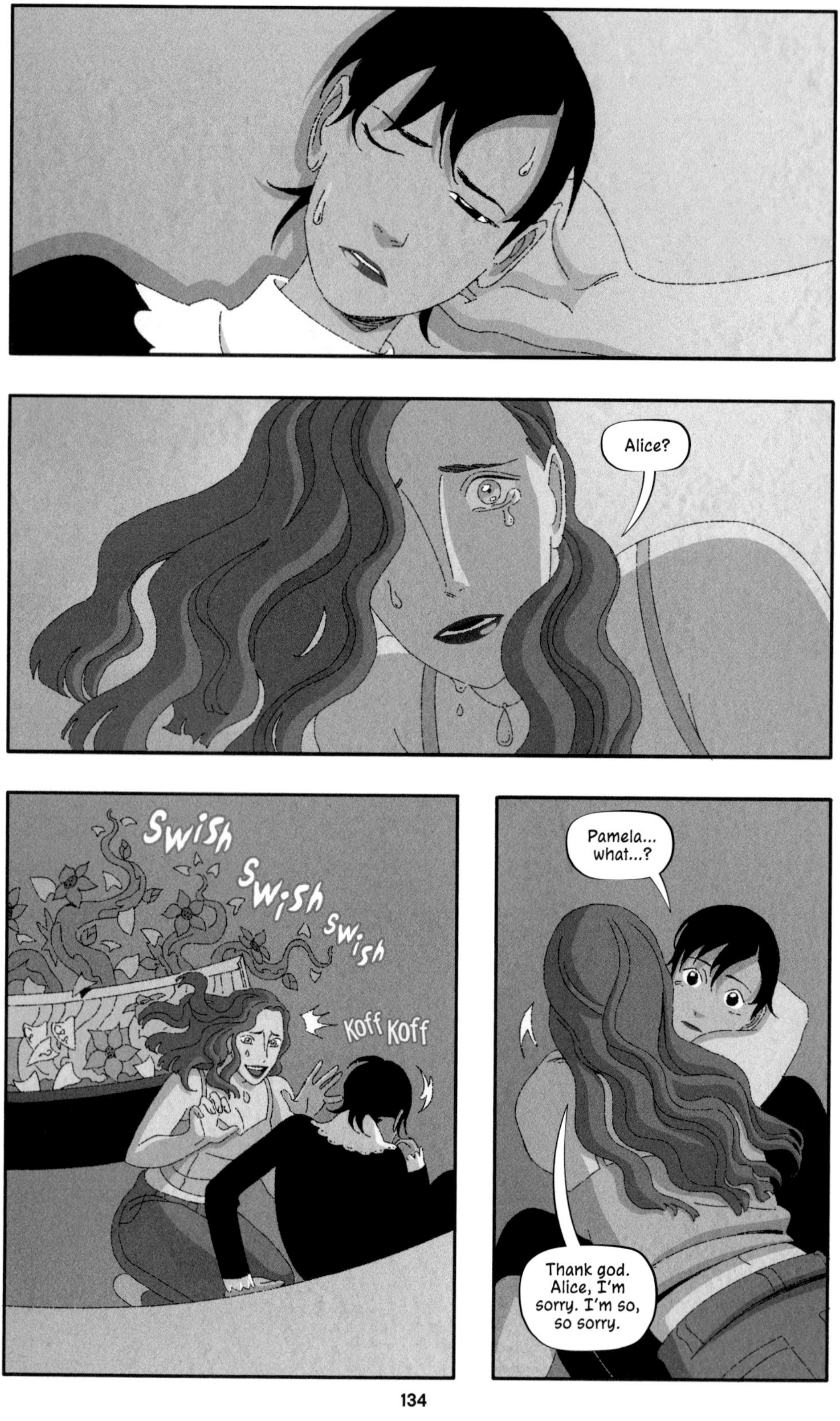
Alice?
SWISH SWISH SWISH
KOFF KOFF
Pamela... what...?
Thank god. Alice, I'm sorry. I'm so, so sorry.

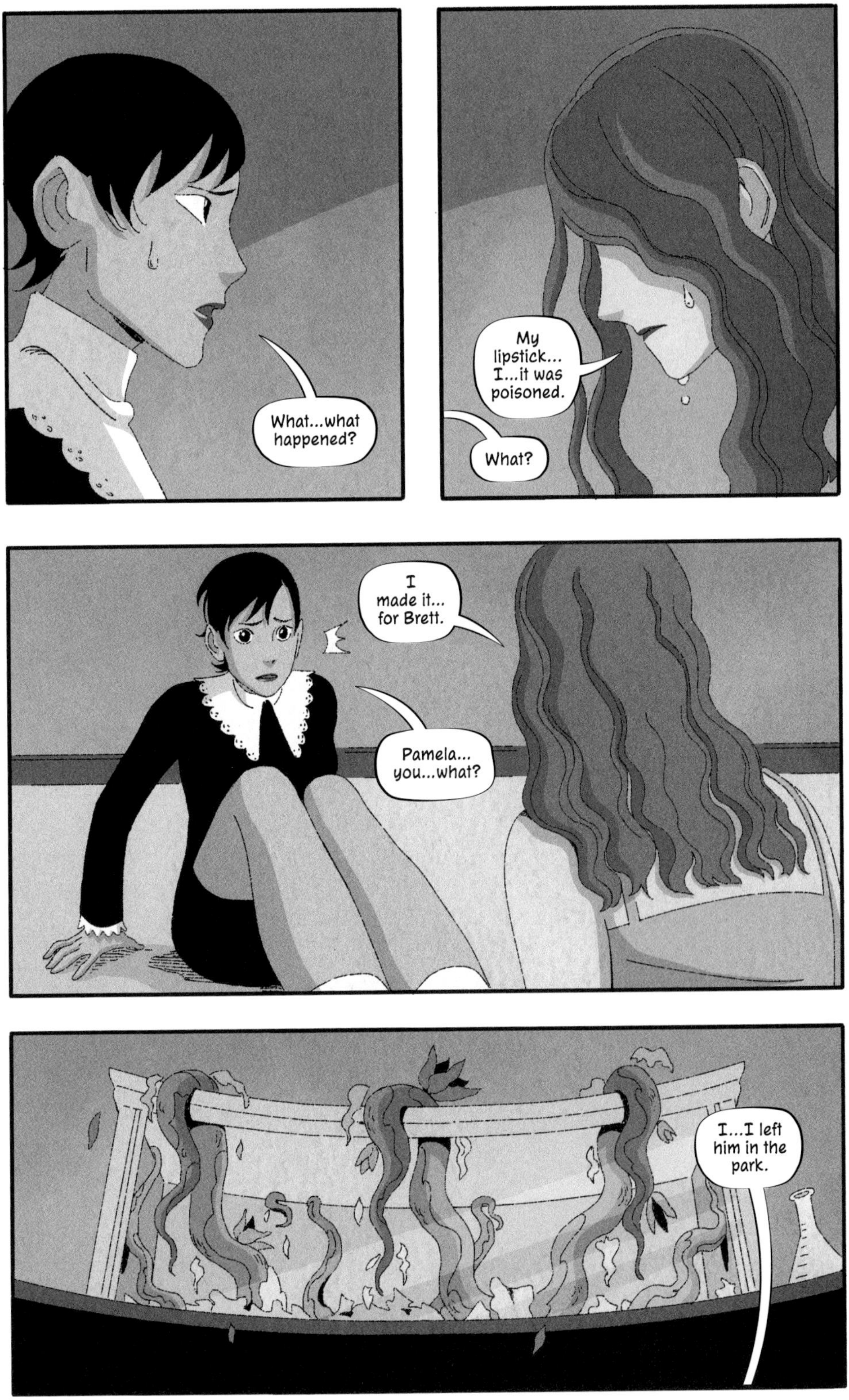
What...what happened?
My lipstick... I...it was poisoned.
What?
I made it... for Brett.
Pamela... you...what?
I...I left him in the park.

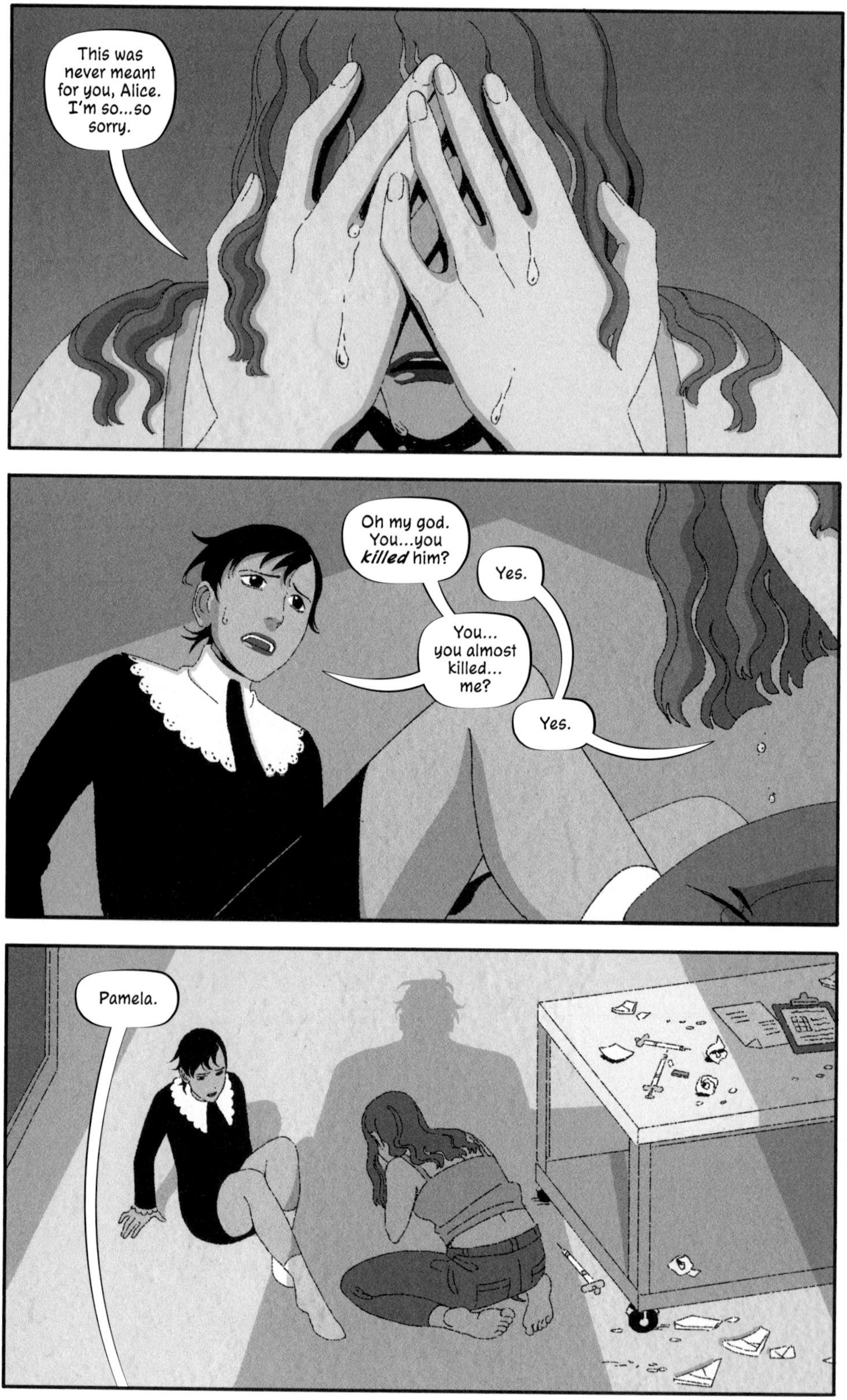
This was never meant for you, Alice. I'm so...so sorry.
Oh my god. You...you *killed* him?
Yes.
You... you almost killed... me?
Yes.
Pamela.

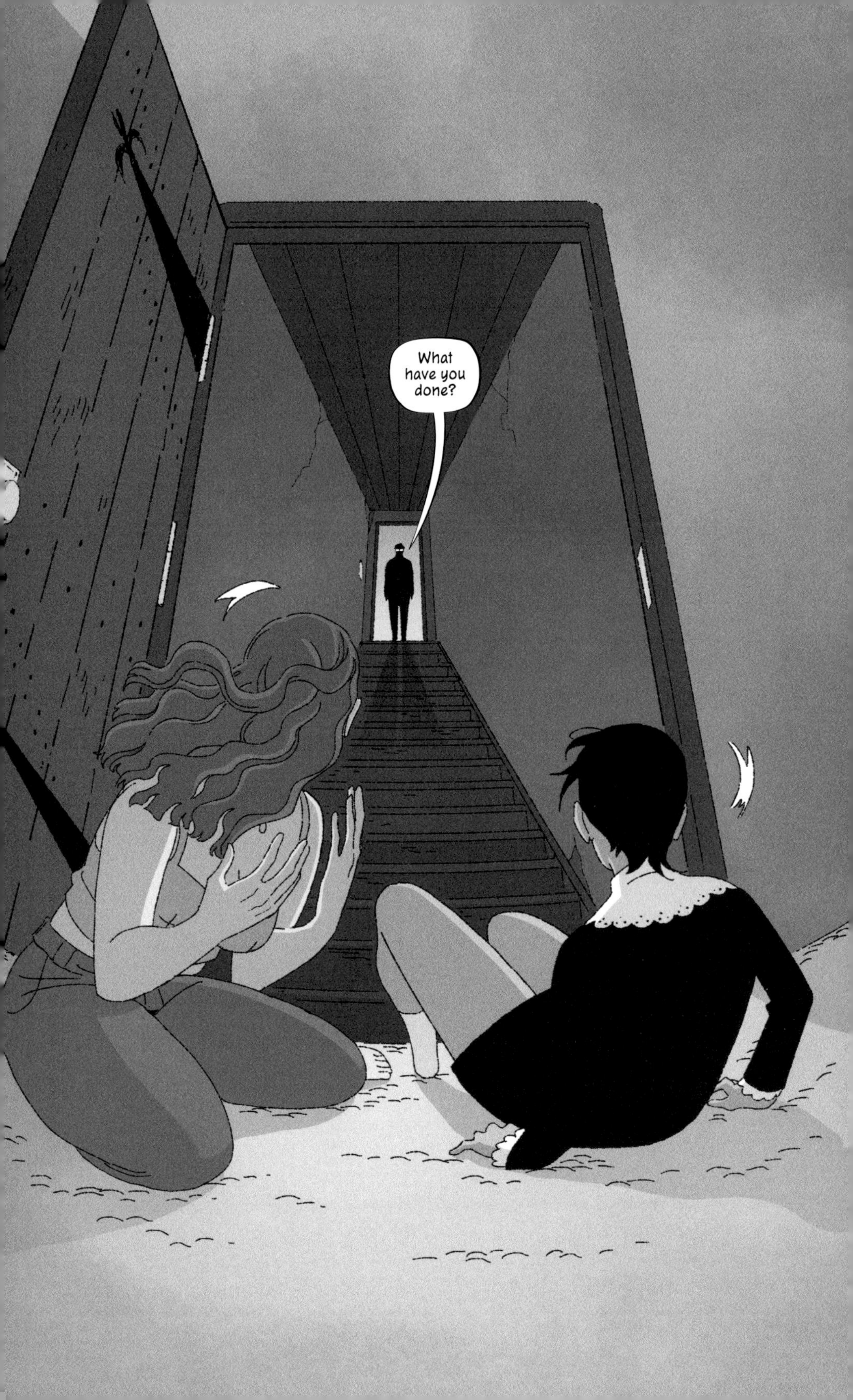
What have you done?

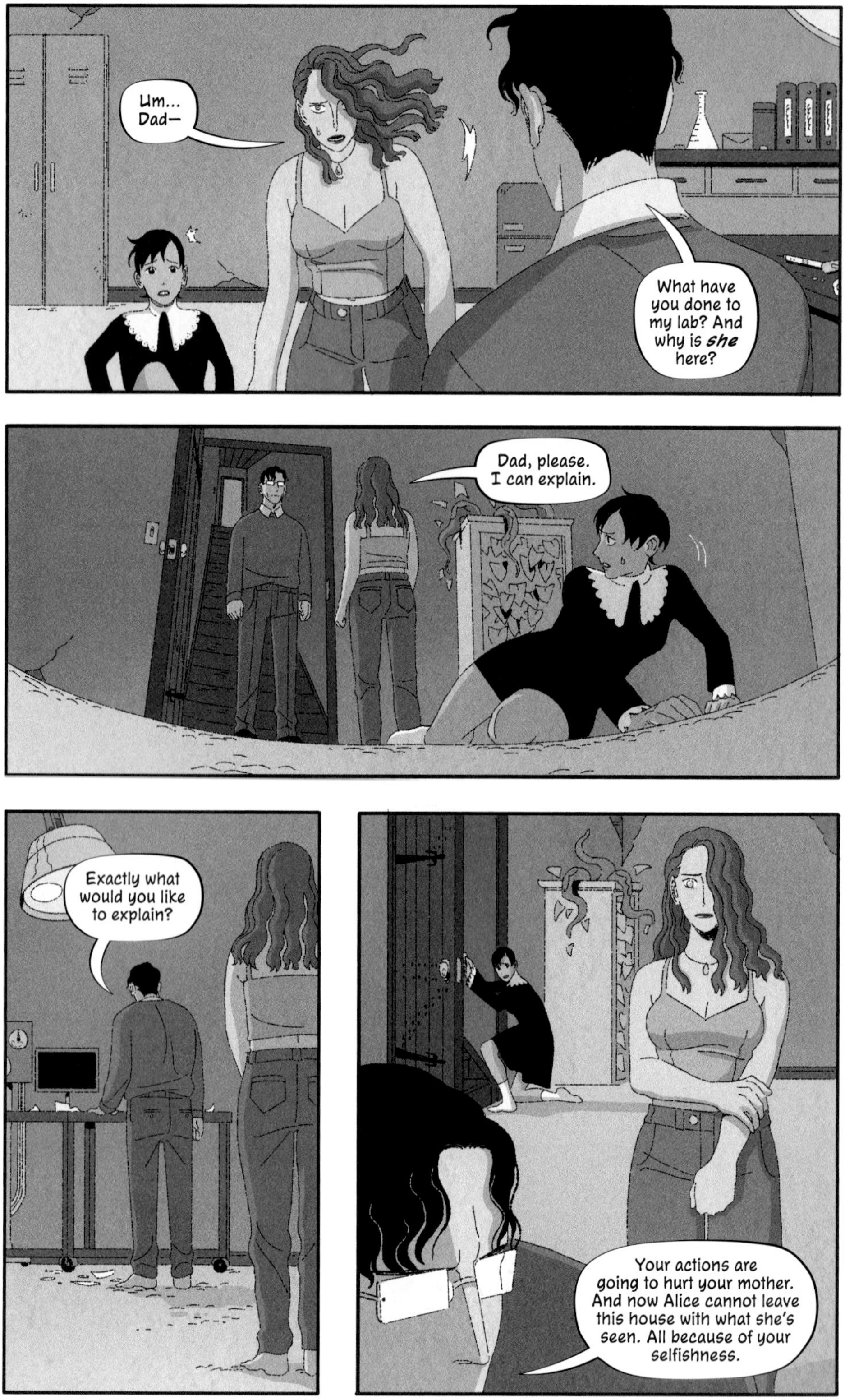
Um... Dad—
What have you done to my lab? And why is *she* here?
Dad, please. I can explain.
Exactly what would you like to explain?
Your actions are going to hurt your mother. And now Alice cannot leave this house with what she's seen. All because of your selfishness.

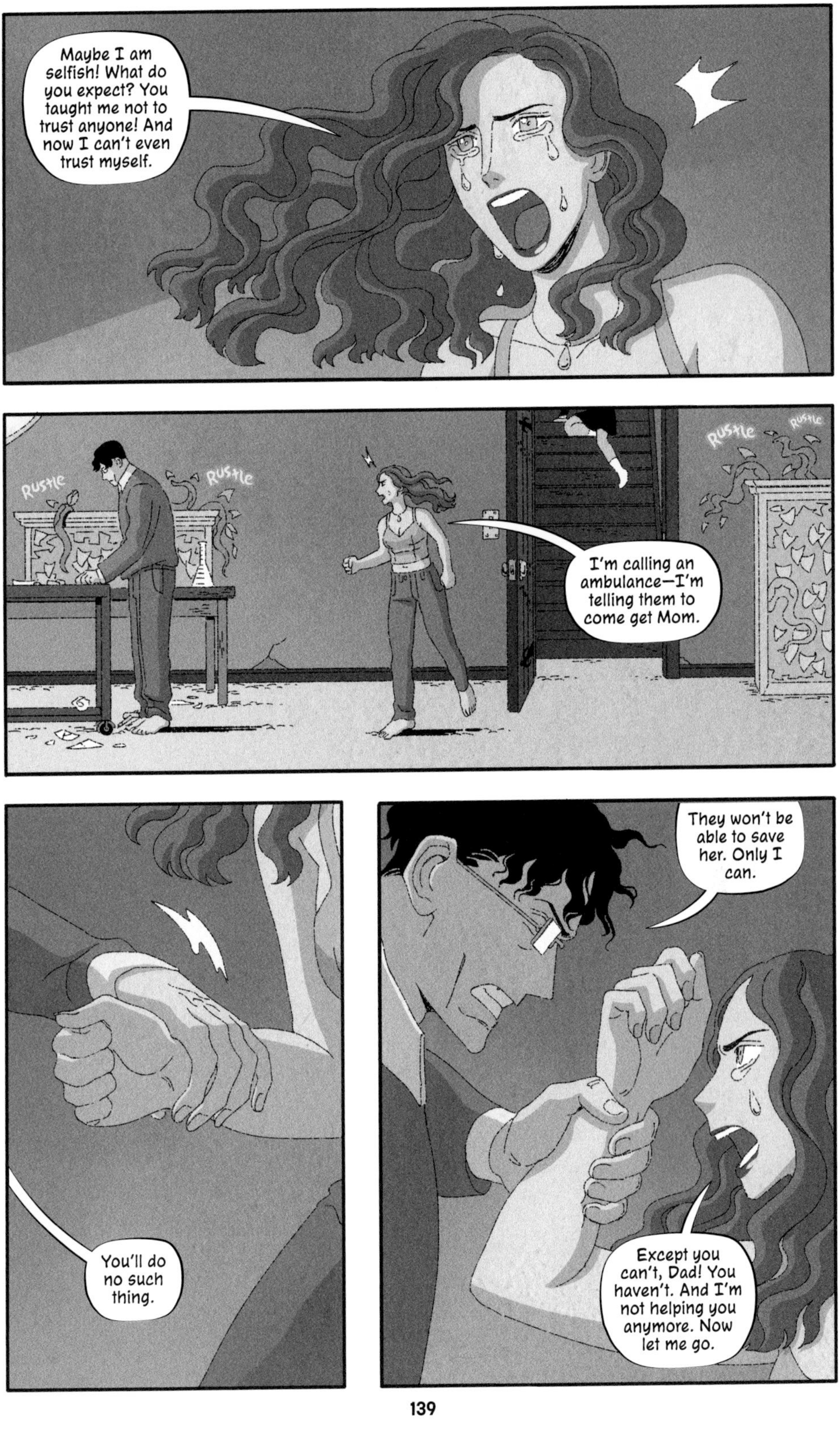
Maybe I am selfish! What do you expect? You taught me not to trust anyone! And now I can't even trust myself.
Rustle
Rustle
Rustle
Rustle
I'm calling an ambulance—I'm telling them to come get Mom.
You'll do no such thing.
They won't be able to save her. Only I can.
Except you can't, Dad! You haven't. And I'm not helping you anymore. Now let me go.

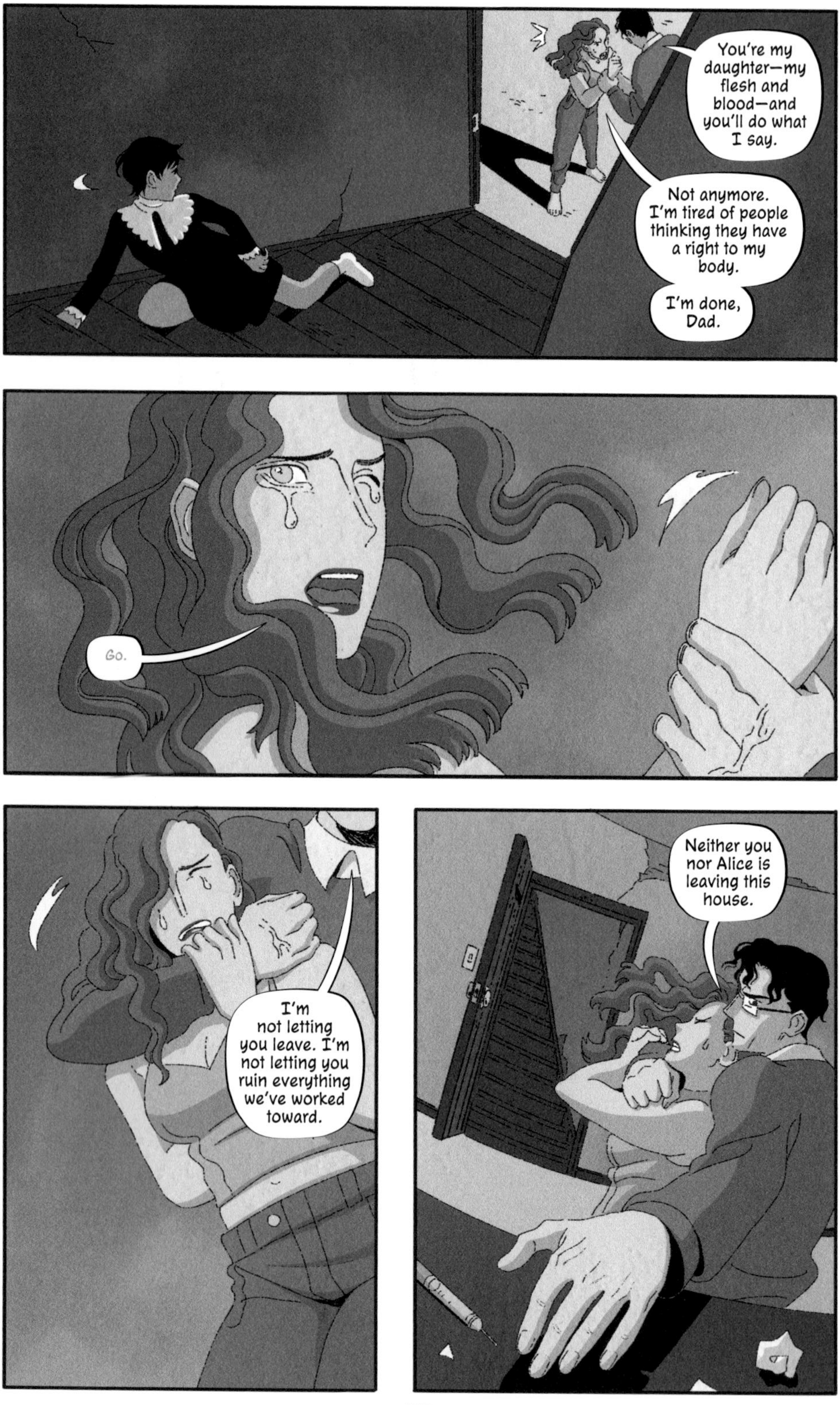
You're my daughter—my flesh and blood—and you'll do what I say.
Not anymore. I'm tired of people thinking they have a right to my body.
I'm done, Dad.
Go.
I'm not letting you leave. I'm not letting you ruin everything we've worked toward.
Neither you nor Alice is leaving this house.

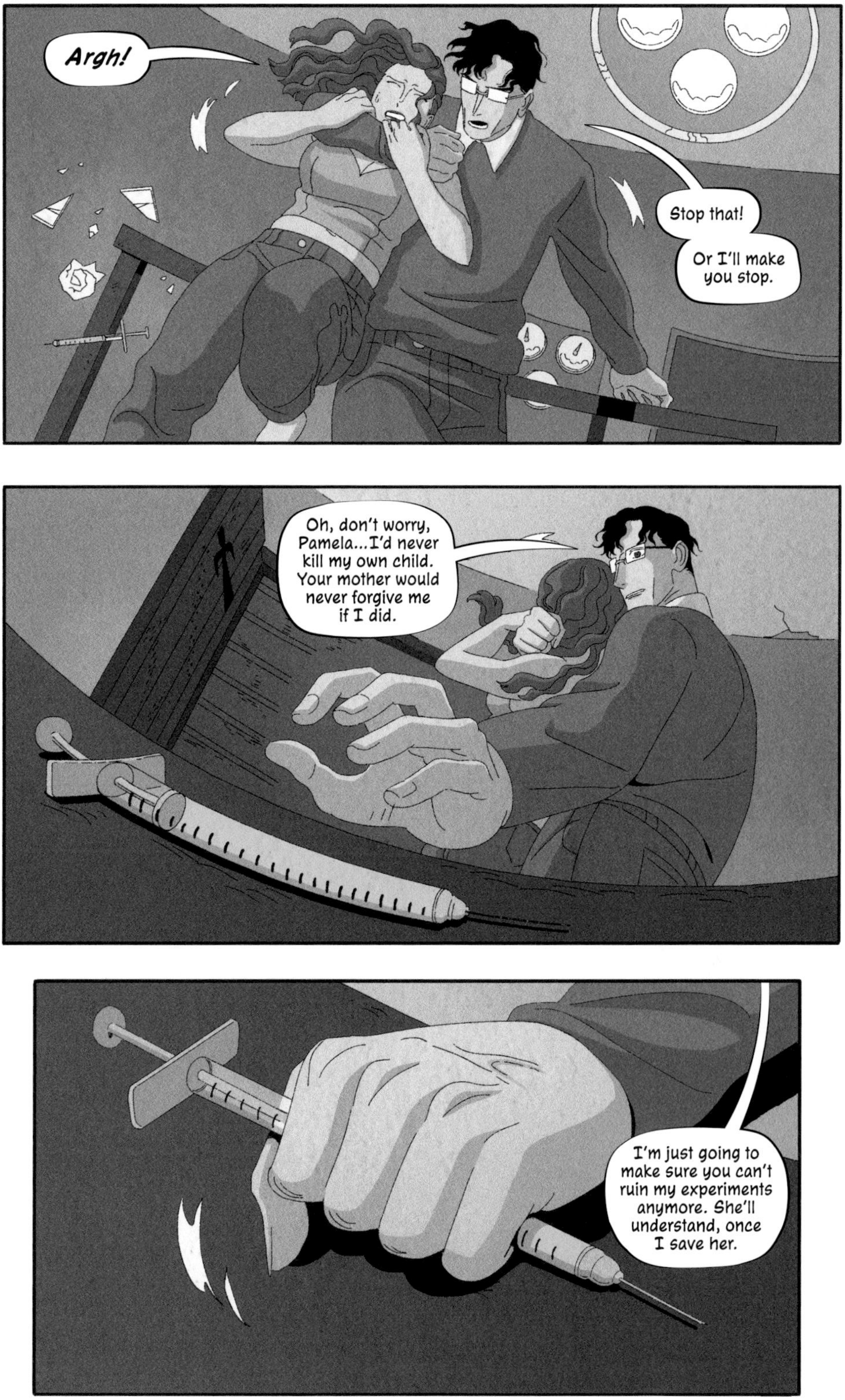
Argh!
Stop that!
Or I'll make you stop.
Oh, don't worry, Pamela...I'd never kill my own child. Your mother would never forgive me if I did.
I'm just going to make sure you can't ruin my experiments anymore. She'll understand, once I save her.

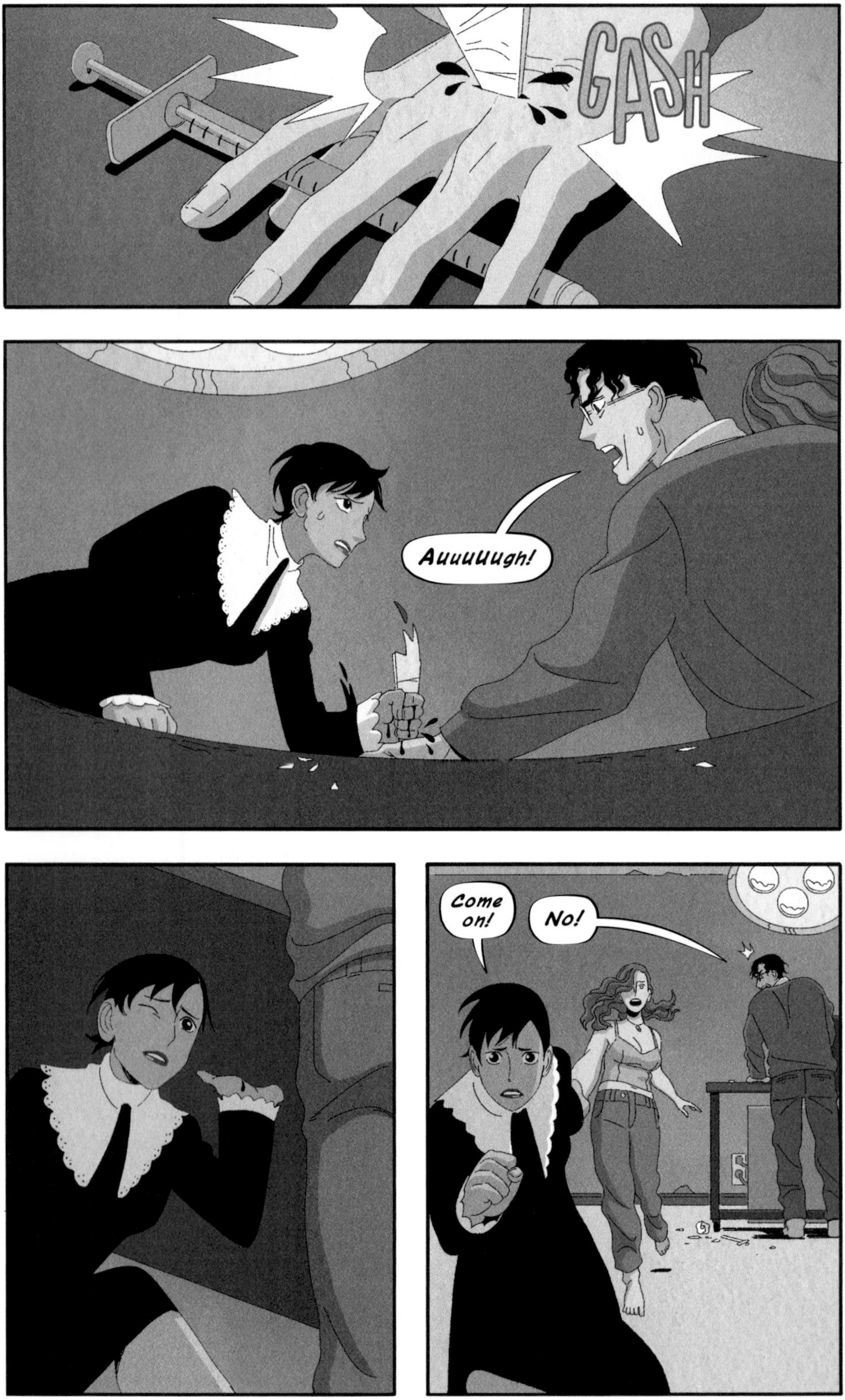
GASH
AuuuUugh!
Come on!
No!

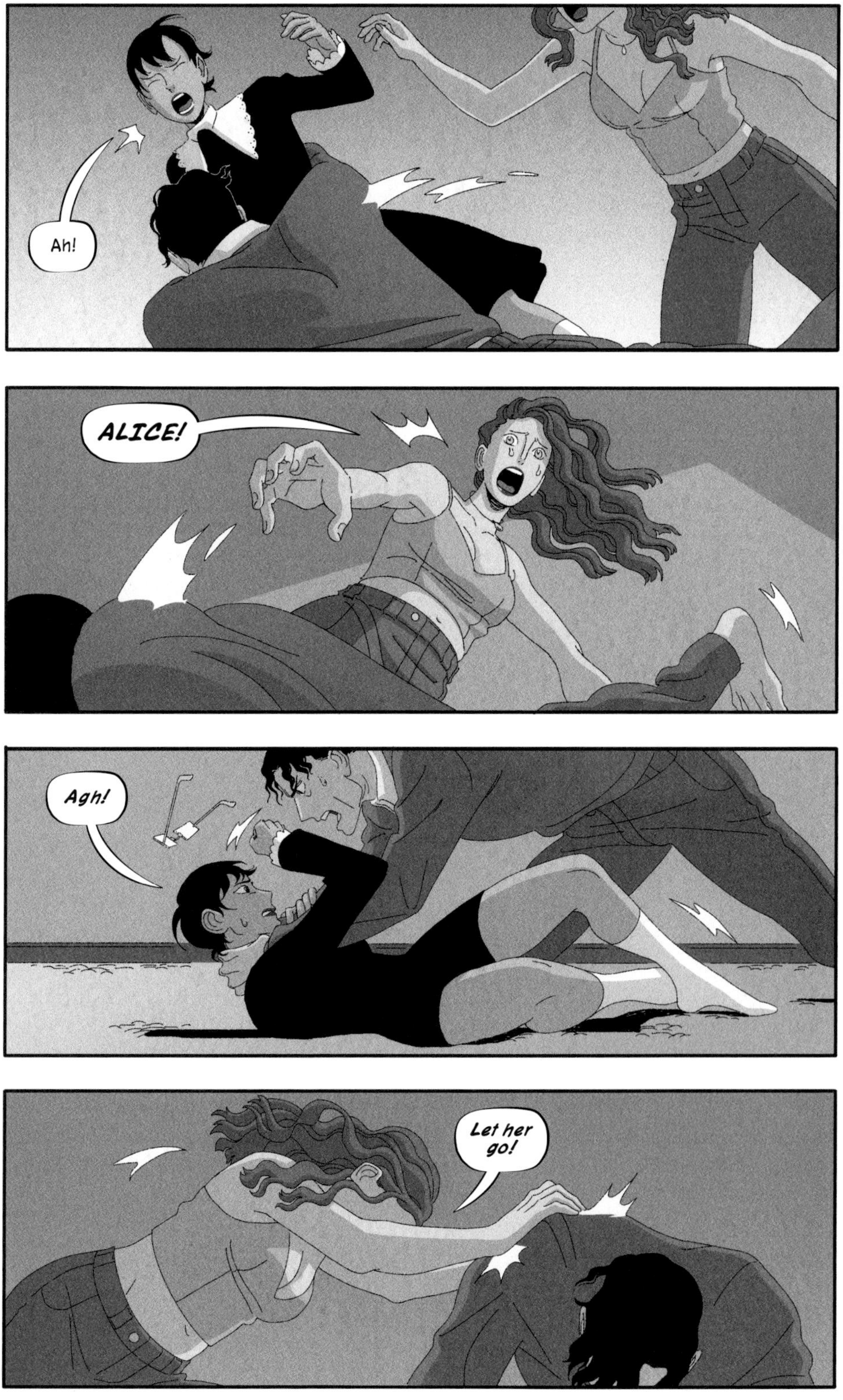
Ah!
ALICE!
Agh!
Let her go!

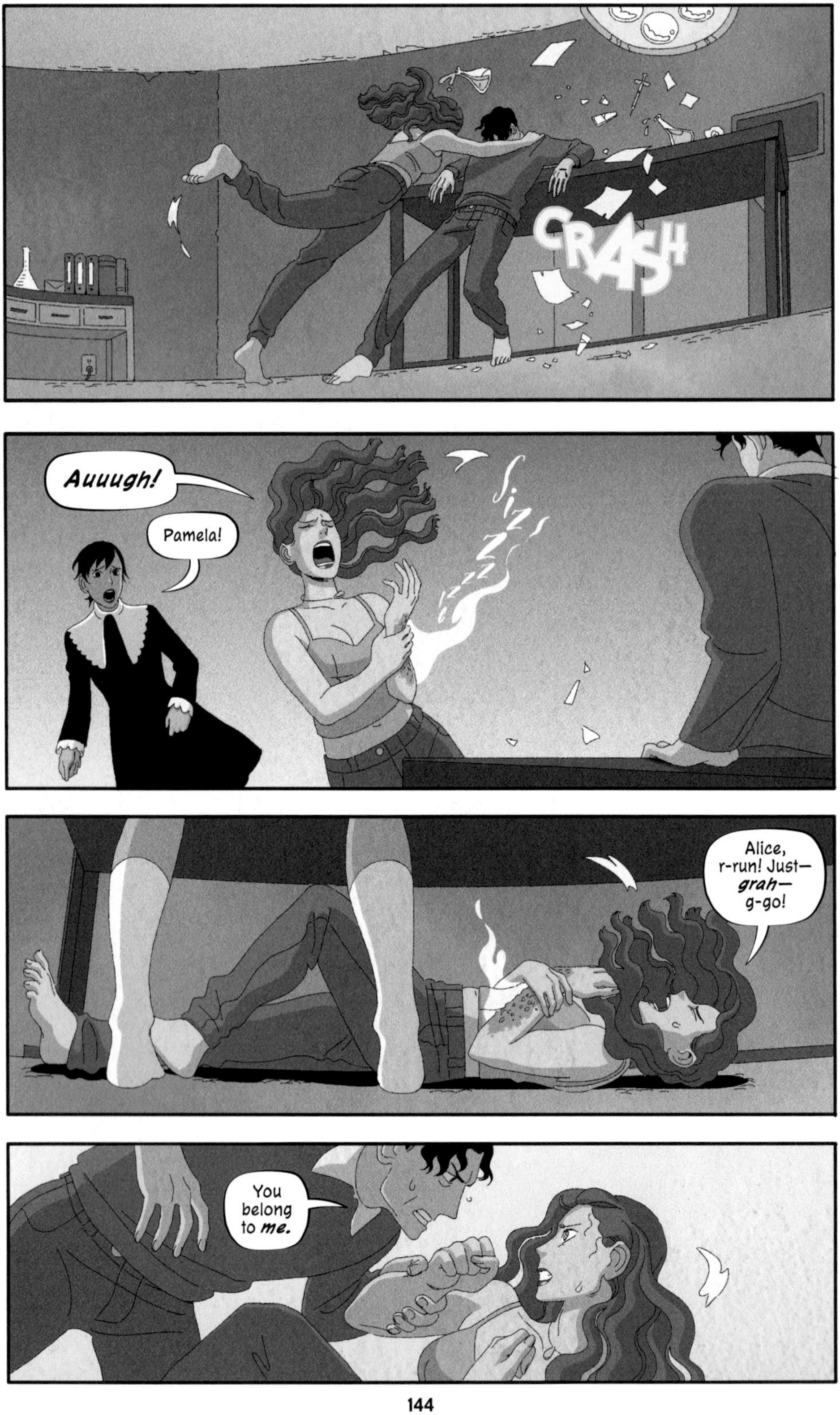
CRASH
Auuugh!
Pamela!
Sizzzzzz
Alice, r-run! Just—grah—g-go!
You belong to me.

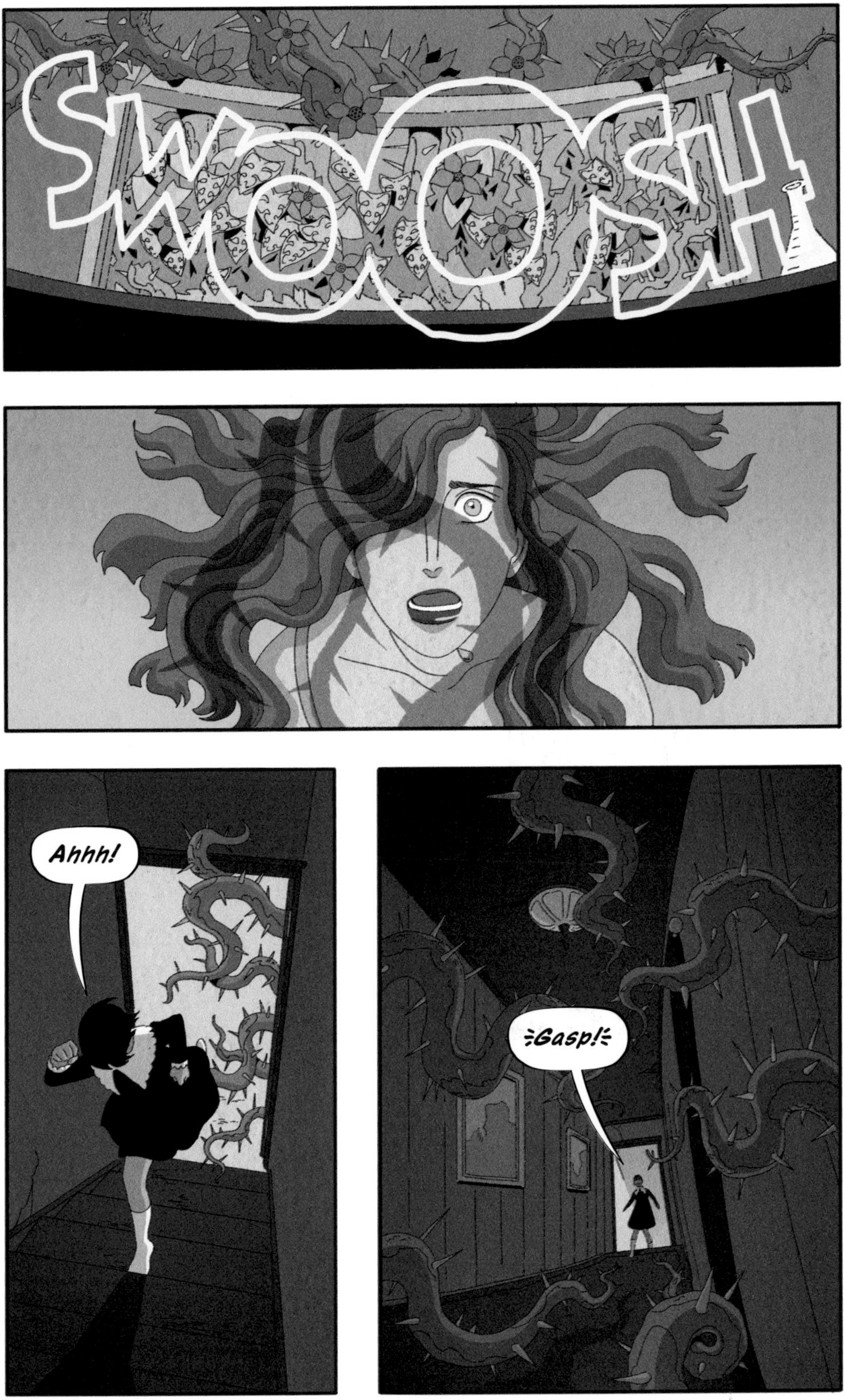
SWOOSH
Ahhh!
Gasp!

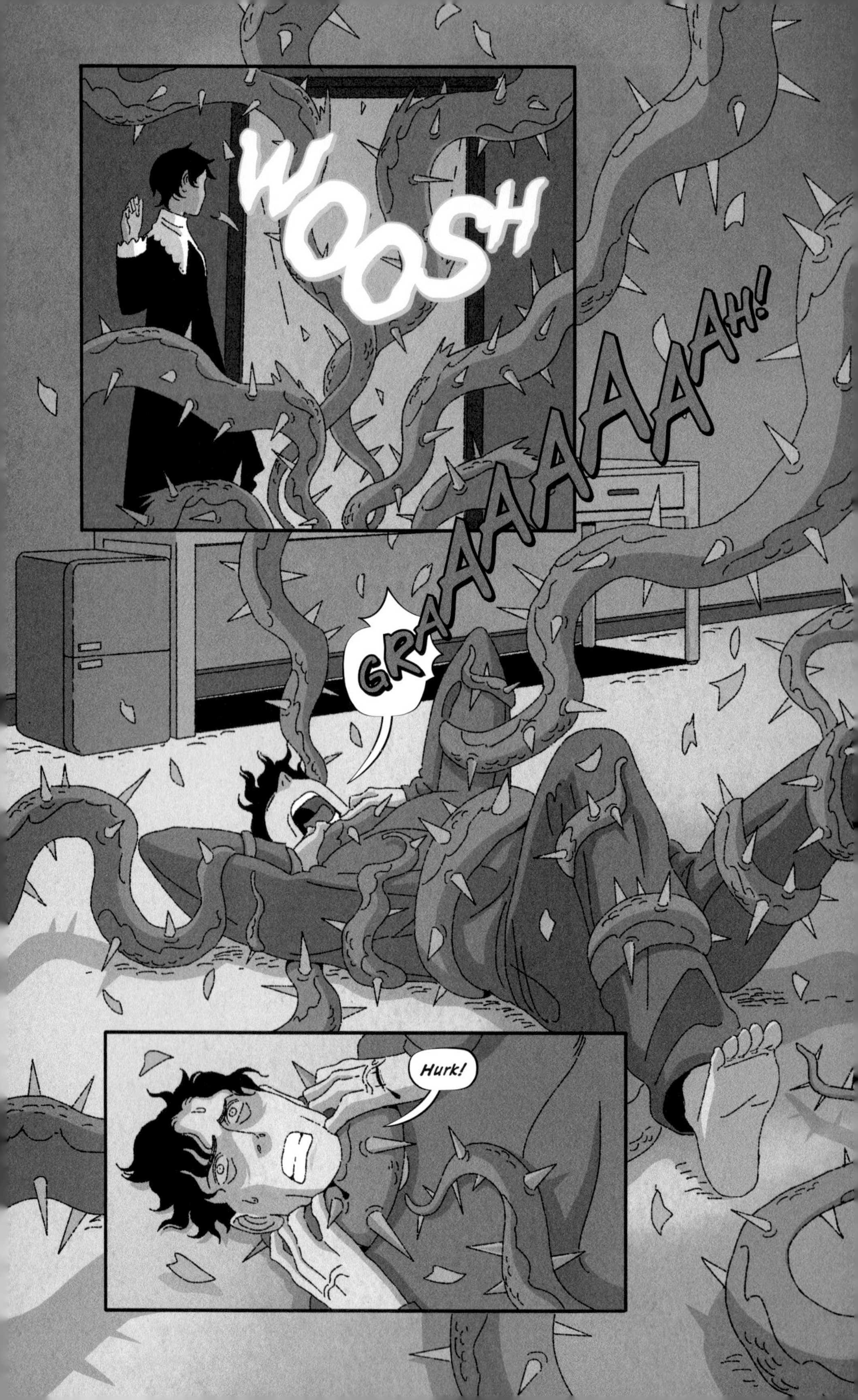
WOOSH
GRAAAAAAAAAH!
Hurk!

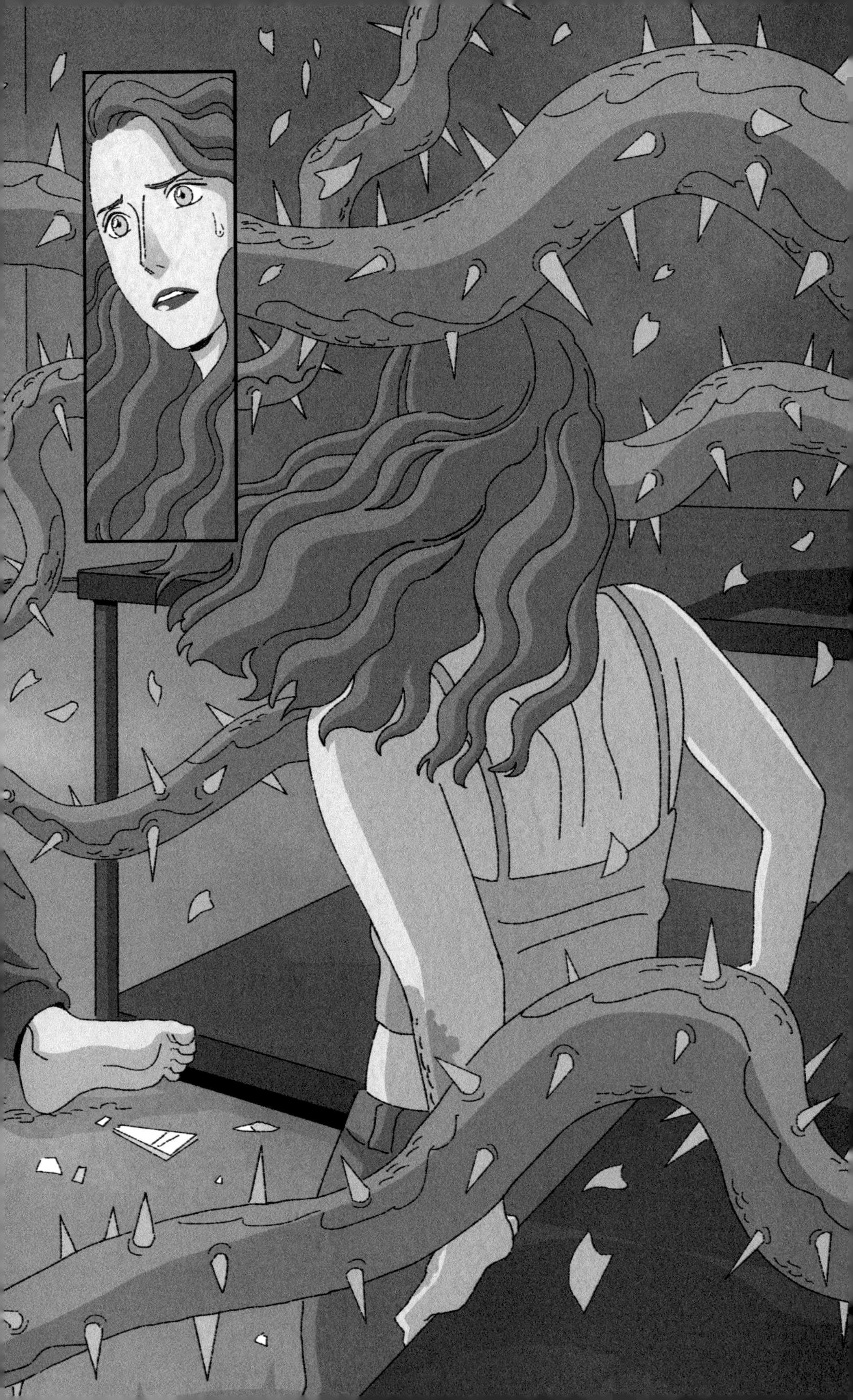

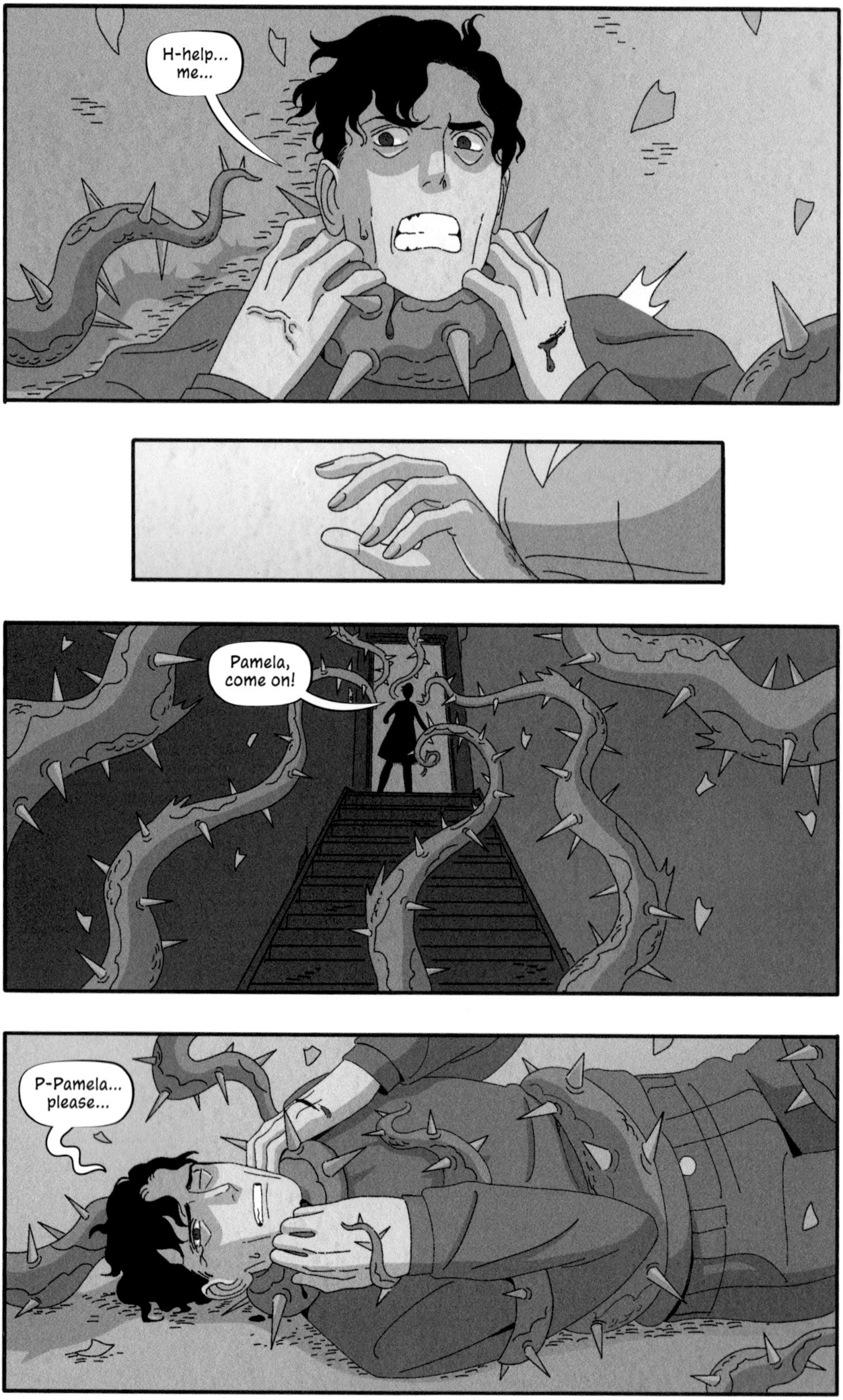
H-help... me...
Pamela, come on!
P-Pamela... please...

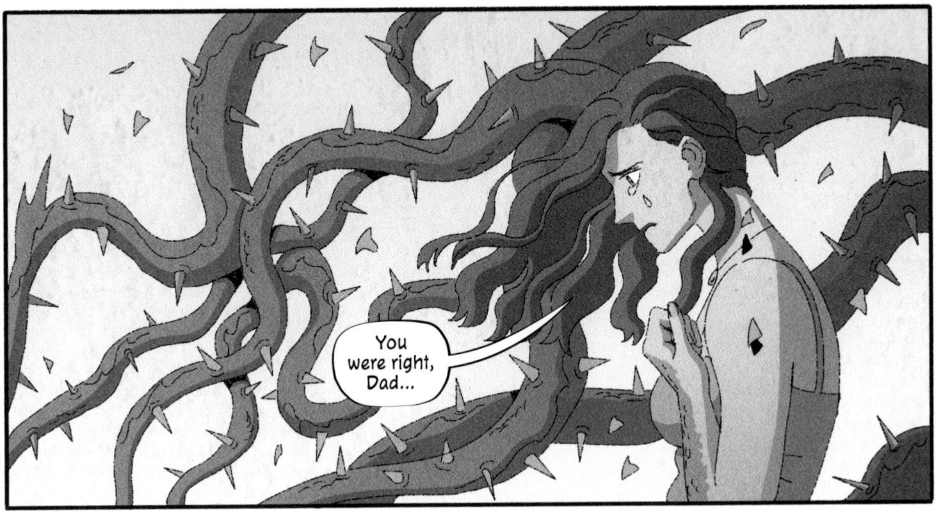
You were right, Dad...

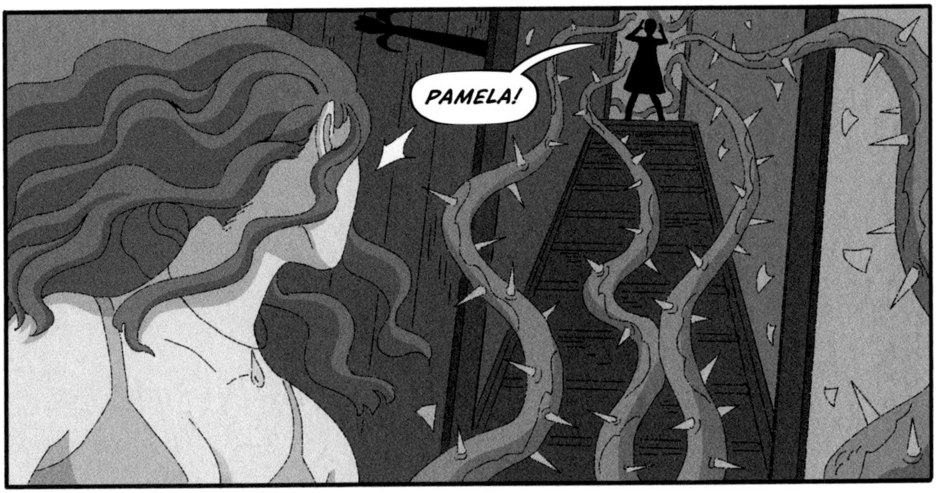
PAMELA!

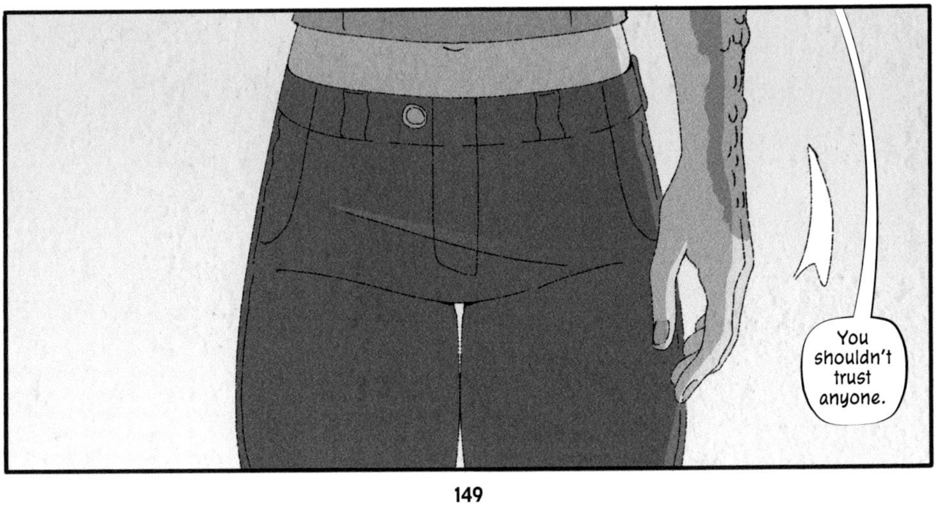
You shouldn't trust anyone.

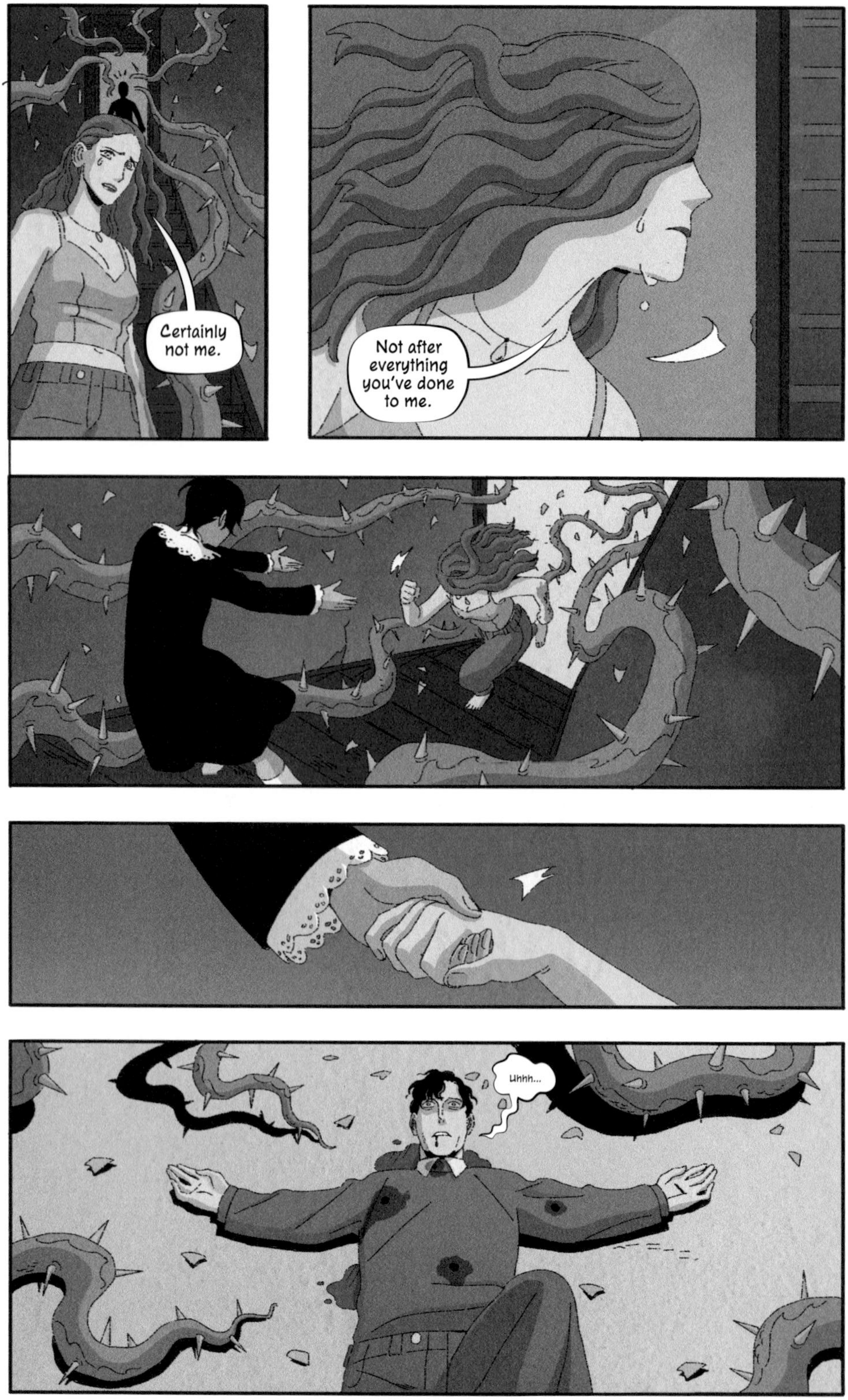
Certainly not me.
Not after everything you've done to me.
Uhhh...

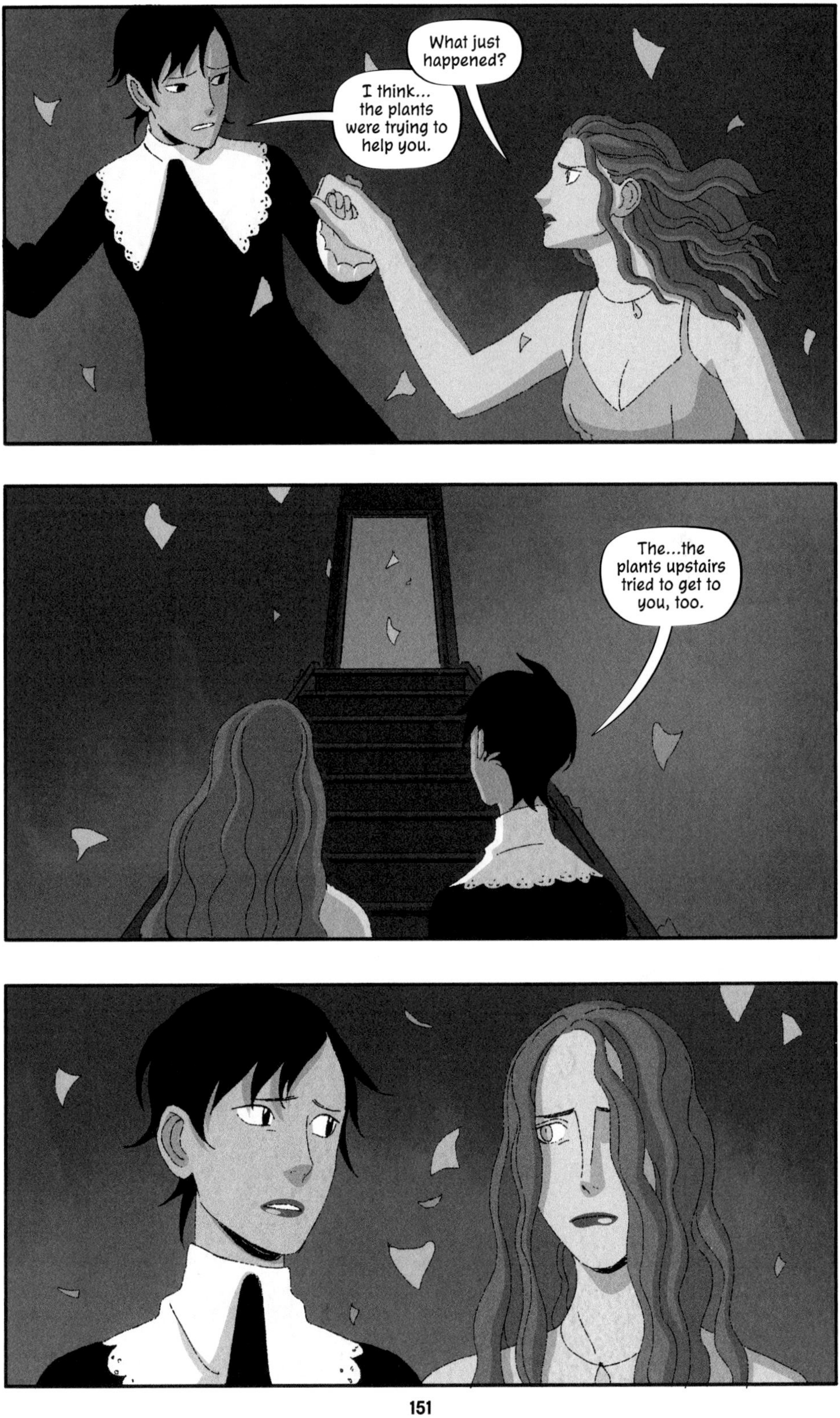
What just happened?
I think... the plants were trying to help you.
The...the plants upstairs tried to get to you, too.

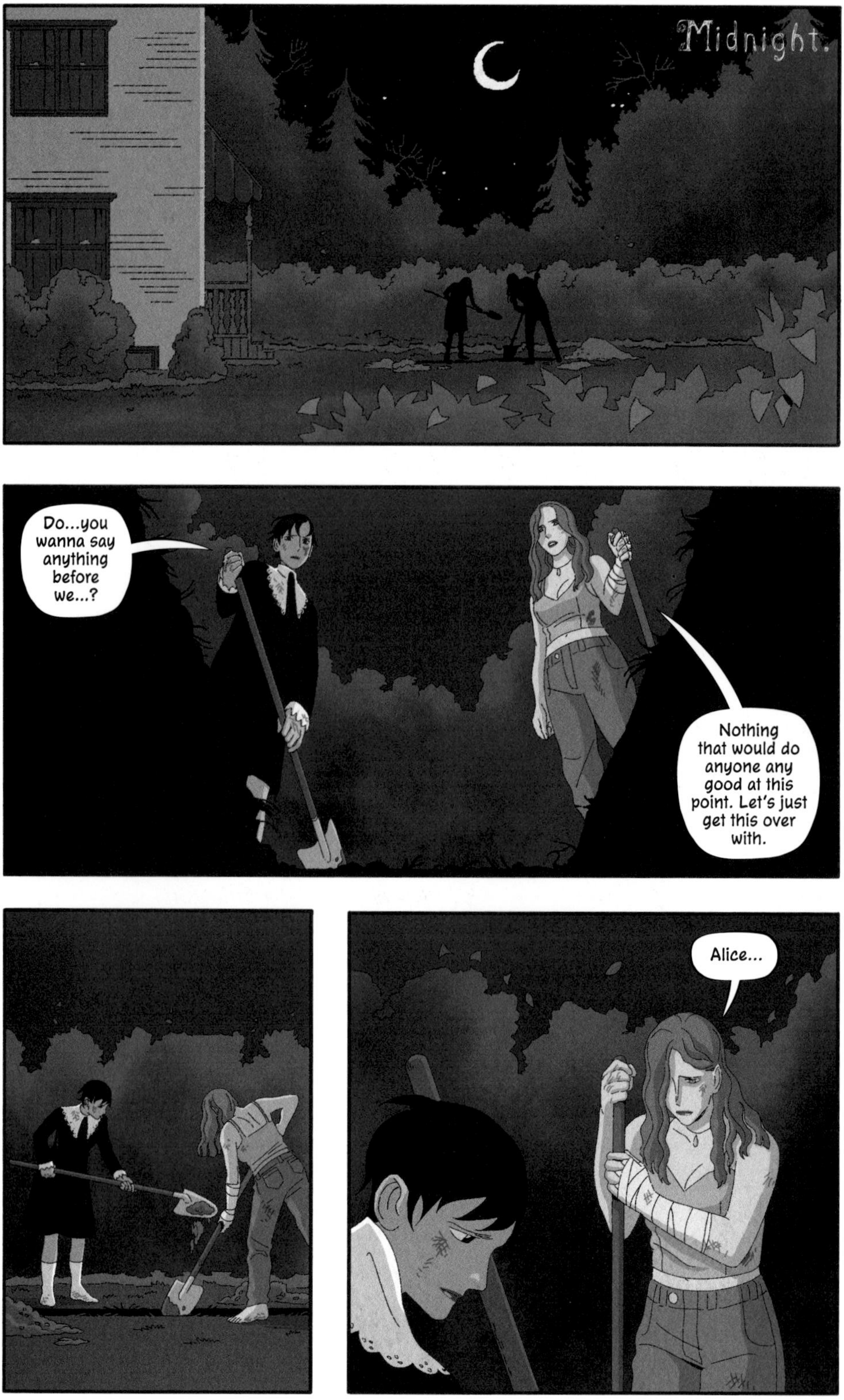
Midnight.
Do...you wanna say anything before we...?
Nothing that would do anyone any good at this point. Let's just get this over with.
Alice...

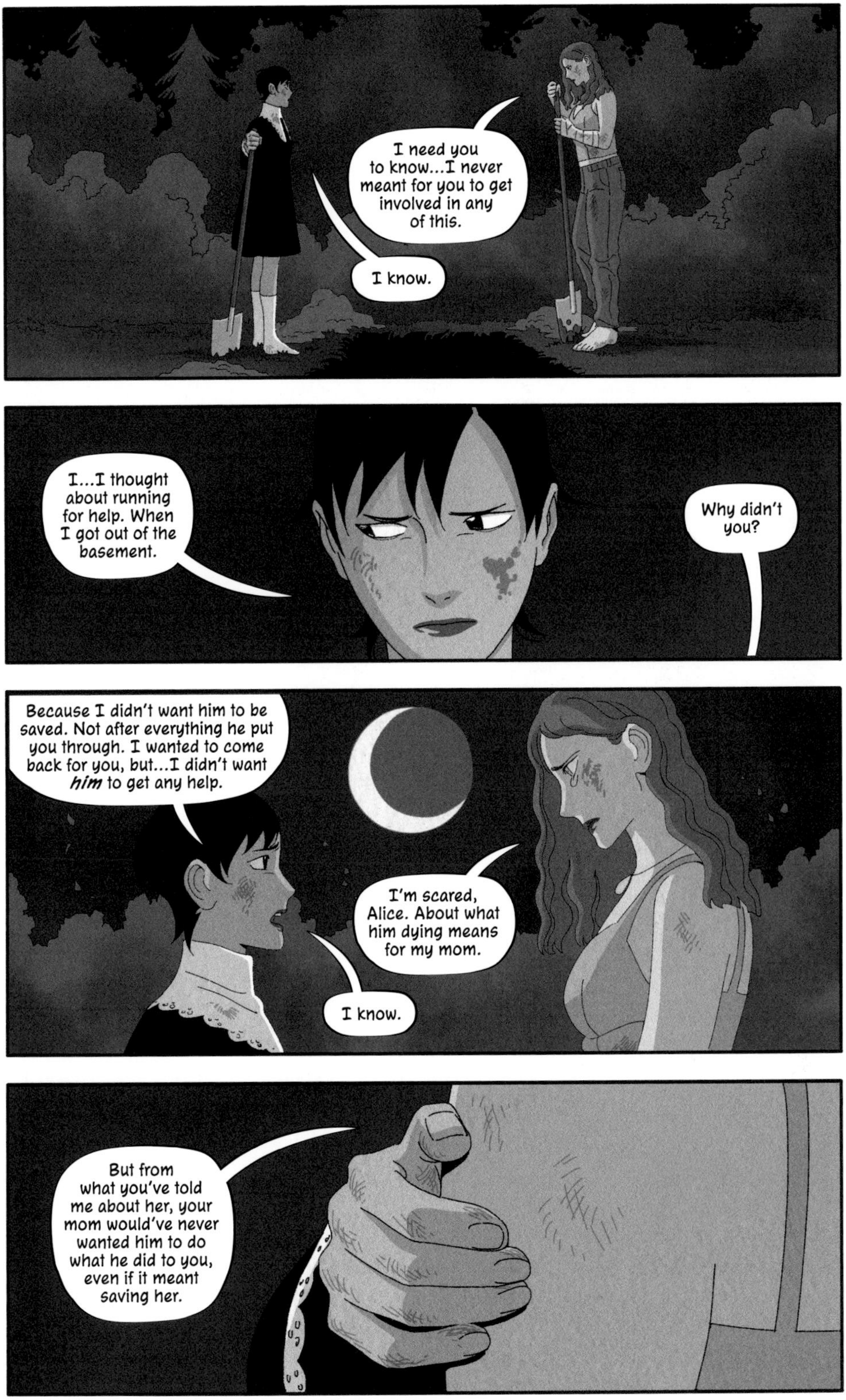
I need you to know...I never meant for you to get involved in any of this.
I know.
I...I thought about running for help. When I got out of the basement.
Why didn't you?
Because I didn't want him to be saved. Not after everything he put you through. I wanted to come back for you, but...I didn't want *him* to get any help.
I'm scared, Alice. About what him dying means for my mom.
I know.
But from what you've told me about her, your mom would've never wanted him to do what he did to you, even if it meant saving her.

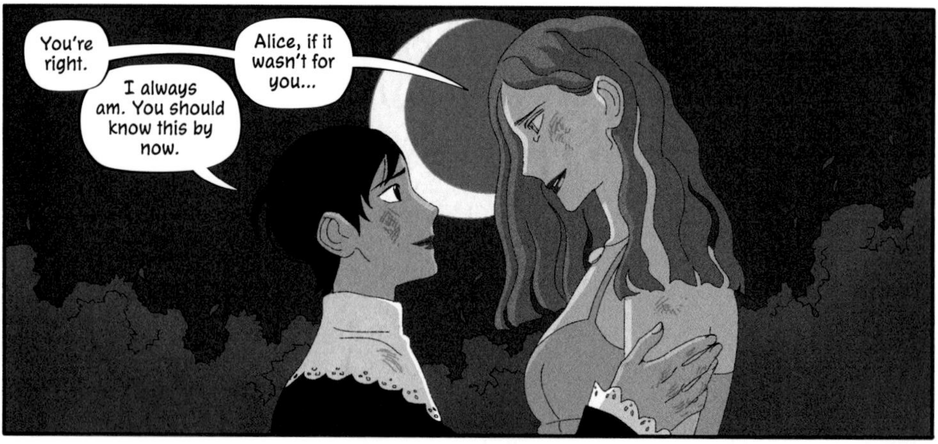
You're right.
Alice, if it wasn't for you...
I always am. You should know this by now.

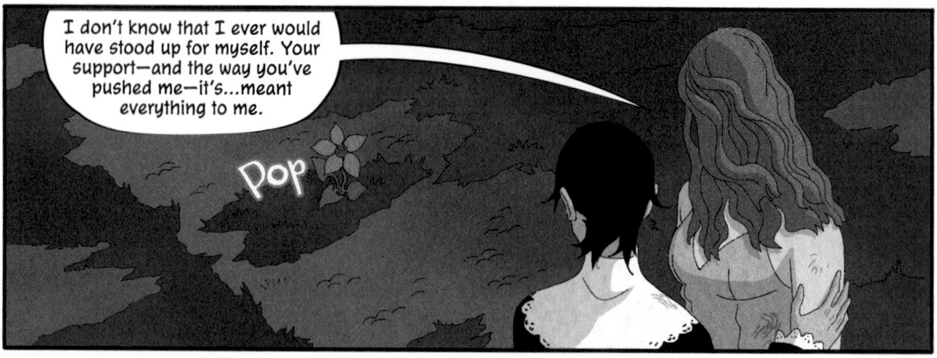
I don't know that I ever would have stood up for myself. Your support—and the way you've pushed me—it's...meant everything to me.
Pop

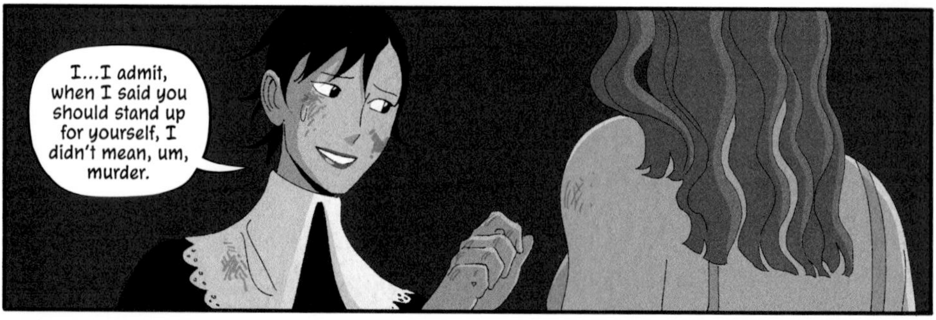
I...I admit, when I said you should stand up for yourself, I didn't mean, um, murder.

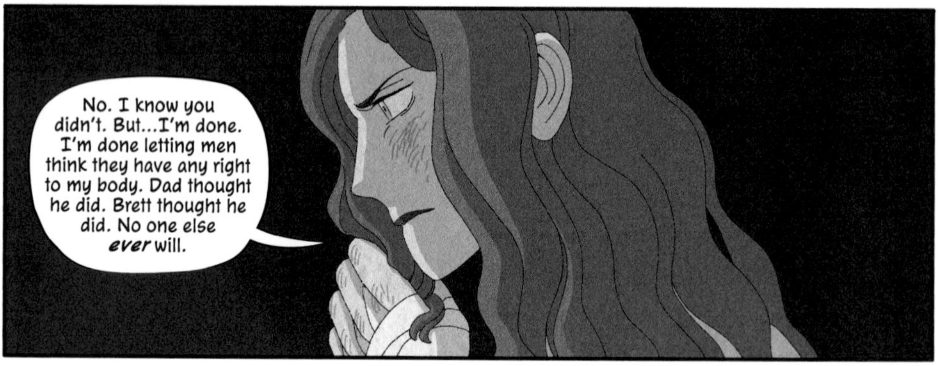
No. I know you didn't. But...I'm done. I'm done letting men think they have any right to my body. Dad thought he did. Brett thought he did. No one else *ever* will.

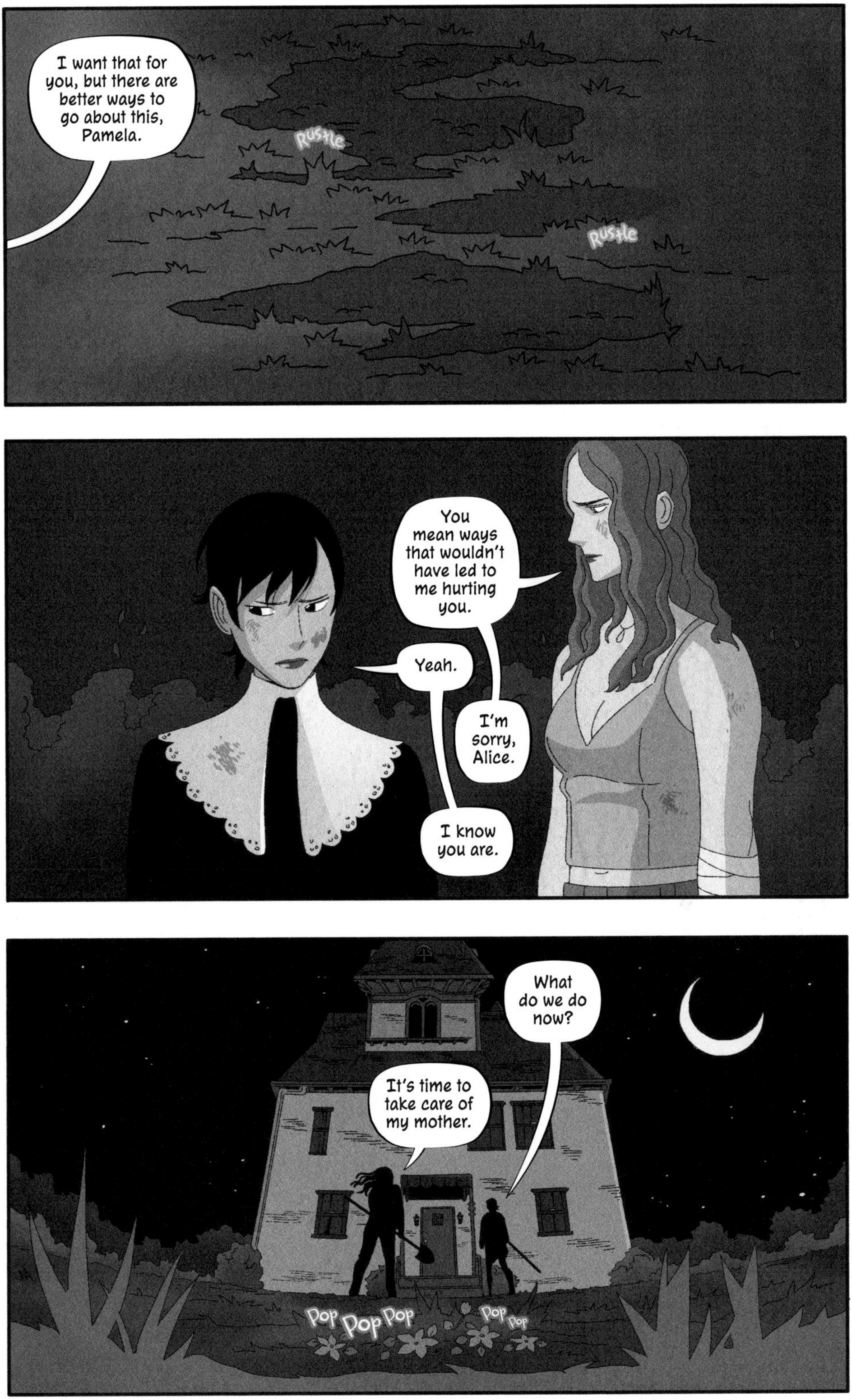
I want that for you, but there are better ways to go about this, Pamela.
Rustle
Rustle
You mean ways that wouldn't have led to me hurting you.
Yeah.
I'm sorry, Alice.
I know you are.
What do we do now?
It's time to take care of my mother.
Pop Pop Pop
Pop Pop

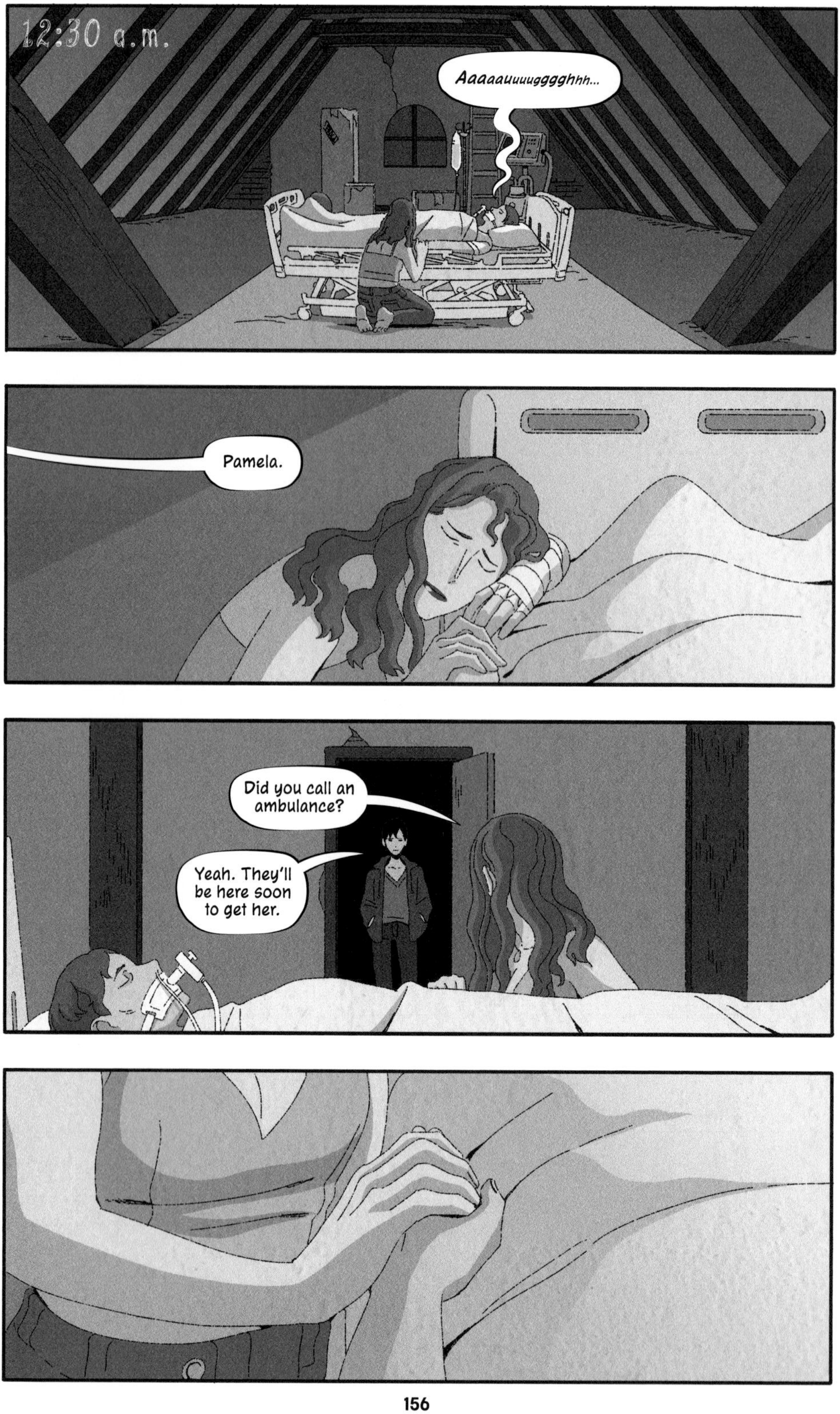
12:30 a.m.
Aaaaauuuuggggghhh...
Pamela.
Did you call an ambulance?
Yeah. They'll be here soon to get her.

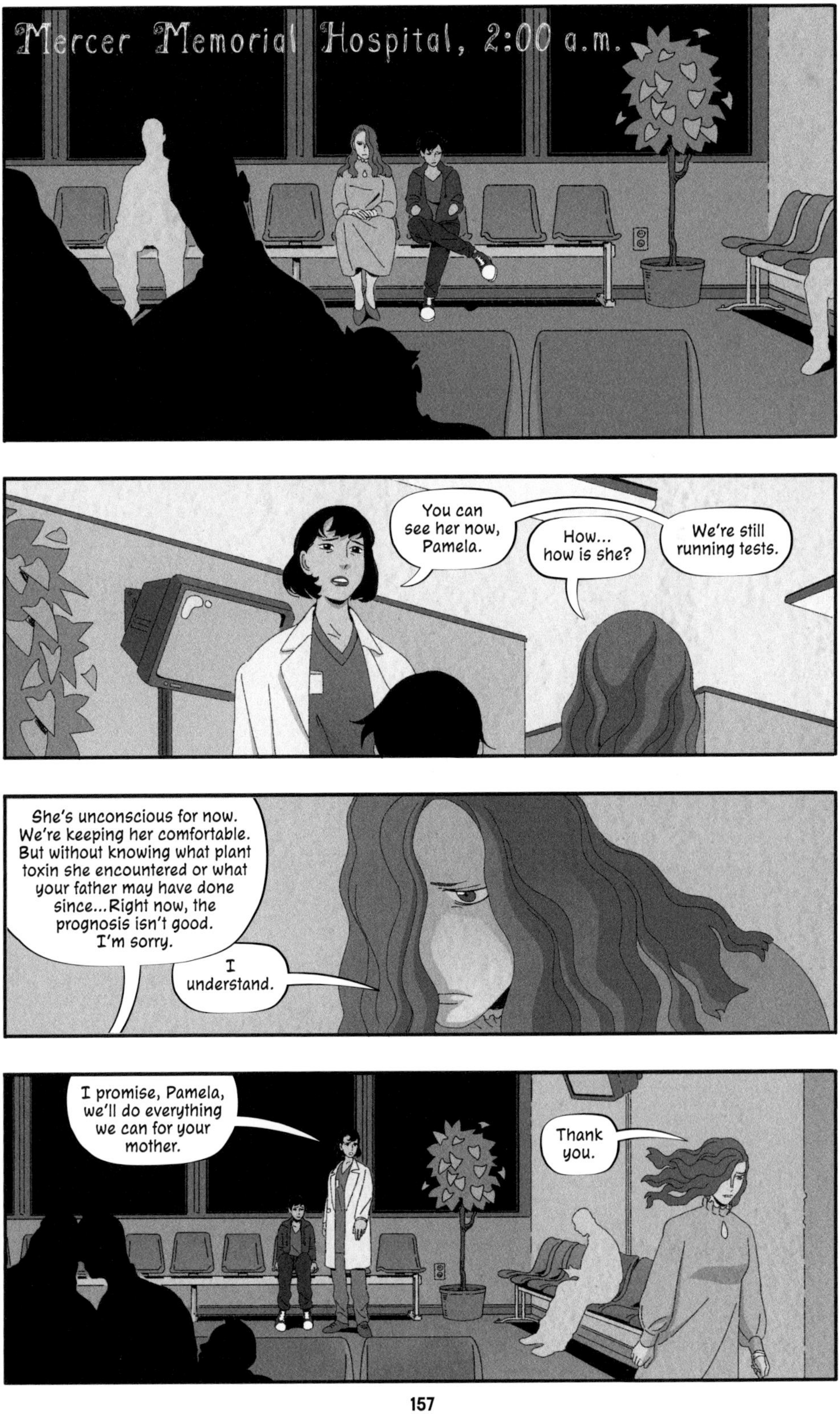
Mercer Memorial Hospital, 2:00 a.m.
You can see her now, Pamela.
How... how is she?
We're still running tests.
She's unconscious for now. We're keeping her comfortable. But without knowing what plant toxin she encountered or what your father may have done since...Right now, the prognosis isn't good. I'm sorry.
I understand.
I promise, Pamela, we'll do everything we can for your mother.
Thank you.

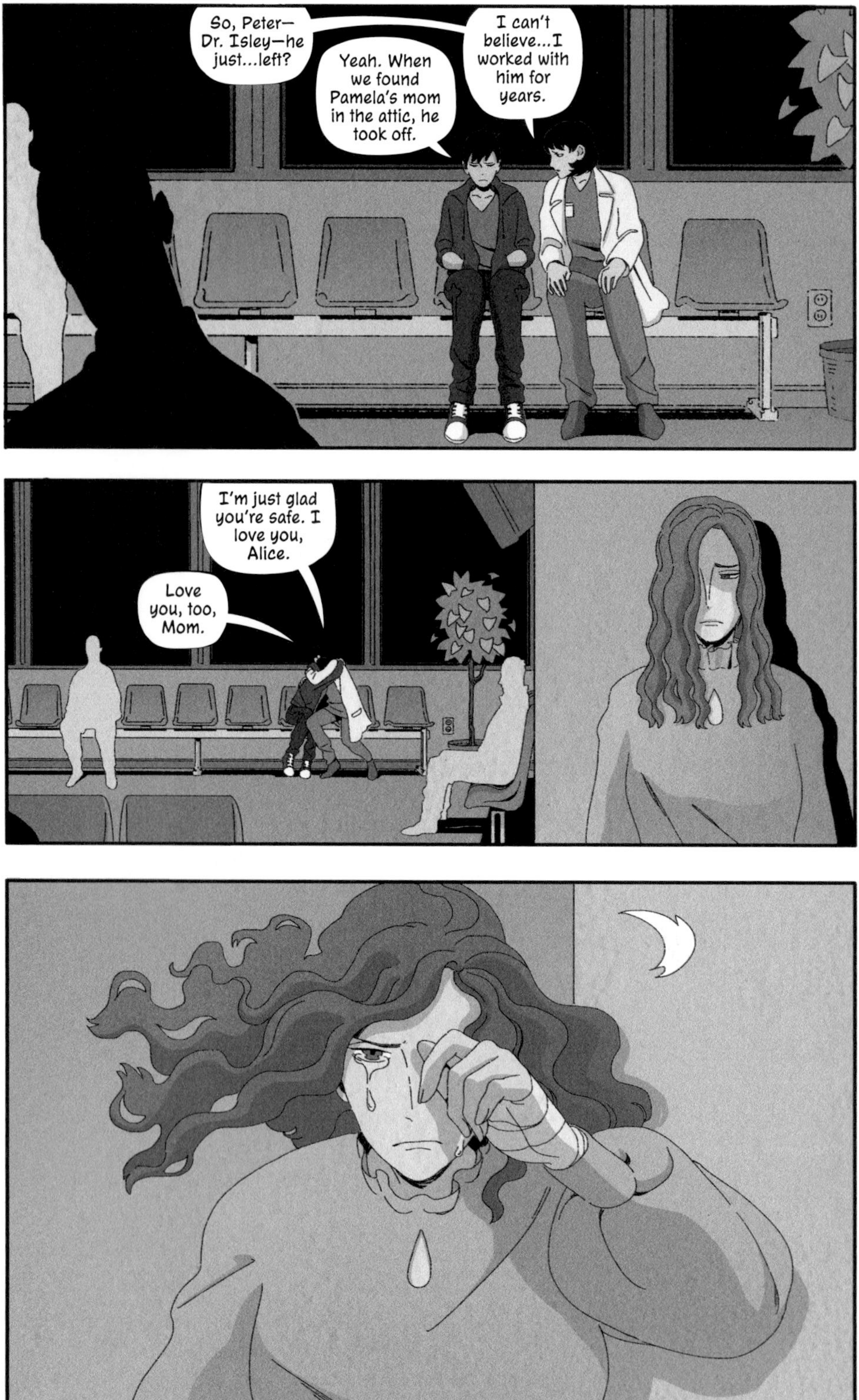
So, Peter—Dr. Isley—he just...left?
Yeah. When we found Pamela's mom in the attic, he took off.
I can't believe...I worked with him for years.
I'm just glad you're safe. I love you, Alice.
Love you, too, Mom.

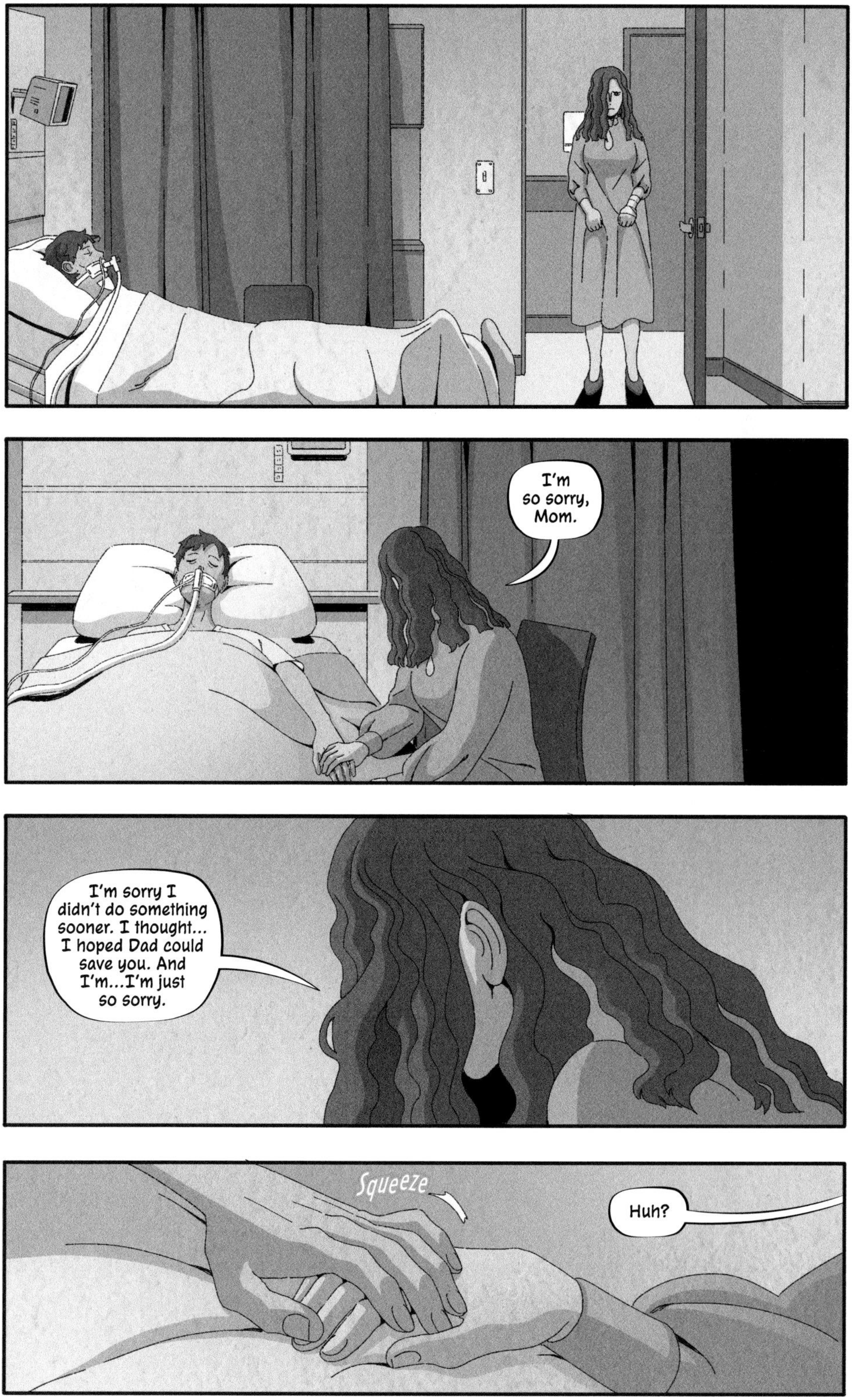
I'm so sorry, Mom.
I'm sorry I didn't do something sooner. I thought... I hoped Dad could save you. And I'm...I'm just so sorry.
Squeeze
Huh?

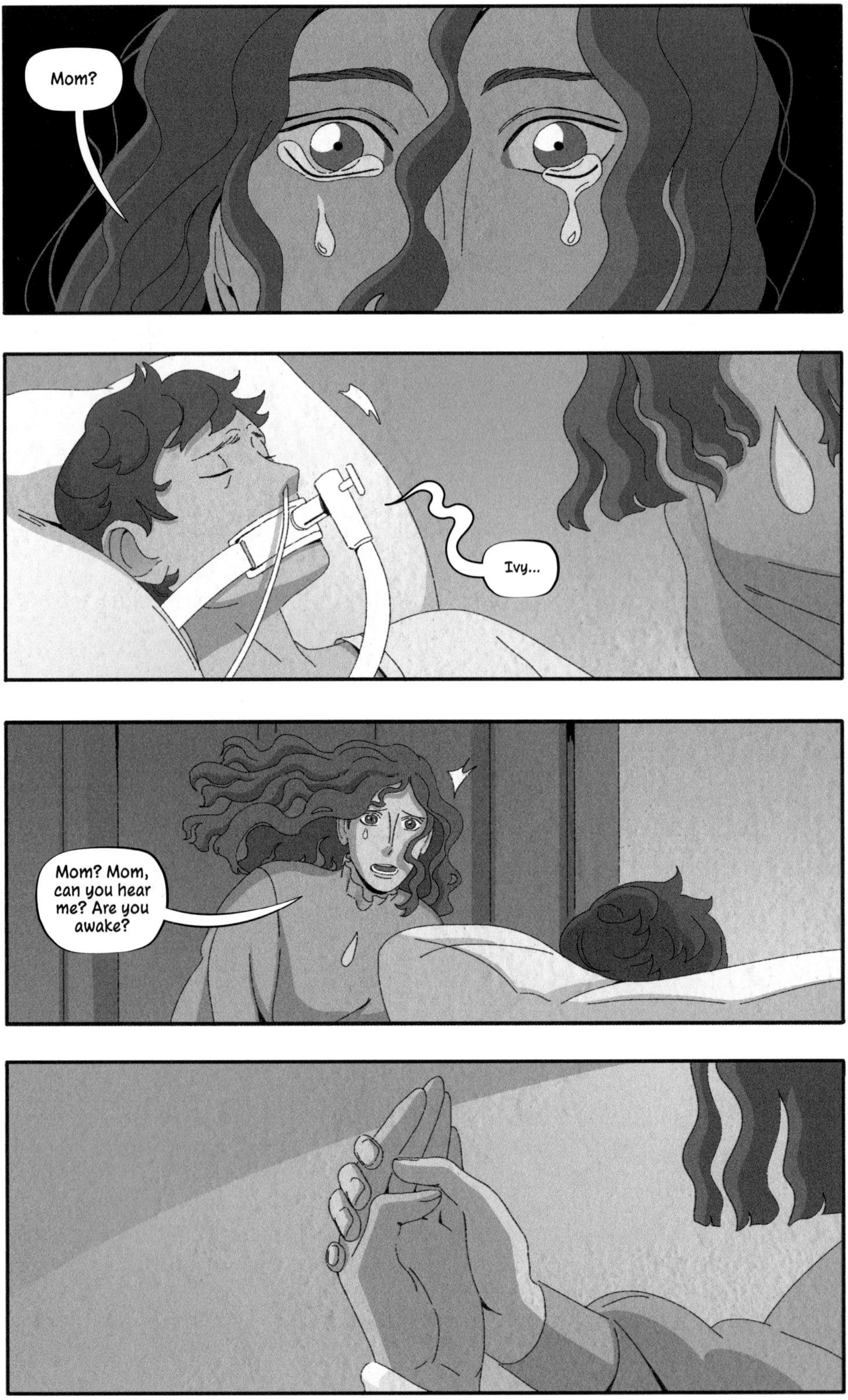
Mom?
Ivy...
Mom? Mom, can you hear me? Are you awake?

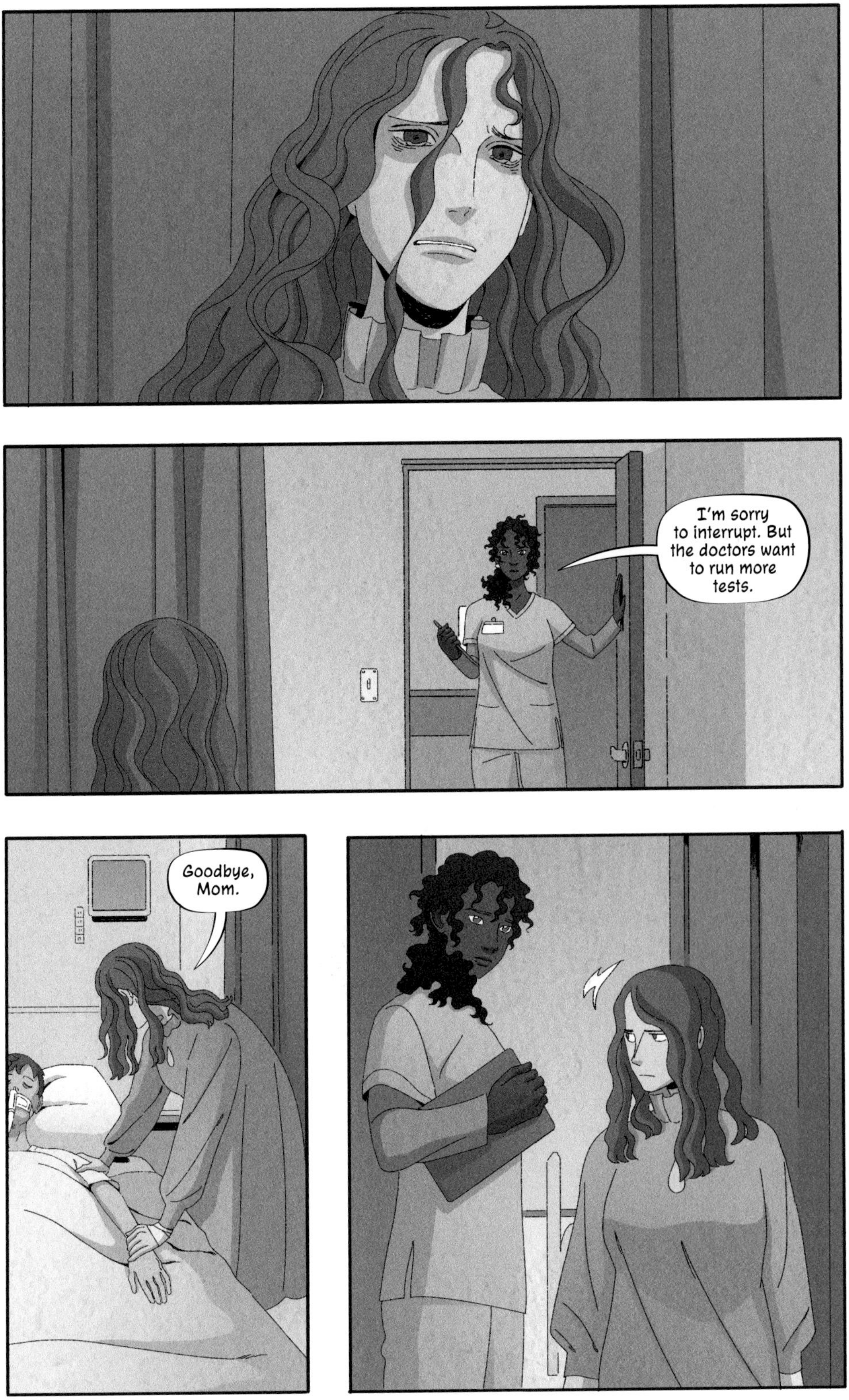
I'm sorry to interrupt. But the doctors want to run more tests.
Goodbye, Mom.

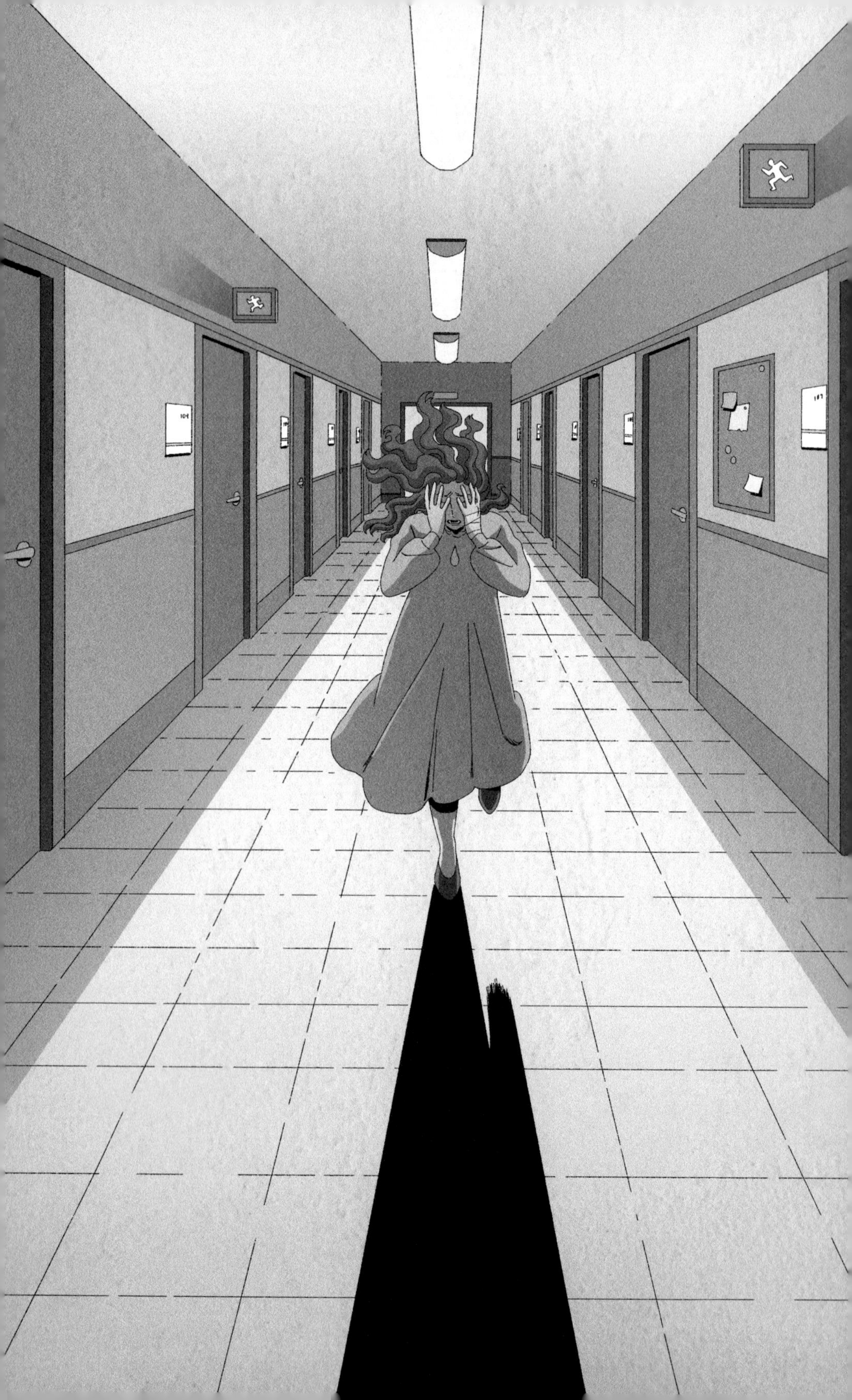

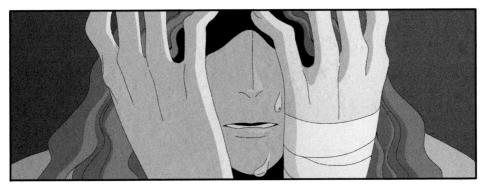

Isley Mansion, 3:00 a.m.

knock knock

My dad just left. I convinced him to let me stay here for the night.

He and Mom will be back in the morning to talk about what we should do from here.

From here?

They're obviously not going to just let you stay here alone after everything that's happened.

But what about your house?

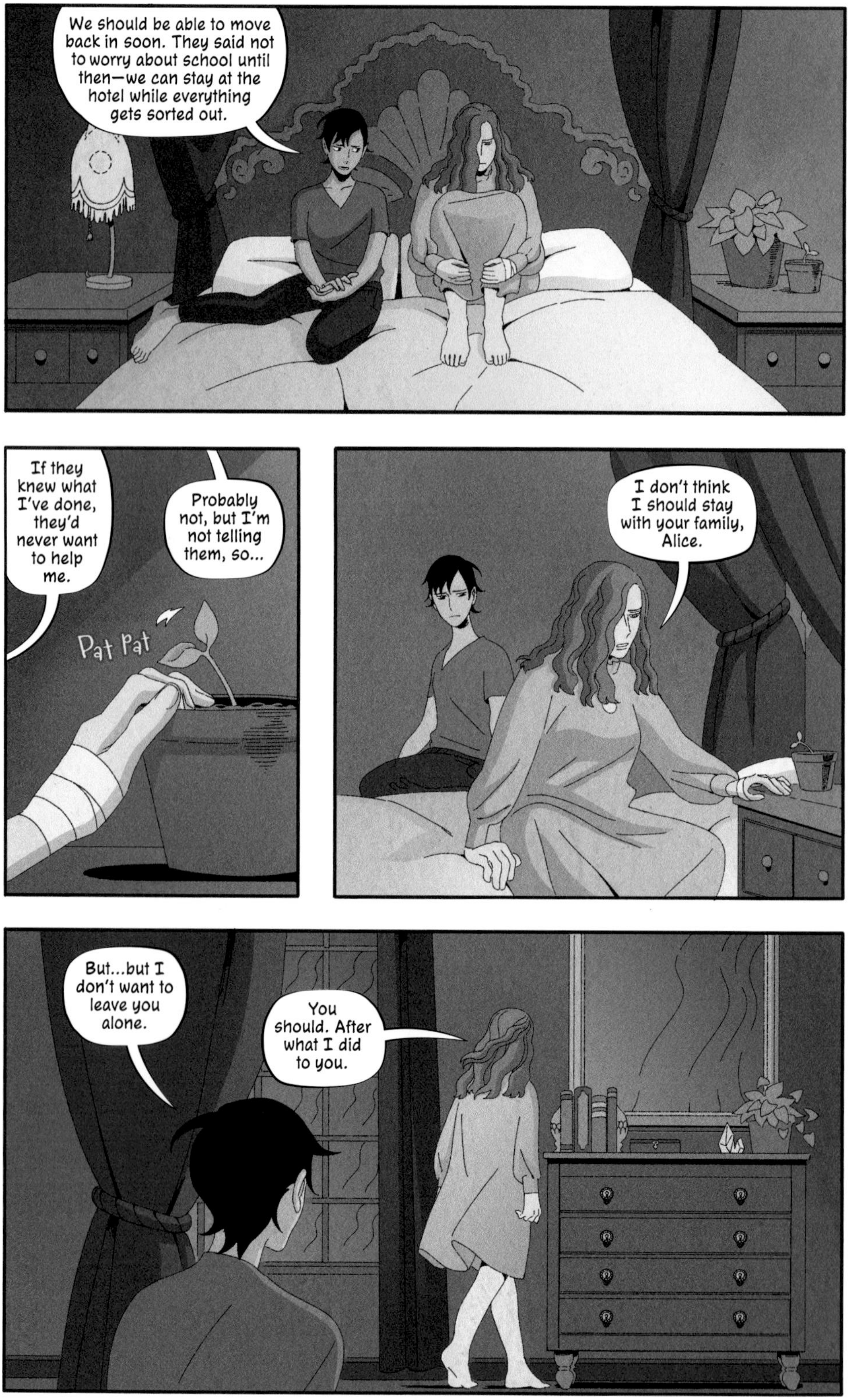
We should be able to move back in soon. They said not to worry about school until then—we can stay at the hotel while everything gets sorted out.
If they knew what I've done, they'd never want to help me.
Probably not, but I'm not telling them, so...
Pat Pat
I don't think I should stay with your family, Alice.
But...but I don't want to leave you alone.
You should. After what I did to you.

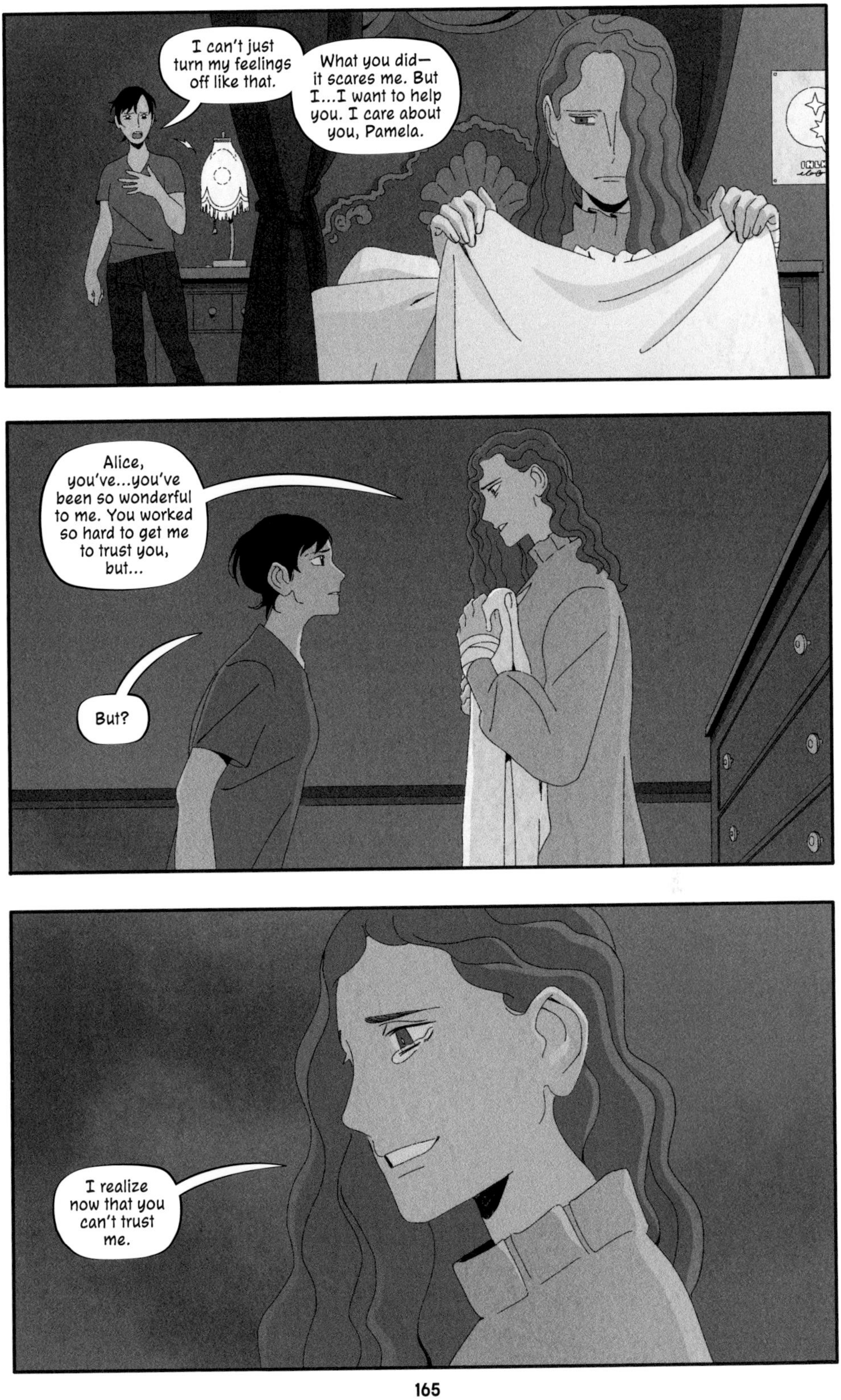
I can't just turn my feelings off like that.
What you did— it scares me. But I...I want to help you. I care about you, Pamela.
Alice, you've...you've been so wonderful to me. You worked so hard to get me to trust you, but...
But?
I realize now that you can't trust me.

You can't keep protecting me, and...I think it's my turn to protect you.

I've been in love with you for so long, Pamela. When we had to evacuate, I felt so guilty because I was just happy I'd get to be near you. And even after everything...

I don't have any regrets.

I'm sorry I didn't end up being the kind of girl you deserve.

Please. Don't say things like that.

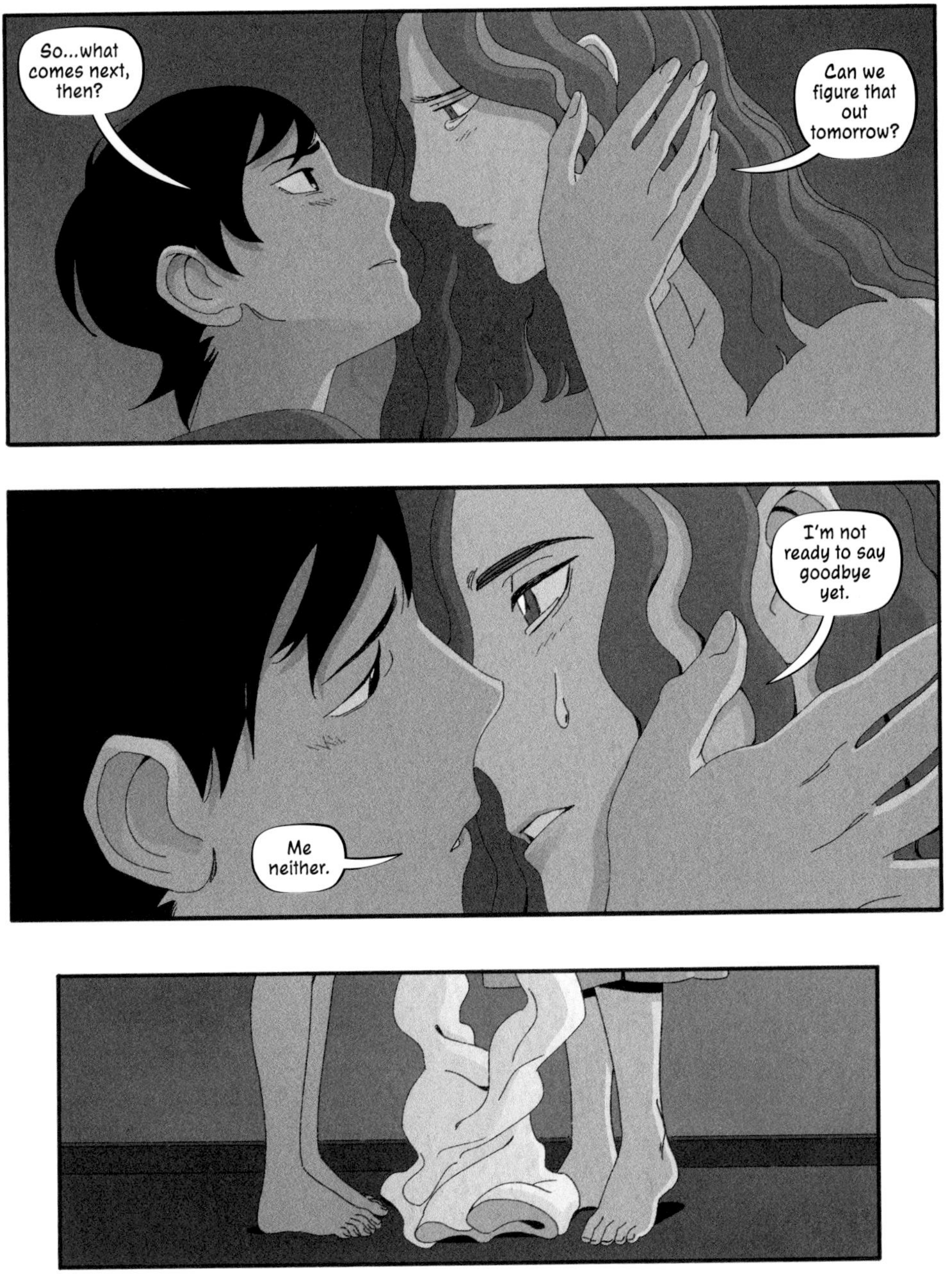
So...what comes next, then?
Can we figure that out tomorrow?
I'm not ready to say goodbye yet.
Me neither.

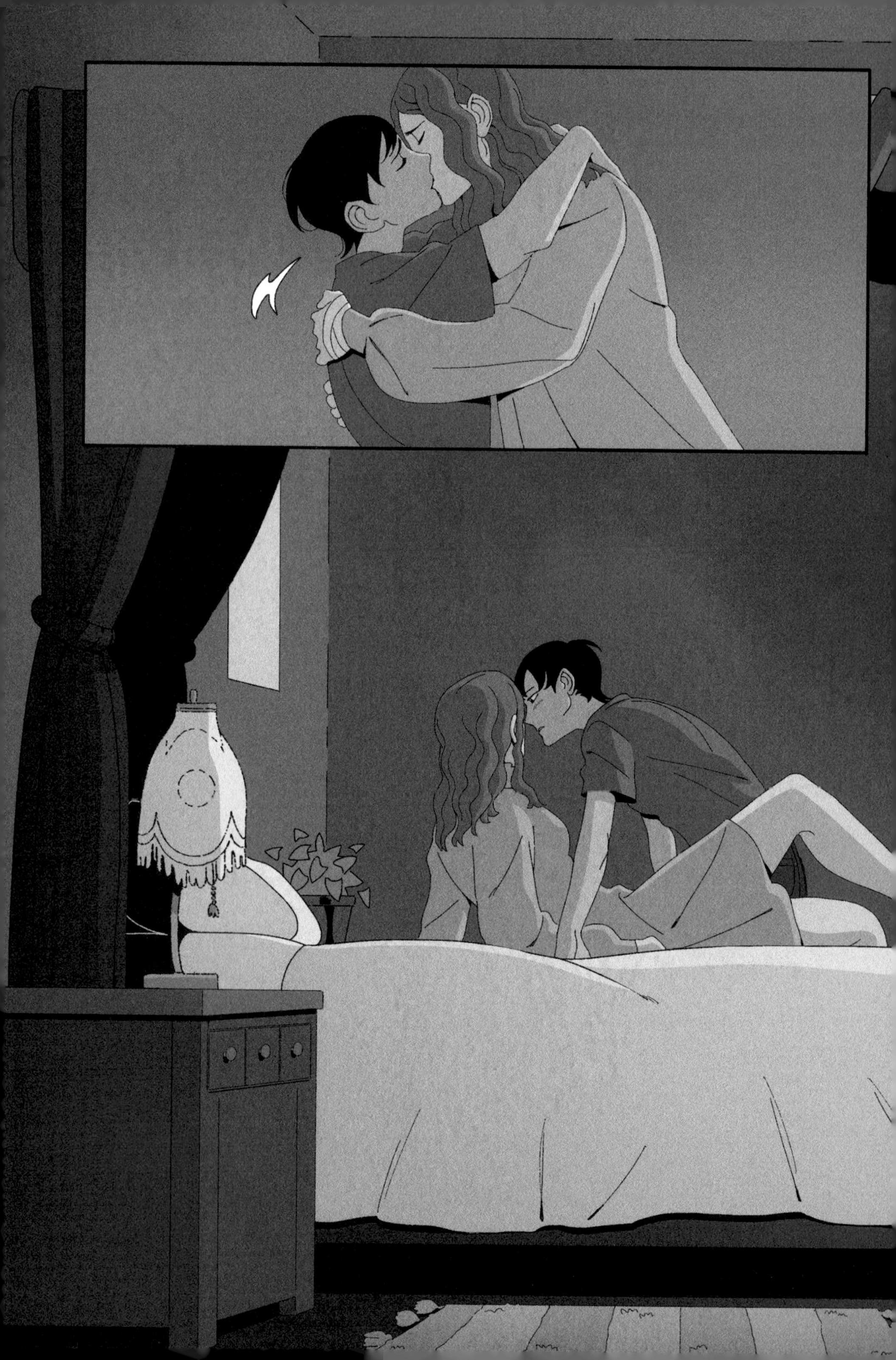

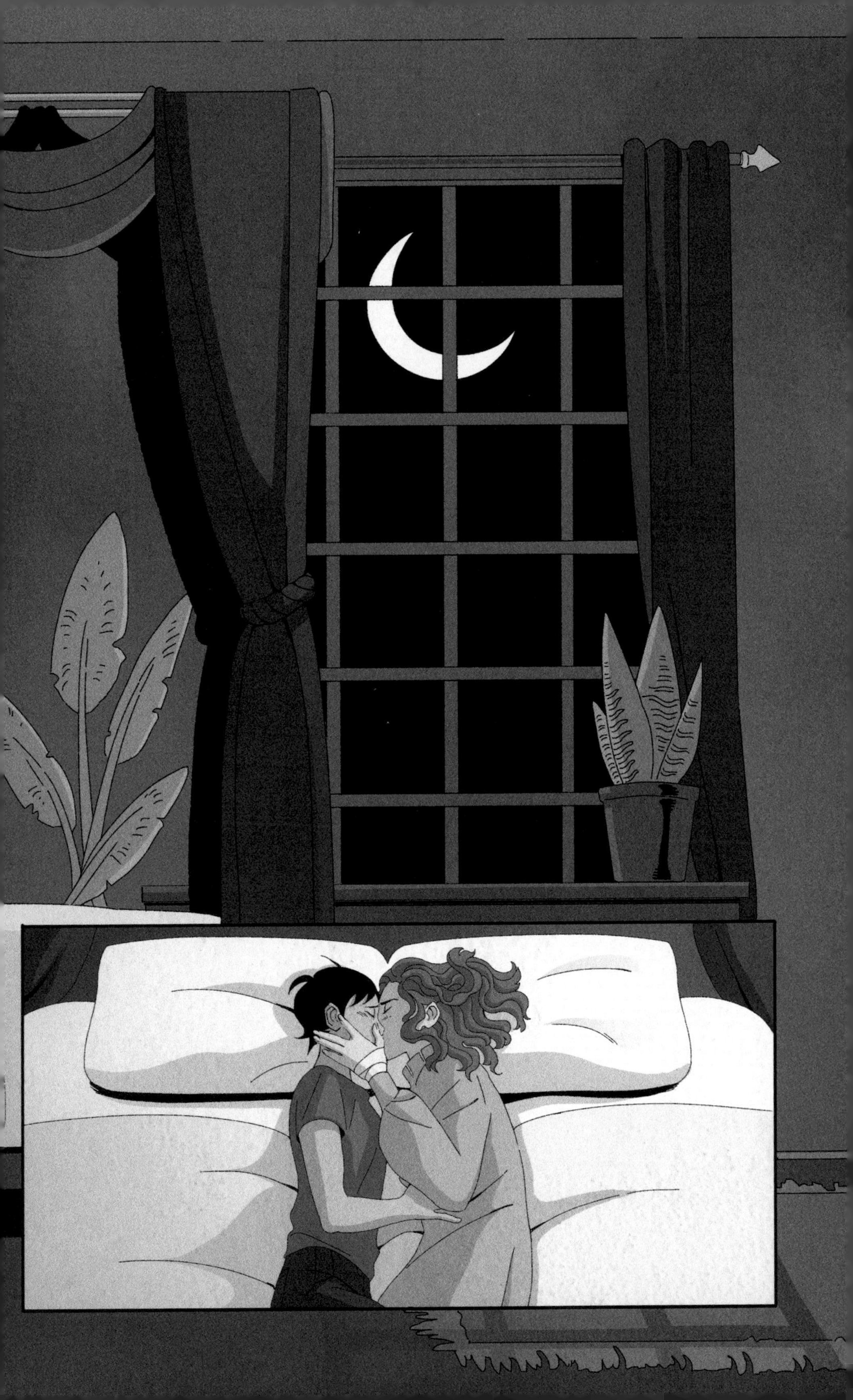

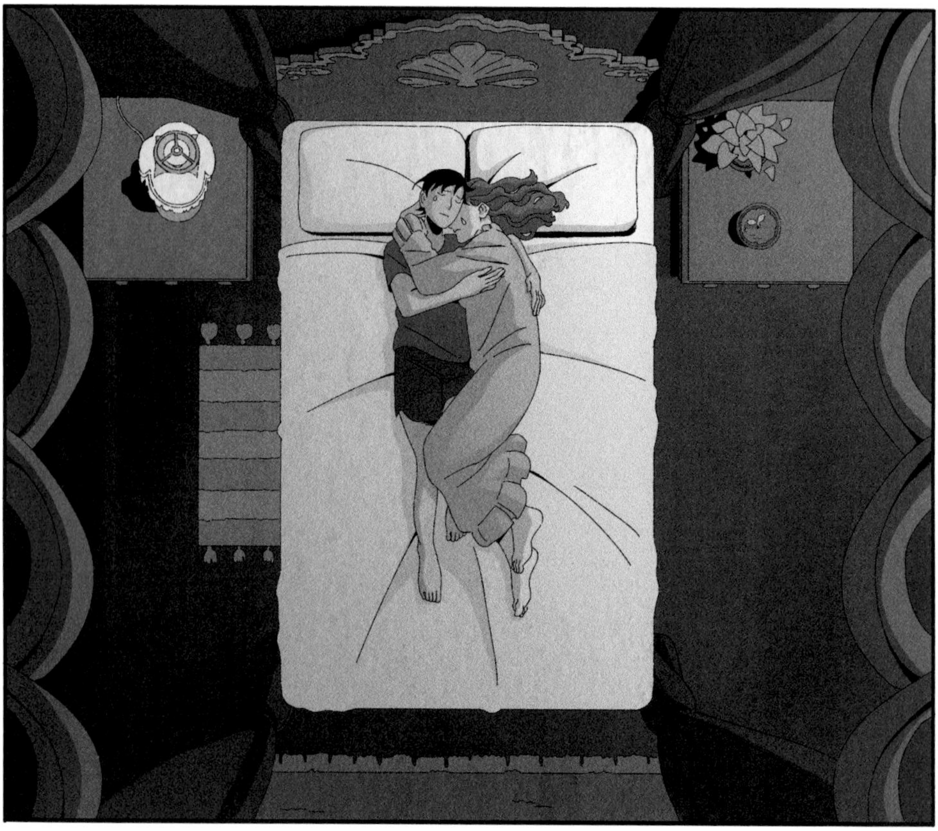

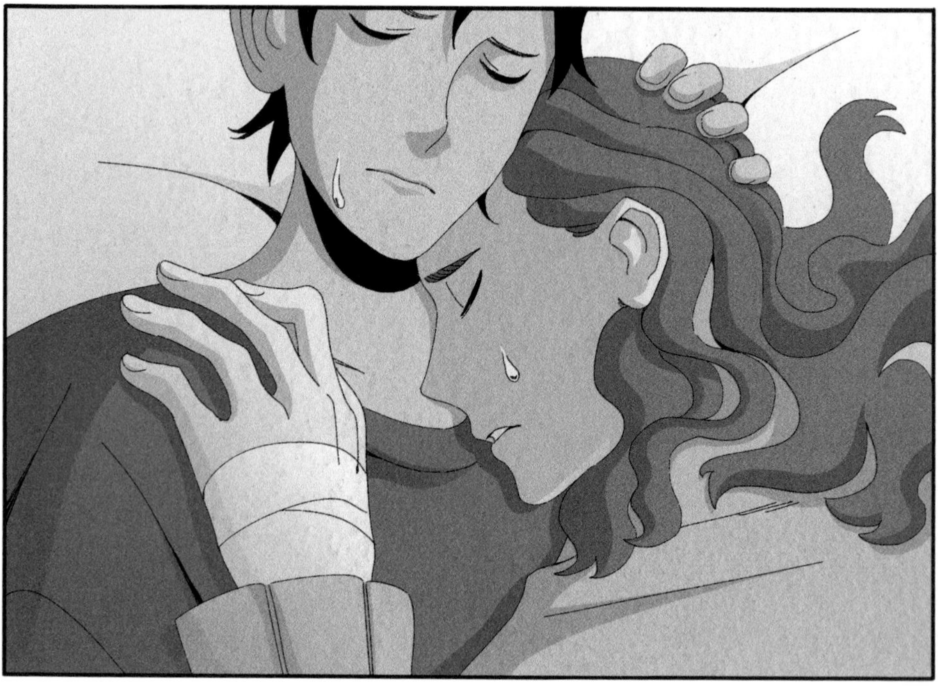

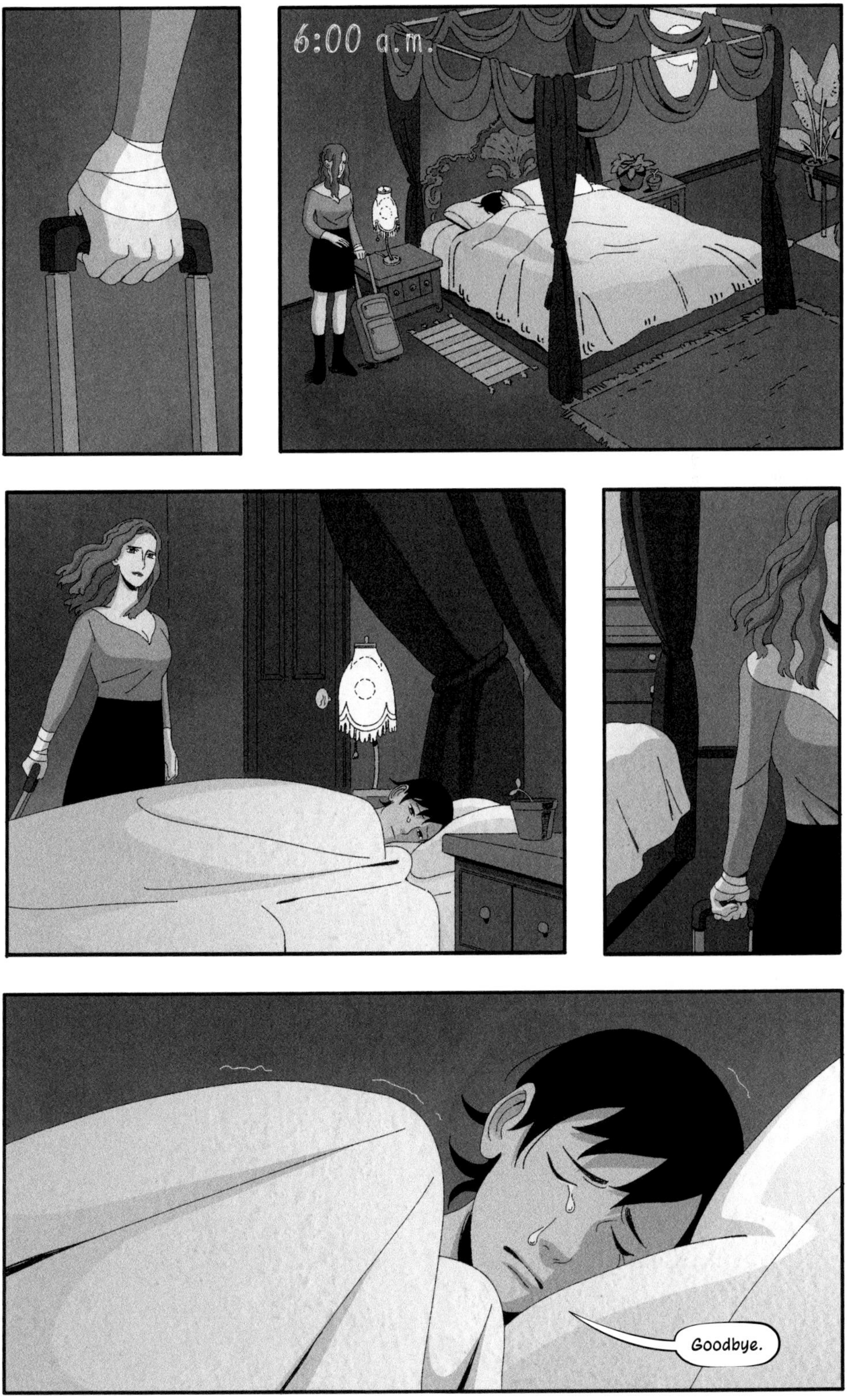
6:00 a.m.
Goodbye.

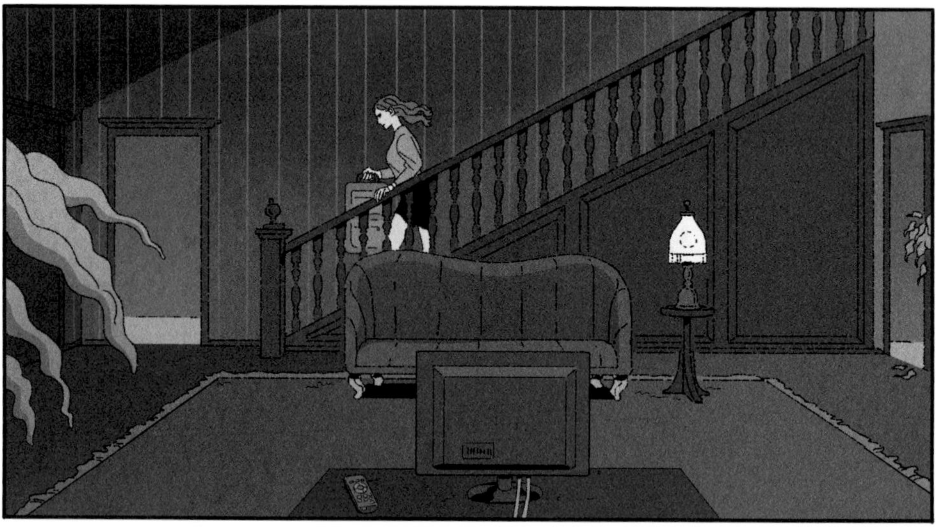

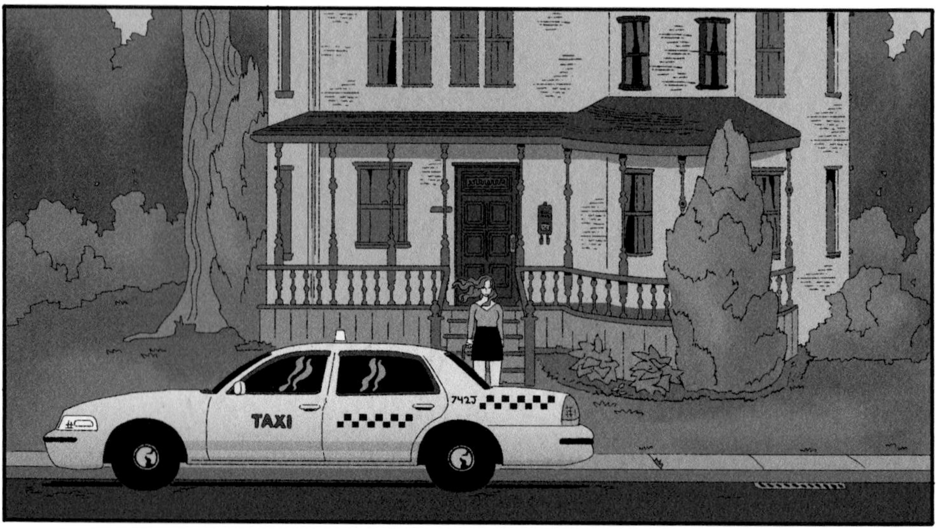
742J
TAXI

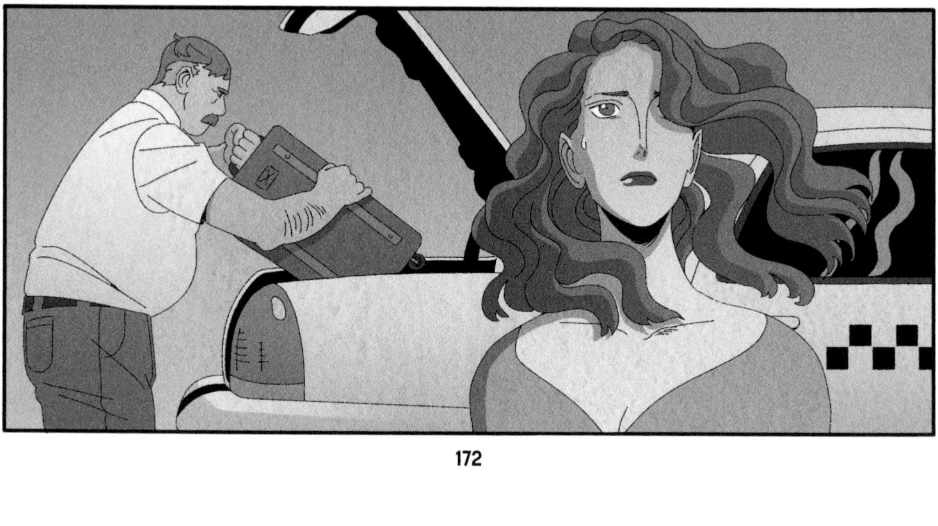

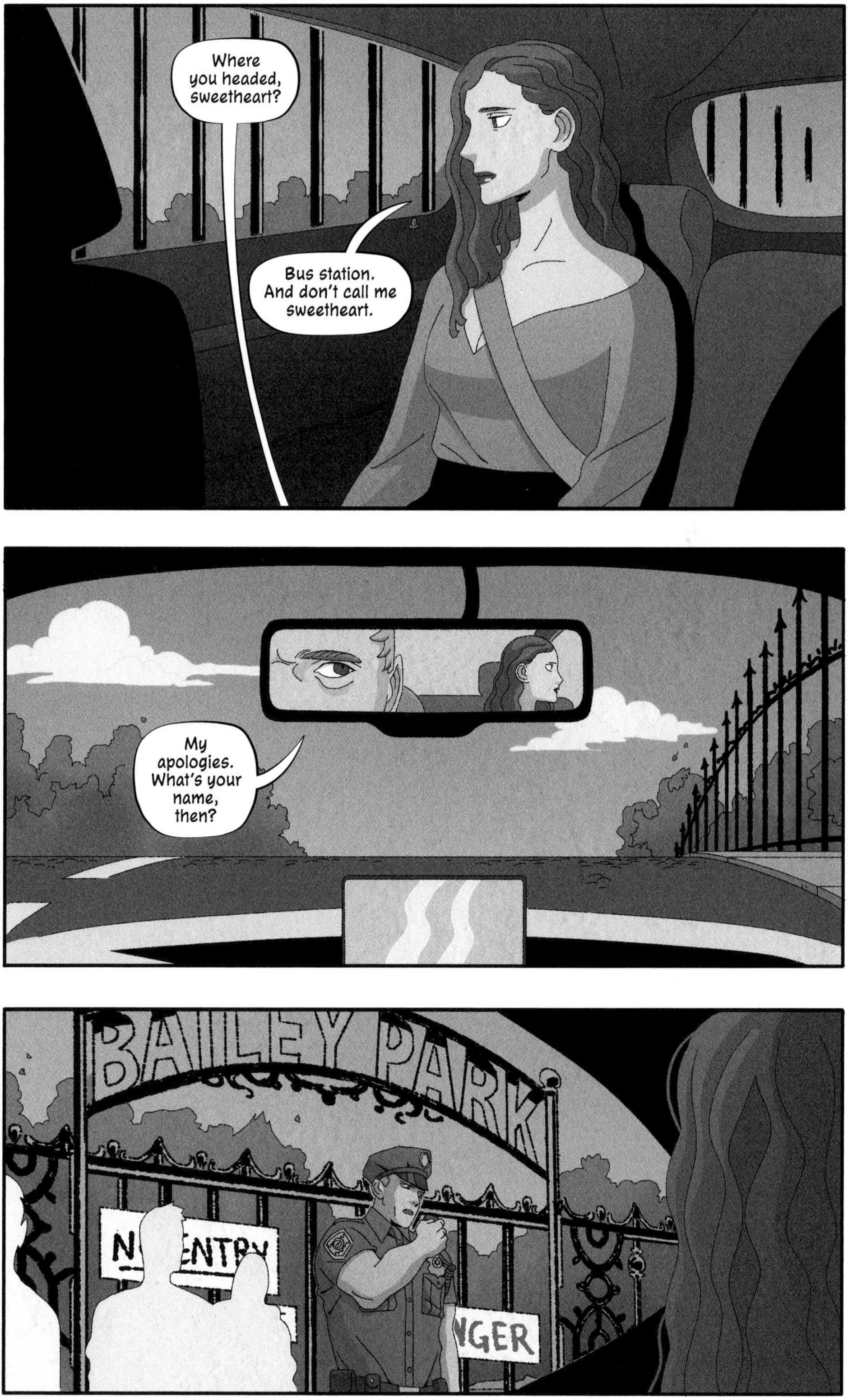
Where you headed, sweetheart?
Bus station. And don't call me sweetheart.
My apologies. What's your name, then?
BAILEY PARK

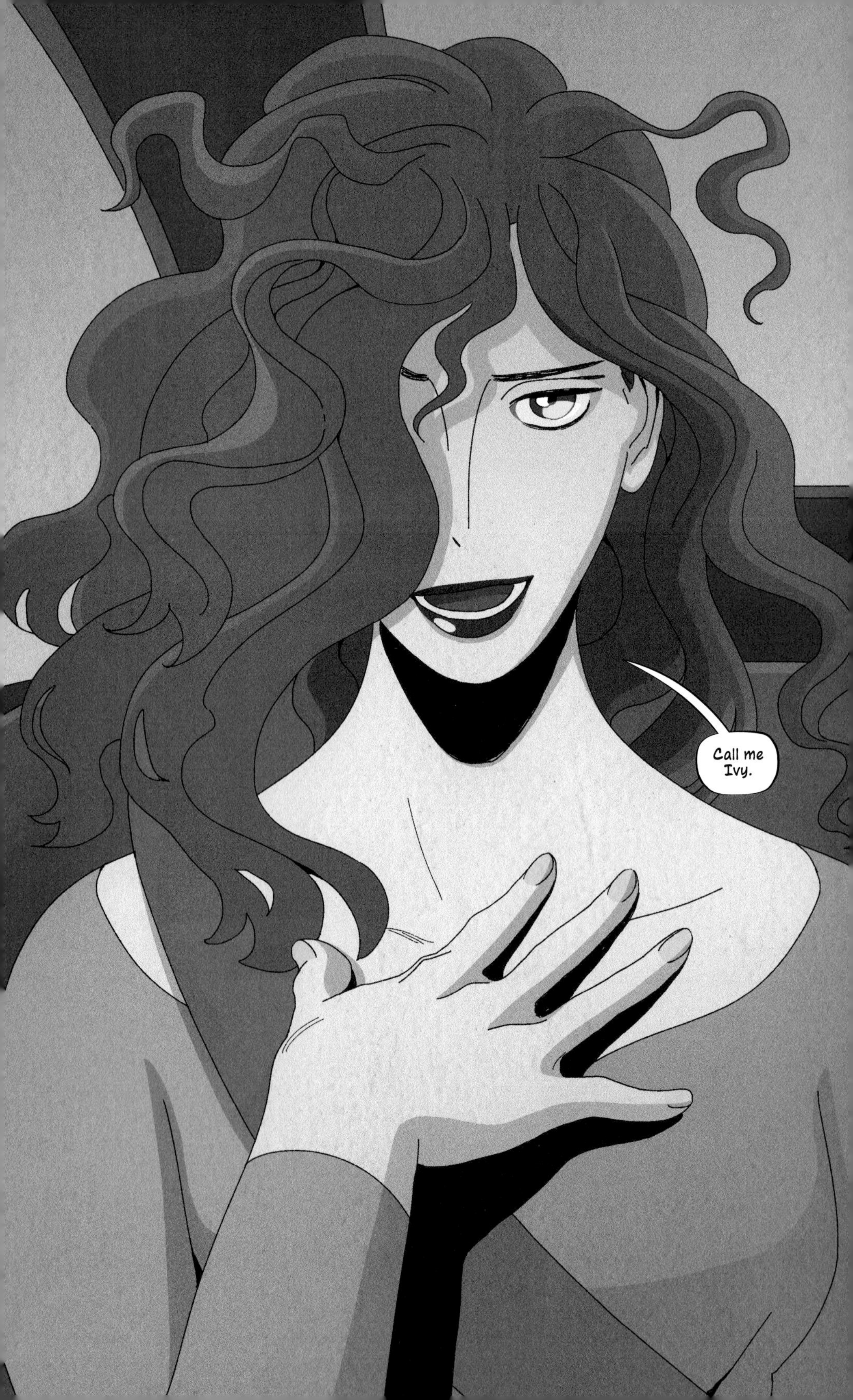
Call me Ivy.

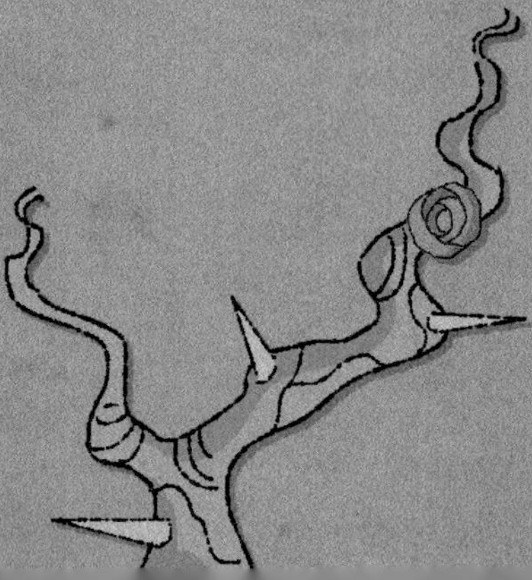

PHOTO BY ALEKSANDR KARJAKA AT KARJAKA STUDIOS

**Kody Keplinger** is the *USA Today* and *New York Times* bestselling author of many books for young adult and middle grade readers, including *The DUFF*, which was adapted into a major motion picture in 2015, and *That's NOT What Happened*. She teaches writing classes at the Gotham Writers Workshop in New York City. When she isn't writing, Kody can usually be found playing *Dungeons & Dragons*, cuddling with her two black cats, or taking long walks with her German shepherd. You can find her online at kodykeplinger.com or @Kody_Keplinger on Twitter.

PHOTO BY SARA KIPIN

**Sara Kipin** is an illustrator and visual developer based out of Burbank, California. She graduated from the Maryland Institute College of Art in 2016 and has been working in the animation industry ever since.

# RESOURCES

If you, or a loved one, need help in any way, you do not need to act alone. Below is a list of resources that may be helpful to you. If you are in immediate danger, please call emergency services in your area (9-1-1 in the U.S.) or go to your nearest hospital emergency room.

## THE JED FOUNDATION

A nonprofit that exists to protect emotional health and prevent suicide for our nation's teens and young adults. Text "START" to 741-741 or call 1-800-273-TALK (8255). Website: jedfoundation.org.

## RAINN

RAINN (Rape, Abuse & Incest National Network) is the nation's largest anti-sexual violence organization. RAINN created and operates the National Sexual Assault Hotline in partnership with more than 1,000 local sexual assault service providers across the country and operates the DoD Safe Helpline for the Department of Defense. RAINN also carries out programs to prevent sexual violence, help survivors, and ensure that perpetrators are brought to justice. If you need help, call their hotline at 1-800-656-HOPE (4673) or visit rainn.org.

## SAFE HORIZON

The largest provider of comprehensive services for domestic violence survivors and victims of all crime and abuse including rape and sexual assault, human trafficking, stalking, youth homelessness, and violent crimes committed against a family member or within communities. If you need help, call their 24-hour hotline at 1-800-621-HOPE (4673) or visit safehorizon.org.

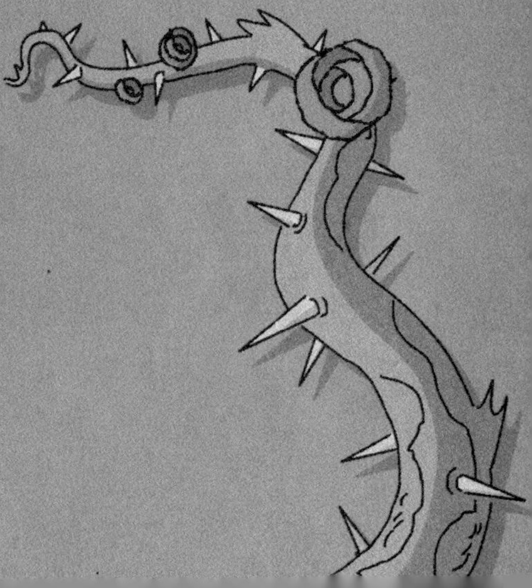

From *New York Times* bestselling author **Mariko Tamaki** (*Laura Dean Keeps Breaking Up with Me, Harley Quinn: Breaking Glass*) and artist **Yoshi Yoshitani** (*Zatanna and the House of Secrets*) comes a story about Mandy, the daughter of super-famous superhero Starfire.

I AM NOT Starfire

*New York Times* Bestselling Author
**Mariko Tamaki**
Art by **Yoshi Yoshitani**

In stores 7/27/2021!
Keep reading for an exclusive preview.

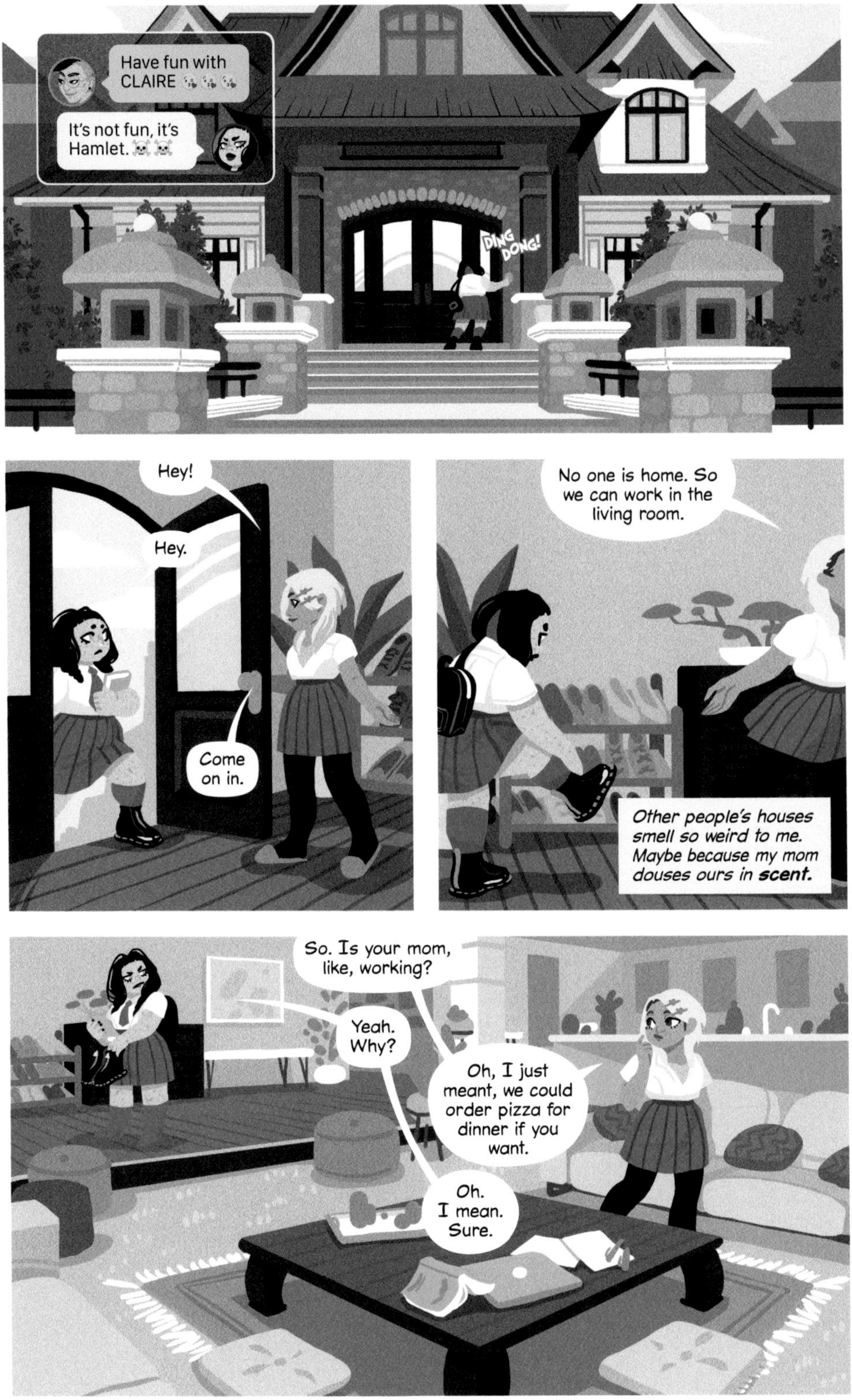
Have fun with CLAIRE
It's not fun, it's Hamlet.
DING DONG!
Hey!
Hey.
Come on in.
No one is home. So we can work in the living room.
Other people's houses smell so weird to me. Maybe because my mom douses ours in *scent.*
So. Is your mom, like, working?
Yeah. Why?
Oh, I just meant, we could order pizza for dinner if you want.
Oh. I mean. Sure.

I mean. What if instead of, like, "mental illness," which is kind of a messed-up way of putting it, we *just* do Ophelia? Like, write about her. Like a new interpretation.
Yeah, like, I feel like the play would be better if Ophelia was written by a woman.
That could be the assignment, right? If we, like, just rewrite her scenes with Hamlet?
Yeah! So she's all like, *"Hamlet, you're a whining ass-hole and I'm too good for you."*
And Hamlet's all, *"But my life is so hard, you need to give me all your emotional resources."*
Right!
DING DONG

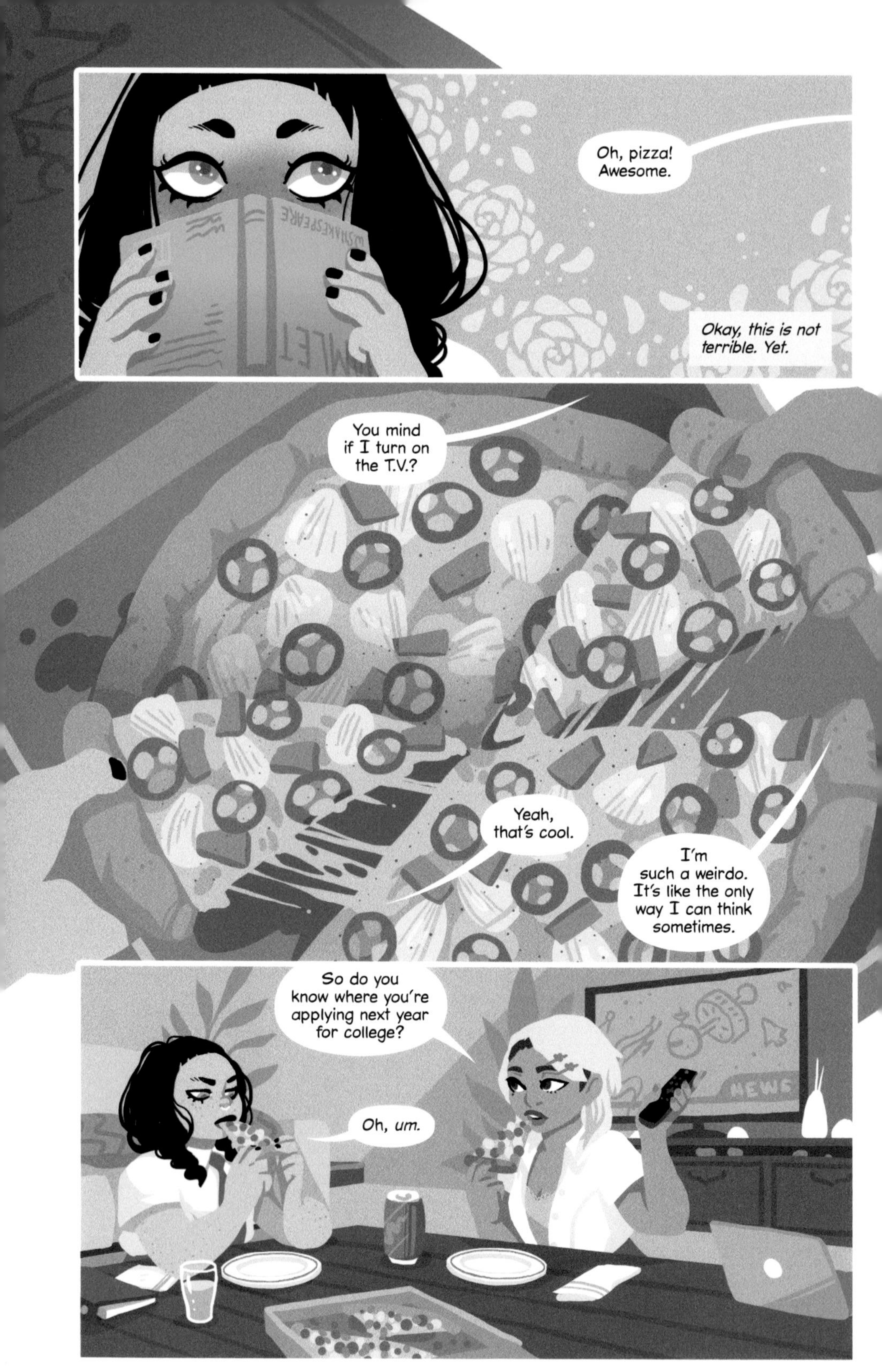

Oh, pizza! Awesome.
Okay, this is not terrible. Yet.
You mind if I turn on the T.V.?
Yeah, that's cool.
I'm such a weirdo. It's like the only way I can think sometimes.
So do you know where you're applying next year for college?
Oh, um.
NEWS

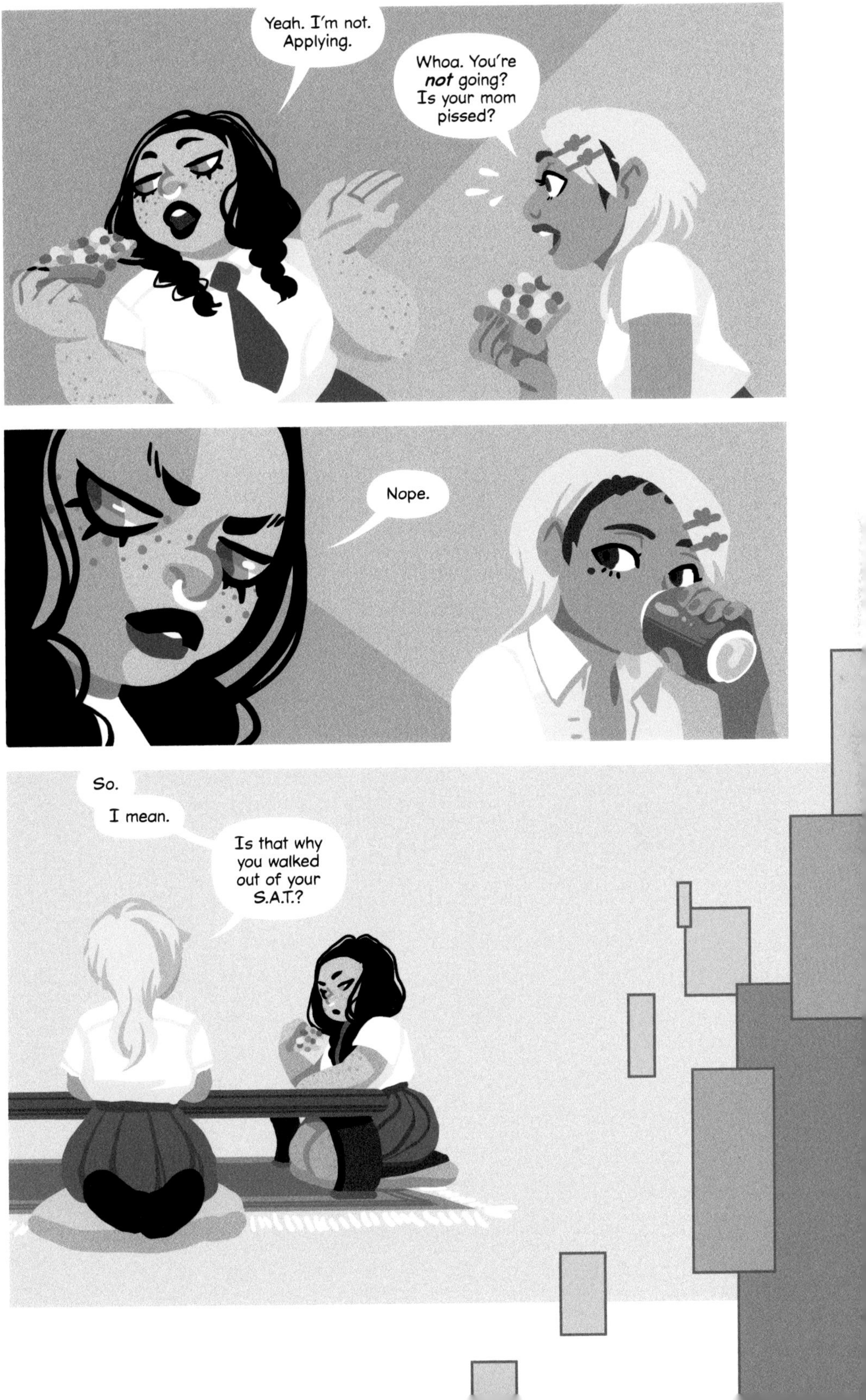
Yeah. I'm not. Applying.
Whoa. You're *not* going? Is your mom pissed?
Nope.
So.
I mean.
Is that why you walked out of your S.A.T.?

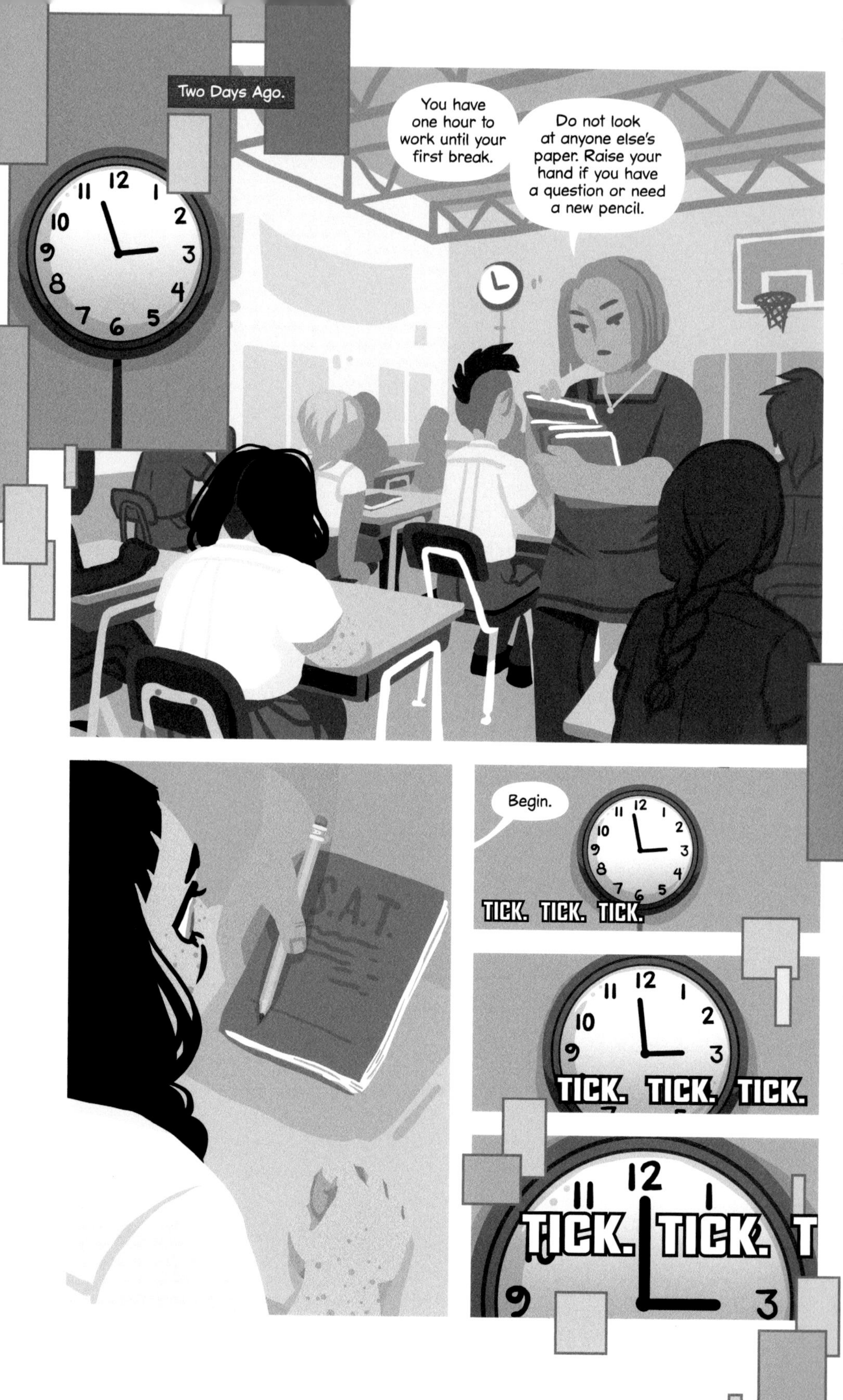
Two Days Ago.
You have one hour to work until your first break.
Do not look at anyone else's paper. Raise your hand if you have a question or need a new pencil.
S.A.T.
Begin.
TICK. TICK. TICK.
TICK. TICK. TICK.
TICK. TICK. T

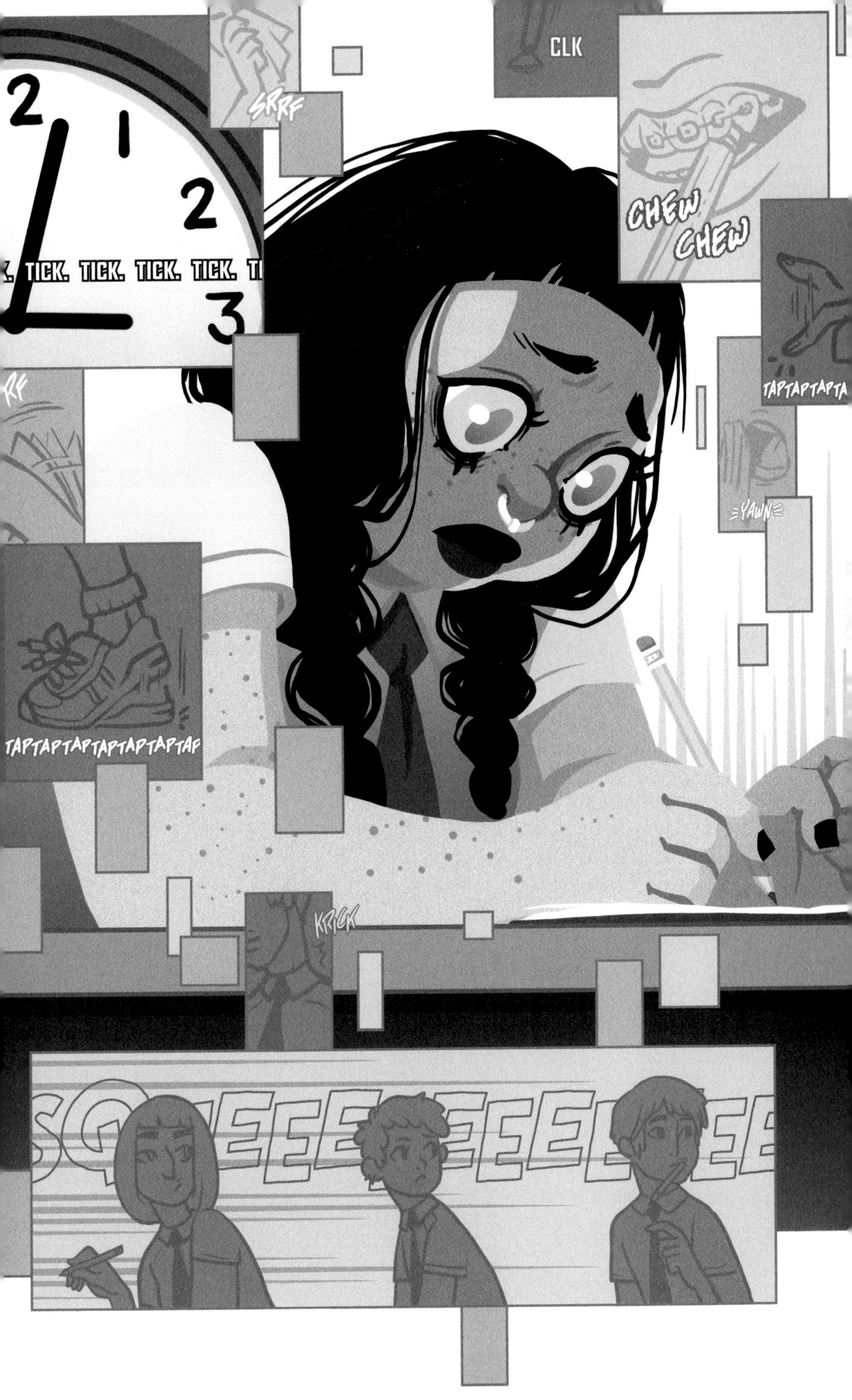

SRRF
CLK
CHEW CHEW
TICK. TICK. TICK. TICK.
TAPTAPTAPTA
YAWN
TAPTAPTAPTAPTAPTAPTAP
KRICK
SQEEEEEEEEEEEEE

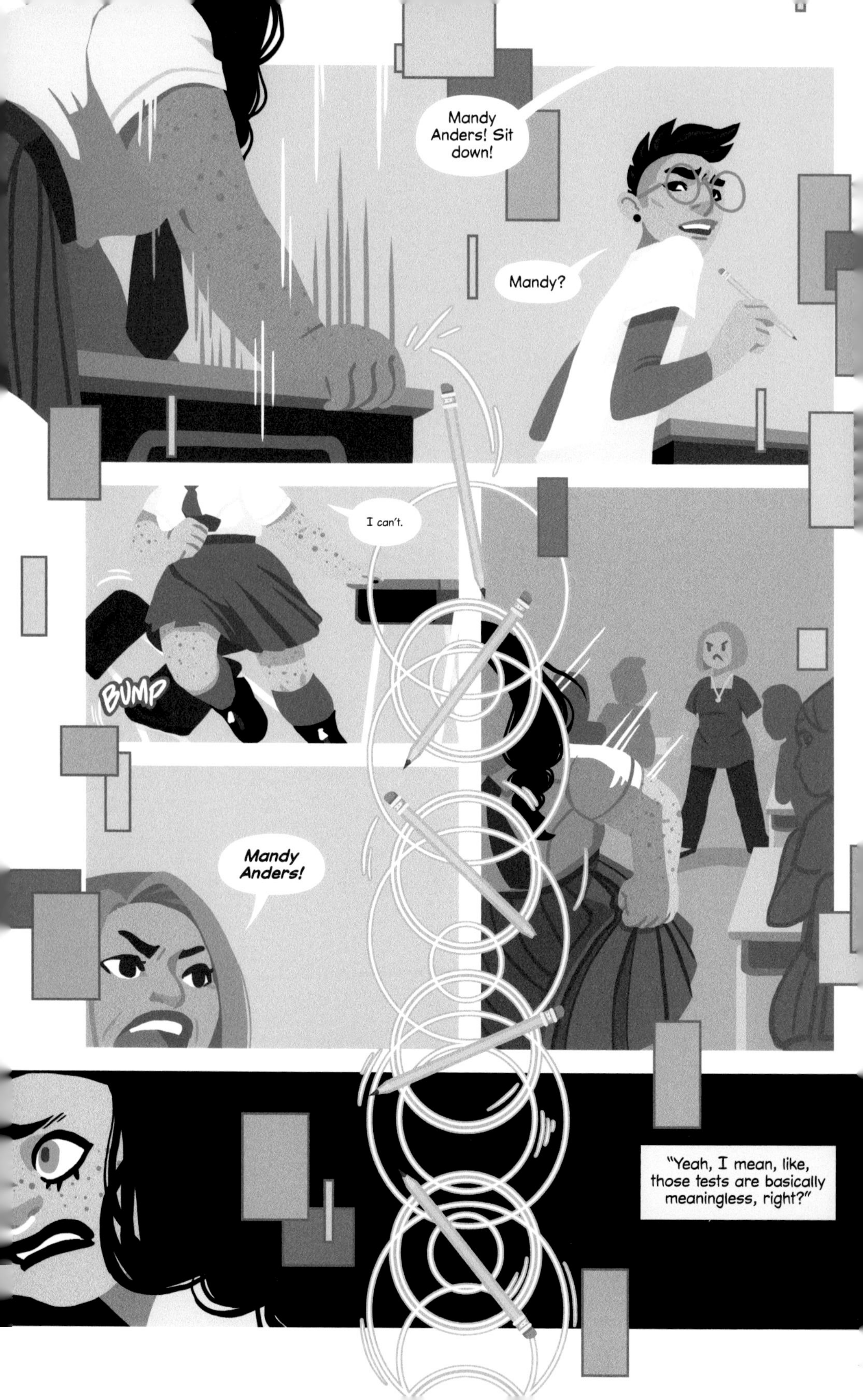
Mandy Anders! Sit down!
Mandy?
I can't.
BUMP
Mandy Anders!
"Yeah, I mean, like, those tests are basically meaningless, right?"

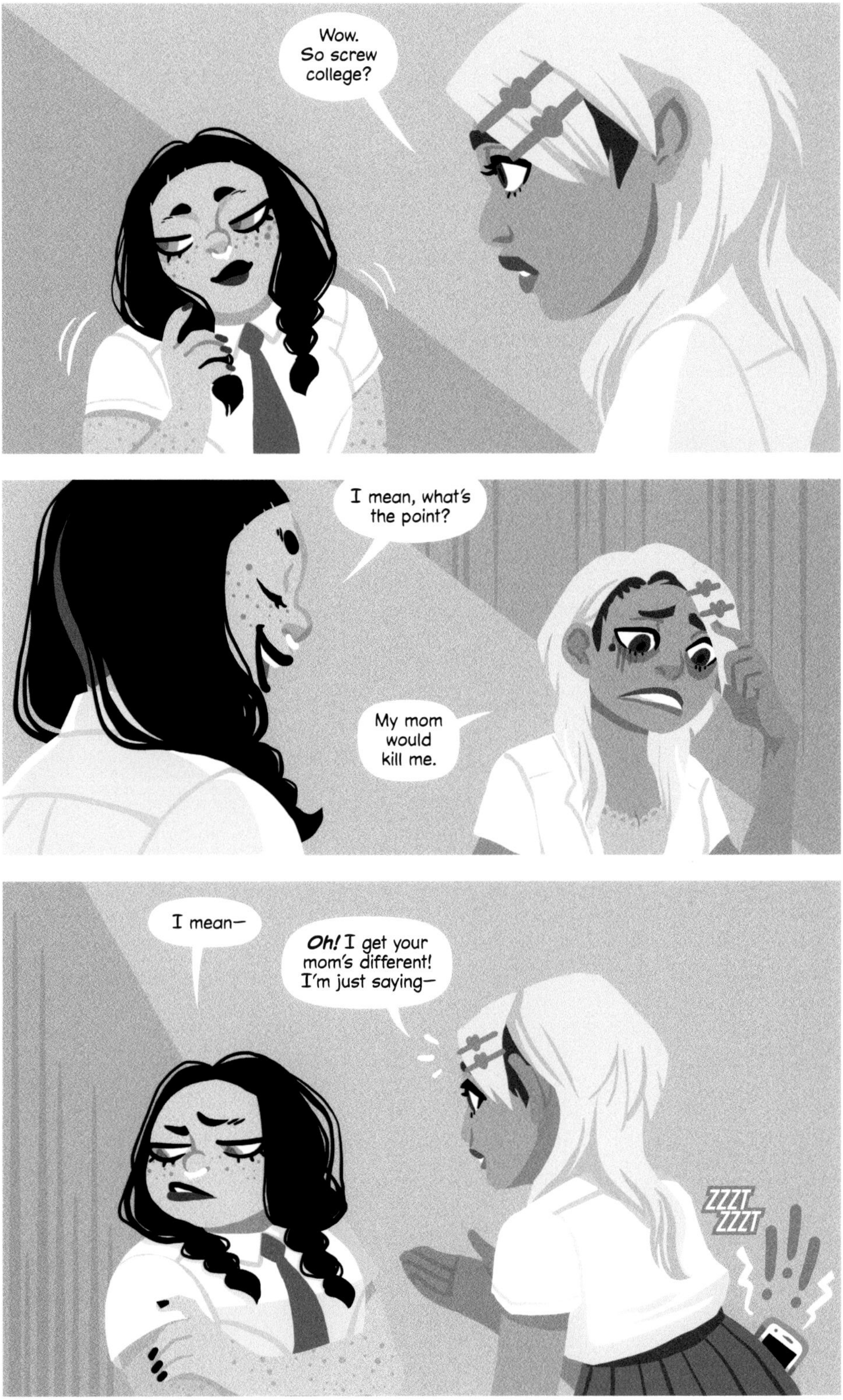
Wow. So screw college?
I mean, what's the point?
My mom would kill me.
I mean—
*Oh!* I get your mom's different! I'm just saying—
ZZZT ZZZT

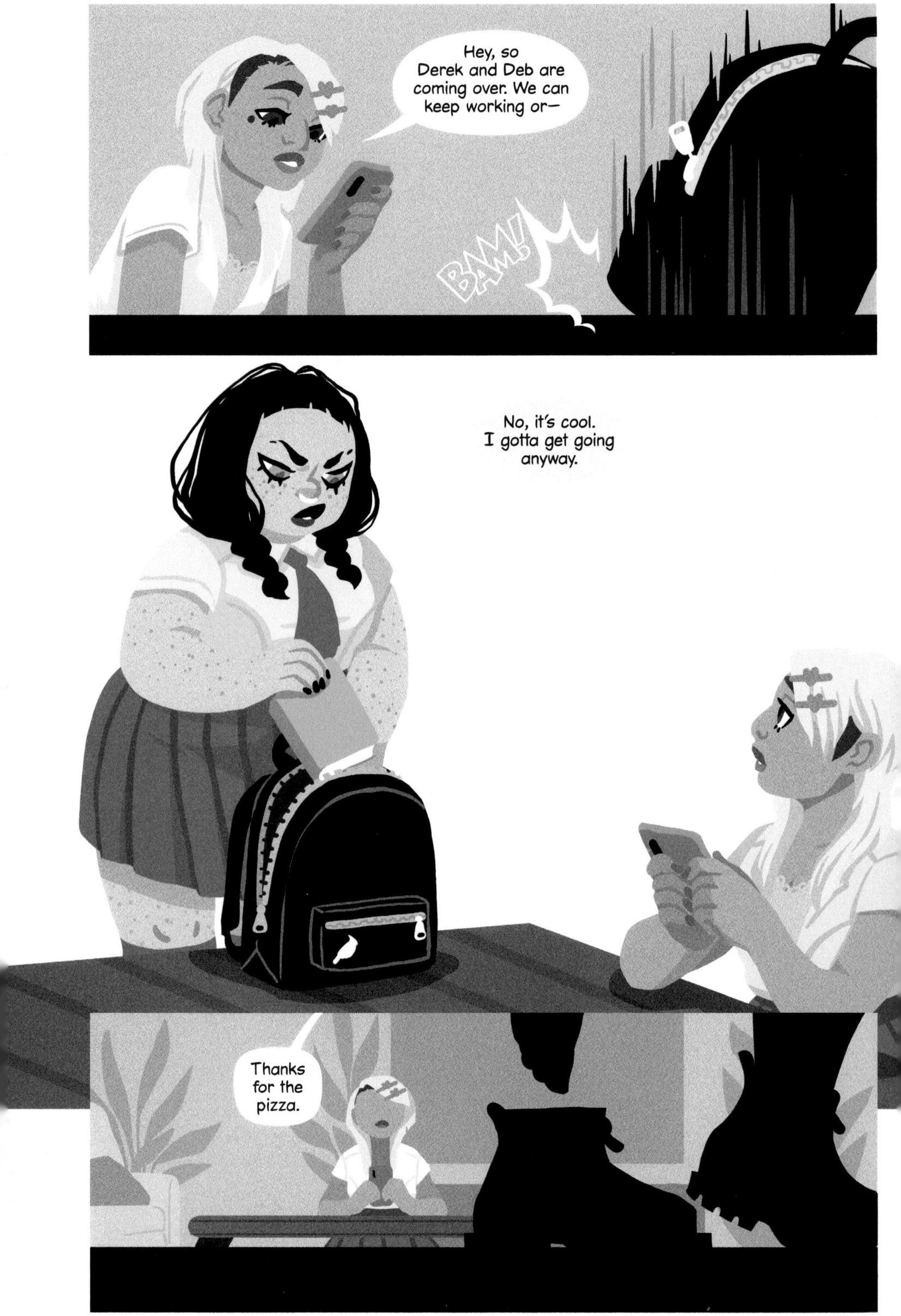
Hey, so Derek and Deb are coming over. We can keep working or—
BAM!
No, it's cool. I gotta get going anyway.
Thanks for the pizza.

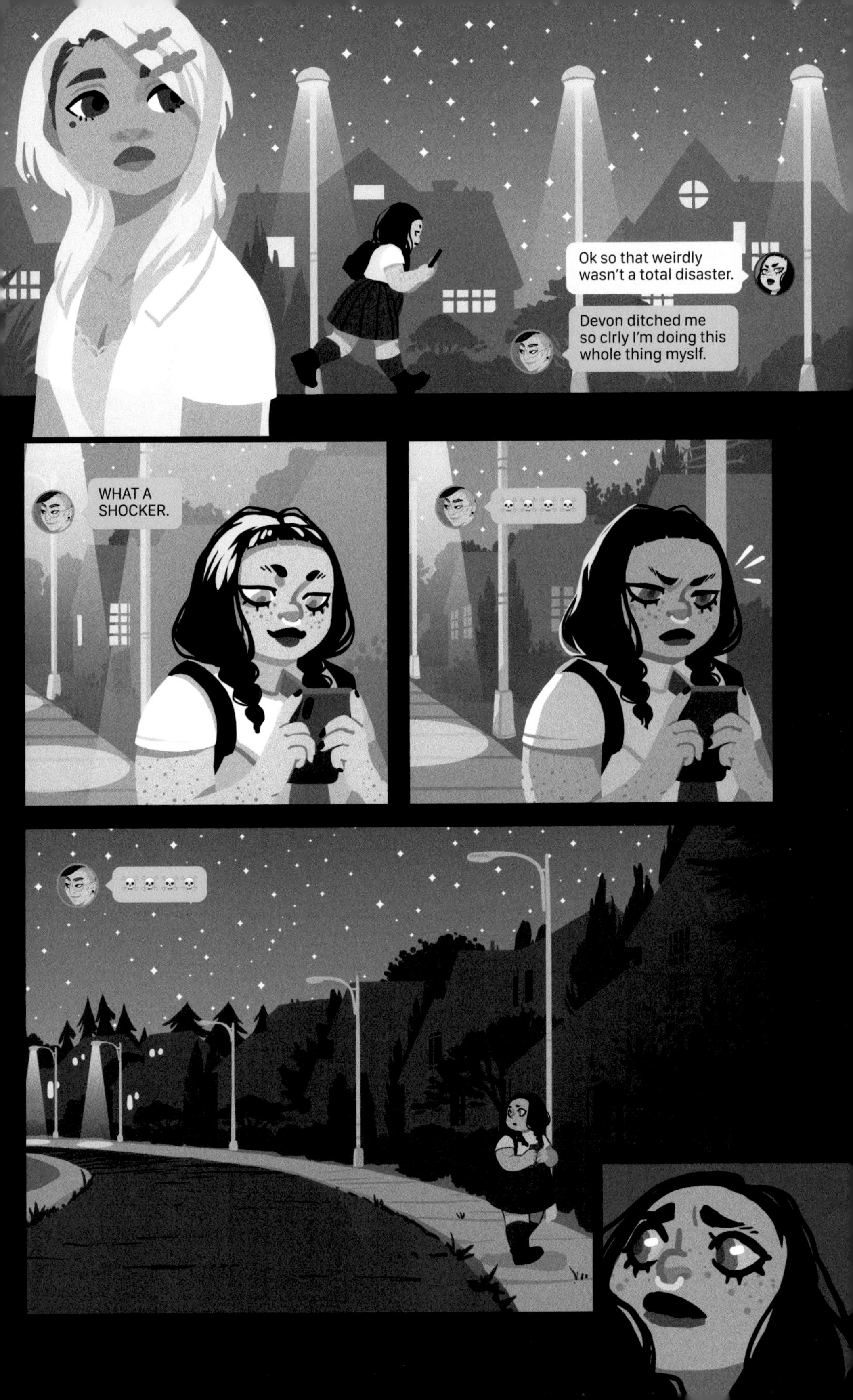

Ok so that weirdly wasn't a total disaster.
Devon ditched me so clrly I'm doing this whole thing myslf.
WHAT A SHOCKER.
💀💀💀💀
💀💀💀💀

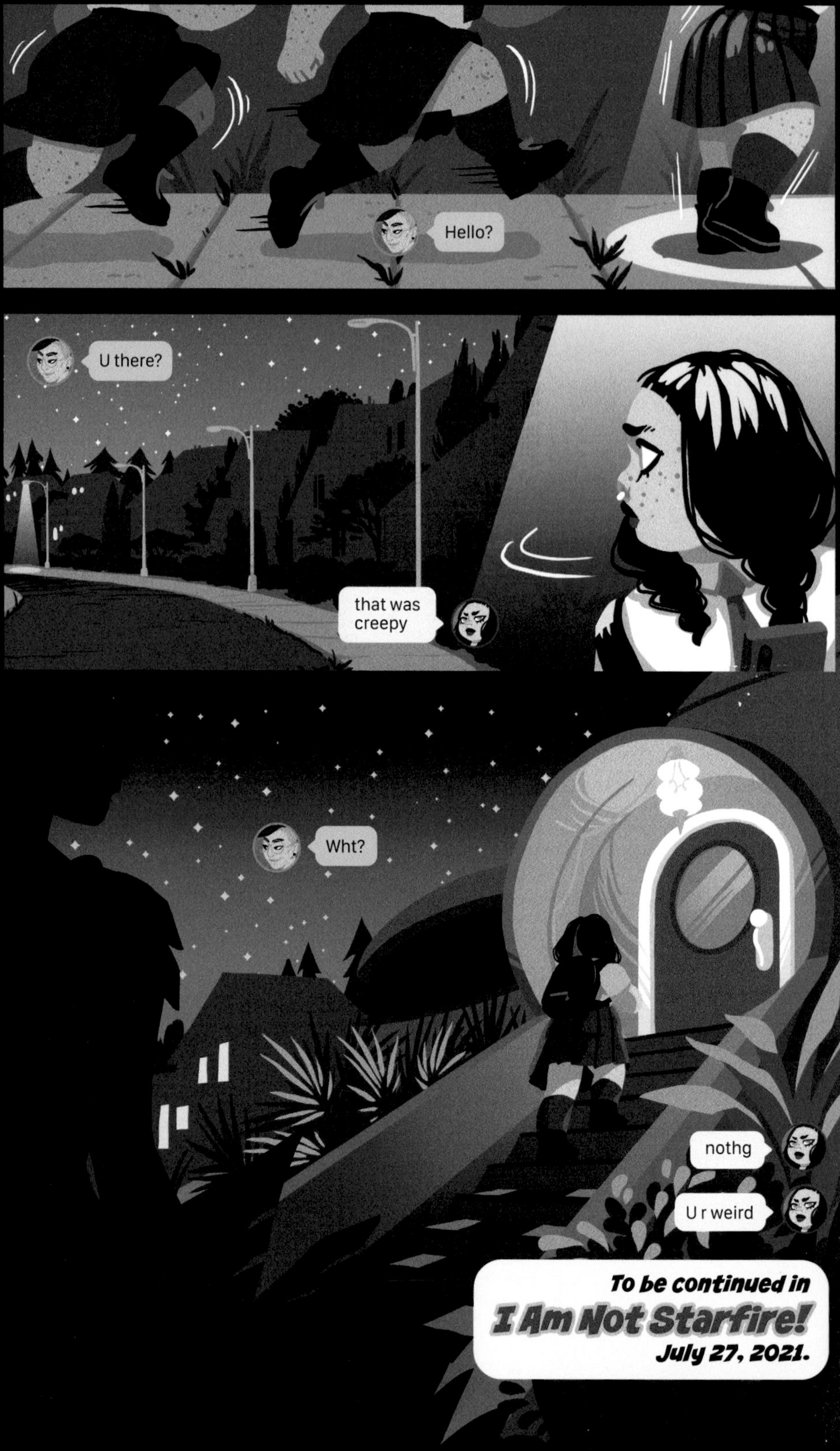
Hello?
U there?
that was creepy
Wht?
nothg
U r weird
To be continued in
I Am Not Starfire!
July 27, 2021.